ELLE "OUR READERS' FICTION PICKS"

•

O MAGAZINE'S "MORE NOVELS TO READ NOW"

PRAISE FOR

Dear Money

"[A] trenchant satire of the '00s."
—*People*, ★★★★

"McPhee has clearly studied traders closely, and *Dear Money* captures their lingo, bluster, willful ignorance and competitiveness."
—*Minneapolis Star Tribune*

"A delicious premise . . . a pitch-perfect send-up of Gotham's literary life, its pleasures, its yearnings and its shocking overhead . . . *Dear Money* entertains while offering shrewd observations about the financial chaos we're still trying to comprehend."
—*San Francisco Chronicle*

"Jaunty . . . In this memoir-cluttered age, McPhee should be applauded for opting to construct fiction from this material."
—*New York Times Book Review*

"The satire here is subtle, understanding . . . and convincing . . . McPhee's characters grow—they win, they lose, they evolve. They appear human, and so are resonant and entertaining."
—*Boston Globe*

"The delicious irony of McPhee's novel is that it deserves to be her own lottery winner, the breakout book that attracts a popular readership . . . McPhee has a lot of fun with a couple of archetypes . . . but what makes this novel work so well is that India continues to engage the reader's empathy."
—*Kirkus Reviews* (starred)

"McPhee is right on the *Money.*"
—*New York Newsday*

"Entertaining . . . McPhee gives perfect descriptions to even minor—or less than minor—characters."
—*Dallas Morning News*

"[McPhee] reveals the full sinister force of our grasping material side—and shows us what we lose when we're so focused on acquiring."
—*Whole Living*

"Although no one can profess to comprehend the complexities of the current economic quagmire, McPhee dishes its jargon with all the aplomb of someone who TiVos CNBC. Delivering virulent social satire with a velvet, humanitarian touch, McPhee's timely send-up deftly parodies the fallout from misplaced priorities."
—*Booklist*

"The characters are lively, and the narrative is engaging and fun to read."
—*Library Journal*

"Deserves to be Martha McPhee's most widely read novel."
—Ron Slate, author of *The Great Wave*

"McPhee is a wickedly good social observer, a writer of beautiful, lyrical prose, and a consummate storyteller. This is a very smart novel that unpacks small surprises and pleasures on every single page."
—Dani Shapiro, author of *Black & White*

"*Dear Money* is conceived with such cutting precision and grace, it will make readers think of a contemporary Edith Wharton, but there's a dark mischief here too, shades of Andy Warhol. Full of beautiful, unflinching sentences, this is an uncompromising, brave, brilliant story."
—René Steinke, author of *Holy Skirts*

Dear Money

MARTHA McPHEE

MARINER BOOKS
HOUGHTON MIFFLIN HARCOURT
BOSTON | NEW YORK

For my astonishing sisters:
Laura, Sarah, Jenny, Joan
And always for Mark, Livia, and Jasper

First Mariner Books edition 2011

www.hmhbooks.com

Library of Congress Cataloging-in-Publication Data
McPhee, Martha.
Dear money/Martha McPhee.
p. cm.
ISBN 978-0-15-101165-0
ISBN 978-0-547-42254-1 (pbk.)
1. Floor traders (Finance)—Fiction. 2. Wall Street (New York, N.Y.)—Fiction.
I. Title.
PS3563.C3888D43 2010
813'.54—dc22 2009029923

Book design by Linda Lockowitz

Printed in the United States of America

DOC 10 9 8 7 6 5 4 3 2 1

PART I

I Can't Keep Up

One

THE STORY BEGINS, of course, with real estate. The heady days of 2003. Maine. Pond Point, the old Victorian cottage tied together, it seemed, with twine, standing as it does before the dunes with a swath of sea grass like a moat, sweet pea shoots, their blue flowers dancing in a late-afternoon breeze blowing offshore. The beach. Miles of sand, flanked by rivers, one large, one small, spilling into the Atlantic. Little islands floating just offshore, connected at low tide by sandbars that reach to them like arms.

Those wonderful July days, as Emma Chapman declared with that fierce enthusiasm of hers that spoke of a desire to appreciate every chance life gives to her. July—each day's weather a mystery, a surprise. Storms blow in from nowhere to entertain the day. From an immaculate sky, fog settles down thick as cotton while sandpipers and plovers dart about. Thunderheads in the afternoon, towering cumulus, then a crack of thunder. Heart-shattering sunsets. Or simply the stillness of early morning in high season, a scorcher in the offing, but for now, an hour past dawn, towels and bathing suits still damp on the clothesline, the sun rising over the river, heating the woods, bringing the strong smell of pine sap into the kitchen where coffee brewed. On the porch, Emma, squarely facing the ocean in a golden bar of sunlight, seemed to have everything in life, and the only thing more she wanted, it seemed to me, was to own this—the salt air and gratifying geometries of the sea, all that came with this house.

I did not like the house at first. The wind blew right through the walls, and chipmunks and mice had made it (even our beds) their home. It was wet and cold. The screen door banged with an alarming thud. The neighbor's house was occupied by a family of Bostonians—you could tell this by the big *B* for the Boston Red Sox that appeared everywhere: on their hats, their barbecue aprons, the kites their children sent upward to broadcast their allegiance to the heavens. They greeted us and smiled stiffly in a way that seemed to register a conviction that there would be no further need to continue down the path of fellow feeling.

The Bostonians' cottage was a bit too close. They weeded their flower beds and assiduously mowed a "lawn" that was mostly sand. They prosecuted a passion for golf by purchasing tiny plastic golf sets for their boys, who whacked little golf-ball-sized Wiffle balls across the lot, and when an errant ball landed on the side of the Chapmans' rundown summer rental, the Bostonian boys sat sullenly staring across the lot at our girls, unable to ask for help. Our girls seemed to enjoy their discomfort, but took pity on them, tossing the balls back, which the boys accepted without thanks, and moved their game farther away. "By their fruits you shall know them," my husband, Theodor, noted. "Yeah," I said. But I admired, actually came to envy, Emma's passion for the house, despite the frosty neighbors, and wanted to see it with her eyes since it gave her so much pleasure. The views took in the open Atlantic, sailboats leaning into the breeze, cormorants and seagulls and, on occasion, even seals, their dog-like heads bobbing in the surf.

Emma and Will had been renting the house for six years, driving up from New York for the month with their two daughters, Will commuting back and forth. Emma had found the house.

Strolling the beach, she had asked various sunbathers camped beneath umbrellas if they rented their homes, the cottages in the dunes behind them. The elderly couple she eventually found did not rent, but they were charmed by her determination: *Oh, that's your house? That one there? The red one with the turret? It's right out of a Hopper painting. No, no, a Wyeth. It's pure Wyeth. It's from the 1880s? Oh, how I'd love to spend a week there, absorbing all that history.*

The couple took her up to the house, showed her around. Every window framed a spectacular view. She could see through the mess of all the guests, the children of nieces and nephews with names like Sacagawea—I kid you not—overrunning the place. The couple had no children of their own. "A view from every window," Emma said. She was exuberant. It was the quality I loved best about her. Emma complimented the children (diapered, juice stained, sticky fingers). "Sacagawea, what an original name," she said. And she complimented the vintage piano and the antique windowpanes, the fraying curtains. In the turret bedroom she complimented the old photographs hanging crookedly on the wall. "Why, they're Bachrach," she said, examining the signature of one of the prints and noticed they were all signed by him. She flashed her smile on Mrs. Hov ("Chekhov without the *chek*," Mrs. Hov would say). "Yes, they are," Mrs. Hov confirmed, and her milky blue eyes brightened. "I grew up in Connecticut," she said, as if in explanation and to underscore her more prominent past, her voice soft and self-assured. An elegant woman still, with slender fingers that had long ago mastered the piano, today she wore a simple housedress, but yesterday she was the smiling girl in all the sepia-tinted prints.

Mr. Hov was a retired Swift scholar and an amateur poet of the A. E. Housman mold, with a firm yet charming manner. The couple was at the house when Theodor and I arrived with our two girls for a long weekend. The Hovs had come to fix the boiler and were just leaving. I would remember them for a long time, a pair, he a smaller version of her with the same kind blue eyes, hazy with cataracts. Though she had a full head of lovely white hair and he was bald. He was in the middle of reciting a poem he'd written, his voice earnest and mellifluous: "I try the fleeting years to catch. / But, mark thee well, this one firm adage of the sea!" Emma and Will listened; she leaned into his caress, standing on the porch overlooking the dunes and ocean. She wore a smile that, having begun in sincerity, hadn't quite anticipated how long a poem could actually go on, and was striving mightily, along with the poem, to prop herself up.

Upon our arrival, Theodor and I found them in a state of suspension, the elderly man holding forth. "For whom our time has come, / And man is laid beneath the sand, the sod, or sea." It was an ode to Pond Point. Hov's wife had been coming here since the 1930s. Together they bought the house in the 1950s, for a song, with the equity they'd accrued in their primary home. Standing there on the porch of their second home, windblown and kissed by the Maine light, Mrs. Hov, her lips curled, just slightly, with love, watched her husband's gentle hands conduct his words. "The sharpened sands their lips do pulse and / Tongueless, whisper songs most sure. / 'Tis we, not thee, that shall endure, / that shall endure!"

A moment of silence followed and then Emma burst into applause. "Just a little something I wrote in 1983," Mr. Hov said, turning his attention fully to us, my girls' eyes wide with curiosity at the spectacle. "Ah, your guests have arrived," he said. "We've heard all about you, Emma and Will's friends. All good, I can assure you! Welcome, renowned New Yorkers! I invite you all to have a wonderful weekend."

We knew all about Emma's cast of friends. She was always telling stories about her collection of elaborate people—friends marrying in the final stages of fatal cancer; a wife whose slender book of poems about her adulterous love affair with a young buck became a bestseller, publicly shaming her (also adulterous) husband with both her betrayal and her success; a young bride who prided herself on her Gypsy ancestors, using her lineage to land her a spot on the reality television show *My Wedding Day*. The Hovs were somehow part of that mix, Emma's menagerie.

Within a few sentences Mr. Hov spilled forth what Emma had told them of us, all of it hyperbolic and with exclamations. Like the Hovs, we were characters in the theater of her life, and it did feel that, if you stuck around long enough, some intriguing plot would unfold for you. Mr. Hov was well into the details of local history, the Sagadahoc settlement: "They came in 1607, same as Jamestown, though the settlers did not fare so well." His expression seemed to appreciate the drama of that antique failure. He directed our attention to the piping plovers nesting in the dune grass—his way of saying to be careful as we walked through it to the beach, not to upset the plovers, as they are rare and protected. "Now, no more of us," he said cheerily. "We are out of your hair." He turned to his wife: "Eunice, I am in the car." He enunciated each word with care. Then he left, Eunice trailing slowly, happily behind.

"Don't you just love them?" Emma said, greeting us, kissing us—the flourish of arrival, folding us immediately into her arms. "I'm so glad you got to meet them, because, you know, I'm going to have to kill them." Emma spoke with mischief. "A pity, because they *are* nice, aren't they?" Then she listed all the other people she'd have to murder in order to buy the place: the ne'er-do-well young niece, her husband, her children and little Sacagawea too. The way Emma talked, you almost believed she would kill. And the way she smiled, lips crimping ever so slightly, like someone who wants to steal a gorgeous piece of fruit from a store's sidewalk display, you almost believed she'd get away with it.

"I love it. I love it. I love it," Emma said, an elegant woman with fine, bird-like bones. She took us on a tour of the house, up and down the stairs, showing us where we would bathe, eat, read, sleep. "In the turret," she said, "the romance of the turret for you." Her spirit, her ecstatic energy, made her seem a good bit taller than her five-foot-two frame. She had straight dark hair that she wore tightly pulled back with a bandeau, blue eyes and a round face, the kind of looks that money easily improved. In her eyes, though, she had the solemnity of a woman who has exactly what she wants.

Will came up behind her and embraced her and leaned down to kiss her on the neck (they were always kissing each other, and I suspected it had more to do with show than anything else, but secretly I wished that Theodor would make a little more show with his kisses) and said sweetly, "I will help you kill them, my love."

"See," she said, turning to Theodor and me, holding us with her eyes, an icy gray-blue. "I married well." She nestled into her husband. "He's so accommodating."

Looking around the place, I could not see the appeal—curtains a hundred years old, the ancient piano so heavy it caused the living room floor to sag. The kitchen hadn't been touched since the Hovs bought the house. The hot water was never hot enough (or so they told us); the floorboards were in need of sanding (my younger daughter got a splinter within minutes of our arrival); fine veins fractured some of the windowpanes. There was a lost museum of cleaning products and insect repellent from the days when gas stations gave such things away with a tank of gasoline, Amway and Gulf Oil products now collectibles worth real money on eBay. Clutter had accumulated in corners where dust bunnies hid, and surely dust mites. I imagined the magnified images of those creatures marching across the television screen, scaring viewers into buying something or other. Some such bug caused my older daughter's skin to itch. "Lice," I whispered to Theodor, lying in our bed, in the somewhat attenuated romance of our turret, that first night.

"Fleas," he whispered back and enveloped me with his strong warm body, kissing my neck.

"I love it when you talk dirty to me," I said.

He saved his affection for when we were alone. We fell asleep to the howl of the wind. It was as if we were camping.

My husband had gone to college with Emma, but they had known each other only by sight: Theodor, the long-haired eccentric who lived in his art studio and smoked Gauloises; Emma, the cute sorority girl with the magnificent smile, cheery friendliness and that good-girl desire to be loved by everyone. We had bumped into each other in a park in Tribeca near their loft (which I later came to envy along with everything else, enormous windows overlooking the Hudson and the sunset, the space immaculate in its spare design, chrome and teak and Senegalese silk around the windows, rosewood cabinets inlaid with camel bone, *objets* here and there, relics of their world travels: a Haitian woodcarving, Polish crystal, a bronze Buddha, Ming vases, a dancing Shiva). Our older daughters, born on the same day of the same year, were toddlers. They began playing and we began talking. We talked all afternoon. We talked until the sun began to go down, a warm June evening, and then, at the suggestion of Emma, who I could already tell bubbled with bright ideas, we walked to a restaurant in Battery Park for dinner overlooking the Hudson and the Statue of Liberty, golden green in the dying light. At the end of the evening our daughters had declared themselves best friends.

Age, of course, stopped us from making such a declaration, but we all seemed high in the way a first date can make you feel. Simply, we fell in love with them as a family, the way that families can do—an appropriate form of dating and romancing for married couples. You see, we each had something that the other wanted. They admired us because we made art and because millionaires, it seems, collect artists (I was a novelist; my husband,

Theodor Larson, was a sculptor), and we (or, I should say, I) admired the Chapmans because they made money (or, I should say, Will made money; Emma was a housewife, a stay-at-home mother or whatever it is they are called these days, and spent her time making their life beautiful). And artists, it stood to reason, were wise to collect millionaires.

Will made loads of money at one of those big Wall Street jobs, and he came from old money, though there was not very much of it left anymore. But he looked like money, with his smooth white skin, his strong jaw that he proudly stroked (though he was not an arrogant man), his soft black hair and those charming green eyes that twinkled with optimism as he spoke: the former created the latter, the way winning breeds winning. Yet he was discreet about his wealth in the way that New Englanders of note have been taught to be. And this house in Maine, falling to pieces as it was, represented for me that discretion and my own inability to comprehend it.

With the Chapmans, our shift away from the companionship of the starving-artist set began. It was something one sees only after the fact: we'd left behind our struggling friends, living in old spice warehouses in Williamsburg—those who proudly spoke of waking in the morning to step into a world described not by quaint cafés offering croissants that rivaled the best of Paris, but instead by forgotten industry and telephone poles, low-slung electric wires canopying lonely Brooklyn streets, the wasteland that fueled imagination. Friends with whom in the early days we spent long hours late into the night conversing about art and the struggle until, tired, drawn, burdened by the pursuit of the masterpiece, we all went around like shades of our former selves, relying on hope as a retirement plan.

For the most part, the world of the Chapmans, by contrast, was so much more beautiful to look upon, more fully realized, a familiar beauty recognizable from magazines and movies. And when they enrolled their firstborn in a private school, so did we, scraping the money together from commissions and advances. And from that point on we entered an almost entirely artist-free zone. Now there were doctors and lawyers and bankers galore, admen and -women and publishers of magazines—a whole roster of fascinating, hard-working people who seemed to occupy positions that made the world go round. They were Oversized People with an outsized capacity to welcome artists into their world. Becoming friends with them intrigued me; they were portals into a whole different manner of living: grown-ups with grown-up concerns, real estate primarily—the acquisition and renovation of. So the struggle and meaning of art was, gradually, imperceptibly, left behind on the shores of the industrial zone. I'd had that conversation. It seemed there was not much else to say.

Will Chapman was not what I had imagined a Wall Street type to be. He could speak about any subject with intelligence and knowledge. He knew art, antiques, literature. He was a reader, a rare thing these days. He knew inside and out the history of the novel, had read *Clarissa* and *Pamela* even, for God's sake, soldiering through them without the prompting of a college class. He dreamed big, and Emma along with him, assisting him in his will and his desire. He wanted his girls to ride camels in the Rajasthani desert, taught them to collect, instructing them on the beauty and precision of Mogul miniatures, encouraged them to draw copies, introduced them to music, signed them up for Mandarin, offered at their private school, because China was the future center of the world and he would do nothing less than prepare them for the shift in the course of empires eastward. (Soon I began to worry, in a way that seems particular to New York City, about the fate of our hapless, Mandarin-less children.) He played the piano beautifully. For him life was a novel, to be lived fully in every regard, with adventures and stories.

"He's a Renaissance man," Theodor would say with a hint of

envy. Theodor's father, son of a Swedish immigrant to the farms of the American breadbasket, had been a salesman of industrial paints, had moved his family a dozen times across America in pursuit of better jobs before retiring to a glorified trailer park in Tucson with my mother-in-law, Gina, where they died young, in their sixties. Theodor's talents were born of determination, self-taught. He suspected the assets of privilege, because veneer and authenticity had too similar a sheen.

"What is it he *can't* do?" we'd speculate. Perfect Boy, we began to call Will (privately). Perfect Boy, because he was perfect, loved Wall Street, loved the high, but would not be limited by it. More than anything, when he looked into the crystal ball that held his future he expected that someday he'd become a novelist. This did not mean that Perfect Boy was less perfect now. No, he was a bubble of perfection making its way, in the fullness of time, through time, as we all were, but somehow he had figured out the proper *valence,* the strength, the capacity, like a chemical element, the proper combining power, to join and be joined in life, by life, through life with a heightened equanimity. He woke early, went to bed late, using the time to write. I admired his tenacity but didn't have much faith in his ability, though I did not tell him that. Rather, I encouraged him just as I did the other wannabe writers I had met over the years. I never made it my job to herald the truth: *Give it a break, buster. You're never going to have what it takes.* If I had a dollar for every person who wanted to be a writer . . . I could have bought a house in Maine.

The house on Pond Point, by the by, was part of their plan: they'd spend their summers there so that Will could write, full time, in the tool room in the damp dark basement, amid the wrenches and screws and nails and hammers and saws and twine of Mr. Hov's remarkable workshop (Hov had fixed the house from top to bottom himself), the great American novel. While his Wall Street colleagues busied themselves building mini-Versailles, temples to themselves, which, really, any knucklehead with money could do, Will Chapman wanted to move beyond collecting, beyond connoisseurship, to the making of art itself. He wanted to be a novelist. He wanted to be what I was. He wanted to have the nerve, the confidence, the bravado and whatever else it would take (ego) to put Wall Street aside and write. He wanted to make the big-money guys, scooting about in their Jags and Gulfstream IVs, look like the foulmouthed Visigoths they were. He wanted to be authentic to the core. He was in love with me thus (and so was Emma) because I was doing that which he wanted most to do. By studying me they could peer into the life they wished to adopt, test-drive it, as it were; they could examine up close the sacrifices and adjustments they would have to make.

And I, on the outside, wasn't doing so badly for myself. I, India Palmer—thirty-eight years old, four novels under my belt, a fifth, entitled *Generation of Fire*, on the threshold of publication, two daughters in private school, sprawling (albeit rent-stabilized) Upper West Side apartment, winner of the International Book Prize and a Monogram fellowship, nominated for the Washington Award for fiction (the only prize I hadn't touched was the Eiseman, the star of all U.S. literary prizes, but always I hoped)—was the object of Will Chapman's scrutiny and fascination. He wanted to be me. And I? How could I not help but be drawn to him, his wife, his daughters?

What he and Emma did not know was all the rest, all the details of how our lives really were, which I kept neatly tucked away because I could not bear to let them see the shambles, the riotous mess that it was. They did not know, for example, that not one of my novels had sold more than five thousand copies, that the awards by this point had been received long ago. ("That and twenty-five cents will get you a Hershey bar—with almonds," a college professor used to say to anyone who inquired too pointedly about what it took to get an A, and I recalled that tidbit of wisdom when I thought of the awards.) They did not know that my advances had become increasingly smaller, that it was not a good sign that I had had a different publisher for each of the four previous books, that they were now slipping, fast, out of print.

"This isn't unusual," my agent said when I inquired about his other authors, whether they too were slipping into oblivion. A young, driven, intelligent man who seemed, every time I saw him, to get younger. Indeed, he was moving in the opposite direction. He was forty going on twenty, with a wide curl of a smile that revealed imperfect teeth which somehow added to his appeal. He spoke slowly, deliberately and always with a bright intention. The Fox, he was known as, and proud of it; the moniker had previously belonged to Maxwell Perkins and had been earned by my agent for his editorial attention. Day in, day out, he'd labor on a manuscript to make it right, irresistible. And like a fox he was coy and tenacious, determined to become the best agent in New York. It did not matter what it took—poaching, dramatic escapades that put him in the media news. Authors wanted him on their side because he made the numbers add up in the writer's favor. They spoke of the high advances he secured for first novels. He did not shy away from the intent of his ambition, always attended with charm. "We're encountering this with Charles Hamilton, fighting to get the rights reverted," he continued, offering me an example of another out-of-print writer. His voice sang with the confidence of youth and time. I loved Hamilton's work. "But isn't he dead?" I asked. "Why, yes," the Fox said, looking up at me. "Yes, in fact, he is dead." But for the Fox that was a minor detail, did not need to be a hindrance. "In fact, being dead," the Fox averred, "could possibly play in one's favor." He offered a wink.

My trajectory was on the downward side of a parabola reserved for the still living. If *Generation of Fire* sold like the others, I would most likely be unable to sell a sixth book (this was my fear, anyway) and my life as a writer would, in effect, cease. I would enter the twilight, after-market realm of teaching at the university. Untenured, my job was not guaranteed. It depended on, at the very least, a splash of reviews upon publication that would draw attention to me and thus to the university. No, the Chapmans did not know the secret, abject heart of our lives—that it was fueled by hope of the sort barely distinguishable from the hopefuls lining up at the corner stationery store to buy state lottery tickets. We worked hard. There was no alternative. The winds of chance had to sail our way. Our lives rested on a fragile set of stilts, supported by money made long ago on a preposterously big, now all but diminished, advance, on Theodor's irregular commissions, on my salary, on revolving credit card debt, on indefatigable hope.

Theodor made little on his art, small gold objects and figurines, a series of miniatures that he'd begun as a dark joke that had, instead, suddenly found a burgeoning cachet, and along with it the faintest glimmer of what appeared to be a market. Odd people began showing up at his studio to examine the figurines. People whose job it was to be on the phone at auctions making bids for anonymous buyers—Russian oligarchs, Indian industrialists, God knows who. Strange people with unpinpointable, transatlantic accents came by to "have a look." No serious money yet, but there was hope.

The trouble was, the miniatures were exquisitely expensive to make and impossible for the ordinary person to afford, but this did not disturb Theodor. He was not a worrier. Actual commissions came in. He'd made a golden chalice for a famous archbishop (who later became infamous in one of those molestation scandals that riddled the Church). He'd crafted a porringer for Lady Amelia Start's firstborn, daughter of Sir Stewart Start and the heir to London's most notorious billionaire. The porringer was a gift from the Queen Mother's cousin. But these commissions, big as they were, never seemed to attract the wave of attention that would bring Theodor steady work. No matter. The idea of giving up (a constant for me) was not an option for him.

He did not rush his work. Patiently he labored over the depth of the porringer's bowl, the shine of the gold, its ability to catch the light. Tirelessly he worked the fine web of the handle's filigree, studying it in natural light and artificial light to be sure the dance played in both. Even if he had the commissions, it would not make much difference for us, in a life-changing way, because each piece took so long to complete. He would not seek help, an apprentice. He would not cut corners. Creating art was a holy calling, a marriage to the mysterious. He would not put it that way exactly, though he did see the relationship as spiritual—a life lived inescapably in the present moment, no end, no beginning, a meditation, a communion with the dead, with Picasso, with Cellini, a destruction of clocks and time. In that moment something was made, emerged from nothing—a piece of scavenged metal now a porringer for the daughter of a billionaire. Like Davy Crockett waking in the morning to step onto the sun.

How did this nothing become something, the unknown known? When I met Theodor he was living on ramen noodles and tap water. I wanted to save him. Add to the broth Korean seaweed and jumbo shrimp bought cheaply from the fishmongers of Chinatown. The challenge drove me, elegance for pennies so that time could still be ours. We hoarded time like some hoard money. It was our currency. But no matter how clever we were, time passed as it always does, and here we were approaching forty, having to reckon with children and their needs and the choices made in our twenties. Theodor remained in the bubble, art's cocoon, indulging my interest in our new, well-heeled friends as a kind of temporary curiosity, one in which he could participate, with amusement and good cheer, for the time being. But he did not, would not, see it as I did. And though I admired that determination, the priest's vow, I had to acknowledge at last that something like a pivot point had moved within me and I now felt, when I watched him busily in his studio, like one of his strange visitors having a look, an outsider peering in.

"I married an artist," he'd say to me. "You don't have a choice."

Is that true, I'd wonder. Is that true? If I was not an artist, then it was not true. And so here I was in this mess, a quandary of my own inelegant design. To make matters worse, I had not shared much of our money woes with Theodor. Rather, I kept assuming the tides would turn for him, for me. But I had published enough books by now to know what to expect, to know better than to trust in all that. Thus the systems that made our life possible and easier all lined up in front of me like those overused domino tiles waiting to topple even if only one should fall.

The Chapmans knew none of this: that I could not afford the babysitter (with us eight years), the private school, the out-of-network doctors (my older daughter suffered from asthma and we didn't have dental insurance), Theodor's studio, my office, the dinner parties I liked to have, the lessons for the girls—piano and skating and swimming and tennis and soccer and lacrosse. ("Mommy, can I take gymnastics too?") I couldn't afford the expensive notions of the other mothers who'd catch you up in their whims, assuming you had as much money as they—private yoga instruction for the kiddies in their private gyms. The girls needed none of it, I knew that, but how could I tell them we could not afford it? Because I had failed? Failed by introducing them to a life that actually did not belong to them, that was a lie?

The problem of the artist who collects millionaires is that after a while you forget you can't live like them. The Chapmans didn't know that catastrophe loomed before me. If a change in our financial circumstances didn't happen fast, our daughters would be yanked from their nurturing school and placed in the terrible school in our catchment (the word alone sounded like some sort of horrid Dickensian workhouse for children), the one that I passed every day on the way to my office and that reminded me of a prison, riddled with the horror stories of New York public schools—drugs, guns, sex in the stairwells, overcrowding. "Oh, but it's getting better," the private school mothers declared in the park, with a nod of affirmation to the idea of public school. They espoused other progressive, open-minded, liberal ideas. They voted for Democrats and against school vouchers, and in most other things embraced a charming, witty, ironic sense of their own exceptionalism—a condition, perhaps, of their residency on an island of exceptions, subclauses and sneaky provisos double-parked off the midatlantic coast.

What the Chapmans didn't know, above all else, was that if things didn't change, and soon, I would have to give up on myself, on the dream of believing that I had made it or could make it, the artistic life so lauded by those who do not live it. In Wall Street terms I had chosen risk for Theodor and me; we'd gone long on ourselves, invested all we had in ourselves, and the investment was not paying off. We had not hedged. We were driving fast, one hundred miles per hour in our seemingly fancy life, but we were heading toward a brick wall.

Even so, I hoped, pumping and puffing and stretching the borders of reality, a kind of insanity. I hoped. *Generation of Fire* was a big book for my small publisher, the new and rising Leader Inc. Books—five bestsellers in the past three years. A "breakout book," they called my novel. They bought it when it seemed no one else would have it. And Hollywood had expressed interest in the dramatic rights. Streamline Productions and Atomic Pictures and Boss Brothers, names cast about like so many diamonds spraying light. Foreign sales were lining up nicely, nibbles on the line. The publisher was hoping for an excerpt in *The Literary Review.*

It was all but a slam dunk. I was high. The editor and the head of publicity called me regularly, checking my whereabouts, making certain I'd be around, telling me about tour date possibilities and magazines that might do profiles, off-the-book-page opportunities. They even considered hosting a book party, a huge deal these days, an extreme vote of confidence. This time it would happen. It had to. *It* equaled success, and success, of course, equaled money. "Don't think about all this," Theodor told me. "Write." Now if only the reviews would be excellent, if only they'd roll in on time, on their wings the book would lift to the stratosphere. The *if only*s really could align just so this time to unlock the sea of elusive readership. In every part of me I felt that desperate hope.

But then a bill would arrive: tuition, life insurance, American Express thick with its charges to out-of-network doctors (I refused to believe I couldn't accept the best medical care), gourmet food stores, lessons for my girls—their endless lessons. Late at night before the blue light of my computer I would check my dwindling Vanguard balances to see if a stock had taken off, if there was a bank error in my favor. Want, want, want. Need. The wish for a piece of America, our own home, was a noble desire, like a good education or the ability to pay a bill without it stabbing you in the heart. For what was the sacrifice? For art? I hid behind my confident smile, my hair pulled back in a neat ponytail, jeans and a shirt from Agnès B., strolling to school with the girls on either side of me, holding their hands, the stroll of a mother who has few cares, the stroll of ease and success. I am a tall woman and I do not slouch. "We're spending a part of the summer in Europe. My next novel is set there," I say to another mother whose days are defined by gutting and renovating her little $5 million piece of America, a Manhattan townhouse. She has asked about our plans for the summer. The words glide from me with ease, not a lie exactly, perhaps wishful thinking. Who is the authentic one? My grandmother used to say, "If I don't like it the way it happened, I just say it the way it should have happened."

A writer is above all this. A writer has the urge, the irrepressible, antiquated instinct to put one word down after another, to create real houses, real cities, real worlds of real people in imaginary gardens. A writer writes because it is necessary—is, dare I say, spiritually sustained by that necessity and not a need for profit. A writer does not care about profit. A writer writes, and because a writer writes, it seems, a writer goes without, and the list is long of the things forgone, all of it on display as Theodor and I happened from one grand summer vacation home to another, refuseniks camping out in the beds of our children's friends' homes. "Socioanthropology," Theodor called it, spinning gamely. This is all that one gives up for art. But the artist does not care.

Will and Emma Chapman knew none of the weight, the slow, steady pressure, crushing with humiliating might. No, no. They did not, would not ever know all of this. They would not see me on the high wire. My life was beautiful! I was a great literary success! Renowned, as Mr. Hov had said. I was at the top of my career or my game or both, and Will Chapman, the endearing fool, wanted to be me. And so I said to Emma, standing there in that crumbling house that would complete their dreams, on that first afternoon in Maine, the light pouring through the fractured windowpanes, casting rainbows of color on our faces, "We will help you kill them too."

"The plot thickens," Will said, raising his eyebrows.

"India is good at that sort of thing," Theodor added. He shot a knowing look at Emma and Will, one that said he knew his wife inside and out, everything that she was capable of, and with that look he knit them into his intimate knowledge of me. I wasn't sure what he meant, nor do I believe did they, but we all smiled anyway. I caught myself up in their dream, pretending to understand it, wanting it too, I'm afraid, because it seemed to my mind, with its desperate questions, that the Chapmans, with this house, their desire for and appreciation of it, were gently pointing me to a kind of answer.

Two

On a clear May day my life began, lilacs blooming, their scent flooding the hospital room, a bouquet on the bedside table. In my mother's tired and happy arms I wailed, her gorgeous girl, everything long about me. She admired each toe, each finger, my rosebud mouth, my long dark eyelashes and my bright blue eyes that held an intelligence, she could tell, that almost scared her with its ferocity. She loved to tell me that, the haunting power of my newborn eyes. They became mythic even for me. It was the responsibility that terrified her and fascinated her and which culminated in my eyes.

I am seduced by beginnings. I yearn for beginnings. I love to start fresh. A new book. A new day. A new dress, slipping into it to become a new person. Before things become messy, before the predicate traps you.

I was the predicate for my father. He sat in an armchair in the corner of my mother's hospital room, a bit stunned by the wreckage of birth—his wife's dark eyes, drawn and tired cheeks. Looking at me there, a newborn baby girl, he did not think I was beautiful. Rather, he thought I looked like him, with my thin hair and round face, the intensity of my big eyes which held a defiance that declared that I would do as I pleased. He knew this defiance. It was his own, had served him well.

Fragile and delicate, a girl who looked like a man, like him, I grew into a woman he could not protect as he watched me in my mother's arms. Nestled and swaddled and tucked against her chest, emphatically driven by instinct and will. Through his thick horn-rimmed glasses it was easier for him to see bills—the doctors, the clothes, the food, the education: the roller coaster ride ahead of him. He knew how to pay bills. But me, impossibly small, rubbery, how would he manage me?

Dread filled him: I was his responsibility. Panic seized his chest. Already he was dizzy, and he hadn't even left the platform. He was thirty-six years old, a successful urologist in D.C., an "intimate of the urinary tracts of senators and congressmen," affiliated with prestigious Washington General Hospital. In a city where proximity to power is the coin of the realm, he liked to say that he had his finger in the Senate. He owned his house, he invested well, he had his daughter, in a few years he would have his son (now a doctor too, living in London with a fancy wife); my mother never had to work. His will had driven him to create this, comfort for his family that his daughter would discard, sneer at and defy. She grew up before his eyes, from mysterious newborn rooting at her mother's breast to a blue-eyed beauty who would not listen. How could he save me if I would not listen?

That I would not listen made him furious. Standing in our living room, my long hair falling in soft curls about my face, I told him I was going to graduate school, that I would become a writer, that I did not need his blessing. When I was a newborn he could hold me in one hand, but even then he'd felt helpless. He had wanted to be able to explain it to me, the helplessness, the fear, how fragile babies are, how punishing whimsical choices can be. Becoming a writer was whimsy, after all. But he did not know how to bring softness to the negotiating table. Fear did not create tenderness. "I would have written books if I'd had the chance, if someone had believed in me," my mother said in my defense as my father raged about my choice—as if it were a choice, as Theodor so frequently reminded me. "Nonsense," my father declared. "You're a smart girl, capable of choosing. Most writers aren't any good. Most of them don't make a dime, even the good ones. Especially the good ones."

Mom defended me again when I announced that I had married (eloped with) the unpromising Theodor. "You really have no idea," my father said. "You don't get it. He will amount to nothing financially. You can't fathom how hard that will be." And my mother sweetly saying, "Theodor is a nice man. I'd have been an artist if I'd had the option." My mother sweetly saying, "Daddy loves you. That is the reason for all this. Daddy is afraid for you." Isn't it always all for love—the rage, the anger? If he didn't care . . . My father's rage swelled beneath his skin, fear getting the better of him, wrapping around him like the snake around the tree because I was throwing my life away. "Don't come to me for money if that husband of yours can't support you." My father came from nothing, was terrified of going back to nothing, afraid that somehow I would lead him there. Art was for the impractical, for dreamers, for people who didn't know any better, who hadn't suffered the consequences.

And that husband of mine.

I met Theodor at a New Year's Eve party on the Lower East Side. He was sitting on the arm of a couch in a smoky room filled, somehow, only with men. His thick black curls, his red lips, the amused and cynical slant of his eyes drew me to his side of the room. He was engaged in a conversation about the messy state of the Union, which quickly led to the perpetual decline in funding for the arts. We were all so young, dressed in fancy thrift-store wear, a roomful of artists and writers on the threshold of something that we hoped would turn into success and the shape of our lives, smoking, sipping grown-up drinks, martinis.

A plate of cheese bobbed above our heads, passed around the room on raised palms. A small ecumenical Christmas tree languished in the corner, draped in strands of flickering lights in a variety of disguises—red chili peppers, lobsters, cows.

The lights illuminated the faces of Theodor and the men he spoke with, casting them in a colorful yet fleeting glow. Young men offered preposterous, ironical proclamations, trying on the preposterous, ironical art world of New York to see how well it fit. Wealth and poverty, at this intersection, were only abstract notions, fodder to support a line of argument—certainly not something one lived in or inhabited as a condition, something that might actually shape, or perhaps, in the case of poverty, warp and derail a person. If some of us lived like monks in abandoned buildings in Alphabet City, it was because we had chosen to do so. It was a choice that came with its own safety net. We were neither rich nor poor. We were simply young. The atmosphere in the room—the music, the laughter—fanned the egos of the young men, each vying to strike pay dirt with a bon mot or two, and thereby receive, like flowers that blossomed only at night, the further blandishments of laughter, the quick and telling smile, the promise of the night that lay ahead and that animated them in their cluster. They were boys, really, well read, equipped with knowledge of art and literature but otherwise largely untested, likely to put quotation marks around a sunset, a willow tree, the V-shaped flight of geese heading south—anything that smacked of an originating source or destination. Boisterous and enthusiastic, they laughed and leaned on walls, on each other, on the shelves of books written by an older generation that had gone on to fame or oblivion.

The railroad apartment belonged to a poet, a woman in her late thirties with long black hair, long face, long body, referred to as Morticia (though her name was Jane), and she played the part like a Dada throwback from that other distant era, reciting poetry at the strike of her cuckoo clock, which was wedged into a corner against one of her overstuffed bookcases. Musil alongside Zbigniew atop Gibbon, the spines reclining this way and that, no logic to the order. "Look out," someone warned as she quieted the room, "the poetry is about to begin." Jane's furnishings had been proudly hauled off the street and restored with care.

"Stunts like the black Jesus do us in," said an earnest-looking man as I insinuated myself into the cluster that held Theodor. The speaker was a tall guy with freckles and flaming red hair. He gesticulated dramatically, knocking the drink of the blond boy standing next to him. It spilled on the front of his pink oxford shirt and he dabbed at it abstractedly with a cocktail napkin. "No concern," he said. "It's fine." I noticed he wore cuff links.

"The what?" I asked as I said hello. I knew some of the cluster from Jane's other parties and from the artistic youth circuit: a gay poet, a painter, two heterosexual novelists—one tall, one short. Jane collected people with interesting faces and thrust them together as some sort of performance art in combustible human energy, but she was well loved for the effort because everyone enjoyed the parties and, we liked to think, since we ourselves were included, she chose people well. Always she engaged in postparty gossip, keen to know the details of who went home with whom. She kept track of these relationships as some people keep track of their stocks, taking a certain pride in the successful match.

I could feel Theodor's doubtful eyes land on me, a tactile pressure as he tried to make sense of who I was, checking me out with sidelong glances and looks of detached appraisal. Unlike the other women at the party, who now made their way into the room, plopping into the chairs, finding cool spots by the open window, a pretty dye cast into clear water, I was wearing an expensive black dress of silk chiffon that my mother had given me for Christmas with the hope, I believe, that it would attract the right sort of man. The thrift-store aesthetic had never been mine. I imagined Theodor saw me as I saw the blond with the cuff links—out of place. I wanted him to know that I belonged, for it was like a club, this world. I had just sold my first story to *The Literary Review* and I was still a bit smitten with the success, but I knew better than to share the news. News like this you let people discover on their own, while leafing through the magazine's pages. Theodor was big and tall with a ruddy broad charm, and the vodka made me feel a little reckless.

"Stuff like that enrages the Christians, the Catholics, the Republicans. It's all over the news," the blond shouted above the din.

"The chocolate Jesus," someone explained to me.

"Oh, that," I said. The artist had sculpted the figure entirely from chocolate and had left him, also entirely, unclothed. A black, naked, edible Jesus, the Christmas Sensation. Outrage poured through the television screen as the Christian holy season fell upon us. Comparisons with chocolate Allahs and Buddhas and the like were summoned up. HOW WOULD YOU FEEL? was one headline of the gossip pages. A photo of the sculpture captured front and center the genitalia blocked out with a black rectangle. Another headline read: EAT ME?

"This kind of stunt—and it is a stunt—is self-serving, but so what?" said the gay poet. "I mean, look at us. We're talking about it. The *Post* is talking about it. It's a success."

"Art becomes advertising—and we're all okay with that?" said one of the novelists, the tall one with enormous hands. He'd received a big advance for his first novel and spoke with authority, though no one I knew thought much of his talent. Everyone liked him all the same.

"That's the oldest trap in the book," the other novelist blurted, sloppily draping an arm around me with a smile, and then removing it with a sincere and disarming apology—he'd mistaken me for somebody else and suddenly became drunkenly bashful and solicitous, offering to fetch me another drink. "Don't mind me, I'm incoherent as a general rule, alas." He was like the rest of us, living on tips from two restaurant jobs and sending out short stories to literary magazines in Nebraska and Seattle.

"Free expression suicide," said the blond with the cuff links, as if trying to convince himself, a bit out of his league, it seemed. I wondered if he was a banker scouting the young art market, looking for long-term investments. Shrewd boy. The discussion turned to funding for artists. The gay poet rolled his eyes. "Writers," he said, "everyone pecking fiercely at a carcass, fighting for scraps of flesh, so little to go around." He turned on his heels, decamping for the kitchen.

Theodor caught my eyes and held them for a moment, and a generous sweetness, mixed with a dash of bravado, poured from him to me. He wore checked pants that would have looked preppy on the blond but on Theodor had a stylish flair, black loafers with no socks and a black T-shirt. He seemed to understand something. I didn't know what. But it sat there on his beautiful lips, making me curious to learn whatever it was. He had a girl's long eyelashes.

"That's what the government wants," said the blond guy. "What do you want to bet at some point this fraud received funding from a government grant? It gives them license. 'See how taxpayer money is being spent?'"

"Don't be paranoid."

"Paranoid? The government wants to control everything—art, philosophy, law, the air even, the air we breathe, you breathe."

"It shows that they really care."

"Art reduced to a state of servility, having to depend on the likes and dislikes of government lackeys," said one of the novelists, allowing himself to be carried far away from the chocolate Jesus.

"Lackeys? Really? You sound like a drunk Socialist Party newspaper." The redheaded man tossed back the rest of his martini. He jutted the empty glass out in front of him. Theodor took an imaginary bottle from his pocket, filled the glass, then raised his own and said, "Here, here. We struggle for the sake of art, and art"—he paused for emphasis, like a car going over a cliff—"*art* is a very important thing." The group laughed. "Interrogate the chocolate," he continued. "What kind of chocolate did the artist use?"

"The artist's aesthetic concern, of course," said the tall, untalented novelist.

"What kind of chocolate?" I repeated. The silliness made me giddy.

"If you can't eat it, the rest is nonsense, right?" Theodor both asked and stated, ceding a little of that something that he understood, like a fisherman who lets out his line only to be more certain of hooking the fish. He raised his glass to mine, eyes sparkling as he estimated the impression he had made on me.

"You mean if he uses cheap chocolate, what's the point?" I asked.

"I mean if it is supposed to be edible—and it's Jesus we're talking about—then it better be good."

"For example, Godiva?" I asked.

"That would do."

"Teuscher?"

"Belgian Callebaut would prove he's serious."

The blond boy said, "The great one speaks." He did not seem to be joking.

"The great one," I said. "So who anointed you?"

"He's just won the Austria Prize from the Kunsthistorisches," said the blond with what seemed to be a perfect accent.

"The what?" I asked.

"Come on," said Theodor—whose name I did not yet know. "No résumé-building. Tonight I think we are all drunken socialists, no?" I didn't believe that. If he was anything like a male writer, résumé-building was exactly what he wanted.

"Do you know each other?" I asked. Someone had knocked into me, pushing me closer to the blond and to Theodor so that we became our own constellation, the others fading away one by one.

"I'm his dealer," said the blond boy.

"Dealer." I laughed. "Ecstasy? Pot? You look like you're still in high school."

"I work for his dealer," he confessed bashfully, vodka flushing his cheeks. He had an adorable mouth, fine straight white teeth. His cuff links were blue Wedgwood. An aspiring assistant. His determination was ferocious. He'd be somewhere in a few years.

"What do you do?" I asked Theodor.

"Is this a test?" he said, tilting his gaze up to meet mine.

"Yes," I replied.

"I'm a collector," he answered. "A trash collector."

"Oh, please," I said. He too was bubbling with the alcohol. "You won the Austria Prize for trash?"

"It's true," he said and looked to the blond.

"Scout's honor," the boy said.

"Just so you know," Theodor said, "and by way of offering a blanket apology, nobody here, including myself, will ever be remembered—for anything." The blond smiled, a telling knowledge of his friend, and retreated quietly to another conversation.

"That's optimistic," I said. "A real upper."

"I'm a realist," he said.

"Trash?" I repeated.

"I collect junk and reshape it and then sell it. It's a value-added service." Then he looked me over again with an awful, awful appeal, and added, "And you're a rich girl."

"I'm a novelist," I said defensively. But I liked the notion, myself as a rich girl.

"But you're also," he said, raising his glass and pointing his forefinger, "a rich girl."

"Will you speak to me if I'm poor?"

"The dress gives you away, my darling." I felt suddenly darling and cocked a cute little smile.

"Perhaps I stole it." I liked that notion too, the idea of stealing a beautiful dress. The idea seemed to give him pleasure. It was hot in the room, everyone pressing together, waves of human movement.

"A thief," he said, raising his left eyebrow. "Interesting." We were shouting above the din. He stood up from the arm of the couch to move closer to me. We were pushed against a bookcase—Waugh and Yeats and Freud and Borges.

"A thief," I confirmed. His eyes brightened.

"It just so happens I'm in need of a thief," he said.

"You're in luck, then," I said. I felt dangerous. A bottle of cheap champagne appeared in his hand and he filled our glasses and we drank them down and he filled them again. The vodka and the champagne mixed in me in a daring combination.

"What are we going to steal?" I asked. "More trash?"

"Trash," he confirmed.

"I don't like that."

"Rich girl!" he said. His curls were wild and unruly, ferocious.

"India," I corrected and reached out my hand to him. "I'm India Palmer."

"And I'm sub-Saharan Africa. Nice to meet you," he said and took my hand in his. He had long slender fingers, a cool palm. A small mole vanished into his dimple as he smiled.

"It was the dress," he said later. "I wanted to take it off of you."

And he had (if my mother only knew), in his studio in Greenpoint, in the brightness of New Year's morning, the sun streaming through the big paned window, the streets below a foreign land with signs in unfamiliar Polish, advertising unfamiliar Polish foods. In the silent hours of the new day, the New Year, I pretended to be a dangerous woman, a thief. I'd followed him home, out of Jane's party and across the Brooklyn Bridge, shivering in the New Year, lips blue, teeth clattering—not a very alluring thief. On the bridge he tilted my head upward, showing me the weave of cables, filigree against the midnight sky, both of us in a drunken rapture over the intricacy of the design. The American flag fluttered boldly from one of the towers. "Hypothermia and romance," he'd declared, enveloping me in his coat and arms. "Beautiful together."

We walked all night across Brooklyn, from the bridge to his studio. I'd followed him along the banks of the Salvage Stream, as he called it, the big swath of garbage that cut through the city like a big river snaking across the continent, or perhaps the Gulf Stream spanning the world's sky, as he plucked from it the garbage of others, metals and ceramics that he intended to reinvent in his sculptures. Beauty from ugliness, he wanted to prove a point, but he was too drunk (and so was I) to be any good at the task. "I'm showing off for you," he said, pulling a cracked vase lined with green slime from rotted flower stems, holding it proudly before me, a trophy of his cleverness. The thing was hideous, almost laughable.

"You need to work harder, then," I said. "The vase smells." It did, of the dank rot of foliage. He looked at me with those curls, trying to come up with an intelligent response, and examining the vase once again, sniffing it, he said, "By George, you're right," and set it gently on the sidewalk so the glass did not shatter. I remembered that detail, how carefully he set it down. As filled with vodka and champagne as we were, he would not let the glass break. As it turned out, I was right about a lot of the junk he wanted to claim. But even so, we had fun. He was trying his mightiest to succeed before me, to pull off a layer of the city like a real estate agent lifting up a shag carpet to show a potential buyer the parquet floor beneath. I'd followed him because what he understood was simply what he wanted. I'd followed him because he was leading me through the gates of Parnassus, showing me that entry there did not depend on credentials. That's what I found in the trash. Alchemy. Something from nothing. You either had it or you didn't. That's why the artist has never had to doff his hat to the king. I followed him. It did not feel like a choice.

"I followed you," he'd say later.

We married at City Hall. Theodor carried a bouquet of daisies, wearing a white suit from a thrift store, his black curls falling here and there about his lovely face. I wore my mother's wedding dress, stolen from her attic, cream-colored with age, long with a full skirt and one hundred satin buttons running down the back to meet a bustle. We borrowed another eloping couple to use as our witnesses and then walked to the subway and took the train to JFK and flew across the country (still in our wedding clothes, showered with the smiles and good wishes of strangers). From Seattle, we took a bus and two ferries and hitched a ride to a small hotel called the Tiger Inn, which was also a commune.

Theodor had heard about it from his nomadic artist friends, heard that they welcomed anyone; they especially loved artists. They allowed their guests to help out in some way if they couldn't afford to pay. We stayed in the "honeymoon suite," a small room built into a tree with a view of Puget Sound and the seals that lay lazily on the inn's small rocky beach. We helped in the kitchen, causing guests and communards alike to love us because we knew how to cook. Theodor carved a Ganesh out of wood, a small offering. The owners were converted Hindus and the property was thick with lingams and Shivas and Parvatis, but it did not have a Ganesh, the elephant god, the god of household harmony and success. We stayed ten days and then flew home to a life in which everything was new and ours, and ours to design.

Our plane landed at dusk, circling the city. The setting sun cast its spell on Manhattan. Pink clouds floated like scarves above the skyscrapers. Far below, the mad rush of work clogged the streets, the taxi horns, the sighing of buses, the hammering of so much development, cranes reaching to the skies, the voice of New York growing. I wanted to be down there, a part of it, hungry for everything that a life there implied, absorbing the love and intelligence, the urgency that New York exhaled. I was impatient for our life to begin, to take on New York like the immigrant who arrives with nothing and ends up the king of advertising. From the plane's window I could see all the landmark buildings, their tops dominating the sky like grand chateaus.

"I want New York to be ours," I said.

"It already is," Theodor answered.

"No it isn't," I said emphatically. "Not yet, but it will be."

Three

NOW WE WERE in Maine, a dozen years later, Emma and I, reading in chairs on the beach in our dark glasses and swimsuits, our legs half hidden in the warm sand. A lazy afternoon, the newspaper flapped about in the gentle breeze and the remains of our picnic lunch dried up in the sun. Seagulls circled overhead, waiting to dart down for a snack. We had brought up the finest stinky French cheeses that Citarella had for sale—Cap Gris Nez and Pont l'Évêque and Époisses and Langres. It was my secret attempt to both impress and stump Will, but of course Perfect Boy knew each cheese and the region from which it came, could pronounce the names perfectly in his perfect French, had toured one of the farms.

Early that morning I'd baked Cuban bread, kneaded it up to the oohs and aahs of the Chapmans. Emma had set up a picnic on the beach, on a green checked tablecloth with wine and an ice bucket and stemmed glasses. She had made lobster salad, the lobsters steamed in a tarragon butter infusion from a *Gourmet* recipe. "But India is the real cook," she kept saying, as if in apology, perhaps in case the salad was not good. But it was just as delicious as she'd intended. Even her girls had devoured it.

And I'll confess, I wished my girls had too. They were polite, of course. They poked at the salad but left it at the edge of their plates, and in the sun, the red lobster tail a bright reminder of the limitations of their palates. "Didn't they like it?" Emma had asked. "Can I get them something else? Something more kid friendly? Anything you need, don't hesitate. We can buy it at the store." I'd assured her they'd be fine and so did they, allowing me to pop runny cubes of Époisses and Langres into their sweet mouths. I hoped they would not spit out the pungent cheese. They didn't. For the most part, they too played the game. They ate well, requested nothing simple—no chicken fingers, French fries or hot dogs. They savored and appreciated and tried, just as we grown-ups did, the delicacies of life, knowing, it seemed, that it was required of them, part of the job description of the New York City child.

The girls played dare with the cold Atlantic, chasing the waves, running away from them: my oldest, Gwyneth (we called her Gwen most of the time), my youngest, Ruby; Emma's oldest, Elisabeth, her youngest, Catherine. They giggled and shouted and carried on. Will and Theodor worked on sandcastles they had started with the girls. I studied them: tanned, fit, stooped over, deep inside their moats, intricate spires rising, bridges spanning towers, secret tunnels, flying buttresses. At some point, Theodor had gone back to the basement of the old house and brought out two shovels, assorted five-gallon buckets and trowels. The sandcastles that slowly emerged as the afternoon progressed attracted beach strollers, who paused to admire them.

I had watched the castles grow over the course of the day, but it was only now that I recognized the ambition in them. I noticed Emma's head rise from her pages to study our husbands too. "Look at the castle builders," she said. "Pretty soon we'll have a local TV crew stopping by for an interview." But we both admired our men. Sand flew from their shovels as they fashioned their towers and dug their moats, sand piling up rhythmically. We could see their backs, the curve of their spines, their hard-won muscles defining their arms.

"In castles, especially, size matters," I said.

"Ontogeny recapitulating phylogeny," she said, lifting her right eyebrow.

"Huh?" I said and thought hard for a moment.

"Biology," she reminded, widening her eyes. I'd heard the phrase a thousand times but could never remember what it meant. "You know, the relationship between embryonic development and biological evolution. But really, all it boils down to is two guys in a hole trying to outdig each other."

There was something slightly awry in her explanation, but I laughed anyway, because I could tell she wanted to impress me, and that desire, and its near achievement, drew me closer to her.

Just then a plane swooped down from the sky, a bright yellow, old-fashioned biplane. Emma's girls started to shout, "Win. Win. It's Win coming to visit!" They chased after the plane, running down the beach as fast as they could as if they believed they might catch it. Sunlight spilled over them, bathing them in gold. As they ran, the plane lifted again into the sky, a fabulous yellow bird.

"What a surprise," Emma said. "It's Win." I had heard them talk about Win before, another one of their storied friends, the millionaire Casanova, always with a different bombshell on his arm, but Theodor and I had never met him, and I had paid only vague attention when they discussed him. He was from the side of their life that had nothing to do with us, *their* Tribeca, Wall Street life of big money and big players and big stakes. The girls raced up to their mother and collapsed into her with giggles and excitement.

"You didn't tell us Win was coming," Elisabeth and Catherine said in unison. Though two years separated them, they seemed like twins, extensions of each other, a pair of butterflies fluttering across life. My daughters were not like that. Gwen, strikingly beautiful, was an independent soul, and though she loved Ruby madly she did not need to be entertained by her. Gwen's beauty lay in the intensity of her eyes; they commanded respect and a desire to pay attention. As pretty as Ruby was, she did not have the same intensity, and I believe it made her need more the reassurance of companionship.

"He didn't say he was coming when he called," Emma responded, looking surprised—bewilderment arranged the features of her face into a vulnerable and refreshingly honest composition. With her children she was sincere. Nothing artificial stood between them, and I always admired the glimpses I'd catch into that side of her, which I wanted to pry open and step inside and become a part of, a hope that our friendship would be able to accommodate vulnerability. Then she relaxed, sank back into her chair, and to me said, "We have an unexpected guest."

"An unexpected guest," I repeated. "I love it in stories when the stranger comes to town."

"Yes, it's a good twist," Emma said, "for your new book about this weekend. Don't tell me you haven't been taking notes!"

"I have. *The House at Pond Point: The Emma Chapman Story*," I said.

"God help us," Emma replied with a smile, pushing her feet farther into the sand in a nervous gesture, as if she liked the notion of becoming a character a little more than she would have wanted to let on. We watched the plane bank to the left and disappear. "He'll be here in about twenty minutes."

"What kind of name is Win?" Gwen asked in that direct way of hers, her hard intelligent eyes fixed on Elisabeth as if to make her prove something. Somehow Gwen had skipped naiveté and gone straight to knowledge and logic. Ruby stood by me now, her arms hanging limply, trying to read her sister to ascertain if Win was a positive thing, or if Win might steal something from their lovely afternoon.

"It's Win's kind of name," Elisabeth answered, protectively. Hers was clearly a world in which everything was good and safe and bountiful, and the light that emanated from her eyes was a protected one. Gwen's question challenged something that was beyond Elisabeth's conscious ability to comprehend, but instinctively she got it. She held Gwen with her big eyes, which softly said, *Leave my world alone.*

"Let me guess," I said. "Win wins a lot."

"Um-hmm."

"It's Win, darling," Will said, approaching from his sandcastle.

"You know that guy?" Theodor asked, approaching too. He was about to say *That jerkoff in the biplane,* I could tell, but had restrained himself. He held a shovel; sand clung to his legs and arms and cheeks, to his lips even, his hair. The sand had turned his black hair gray. Somehow the sand had not managed to make such a mess of Will. ("It's because I was working harder," he would say to me later. "Hah," I'd respond triumphantly, "so the rivalry does exist.")

"We should bring down some champagne," Will said.

"Absolutely," Emma said and stood up, took her girls in hand and ran off to the house, racing through the pea shoots and the dunes and the sea grass, returning a short while later with champagne flutes, a chilled bottle, the ice bucket refreshed, and Win trailing behind like her prize. He wore goggles around his neck and blue jeans and black combat boots and a leather jacket over a white T-shirt, an ersatz Howard Hughes. He was almost tall and definitely full (indeed a little thick), as if he had enjoyed a few good meals, the kind of person you wouldn't look at twice if he didn't own confidence—and money.

But Win did. You felt it immediately. His I-don't-care attitude lent an aura of self-assurance to each step he made toward us—a swagger, actually, more than a step. His paunch pushed against the white T-shirt; the jeans were too tight. He was not handsome. Not one bit. But it did not matter. He oozed bravado, and that was what got you interested in him—he was a puffed-up little man accustomed to getting just what he wanted, I imagined. Asshole, I thought. His sandy hair was thin and windblown; his face and nose were soft, round, as were his eyes. A platinum watch wrapped his wrist. He reeked of money, new money, recently made and thoroughly enjoyed in the sloppy sort of way that was as much about waste as it was about the possession of some fine *objet.* Aside from the goggles, which themselves were preposterous, he had succeeded in affecting the high-rolling winner I had envisioned when his plane swooped down upon us.

The Chapman girls, dizzy with excitement, tugged at him, competing with each other for his ear. They wanted him to know certain recent accomplishments: Catherine's blue ribbon in the riding show; Elisabeth's first place in the fencing match; Catherine's prize in the summer spelling bee; Elisabeth's plan to take Hindi lessons. "We're getting an Indian au pair," she declared. My, what a lot these girls have accomplished, I thought. But I was more fascinated by their idolatry. Idolatry is born of influence and suggestion. I could intuit that their fascination was Emma's. Win flirted with the girls, scooping them up and heaving them into the air to catch them. I imagined he had tossed them many times when they were tiny and had forgotten that they were now too old and heavy for this. But he did not let on when he caught them. He ruffled their hair and then pulled from the pocket of his leather jacket the small, unmistakable green boxes of Teuscher's truffles. He had brought four boxes, two of them for my girls, which he gave to Elisabeth and Catherine, instructing them to take the chocolates to their friends. A thoughtful asshole, I thought.

As he approached us, he absorbed us: Theodor at work on

his castle with our daughters once again, legitimizing the effort; Will, who had been talking about *Generation of Fire* and its publication, about tour plans and anxieties I might be feeling (he was a genuine, warm and caring person, attentive in a way that made me admire him for taking such good care of Emma and their girls, suppressing his own literary ambitions because it would cost his family too much. I almost felt I could be honest around Will, reveal all, money concerns and woes, and that if I did open up, he might try to fix them for me); and me with my legs stretched out, *The Mayor of Casterbridge* resting on them. And then Win was above me, his shadow pressing over me.

"He sells his wife," Win said and offered a smile. It was a bold smile yet warm, and that sent a thrilling rush through me, one of possibility that surprised and appalled me and that I immediately dismissed, embarrassed, almost as if the rush had been visible. I did not like this man.

"What is it with you Wall Street types? You all read. I hadn't thought you read," I responded, trying mightily to conceal that he had knocked me off balance. Will and Emma laughed. They were familiar with my wonderment at the literary intelligence of the Wall Street type.

"How do you know I'm a Wall Street *type?*" he asked, emphasizing the word in order to draw attention to my reduction of him. He stared hard at me, scrutinizing me as if reading me, as if it were that easy for him, as if deciding for himself that he would buy me, should I be offered up for sale.

"I don't know. Arriving in a biplane, the boots," I said. Everyone rose suddenly, sensing tension, and shook hands. Win was not as tall as I had first thought. It was the confidence that lent him height. I, tall for a woman, was almost his height. I looked him in the eye, brown, like a deep dark expensive Swiss chocolate, like the chocolates he had brought for the girls.

"You're a bond trader," I said.

"Mortgages," he replied. "You're a writer."

"Novelist," I said.

"She's publishing a novel in the fall," Emma fairly sang. "We're going to have a huge party for her at the loft and invite hundreds of our friends and they're going to be required to buy dozens of copies of her book and to spread the word to all their friends."

But it was clear from Win's face that he didn't need Emma's help deciding if I was legitimate or not. In an instant he sized me up, formed an opinion, and though I would never reveal that I wanted to know what that opinion was, I did. I had never before been summed up so fast and so blatantly, so audaciously. Emma carried on with her exuberant plans, which seemed to have more to do with Win than with me—as if I were some sort of commodity being traded, though I didn't understand for whom and for what gain. Or perhaps it was just the excitement of the moment.

"You'll let us, won't you?" Emma asked, and I smiled my assent. Will popped open the champagne and soon we were all talking and drinking, and the chill of the Maine afternoon gave over to the warming sensation of the champagne.

We were standing at the edge of the Atlantic, the sun beginning its slow descent, the tide closing in on the castles. Will engaged Win in business talk. Emma chimed in—derivatives, yield curves, investment opportunities, bets involving the mortgage market, company scandals, the stuff of their world that meant nothing to Theodor and me. Their conversation sounded like another language.

"More socioanthropology," Theodor whispered under his breath. This was not where we belonged. But isn't this how it happens? It is said that there are only two real plots: someone leaves town or someone arrives. Win arrived like the stranger in the fiction I love so well, to take me, our lives, in a direction that, as clever as I can be, I could never have designed. A stranger had arrived, Win had arrived, fresh, new, sudden, in a biplane like the *deus* in the *machina*.

Four

HIS NAME, BELIEVE IT or not, was Wayne Johns. (His parents had met at a drive-in screening of *Stagecoach* and fell in love over their mutual admiration for the actor.) Firstborn. Mathematical wizard. Father was a math teacher in Akron, Ohio. His mother taught home economics. Republicans. Financially sound if not wealthy. They owned their home, owed no debt, taught their children to be precise with numbers. When I met him in Maine on that July day he was thirty-four years old, four years younger than I was. He had three younger sisters. The baby's name was Betsy, and as a toddler Betsy had the hardest time pronouncing Wayne's name, so gave up altogether and called him Win. He became Win, adopted a John Wayne swagger and a half-cocked smile and learned not to bother with apologies.

Win went to Yale and then to Columbia, from where he was taken in by Bond & Bond Brothers because he'd met the wife of a senior partner (her name was Pretty) at a party on the terrace of a Park Avenue penthouse with a 360-degree view of the city. Pretty liked Win's smile and approached him as he admired the view. She also liked the fact that he had gone to Yale (like her husband) and that he was finishing his MBA—his career trajectory unfolding over sips of citrus martinis. Her husband had not gone beyond a bachelor's degree, but when he started out a good fifteen years earlier, higher degrees were all but unheard of, especially in the field of mortgage bonds.

Pretty's husband, Ralph Radalpieno, had been at the forefront of the mortgage bond market, instrumental in the mid-1980s in the dissemination of the collateralized mortgage obligation (CMO)—an invention that made home mortgage bonds look more like other bonds, which greatly increased their appeal, turning them into viable bank and insurance company investments. (For a long time this would mean nothing to me, but back at the beginning of it all, I tried to pretend, at the very least, that I cared.) Radalpieno made money, lots of money, and that money, as it will, translated to power, not only his own but also his wife's. Pretty was a power broker and got Win a job because she liked him, his name, his smile, his sparkling brown eyes. Win followed Radalpieno to Bond & Bond Brothers, apprenticed with him after completing a required training program meant to weed out people who really belonged elsewhere—down in the world below, where you and I live with our quaint, picayune cares—began trading mortgages after six months and within a year was raking in millions of dollars for the company. Win had brains and stamina and an unending supply of clever ideas. He could work eighteen-hour days and schmooze until dawn. He had market savvy and a knack for predicting trends and habits on the big scale and the small. He found himself launched into an Olympian milieu, and as luck would have it, he soared.

Every now and then he would look back on it all—say, when his personal driver had somehow gotten derailed and he couldn't catch a cab uptown, a cold rain blowing sideways, and a shudder would go up his neck—how easily it could have been otherwise. But no. He was resourceful, with resources—a clip of hundred-dollar bills to feed to a pedicab driver who would wrap him in a snug blanket and wheel him uptown for all he was worth, and Win would make better time than he would have in a taxi. Clever Win. Smart Win. The little brown-eyed, pudgy boy from Akron grew into his name, embraced the bravado, bought a few too many sailboats and planes, as might anyone who received $10 million bonuses (the biplane, by the way, was only an amusing toy; for serious travel he was flown in a G-IV). He eased his way into conversations, into beautiful women, into fast cars and quick thinkers in Davos and Cupertino, and he rose—how else to put it?—to the level of kings.

I learned these details from Win's unofficial biographer, Emma. He was with us in Maine for exactly twelve hours, and as we walked across that afternoon and night, whenever the chance arose Emma took me aside to fill me in on Win and his life, speaking with that same intense enthusiasm of hers, revealing for me a new shade of Emma, a deference I had not observed before. She hung on Win's words, smiled up to him solicitously when he spoke to her, asked him about his plans for the summer, and you could read an inner calculus, a way of measuring whether she'd planned her summer with enough savoir-faire. Later, in August, they were headed for Paris, an apartment in Saint-Germain-des-Prés. Win approved. "Rue Christine?" he asked. "Well, yes," Emma answered with a bright smile—rewarded by his approval.

Money had that power too, and I felt a further warmth for Emma, knowing she was not immune to the consuming fire that sometimes raced through me. Her family, after all, were not New England blue bloods; they were from Indiana. Her mother, a professor of nineteenth-century English literature at Bloomington, had the annoying habit of asking me if my books sold well. The few times I'd met her it was her first question, and she'd ask, "How can you possibly make a living?" An attractive woman with striking white hair and silver eyes. For the most part, Emma's family stayed in the Midwest, leaving Emma to be absorbed by Will and all his sisters. He had five of them—lovely, opinionated women, all with serious careers, who would chide Will for how he cultivated his girls. "Gstaad," one of them once said. "The girls don't need Gstaad. That's entirely unnecessary and a waste of money. They'll have Gstaad when they grow up."

We were taking a walk on the beach and Win strode in front of us with an annoying bounce of the heel, as if, even when it came to putting one foot in front of the other, he were somehow more ready to ambulate than we common bipeds. Theodor and Will, kicking a soccer ball, kicked it to Win. The four girls collected sand dollars at the water's edge. Each find caught them by surprise, as if each sand dollar were a sterling coin. Emma whispered, though the wind would have hidden her words: "Will says he's the best mortgage trader on the Street. He's untouchable, a seer." Watching Win run after the ball, he seemed more like a guy who never made the varsity team, but the way Emma spoke about him, the way she held him up and turned him around for me, telling me about his G-IV and his sailboat and his apartment on Park Avenue and his ski lodge in Cervinia—the care with which she told his story, it was as if she were telling the tale not of a friend but of a mythic figure.

He turned and kicked the ball to me, a little too hard to be just play, and I, who did make the varsity team, sent it whistling past his ear, which got him racing with Gwen down the beach, her hands clutching sand dollars. The stiff shore breeze caught the ball and carried it very far, and soon everyone was running to save the ball.

"Where's Casanova's girlfriend?" I asked.

"Which one?" Emma said.

"Oh, right. Of course," I said.

They were all showered in the late-afternoon light that painters love so well, racing along the water, splashing it up around their ankles. Win had the easy manner of one who wanted for nothing. Will made plenty, sure, but he was not pursuing his dream in order to keep Emma's wants at bay. He wanted to be a writer; already he had written hundreds of pages in the wee hours of the morning. She wanted a house, and I wondered if she would continue to want it had she all the money in the world. But Win was something else again. Win had the heel bounce. He was doing exactly as he pleased.

I had no idea what a mortgage trader did or what a mortgage bond was or why and how so much money could be made off of other people's puny debts, if indeed that was the case. For a while yet I would not understand that these puny debts were packaged and put together and compiled, which in turn created not just a revenue stream of batched, bundled and tranched mortgage payments but a colossal revenue river—a Mississippi, an Orinoco megaflow. I had no idea that homeowners as a consolidated group of borrowers accounted for $8 trillion of debt, exceeding by a long shot the combined United States stock markets as the largest capital market in the world. I did not appreciate, because I had not contemplated before, that these traders moved massive quantities of this debt between borrowers and investors and back again with the press of a button, with all the ease of a gambler rolling a pair of dice at a Las Vegas casino—luck mixed with savvy and not a little appreciation for the sentiment of the market.

I knew nothing of that. I was ignorant in a very basic way, because the subject had never meant a thing to me. My world, down here among the masses, had never collided with the intricacies of high finance. I didn't own my own home, so a mortgage was an abstraction, something that other people had. More adult people. Not artists, for instance. Owning a home was something I longed for. A home mortgage was the vehicle by which one lifted oneself by the bootstraps into the realm of adulthood, into commerce, into seriousness, into the general franchise. But debt, so assembled and gathered as I would come to see it, was a bracing chasm. Across it we walked even if we had no idea of the depths of this dream, how it was becoming the blood of our economy. So, naturally, I knew nothing then about CMOs and Fannie Maes and the LIBOR rate and tranches and thrifts and prepayments and interest rate swaps and amortization and negative convexity. I did not appreciate or understand the influence of a change in interest rates, the ups and downs of consumer spending, company forecasts, the price of oil and natural gas, fluctuations in currencies, the weather (mudslides and hurricanes and tornadoes and extreme heat waves and blizzards) and personality types (the ability to herd people like sheep) on the value of debt. Subprime loans and ARM loans and hybrid adjustable-rate mortgages and balloons and Alt-A's and prepay penalties meant nothing to me either.

But I did know that Win made money, lots of it, so very, very much of it. The kind of money he made had nothing to do with the kind of money Will made, that was clear. I hadn't understood that there was a hierarchy on Wall Street, that hedge fund guys and traders ranked at the top, that people like Will, who brokered financial deals for enormous corporations and who made more money, by a long shot, in a month than we made in a good year, were lower on the totem pole. Making little, in comparison, had made me curious about a person's ability to earn so very much. Who were they and what were they and where were they and how did they think and what drove them? There was something of the romance of the cowboy, of John Wayne, out there riding the range alone. The fearlessness, the cool confidence, needed to risk so much. Most of all the idea of pooling people, of trying to understand how they operated psychologically (all the yous and all the mes with our various styles of spending and saving, our susceptibility to trends, our ridiculous hopes that place all our bets on tomorrow, thus making us so foolish today) as a collective lot, reading them and translating their likely actions into the amassing of money on a colossal scale, a scale bigger than the entire combined U.S. stock markets—this was better than the plot of any story I'd read in a while. This was a story line on an Olympian scale. This was imagination at work, imagination with consequences—nothing less.

We were seated at the picnic table, alone on the deck, Win and I. He was before me, not one bit handsome but attractive all the same. Between us flamed a candle casting shadows on his face, highlighting his thin hair. He had shaved for dinner, and the illuminated portions of his face shined like the surface of fine china. He made no concessions to L. L. Bean. He wore a pink shirt with silver cuff links that splashed the candle's light whenever he raised his hands to gesticulate about one thing or another. The others were inside: Theodor putting the girls to bed, Will steaming lobsters, Emma preparing drinks.

From the kitchen we could hear lids banging against pots. Will was in charge of the dinner and had forbidden Emma and me from helping. He wanted none of our fancy recipes. The clams and lobsters would be steamed simply in sea water, with the seaweed he'd collected from the ocean, carrying the big pot to the water's edge wearing his flip-flops and khakis. Studying him as he went, I understood that simplicity was a vacation for him, a connection to what he quested for: the plain expanses that described the life of a writer. If he only knew.

Emma had instructed Win and me to watch for the moon, which was to rise, full, in a few minutes from behind the northernmost of the small islands. It was low tide and you could see the sandbars reaching to the islands floating just offshore. The sun had set and it was getting dark, but paths of fuchsia spilled across the sky. Lobster boats puttered toward the harbor and a few sailboats drifted on the horizon. The house might be nothing much, but Emma sure had the view right. It was gorgeous, and Win agreed and started talking about how the present owners would probably have to sell someday soon.

"That little girl—what was her name? Sacagawea? Really?"

Win shook his head and smiled. "That little girl with the ridiculous name's parents will inherit the house from the childless Hovs, but little Sacagawea's parents have three other children and no money. But they love the place and will want to try to scheme and hang on." A nice sum dangled before them, he explained, would certainly outweigh sentimentality if dangled at the right time. "The trick for Emma," Win said, "will be the timing of her offer. Too soon, and she'll alienate them; too late, and she'll lose it to someone else. If she can gauge just when they'll be desperate enough but without taking umbrage at an offer, she could do very well."

"The Hovs aren't dead yet," I remarked.

"Details," he answered, and I thought of my agent, the Fox. "I'm simply telling the story." I was at first touched that he cared enough about Emma's dream to figure it out for her, but realized it was the game that engaged him here, the sheer sport of picking off what you wanted from life. How could someone be so smug about other people's fortunes?

Emma appeared through the screen door to offer us champagne. Her hair was wet and flat, severe and beautiful; she had Cleopatra's hair. She smiled at us as she pushed the flutes into our hands. (She'd brought the flutes from New York because she could not bear to drink champagne from anything else.) "I'm going to help Theo put the girls down. He's so wonderful, India, so delightful with the girls. But I fear they'll do more giggling than sleeping if I don't oversee a bit."

Theodor never went by Theo, only with Emma. In the beginning I had tried correcting her, but she'd persisted, out of fondness, and so we indulged her. She turned to head back inside, glanced over her shoulder at us and said to Win, "Watch out for all of India's questions. She's a thief. Anything you say could end up in one of her novels." Her expression held a knowing smirk, one that possessed me entirely for the benefit of Win.

“She’s already working on one about me. What is it again? *Pond Point: The Emma Chapman Story*?” She threw back her head and laughed.

“Just keep talking, Emma,” I said.

“See, Win? I’m warning you.” The screen door slammed. She and Will were always teasing me for taking notes, doing research. They were certain that in one form or another they’d appear in my next book. I thought perhaps she’d make a good character, maybe not as a lead but in a lesser role, the supportive wife of a man who gives up everything to write a novel. “Will you still love her if you appear in a book?” Theodor had asked Emma once. She had looked at him incredulously and said, “How could I ever stop loving India?”

Win watched Emma go with a look of admiration—her determination to sip champagne only from flutes, to desire this house, to possess me. “She’ll get this house if she wants,” he said. I felt unaccountably annoyed. Not because I wanted the house too, but because Win would guide her toward the winning of it and thus the completion of her dreams. And she had that ability always to have just what she wanted. She never languished too long between want and have. And I felt, as if by cosmic design or simply by my choice of profession, I would always want.

“Would you buy this house?” I asked.

“Wouldn’t you?” Win said.

“Why, no,” I said. That was the truth, but I hadn’t meant to say it. I had meant to agree with him. He was a man who could buy himself any view, anywhere. I had not expected him to respond positively.

“You don’t like the fleas?” he asked with a teasing smile.

“Is that what they are?”

“Emma even loves the fleas. Bless her,” Win said.

“Is she immune to their bite?”

“You will want this house,” he said. “If you stay here for more than a few days, you’ll want it just as Emma does.”

"Is this the seer speaking?" I asked. "Emma says you're a seer." His silver cuff links caught the flame.

"Well, I did happen to bring my crystal ball," he said, pulling an imaginary orb from his pocket and polishing it with his shirtsleeve. "I see you fighting for the house, a bidding war between you and Emma."

"She'd win," I said. "No competition there. Remember, I'm a writer." I didn't often announce my lack of money, but there was something about Win that made me feel I had to say whatever was on my mind. I wouldn't be able to hide. I had to be honest, and for a moment that was refreshing, not at all scary. I assumed that quality served him as a trader—he had the effect of making people honest, and thus they were easy to read.

"Tell me about you. Are you really a thief?" he asked.

"My brain is a tape recorder," I said.

"So is mine."

"But you're not a writer."

"I can use what you say all the same."

"Mysterious."

"I've heard quite a lot from Emma today about you. I'd like to see how her version compares to your own," Win said.

I wondered how Emma had the time to tell us each so much about the other, imagined her busy as a bee pollinating so many flowers. This was another trait of hers that I admired: she loved people, loved their quirks and idiosyncrasies, wanted her friends to all get on, find in each other that which she treasured in them.

"What did she say?" I asked.

"That you're the winner of such-and-such fellowship and several other impressive prizes. The Monogram. The Washington—good Lord, girl, you've been busy." He paused and looked at me with a twinkle. "And Emma no doubt has been saying all sorts of rubbish about me, I'm sure."

I nodded. "Good reviews."

He laughed, and the conversation turned to *Generation of Fire,* the promise of which still hung out in the ether. I told him the story in a nutshell—two sisters marry the same man. The novel had been my attempt to write a book that might appeal to a larger audience, though I didn't generally share that ambition. Rather, I always felt I had to qualify the story line by saying that what I was really looking at was the depth of love and loyalty in the face of excruciating betrayal. How far will a sister go (or not) for another? And I did so now with Win so that he didn't think the book trite.

"How far does she go?" he asked, holding my eyes. They were bright, intelligent eyes, and I understood just then that they alone lent him his magnetism. I did not want to look away, though it was hard to hold his eyes.

"You'll have to read the book," I said. I wanted him to read my novel and wanted him to love it and admire me the way I admired him, for doing and saying anything he liked.

"With your royalties you'll buy the house," he said.

I laughed and rolled my eyes. "I'll be lucky if I earn out my advance. If I don't manage that, I'll be finished as a novelist." The moment I completed the sentence, I regretted having uttered the words, like a drunk, *in vino veritas.* I took a sip of champagne and noticed the moon, big and full and red, rising just as Emma had declared, just as big. "The moon," I said, hoping its arrival would change the subject. I could hear a window being shut upstairs and imagined my girls curled around Theodor as he read them to sleep. A perfect image that still somehow was imperfect to me because we could not quite afford it—the two children, the nanny, the private school, the relaxed father putting them to bed. From the kitchen came sounds of Will clanking away with the cumbersome pots. I imagined the lobsters plunging into the steam. The foghorn on one of the islands sounded regularly and rhythmically even though there was no fog. I took another sip of champagne and Win stood up to get the bottle and poured us both a little more.

"Is that how it works?" he said. "The writer is held accountable for bad sales?"

"Yes," I said, but I did not want to be talking about this. "Should we offer our help in the kitchen?"

"Our help is not wanted," he reminded me, but of course I didn't need reminding. "We've been asked to stay outside." I wished Theodor would come save me so that we could stop addressing a topic we seemed to be rapidly approaching, the *roman à clef* I was writing daily: *The Shambles of My Life.* I knew Win didn't mean any harm, but he persisted with his interrogation.

"How many copies does a book, does *Generation of Fire,* need to sell to be a success?" He was studying me with those eyes, scrutinizing me, reading me. He'd spent so much time around people who made so much, he had no idea what struggle was, no idea what it might be like to have forces larger than oneself driving one's ability to become successful. He was in charge of a large Wall Street firm's mortgage department. There were outside forces, sure, but they were all part of an equation that he could manipulate to positive effect. For the most part, a writer could not do that. The only thing a writer had control over was the work, the writing. After that, it was up to forces so mysterious not even the publishers understood.

"Thirty, forty thousand would be excellent." I had no idea how to take back control of the conversation. "I'll come to Wall Street if it fails," I blurted, in another attempt to change the subject. He didn't laugh. I tried moving on, to Scotland, the trip we might be making there, the castle my brother was renting with his wife and her sisters on the sea in Kintyre, the three sisters always fighting, then loving, then fighting again—dramatic crescendos from which return to cordiality seemed impossible, so very un-English, but every single time they got back to it with laughter. I rambled nervously. "The Weird Sisters, Theodor calls them," I said, but Win didn't seem to be listening. He had a ponderous gaze that seemed to look through me, something remote swirling through his head.

"What fun," he said. He scratched his nose contemplatively. I had never known that brown eyes could be so light and jewel-like.

"The Weird Sisters?" I said, picturing the pretty sisters all in a rage and then in fits of laughter. Oddly, I was fascinated by their passion; they made me want to be one of many sisters—more even than Will's group of five. It seemed that they, their concerns, mattered most to one another. I didn't have that sort of clan relationship, and the bond with my brother was a more formal one.

"Would you do something like that?"

"Have sisters?"

"Wall Street," he said. Now his eyes were fully engaged, like stars. "Would you come to Wall Street?"

"Is this an invitation?" I asked.

"Perhaps."

"Well then, perhaps."

"I like the notion," he said. "It would be fun."

"Absolutely," I teased. I didn't let go of his eyes.

"You'll work for me, then," he said. He wasn't smiling. In fact, there was something serious in the way he said that. "You'll be my protégée. I hope your book fails."

"Thanks," I said.

"Did you take calculus in college?"

"I didn't go to college."

He looked puzzled. I felt relieved. The conversation was mine again. In that one instant of throwing him off I was able to retake control. I liked Win. I liked him very, very much.

"You're a tease," he said.

"And so are you," I said. "I was excellent at math. It was the only subject in which I received straight A's. But my book will not fail, and I would never go to Wall Street. I couldn't imagine having to ride a subway every day." Instead I imagined myself with my own car and driver, and a parallel life rose before me like an expensive helicopter, clear up and into the night sky. That life, filled with splendid luxuries and great abundance, so vivid, settled around me, gratifying my craving for the beauty of life's external finish.

"Give me eighteen months and I'll turn you into a trader. And no ordinary trader."

The door to the kitchen banged shut, and Will's smiling face appeared over a pot of steamers. "What?" he said, looking at both of us. "You're both a pair of possums."

"Win's just propositioned me," I said.

"Oh, here we go," Will said, snagging a clam and shouting upstairs, "The weekend is getting weird. Theodor! Win's seducing your wife!"

"Tell him to stop doing that, please," Theodor's muffled voice shouted down from an upstairs bedroom.

Emma emerged, declaring that we had to eat the steamers immediately or they'd be no good. Then Theodor arrived, sitting down next to me, cleaned up with a nice shirt, his shock of thick black curls so very handsome. "Now, then," he said, lifting my hand and kissing it, staking his claim, "what in God's name are you wild swingers up to, anyway?"

Then we were all digging into the clams, slipping off the skins covering their long black necks, dipping them in butter. They tasted like butter, just as silky, just as soft. The Atlantic air wafted over us, carrying a mist.

"How are things with Europe?" Will asked Win.

"Not happening," he said. "All the different laws get in the way. Too many countries."

"The European securities market," Will offered to Theodor and me as an explanation. I had no idea what a security was.

"Win's company wants to export our securities structure, but the Europeans have stringent, antiquated laws protecting inhabitants and that are different in each country."

"People don't take out mortgages in Europe in the same volume as in the U.S.," Emma said. This was all over my head.

"Better to let them buy ours," Will said. "We're rich with them anyway."

"Actually, I have a new sort of business plan," Win said and looked at me conspiratorially. Emma and Will were all ears. "I'm going to hire India."

"Oh, *that* kind of proposition. *Whew!*" Theodor said with an exaggerated swipe of his forehead.

"He's going to turn me into a trader," I said with a coy smile. I liked knowing something they didn't know.

"A Pygmalion story," Will said.

"That's right," I said. Make me new, make me rich like you, I thought. Leave it to Perfect Boy to give a literary flourish to a ridiculous business proposition.

"I'm having problems negotiating with her, though," Win said.

"Do tell," Will said.

"She doesn't want to take the subway," Win said.

"She wants a car," Will said knowingly.

"*And* a jet," Theodor added helpfully.

"Don't forget to backdate the stock option package, India," Will said.

"That'll be touchy," Win said.

"A jet would be nice," I mused.

"We'd never let it happen," Emma said protectively. "Wayne Johns, you are not going to corrupt our artist."

"Oh, yes, he most certainly is," Theodor said and looked at me as though I were crazy, seeing into that side of me that he knew was corruptible, and wondering, I imagined, if I was taking this at all seriously, wondering if I'd gotten myself into a mess. I raised my eyebrows suggestively, popped a clam into my mouth and lifted my glass to Maine and the house and to its someday belonging to Emma, though I was beginning to fall in love with the house myself—or, I should say, the spot. The moon, now a bit higher, cut a path across the water from it to us, so bright it seemed you could walk upon it.

In the morning, a thick fog had settled in. I could hardly see the dunes just in front of the house. The change in the weather sent an unexpected rush of hope through me. A beautiful white fog that drifted like a veil over the beach and the morning. I wished, as I sat up in bed in the turret with my husband asleep at my side and the house very quiet, that the fog would prevent Win from leaving. There was no way he could fly in weather like this. I wrapped my robe around me and slithered downstairs. I hadn't felt this excited about getting up in years. I wanted to see Win again. I wanted to see his smile, his eyes, and hear his presumptuous declarations. I was giddy. I wanted to find him in the kitchen sipping his morning cappuccino (Emma had also brought along a cappuccino machine), go for a dawn stroll on the beach.

But he was gone. (People with all the money in the world, it seemed, weren't held up by such a nuisance as weather. I imagined a limousine whisked him to a fogless airport and his idling G-IV.) In his place were four kites, colorful and neatly wrapped in cellophane, and beneath them lay a note of thanks with a promise of clear skies and stiff winds in the afternoon. I stood on the deck, the fog washing over me, so thick that at times it was impossible to see even my own extended hand.

Five

I WOULD NOT SEE Win again until a bitter cold night at the end of November. He would invite Theodor and me along with the Chapmans to a fundraiser at the Metropolitan Museum of Art, beside the Temple of Dendur, snow falling heavily into the glass wall overlooking the park, the temple illuminated, seeming to float on the dark pool that lay before it as people in holiday spirit drifted from one conversation to the next, canapés and champagne bobbing above them on silver trays held by servers wearing long white gloves.

Emma, in a red velvet gown, her hair in a French knot, blue shadow about her eyes, would lean toward me to let me know that a benefactors' table, at which we were to be seated, cost $50,000, her whisper thrilling with the absurdity of such a sum spent for a few hours' entertainment. Then Win would be before me in a smoking jacket with a pale pink cravat, his thin hair combed smoothly to one side, a wicked smile lighting his face, his chocolate eyes, as I approached him, forcing my lips into a smile, and I would fill once again with potential and hope. "Ah, my protégée," he would say, and kiss me on the forehead like a good brother, his lips warm, his embrace solid and reassuring. "I've been waiting for this." Then he would hold me out from him with both hands to admire. I dressed specially in a full-length gown (charcoal silk chiffon over silk satin, Empire waist), knowing that I would see him again. He would turn me around slowly, in a proprietary way, as if he owned a part of me and could do with me as he wished. I would let him believe that he could, because feeling possessed made me somehow stronger, more alive. "Smashing," he would say. "I have missed you."

But that was later. Now I was leaving Maine. We left the day after Win did. It was the end of July and I found myself downcast, though I tried to hide any appearance of it. We were headed back to New York, to five weeks of writing before teaching began. It was my plan to start a new novel so that I wouldn't have time to fret over the publication of the current novel. I had learned long ago that it is better to be involved with a new project so that you care less about the publication. That was the myth, anyway. Once, it had worked. I had soared through publication on the high of writing, with no concerns, and everything had gone fabulously—glowing reviews and the like—except for those elusive sales. My problem this time was simple: aside from the imaginary Emma Chapman Story, I had no idea for another book. So in front of me now, if I could not work, lay instead the stretch of time before the publication of *Generation of Fire*. "The calm before the calm," as a friend and fellow novelist once put it.

Leaving the Chapmans always made me a little blue. I was familiar with this sensation. It would happen after a simple dinner party at their Tribeca loft. Driving home along the West Side Highway, past the heliport and the *Intrepid*, I always longed for something ineffable, some part of them, perhaps, that I could take with me, a souvenir that would be infused with all those answers they seemed to know so well. We were approaching forty, Theodor and I, we had our two girls, but we lived like a couple just starting out—with the expectation that circumstances would change, that with the growth of our careers we would trade up from our apartment to something a little more grown-up, replace the hand-me-down furniture, stuff hauled in off the street. All the pretension, all the hiding and the juggling, couldn't keep that reality from me as we faced all that was—or wasn't—ours. With each novel, with each impending publication, I longed for our circumstances to change. However much I'd built my life around my art, I'd also come to hope that my next book would be the winning ticket in the literary lottery where art met commerce and bought you a fancy new coat for your trouble.

This was the writer's paradox—ego fueled the belief that one was about to become the exception. This is what kept me writing, the humongous ego, a necessity of the trade. How else to go forward? I longed. I longed to prove to my father that I could afford my life, that I, with my talent, had earned the ability to do so against his proclamations of failure. For him and for so many others, success was defined by one thing only. And we all know what that is. So I hoped. I hoped mightily, and the trouble with hope, yapping at your ankle like a hyperactive poodle, incessantly clamoring to be believed and heard, is that it turns into expectation, and given enough time, expectation skips over a fine line into something else again, into conviction—that you deserve.

Who except for a scant few among us doesn't deserve more? Riding on the subway, home from an early evening out, Theodor and I were discussing what a real artist would do. A real artist would not want as much as I do, I was saying. A real artist would be happy in the act of creation. Sitting beside us in the subway car was a tall, bald, young, familiar-looking man. He had one of those faces that could have been familiar because he was famous or because I'd known him in college. He wore a pale green, clean, pressed shirt, tucked neatly into his jeans, shiny loafers on his sockless feet—a preppy look, but on him there was style, as though the clothes were speaking against the persona. He had his nose in *The Literary Review*, absorbed.

As the subway bounced us uptown I tried to place him. The logo on the side of his glasses said Prada, the logo on the side of his watch said Prada. He continued to read. I continued to wonder how I knew him. He got off at our stop and we followed him for a few blocks. At home, I Googled Carlyle P. Smedes, the hip and famous It Boy, best-selling Scottish novelist, literary superstar, *imaginative, dynamic, inventive, nothing like him has come along thus far to stir up contemporary literature, his style is acrobatic, he's the voice of the turn of the century.* The praise for him was universal, and there was a picture of him—the It Boy himself—the same man I'd seen on the subway. "He was probably reading his own story," said my friend Lily Starr, also a novelist, on the verge of her first publication, when I told her of sitting next to him, carrying on about the real artist versus the fake. "Prada glasses, Prada watch, you got your answer," she said. "Didn't Twain go bankrupt? Didn't Melville bet his farm on his work and lose?" she asked.

"Don't forget Shelley, who made precisely forty pounds from his writing, and most of that was for a novel he wrote while still in school." We enjoyed this game.

"Joyce, Pound, Milton, they all died in miserable, impoverished circumstances."

Fools, I thought heretically. Win came again to mind.

Being grown up would mean this: buying an apartment like the Chapmans', having the walls skim-coated and detailed, choosing the smallest things for it: the switchplates, the doorknobs, the faucets and all the rest of it would allow us, finally, to take part in the real estate conversation that was the very air of our New York life. Carlyle Smedes famously paid $2 million for a double-wide brownstone in Sugar Hill that he bought for himself and his dog, spent $4 million renovating—garage, the whole nine yards—turning the neighborhood into the new trendy dwelling spot for hip artists, causing prices there to shoot toward the moon. "He calls himself an artist, for Christ's sake," declared a blogger on a website devoted to Smedes's domestic purchase.

Being the grown-up would mean inviting my father and mother for an elegant dinner, putting them up in the guest bedroom, having them see what I had made of myself, proving them wrong. This would mean more than any book I could offer up, but that this was paid for by the success of a book would mean triumph. My father had nearly disowned me when he learned that I had paid for the lease to a rent-stabilized apartment. (A deal I had been proud of, which involved risk and the reading of chance on the face of a tenant with slender fingers and long, manicured fingernails, a man, and his realtor, a woman with one leg; $15,000 dollars in a paper bag and we'd receive a lease that would allow us to live in New York City on a shoestring. I used my graduate school fellowship and student loans, figuring I'd pay it all back by getting roommates so we could live rent free. "You should have gone to Wall Street," Theodor said when we'd paid off the fifteen grand, gotten rid of the roommates and had the sprawling apartment to ourselves—it had seemed big before kids. To pay off the fifteen grand took exactly one year.) But for my father, rent stabilization was a disgrace, a system designed to screw respectable business owners. It was a socialist relic from a time when Democrats had too much power. It was welfare, nothing else. I would regret it someday, he had said, because later in life I would own nothing, no equity, a shame. He was a Republican and I was an artist, but I did not want to live like one. I never had. Without my stabilized lease we would not have been able to live in New York City.

When we drove away from the Chapmans, their glittering orbit filled with champagne and fine cheese and characters like Win, a hole would start to widen in the center of me into which you could drop a house. Now, leaving Maine, the truth was the impending publication of *Generation of Fire* and what its failure would signify. This is what stared me in the face as we left the sea air and the pines. Somehow I knew, though I hoped so very differently, that the publication would not go well. The odds favored that outcome. I imagined that Emma understood this. I could see the understanding fluttering in her eyes—a mix of sympathy for me and relief at her own good fortune.

Indeed, it felt as if Theodor and I were being banished from the Chapmans' world, renters cast out from the comforting blandishments of home equity. (For example, Maine wouldn't be theirs unless they owned it. They strived to own it.) "When I see you next, you'll be on the verge of giving birth," she said with those eyes of hers on me. A stupid expression when related to the publication of a book. Could I see in those eyes the flit of desire that we all have, the glee one feels while standing witness to another's fall? It was I who was creating this, my reflection in her image. She loved me, and had she known the layers of fear and self-doubt, and yes, ego, she would have tried to prop me up.

As we all stood in the yard of the Maine house, near our car, heavy with all the paraphernalia—games, puzzles, kites, bikes—that a vacation with two kids necessarily entailed, Emma's willowy arms draped about her husband, I felt that we were the Joads to their Joneses. "Be safe," she said kindly. And the image of Will and Emma, wrapped protectively in each other, gave a sharper edge to our departure.

Somewhere in Connecticut I called home to our machine to check the messages. Nearly a week's worth of them. I pressed the phone to my ear with my shoulder, told the girls to keep quiet. With my other hand I jotted down names and numbers. I deleted. I saved. And then there it came, just what I had been hoping for all along. I smiled. "What is it?" Theodor asked. I shushed him as I jotted down the number. Then another message. Better than the last. Then another. And yet another. Bonanza.

"It's worth it to go away for a week," I said.

"What?" he persisted.

And I told him. *The Literary Review* loved my novel. *Loved it!* It was the editor calling. *Loved it.* The best novel they'd read this year. They wanted to excerpt it. *Woman* magazine wanted to run a piece by me; could I write it in ten days? Any subject I chose as long as it wasn't too literary, appropriate for a magazine that targets smart, intelligent, fashionable, busy women who like to read but don't want to think too hard. They want to run it in October, simultaneously with the publication. A message from my agent reporting interest from three foreign publishers, all of whom wanted to meet me on their September trip to New York. And last, the *New York Morning Show* wanted to know if India Palmer suffered stage fright, as they were considering a segment with her. Theodor let out a whoop and the children cheered.

"My star," Theodor said. But I hardly heard him. It had just rained and everything glistened. The trees were emerald. I was eager to get home.

"Europe," I said. "Let's visit my brother."

Heath, my brother, had invited us earlier in the summer, and his wife, Clarissa, had been calling ever since, pleading. There'd been a message from her too. I hadn't wanted to admit to them that we couldn't afford the trip, so I'd declined, using my novel and all I had to do for its publication as an excuse. "Clarissa's begging us to come." And I thought of Emma, of calling her to say thank you for the long weekend, of telling her we were headed to London and then to a castle in Scotland, "on the Firth of Clyde," I'd say, "the Mull of Kintyre." Beautiful name.

On my cell phone there was one message, from Win. I wondered how he got the number. "You shine, India Palmer. I read *The Way We Do Things Here*"—my first novel, out of print; where had he found a copy?—"on the plane ride home. Prose so sumptuous you don't read it, you live inside it. I look forward to making you blush when I see you next."

I did not tell Theodor that Win had called.

Six

PUSSY JONES WAS the first Jones. Yes, we all know the Joneses. They are the anti-Joads. Before marriage, as it happens, Edith Wharton was Pussy Jones, daughter of George Frederic Jones, a "gentleman," with inherited social position and wealth from shipping, banking and real estate adventures gone wildly well. He was a man of leisure who took his family to live in Europe, who owned property in Manhattan and Newport. It is said that his name and lifestyle (and the ensuing envy of others) gave rise to the expression "keeping up with the Joneses," which the cartoonist Arthur R. Momand, known as Pop, mined in his satirical column. In 1913 he created a cartoon series entitled *Keeping Up with the Joneses*. It ran for twenty-eight years and chronicled the comedy of American striving, which did not end, of course, with the closure of a comic strip.

Of my students I always asked, "What does your character want? Your character must want something. The desire will make us curious, make us want to follow the character on a quest, whether the outcome is successful or not." I had my students read a passage from *An American Tragedy* in which Clyde's girlfriend, Hortense, wants a coat. She will stop at nothing to get the coat that, simply by her owning it, will change her life. For twenty pages she schemes and manipulates and bribes, coming up with strategies until the coat is hers—twenty riveting pages that pursue a coat.

The thing about a writer is that want is part of the job description. Without want, a writer is nothing. A writer must want to sit alone at a desk for days on end. A writer must close out the world and wait. The reward is the chuckle, the quiet laugh that only the writer hears alone at her desk. She is laughing at her own work, her own imagination nailing a particular phrase because she knows, as one just knows some things, that the phrase, the scene, the story will make others laugh. Who among us, no matter her trade, has not made something bigger, at some point, simply by virtue of sticking with it? She must want this even while knowing that few others will care.

But want, as we say, has a problem with boundaries. It bleeds. What young writer, sitting at her desk, doesn't also crave to be in the world? The blue day, the summer heat, they pull her outside, toward shops and cafés, toward the land where life is real and filled with temptation and expensive desire: the cappuccino, the magazine, the taxi, the pretty dress. Want proliferates with age: she wants a baby, then another, then a babysitter to go with them, a house, a car, a good school for the kids, lessons, camps, more of those nice dresses, perhaps a better neighborhood to settle in. She'll become practical, money for retirement, stocks, perhaps some bonds. She'll want theater tickets, to dine with her friends, an office, books, a vacation, a new wedding band, another bedroom. On it will go from one thing to the next.

What did I want? I wanted to know what it felt like to be able to have whatever I pleased, to cast aside worry. I wanted to partake of the dessert tray. I wanted to invite people for dinner without worrying about how I'd pay for the wine. I even wanted to get a parking ticket—$115—and not have it feel catastrophic. I wanted an apartment that was mine. I wanted to be able to want the house in Maine, have it be within my means. I wanted to see Win again. I wanted to be desired again by someone new. I wanted to feel the gaze of someone's curiosity. I listened to Win's message several times and saved it. *Prose so sumptuous you live inside it.* (You could tell what that sentence wanted.) I wanted everything.

We had come home from Maine to discover a leak in the ceiling above our bed. Water from the storm that had draped Connecticut in a glistening beauty on our return had penetrated the roof of our apartment building and dripped through the ceiling and onto, and then into, our mattress. The plaster above the bed buckled, an enormous gray and sweating welt. Flakes of dried paint fell softly to the bed like snow. I will confess, I was delighted. This is what made our life affordable: our ceiling was constantly falling in. Hurray, I thought, but didn't say it. We lived on the top floor, and for fifteen years the various landlords who'd bought our building tried to have the roof repaired, but they did so on the cheap: when a big storm blew through, leaks sprouted. As a result, we had an abatement from the city, making our already inexpensive rent even cheaper. We lived practically for free. So, though I found the rain irritating, and though I feigned upset with the super—"When will this ever be fixed? Do you know what we live with? And we have young children"—I secretly prayed for storms. My ears perked up when the news forecasted the worst season for hurricanes in decades. "They're going to roll in like Frisbees, drenching the region. There will be potential for catastrophic flooding," said the weathermen. "Excellent!" Theodor would say, catching me before the TV screen.

Theodor taped plastic over the damage. Calls from the landlord promised it would be mended. But it was the leak that offered me relief as I lay in bed. And there I thought of Win. I wanted him to make me blush. I wanted to see those brown eyes as he said magnificent things about my work. I couldn't sleep.

"What is it?" Theodor asked at last. It was 2 A.M.

In the dark of our bedroom, it was time for a little truth salvo. "My desire to write has been swallowed," I said.

The streets outside were quiet. I wanted to confess that I was so consumed I was imagining a life with a rich husband. I thought of Becky Sharp and Undine Sprague, the force of their wills to get exactly what they wanted. I thought of Scarlett O'Hara. Who else? Lily Bart? She decidedly did not get what she wanted in the end. Who would those women be today? The religious nut who wandered the streets every night chanting hallelujah; even he had gone to his bed. The ceiling fan rustled the plastic. "I have absolutely no ideas anymore. I'm consumed." Theodor turned in the bed. Outside, it was beginning to rain again. The city's light sneaked in at the edges of the shades.

"I'm tired, darling."

"But I'm consumed," I said.

"Sleep and you'll feel better."

"Please," I said. I wondered what Win was doing right now. Theodor shifted again, toward me. He stroked my hair. His fingers felt good against my scalp. "You don't understand," I said. "I've been blown off course." I thought of all the female writers I admired when I was starting out. Where were they now? How many had kept publishing? I could think of only a handful, and all of them had big-salaried husbands with big-paying jobs.

Was it motherhood? Did motherhood make me lose my drive? He was still stroking my hair. I'd had this conversation with him in many different forms. I wanted him to speak. It made me mad that he didn't speak. I sat up sharply. He was in this too. I wanted him to care. "I hate that I love our leaky ceiling. I don't want to pray for storms, especially if you can't be bothered to. Why should I be doing it all alone?"

"India," he said and sat up with me. He tried to pull me close to him, but I wouldn't let him.

"We're nearly forty."

"We're artists."

"I hate that excuse."

"Don't do this to yourself."

"Why do we like to keep our writers poor? Men, women alike, bankrupt, dying without a *farthing*. Women are just smarter. They give up earlier because they can turn their attention to their kids." I thought for a moment of Gwen and Ruby—all the magazine articles I had written over the years to pay for April, their nanny. "I want to become a full-time mother. I want to take care of the kids. I want you to make the money for a while and let me take care of the kids. I want to plan their days, help them with their homework, do their laundry, clip their nails, meet other mothers in the park and complain about things like bad child care and how long the renovations are taking, the slow contractors, the food served at school—too many sweets, not organic enough."

"Please, my love."

"Please what?"

"You don't want that."

"How do you know?"

"Because I married an artist."

"You're just saying that so you don't have to take responsibility. I do want that, and that's not all I want. I am consumed by want. It's eating me alive. I'm just one big mouth."

"It's a good thing you have a beautiful mouth."

"Don't make light of this," I said. "I'm serious."

"I'll be serious too. I am being serious," he said in a stern, serious tone. He pulled me into him again, and this time I surrendered. "Let's hear everything you want."

"Bad things," I said. "Things we don't need. Things I'm not supposed to want because I'm supposedly an intellectual. Intellectuals don't want things like I do."

He reminded me of Carlyle Smedes, nominated for the London Fucking Bridge Book Award for International Literary

Fucking Greatness. "Prada glasses, Prada watch. What do you want?" he asked. "You can whisper," he whispered, "so that no one hears."

"A butler," I whispered.

He laughed. "And a chauffeur?"

"That too," I said. "What a wonderful idea."

"And what else?"

"No, seriously," I said.

"Okay, seriously," he said.

"I want to be able to pay April without worrying about where the money is coming from." A maid just for me, I thought. Someone who asks nothing but anticipates my needs before I can. The mother of a friend of Ruby's once said that to me, and I'd been horrified. She'd said, "I want my staff to anticipate every need so that I don't have to know what it is that I need." What a relief. I wanted to be free of wanting, rid of needing—have someone else do all of that for me. This woman, she'd carried on, "I pay my maid well. She wears a maid's uniform. I treat her nicely, give her extravagant gifts, but she knows the line. The boundaries are clear. She's my maid and I'm her boss."

"Okay," said Theodor. "What else?"

"A room, an empty room," I said. Another mother I knew had an empty room in her Park Avenue apartment (Ruby's preschool had been on the East Side). The room was completely bare and she had no intention to furnish it. Her apartment was enormous, with an internal intercom system installed so she could find her kids. Ten windows faced Park Avenue and ten windows faced the cross street. In all of them hung the same drapes so it would be clear from the street that all twenty windows belonged to the same owner. She wanted the room to remain empty simply because many people in New York wanted to have just one more room. She wanted to have the room that everyone wanted.

"Interesting," he said.

"I want to hoard space," I said.

"And?"

"A house in Southampton."

"You've got to be kidding me."

"You mean all the other stuff is all right but not a house in Southampton?"

"The traffic," he said.

"We'll take a helicopter."

"All right, then."

Another mother had had a tea party and invited me to come as the entertainment. I was to discuss what it was like to be a writer and a mother, because the mothers were curious about that; they really wanted to know. How did I *keep it all together and still find time to express my creative side?* On her white plush couches in her enormous living room I spoke to her East Side friends—all the lovely ladies, their faces had been rearranged so they all looked the same.

"What is it you'd like to discuss?" I asked the hostess as we sipped our tea after the lunch (a small piece of chicken on a bed of frisée with a spritz of lemon—"They won't eat it anyway," the hostess had said, "they're all on diets"). Her name was Janice and she was not as thin as the others and she had not rearranged her face. She was wholesome and full-figured, and I found her beautiful. Janice brought silence to the din with a clink of her glass and announced that I'd be happy to speak about anything.

"Well, not anything," I said and smiled, trying to interest them in me with my humor. They all stared at me politely with their lips pursed, and the silence remained for a spell. "At our children's school a teacher was just fired for using details of his teaching experience as fodder for his fiction," one woman said. "Most of the students were incensed by the firing. Freedom of expression, you know. Artistic prerogative."

"I haven't read the book," said another lady, "but Balinka Smith gave it a terrible review in the paper."

"Balinka Smith hates everything. She certainly helps you weed out the possibilities," said another lady.

"She's usually right."

"What's your position, Ms. Palmer?"

"On Smith or the book?" I said, chastened by these women. "I don't know the book."

"It's about spoiled New York City prep school kids who spend wildly, consume everything and are indulged by their overworked, high-strung, competitive parents, who are also all busy having affairs."

"Sounds delightful," I said. I thought of the chocolate Jesus from so many years ago. "If it is good," I said, "isn't that what matters?" And then they were speaking among themselves again, about the teacher, the school, the students' campaign to get the teacher rehired. Art and its creation, as a subject, was over. I made my way to Janice to say goodbye, coming in on, "He must get it for you. Stake your ground. Do not back down. You deserve it."

"What?" I asked, curious. What was it that this woman deserved?

"A house in Southampton" was the reply. "She's earned it." I pictured a big man alone at a big desk, writing checks. I pictured Theodor in his studio, carefully soldering gold to silver, placing a jewel between prongs. Deserve? What is it we all deserve? Long before, Theodor and I had traveled to Sri Lanka. A tout on a beach there had tried to sell me marijuana. I'd declined the offer, and he'd been mad that I rebuffed him. He looked at me with his harsh, liquid eyes (they seemed to want to spill from his face with fury) and said, "You deserve to be a Sri Lankan. In your next life you will be. Wait and see." And then he'd lumbered off down the beach.

Back in our bed on that rainy night, with the rain quickening its pace:

"And?" Theodor asked.

And we played this game for a while. I knew why he was doing it. He wanted to push me back to the other side, to the artist's hunger for the next trick up her sleeve, the next flash of language on the page. This was how he dealt with the unpredictability of our lives, to keep pushing forward and to use everything as a means, as he did with the scraps of metal he'd scavenged off the street. Beauty was everywhere, even in things that were ugly, and the alchemical desire to transform things was indeed a respectable fuel.

At the moment Theodor was working on a piece for a museum in Fort Worth that had been commissioned and funded by a venture capitalist who applied his knack for finance to his love of art. He, a large, boisterous and intelligent Texan who wore the boots, hat and bolo tie, was Theodor's patron. He was betting on Theodor as he would bet on an idea for a start-up. Initially he funneled plenty of money to the commission to pay for supplies and time and anything else, but now he needed to see results. He asked for them in a kindly way, and in a kindly way Theodor told him he needed more time; he'd rather get it right. The work was to be the centerpiece of an exhibition that the museum planned, a retrospective of Theodor's oeuvre. The museum intended to track down his work and take it on loan from the present owners. The show would include about thirty pieces and be a career maker—all of it instigated by the patron, Warren William Sullivan.

But the commission was not coming along well at all. Gold leaf on silver, extraordinarily expensive; and working with the gold leaf was like working with butterfly wings. Beyond that, I knew very little about the subject because Theodor never discussed what he was working on, only the struggles in the abstract. I did know we were out of pocket a lot of money now, and unless he could finish and be paid for the commission our bad financial situation would become even worse. "Don't worry," he would say. Once, long ago, he had said to me, when we were first starting out in New York, his black curls bouncing around his sculpted cheeks, "I'm going to keep wanting. That's what it's all about. Stay poor, my girl. Poor with me, to make this work."

"What do you want?" I asked him now.

"I want, and I have, you," he said, and he pulled me deeper against him.

In the morning I received more good news. Streamline Productions wanted to option *Generation of Fire* for film. The option was for $2,000, not much, but money all the same. The *Woman* magazine article would be about $4,500; the *Lit Review* excerpt could be as much as $8,000; several thousand for the three pending foreign sales. Yes, things were coming along quite smartly. In a small notebook I kept hidden in my desk, I wrote down the figures, adding up our potential extra income. All the zeroes smiled like round and jolly faces. And I didn't even include Theodor's commission or the possibility of the film's coming to fruition. On the first day of shooting we'd receive a check for $250,000. That sum sat in the back of my mind like a lozenge. Of course, I didn't calculate all of our expenses, all that we owed, the tuition bill that was coming due in September, Theodor's gold and jewels. Instead I met Lily Starr for lunch in midtown.

Lily and I had been to graduate school together, and since then she'd published no novels and I'd published my four, with the fifth imminent. In general, I did not like to surround myself with writers. I preferred the bankers and the ad executives and the lawyers for whom I was a curiosity and with whom I had no overt professional competition. But Lily and I had hung on to each other. We liked each other, but for her there was also a bit of envy and masochism—each of my successes a reminder to her of her inability to finish a book. And I'll confess: that inability of hers, and her envy, made me feel better about my own career and its degrading lack of sales. Things were about to change, with Lily's first novel publishing one month to the day before mine.

"They say publishing in the fall is the new spring. Everyone, all the big names, now pub in spring, so the fall's opened up again for fresh voices," Lily said.

We were walking up Park Avenue in the Fifties. We'd been together for an hour and I was beginning to feel that unease of writerly competitiveness. Ungenerously, I decided she had the irritating characteristic of pretending to be a novice even though she knew all about the business. She'd had years to study it, and believe me, she had been. What she knew made me jealous and fearful. She knew that a debut novel was a potent aphrodisiac to those in the industry. A first novel was a blank slate that an enormous career could be written upon. A first novel was the wildcard in the deck; it had the potential to become anything, everything. I was a known thing, harder and harder to launch. She was the new thing: a few smart words, a brilliant book jacket, and entry through the gates of Parnassus was hers.

Truth be told, Lily had been a good friend to me long ago, had read my first novel and encouraged me with every sentence, giving the first chapter to her boss when she worked as an intern at *The Barcelona Review,* and the boss had loved it and they'd published it, launching me into the New York literary scene. It was based on that chapter that my agent first contacted me. *Barcelona* had published three chapters from that novel, all while Lily slaved as a lowly intern, receiving high praise too, by the by, for having "discovered" me.

"Is that so?" I said about spring pub dates. I'd read her book, *You Didn't Want to Know,* and thought it good, in fact very good. But I also knew how hard it was to publish. Her book would languish out there with the rest of them, and she'd come to understand what it felt like to be an author—revered, hailed. Piccadilly was publishing it, and though they were the best for literary fiction (they'd published my second novel, *Scion*), I knew they gave little attention to unknown writers, let them sink or swim on their own. ("The book will abide," or some such, the publisher, the Dashing Cavelli, had famously said.)

Piccadilly had a reputation for doing nothing for the books. Indeed, their logo, a pair of trumpets, did everything for the books. I played up the air of indifference, as if publishing were rote, run of the mill, as if everything didn't depend upon it. It was a sweltering day and I wore an old sundress that I'd bought at Marshall's for $5. One of the shoulder straps was slightly torn. But it was a pretty dress, had once been stunning, and I'd prided myself on how good it looked for so little. In fact, with some other graduate school friends we had a running competition: who could buy the cheapest dress and look the most expensive. This particular dress made me look like an artist, I fancied, and a woman who looked fabulous in anything.

Then I saw it, the sign, big roman letters—two B's and an ampersand intertwined, the unmistakable logo of Bond & Bond Brothers. I had no idea it was here. I had thought all finance was centered around Wall Street, most of it anyway. Park Avenue, I now noticed, was thick with businessmen, and a few -women, dressed in their suits, marching between office and restaurant for the midday meal. The buildings loomed above us, terraced with gardens, trees spiking above steel and glass. There seemed to be a rhythm to the stride of the avenue, a steady beat, a pulse—the not so subtle pulse at our temples. The pulse of a flower emitting its fragrance, the fragrance of America. Flags fluttered like kites. A klatch of limos idled at the curbs. St. Bartholomew's Church seemed an oasis of reason in the midst of all the banks. Big bank after big bank, and then here we were beneath B&B, caught in its shadow.

A stream of taxis flowed by. One stopped in front of us. Lily said something that I did not hear, her voice small in the street. A woman stepped from the cab. She wore a nicely pressed, white linen suit, her dark hair swirled in an up-do, her eyes shaded by big black glasses, her lips a startling red. Under her arm was a folded *Wall Street Journal.* In her right hand she clutched a leather computer case. She slammed the cab door and disappeared into the revolving doors of the Winchester building.

"Do you know her?" Lily asked, gawking at me as I gawked at the woman.

"No."

"She's a different species. Can you imagine?"

"They're all a different species," I said, sweeping my arm around to include everyone walking down the street. I felt protective of the woman, but also smaller in my smart $5 dress. Why weren't we at our desks? Why were we out in the middle of a New York working day? I felt like a little girl, a truant.

"What a life," she said. "Every day I thank my lucky stars. Time is mine and I do what I dream."

I didn't say anything, but I thought, How naïve. I looked up to the top of the building, then to the doors. When the doors opened, cool air gusted over us. Here the engines of commerce hummed. Mortgages were packaged, lumped into a vast money flow.

"Gorgeous," I said.

"Bond and Bond Brothers?" Lily asked with an incredulous huff.

"I met a trader who works there," I said.

"And—"

"And he propositioned me."

"You've got to be kidding." Then, "Attractive?"

"Not at all."

"And Theodor?"

We were walking again, but then Lily stopped me and looked me in the eye, all genuine concern, it seemed. I left the notion suspended for a moment so I too could live in the bubble of misperception. Imagine: *India Palmer on the verge of an affair with a billionaire banker.* Even the best of us loves gossip. I certainly did. Gossip was storytelling, after all. *And what about adorable Theodor? I knew they'd married far too young. Two artists? It just is not possible.* I looked at Lily, letting her eyes try to read mine. She was a pretty girl with high cheeks and a sweet oval face with all its features neatly arranged, as if someone had placed each one there carefully, by hand. She was short and a little chubby, but her body was incredibly strong and agile, able to contort into difficult yoga positions.

"Not that kind of proposition," I said finally.

Why weren't we talking about Duchamp and Mina Loy and Wallace Stevens and William Carlos Williams? Why weren't we discussing the history of the novel or Thackeray's cynicism or Eliot's objective correlative or Dreiser's patience? Why weren't we competitive with our knowledge and our artistic desires? Why weren't we sharing ideas and thoughts of work? Deciphering the struggle, making it urgent and necessary? Why weren't we creating our own *ism,* an aesthetic revolution like those other aesthetic revolutionaries who came before us and paved the way for what we try to write now?

Before kids, before now, before life got in the way, we'd spent long evenings with our grad school friends parsing the structure, the very sentences of the works of little-read novelists like Heinrich von Kleist. Sure, we'd been interested in his biography, his double suicide with his terminally ill lover on the shores of Lake Wannsee. Sitting in one of our gloomy apartments, drinking cheap wine, smoking hand-rolled cigarettes, so very very late, we had all agreed that we'd be successful if we didn't kill ourselves by thirty-five. But we'd also cared about how Kleist had made the work happen, how he'd managed the famous first sentence of "The Marquise of O—." An Italian woman of unblemished reputation finds herself mysteriously pregnant and places an ad in a local paper with the hope of learning the identity of the father. Now that's a brilliant plot, and it was held in one burst of a sentence, an opening sentence. An explosion of curiosity, every part of the sentence made you want to know more. If your character must want something, the reader must too. Why, at the very least, weren't we talking about the wars? There were two wars going on, and no one seemed to be aware. Who and what had we become? But it wasn't any of that that came from my mouth. I thought of a talented and acclaimed writer I knew who, at a book party for her new novel, wore a black dress with straps that cut across the wings of her shoulder blades, accentuating her fine muscle tone. I admired the dress. She said, "I love publishing a book most of all because it's an excuse to shop."

We slipped over to Madison as I described Win and his proposition. The street smelled of perfumes blasting from the doors of the expensive stores. People walked fast, eager, anxious, a ferocity propelling them down the street, passing newsstands and newspaper vending machines, the headlines announcing military and civilian death tolls, troops searching for the missing, car bombs, suicide bombers, training camps in Afghanistan. The smell of lemons and honey-roasted peanuts, the sighing of buses coming to a stop. A woman rushed past me, knocking her Chanel shopping bag against my hip. She turned, sneered, continued on. Horns and sirens and all those beautiful stores, like pretty flowers so carefully arranged.

I loved giving Lily the details, resurrecting the evening in Maine—the crystal flutes imported from Manhattan for the champagne—a world far removed from the one we lived in that was glamorous and somehow easy in that it was rid of so many concerns. Lily Starr had two kids and a husband who taught in a public high school. They crammed into a one-bedroom apartment that she referred to as a mini-loft. Great location on Riverside Drive and they owned it. But their ticket out, like ours, had always been and still was her novel. She'd been writing it for fifteen years. For fifteen years she'd done what all of us writers so pathetically do with our humongous egos. She'd believed that a novel, her novel, could defy the novelists' track record for dying unknown and impoverished. She'd believed. We all believed. And why not?

"India Palmer: bond trader, mortgages. Bond, James Bond," Lily said. "What is a bond, anyway?" she asked. Her eyes were a bright blue, sparkling as she had fun with this notion in a way that reminded me of why I always adored her. She was fun. She could look down the road and fully imagine it, decorate it with all the details and then decide, all in an instant, if it added up. "Whatever a bond is, your trading them is an exquisitely stupid idea. Was he serious? Has he read your work? *Generation* is your best novel yet. I couldn't put it down."

She *has* read it, I thought, and a lovely sensation wafted over me. She still believed in me. My first review. I'd given it to her months ago in manuscript, but she'd said nothing. *Best novel* and *couldn't put it down* translated to: she loved it. Writers were like this; they always believed everything positive they were told—praise from their readers, their friends. When they say they love it, the writer never doubts. She believes she's a genius. She's brilliant. A shining star. She believes even though she knows how many times she has lied in the same circumstance.

But as Lily carried on, I realized just how seriously I had taken Win's proposition even if I hadn't given it much thought, wondered would I be capable of that, of becoming a trader. Yes: India Palmer: star trader of mortgages: one of the few women on the Street: heralded: me: Mistress of the Universe. Well, I'd have to work on my moniker, at least. Yes, I hadn't dismissed the idea as quickly as Lily had. It meant that I was second-guessing myself as a writer. Did Lily know this? Was this also part of the fun she was having with me? I realized how far apart we were. She sat atop a Gibraltar of belief in herself. Looking at her was like looking into a kaleidoscope, a colorful swirl of affection, jealousy, malice, admiration, untoward intent.

"It's actually fascinating, you know. Mortgages, anyway. They've figured out how to amass mortgage debt and turn it into bonds that are larger than the entire United States market overall." I had forgotten what it was larger than, but I knew she'd know no better. "Imagine how clever that is, taking all the puny mortgages, compiling them. It's a guaranteed fixed coupon of five or six or seven percent for the duration of the loan, thirty years in most cases, and now they've come up with endless variations that make making loans possible for just about anyone."

I carried on trying to render the story as interesting as it had been to me in Maine, feeling as I spoke a passion to know more, to understand better, not unlike the feeling I had felt long ago about getting to the bottom of a writer's masterly sentence. I thought about Win, of seeing him here. Of bumping into him, of having him invite us for a cup of tea, a glass of champagne. I could feel Lily's eyes on me.

"Fascinating," Lily said, yawning playfully, patting her lips. She pointed while still watching me—like a ringside doctor examining the eyes of a boxer—to a bathing suit in a shop window. It was a sharp black bikini. The bottom, a square-cut brief: $250. The top, a halter: $195. We loved it. She encouraged me to try it on, flattering me with compliments about my body. So I tried on the suit, thinking it was only a fraction of what I was to be paid for the article in *Woman* if it wasn't killed. The idea I'd chosen was on beauty and my relationship to it. "I'm a whore," I'd said to Theodor. "I'll write about anything."

"As long as you're my whore," he'd said.

The bright lights of the store were also somehow soft and flattering, the mirrors tilted so that they added length to the body, elongating the calves and thighs. I looked elegant. The store was spare, only a few lacy bras and panties hanging here and there, carefully selected for exquisiteness, no need for excessive choice. I felt expensive, worthy. My skin was softer, smoother.

"Indulge," Lily said with her sweet smile. "You deserve it." Like a Hamptons house.

"Indeed," I said, feeling, however, that it would be more fun if there were some big man at a big desk blindly writing checks to pay for my indulgences. Rather, I thought of Theodor in his studio. "How about you?" I asked Lily. I thought of Emma admiring the bikini as we went for a swim at her rooftop pool club in SoHo. She would know exactly which store it came from; she'd take note of it and believe that I actually must be doing well as a writer—either that or I was a fool, and I knew she would never believe me a fool.

"That's a month's worth of food for my children," Lily said. And I thought of mine, Gwen and Ruby, their beautiful little faces, their mouths pursed, opening like fledglings'. I bought the suit, impressing Lily Starr with the ease with which I pulled out my credit card. I worked hard; I worked as hard as the next person.

At Bergdorf's I bought a new dress, a rich brown macramé for fall. The price: $775. A tax deduction, I thought. I just had to have it to wear to my book party. I shared my strategy with Lily, and we both laughed about the deduction. "An absolute expense," she said. "I'll serve as witness if the IRS comes after you. Kind sirs, she only wore it that once. She had to look like a million bucks, otherwise who'd buy her book?"

I stood in front of the mirrors, cocking my head to the left, watching myself in the dress as Lily enacted my defense. Illusion: the dress hugged every curve of my body, my skin like pale silk seen through the macramé. Money certainly could help one become thoroughly ravishing. I bought the dress. "I'll put it in a novel," I said. "And then it will really be a valid tax deduction." Why did I want to show off for Lily by spending so much? Why did I care what she thought? Somehow it helped me feel that I had succeeded, I supposed, part of the fabric of a lie I'd been telling myself for some time, that as an artist I could live this life in which the value of my work was equal to the value of other people's work.

Then a little later: "Book party?" Lily asked, slanting her eyes toward me.

"Emma Chapman is having one," I said. "Save the date, my pub date, October sixteenth. The publisher's helping." That was a lie. In the end, they had wanted to keep the private party separate from publicity so they had declined to help, promising their own wine-and-cheese event at a bookstore. "We must do something for you," I said.

"I didn't tell you?" she asked, as if just remembering now, as if this hadn't been on her mind for our entire afternoon together, as if this hadn't been the reason she'd called wanting to see me.

Was I being terribly unfair? Writers could be like this, were like this—a combination of that ego and deference, wanting to both hide and trumpet. Her face brightened. No, I was not being unfair. We were riding the escalator down, our faces reflected into infinity in the mirrors, my bags draping off my arms, as if I were a lady who could afford the $1,500 I'd just dropped in an hour. The day before, I had spent $3,000 on our last-minute tickets to London.

"What?" I asked. "Good news?" I knew it would be good news, and I also knew I didn't want to hear it. I saw the future suddenly. Her book would become fabulously successful. She'd become the anointed It Lit Girl. She had a story after all: fifteen years to write her first, smashing novel. *Worth the Wait:* I could see the headline. Lily Starr, the truth transparent in her name.

"Leonardo Cavelli called me. Piccadilly is hosting a party. This is a big book for them," she said, glee oozing out of every part of her. And why shouldn't it? She should be flooded with glee, drowning in glee. And I should, *should* be happy for her. The brilliant smile of hers shining with success.

I could not share in the glee. Why hadn't I understood the glee before? Before spending all this money? Her voice nearly a squeak, she knew full well the news had to come quietly. This, for Piccadilly, was unprecedented. A call from Cavelli for a book party was like a call from God, reserved thus for the biggest names.

"I got a star on the *Advance* review and a star on the *Cramer*. I'm still waiting on the others. But *Advance* and *Cramer*—that's like hitting a double-header, or whatever you do in baseball. Bull's eyes?" she said. "*Advance* is going to run a profile!"

Who, anywhere else in the world, anywhere but in New York City, would care about a *Cramer* star? Who? No one. Nowhere. But I was here and I cared, and I hated myself just then for every sensation that rushed over me. Most of all, for imagining she knew just how I felt.

"A what?" I asked, referring to the double-header—a football term? Baseball?

"It's great, isn't it?" she asked with false modesty, asked as if it could be possible that the stars were a bad thing, as if a book party hosted by Cavelli were an irrelevant occurrence. An *Advance* profile, to be avoided at all costs? In the machine that knits a selling book, these were the founding threads. Worse was that she was pretending to defer to my experience when she knew that with this first book of hers she was on the verge, with one giant leap, of surpassing me in sales, and we all know that sales are all that matter.

"Well, of course," I said, those bags pulling me to the ground. I was a fake. That's what it was. If she was pretending, so was I. I was living inside the inauthentic, trying to prove that the writer could live like everyone else, all those honest, hard-working souls. That we could keep up. I was pretending for Lily Starr so that she'd think I was doing well. I had been her role model. I was pretending with the parents of my children's friends that I had the money to pay for the vacations they invited me to join them on, for the birthday presents I bought for their children, for the dinners out at fancy restaurants. I was pretending to the children's school that I could afford the tuition we had no business affording.

Lily, bagless, was as light as a feather. I could feel her stars and her Cavelli in every part of my body, sick, nauseated, as though I'd just eaten grease. I wanted to return the swimsuit, the dress. Outside, the sun was blistering. Writers, I'd learned, don't stab you in the back. They insert the blade gently right between your ribs while staring you in the eye.

"They're planning a first printing of fifty thousand," she said. "I'm in shock, really. That's a lot, right?" Then, "Have you gotten your prepubs?" she asked.

I hated her using publishing jargon. I hated her.

No was the answer. No, I had not.

Speaking of the Joneses, Win was the first to teach me their secret, to let me in on the fact that the Joneses, as a category of consumer, were in fact more volatile than the neighbors who tried so hard to keep up—in the olden days, that is, of the mortgage universe, before the flourishing of subprime. The nature of the neighbors' relatively predictable (and small, also relatively speaking) incomes made betting on them—or against them, as the case may be—easier to get right. They tried hard not to fall, but when they did the loss was minimal, easily absorbed. Not the case with the Joneses. First, they believed so invincibly in themselves that they didn't protect with wide margins; second, when they fell the enormous sums were not so easily absorbed, making them a riskier bet but also potentially far more profitable.

Emma had brought up the Joneses. "The Joneses of Pond Point," she had said, speaking of the family in the neighboring house, the Bostonians with the Red Sox paraphernalia everywhere. We were gorging on lobsters after the clams, that night with Win in Maine. The Joneses had just arrived for their weekend stay. It was dark already but their house was lit up, a lamp in each window, above the front porch and the back. The house shimmered and one broad floodlight blanched the sea grass for fifty yards, then darkness.

As the lights went on we admired it again as we had done during the day, walking on the beach. It was well cared for in contrast to the Chapmans'. The place was freshly painted. Window boxes thrived with red geraniums, along with a garden of hardy flowers in front of the house. An American flag snapped smartly in the breeze. On weekends they worked tirelessly on the property, Emma told us—mother, father, aunts, uncles, even the children. They weeded and scraped and banged and fixed and swept and cooked and mowed the small lawn. They hung out their clothes to dry with tidy precision. Never would they dream of renting the house. "Even the dog struts around with a sense of having done a helpful chore, carrying his bones here and there, digging clean holes," Emma had said.

Now the family was inside having their dinner.

"Emma rubs shoulders with the Joneses," Will said. "Wherever we go, she gets their number."

"I hadn't known she'd found them on Pond Point," Win said. "You've got a knack. Middle-class neighborhoods are the new posh."

"Funny you should mention the Joneses," Theodor said. "We're related to a pair over in England."

"Oh, not *that* story," I said as Theodor launched into it. This was a little dig at my family, my brother and his values, but I liked that Theodor was telling it; I liked appearing to be above the Joneses in that I was all right with admitting that I was beneath them. After all, that was what Emma liked about them. We weren't so very different in many ways. Theodor set the scene: Heath and Clarissa, the American doctor in London and his expensive English wife, with her Oxbridge accent. "Darling," my brother would say, drawing out the word until it was as long as a dachshund, "don't forget the schedule"—pronounced *shed-jewel*—"and tea this afternoon with the Harringbones." Their four daughters: Ginger, Chance, Olympia and Happy—yes, Happy, as in Rockefeller, as in Felicity—all blond and blue-eyed and entitled. My brother earned bundles servicing the American expatriate banking community, charged American prices to those suspicious of the National Health Service. The family lived in a gorgeous townhouse in Cadogan Gardens—recently purchased for many millions of pounds—red brick with white wood trim and paned windows two stories high. Each house on the square was prettier than the next. But my brother's house was the prettiest, the largest and the most lavishly redone, but only upon close inspection, only if you are one to notice the finest details. Clarissa passed her time with interior decorators, examining swatches and paint chips and doorknobs and finials, making decisions about windows and equipment and appliances.

Visiting them just after they bought the house, taking in the whole picture, endless minutes on the couch with fabrics and window treatments, Theodor had said to my brother with an inside nudge, "What's it like keeping up with the Joneses?" I had laughed both nervously and sincerely, for he was teasing my brother, who was difficult to tease as he took life very seriously. We were swimming in too much delicious chocolate, up to our necks in it, drowning in it, and no one seemed to be aware except Theodor.

"The who?" Clarissa, looking up from the couch and out the window at all the other, inferior homes on the square, asked innocently with her sweet small voice.

She had always had and would never need. She knew exactly who the Joneses were. They had reached all four corners of the developed world. Everyone knew the Joneses. "The who?" Theodor nearly burst out laughing. Then so did she. She hadn't heard, but now she had, and so she laughed at herself, at the misperception, feigned ignorance because the Joneses were an

American construct and she was too English to allow them admission. "The who," she repeated, mocking herself, and I knew again why Heath loved her.

Heath was a big man filled with a doctor's bravado and a small, adorable boy's desire not only to please his father but to outperform him. He looked at Theodor and said without a trace of irony, "We *are* the Joneses."

"He didn't say that," Emma said to Theodor, bubbling with laughter; and then everyone laughed. You could pretend all you wanted to be beneath the Joneses, but God forbid if you place yourself up there with them. What kind of a person would do that?

"Power to your brother," Will said, stroking his strong chin, pushing back in his chair, admiring my brother for the boldness of his character, finding the complexity in something seemingly silly. "At least he calls a spade a spade."

"The Joneses," Win said, turning them over in his mind. On his plate lay the lobster carcass, picked clean, even the head. Will had instructed all of us to dig into the small crevices of the head to find the lobster's best meat. "They always fall. The trick in trading is to assess when, understand how and when the illusion will get the better of them, you know, in terms of the general feel of the market. There's a whole subcategory of bonds designed for the collapse of high-end mortgages, bonds that thrive on the failure of the Joneses."

Win sat there with his pink shirt and his glistening cuff links, perched high above the rest of us.

"True enough. But for now he's a Jones, and for now he knows it," Will said. And my brother was deflated and inflated in what I could see was a dialogue about their perspectives on the market. Will worked in the present. Win worked in the future. And character, as it always seems to be, was at the center of the argument.

• • •

Again, in my bed, I awoke to a thunderstorm violently ripping the night sky, lightning darting about, streaking light here and there. I heard water dripping onto the plastic above my head. I lay watching the storm out the window. Theodor had moved to the girls' room to comfort them. The water would become too heavy for the plastic and the tape. Eventually it would all fall into the bed. I would drape more plastic over the bed in order to protect it and then move to the couch.

But for now I lay here listening to the sound of the leaking water that made our lives possible, allowed us to live well. Was there a category of bond for us? Of course not, for we were renters. Even Lily Starr made it into Win's fabulous subcategories of mortgage bonds. She'd be good and reliable and stalwart. The crash of thunder was so violent and loud it seemed New York was being carpet-bombed. The thunder obliterated the drip. For so long I had been outside the forces of the market. I, my family, a stealth force, operating beneath the surface, unable to be tracked. If Win was above it, we were beneath it. In either case, we were both outsiders, able to sit back and watch the play unfold at a distance, with perspective. For all my longing and indulgences, I was fascinated by the mechanics of the system, all our minor yet essential parts in creating desire's narrative.

Seven

IN HIGH SCHOOL, a teacher of mine, Miss Fine, gave me an extra-credit assignment to help me improve my grade in language arts. She asked me to describe my bedroom, to go home and look at it carefully, to observe the details. I lay on my four-poster bed, my back pushing into the thick, full down comforter, looked into the crocheted canopy above me and studied the design therein. For a long time I looked only at the canopy cover—four-inch circles, each like the eye of a cobweb, spun by hand and repeated a thousand times. The canopy cover was enormous. It spanned the four posts and draped down each side to meet at the mattress. My great-grandmother had made it for my grandmother's bed when she was a toddler, some eighty years before. I never knew my great-grandmother, but I could see her hands as they worked the crochet hook and the needle, sewing the canopy cover together. She was an elegant woman named Margaret, and she lived with her husband and two daughters in Philadelphia. Her husband, Heath (like my brother, his namesake), was a financier heavily invested in railroads and in the city's infrastructure—trolley cars and garbage disposal and the like.

Margaret was a young woman when she worked on the canopy cover, her hands less marked by age than my own, at thirty-eight. Smooth, white, unblemished. She did not wash her own dishes. The eye of the web was detailed with balls (popcorn, the stitch is called), the fine cotton yarn teased to form a cluster of eight. If there were a thousand circles, and each circle had eighty tiny balls, that would make at least eighty thousand balls stitched by her hands. It took her less than one year to make the canopy cover. She worked on it in her parlor by the fire while her husband read the evening paper, while my grandmother India was still in a crib and while Margaret's baby, Nora, was in a bassinet.

Looking into the canopy, it was as if I were sharpening my eye. There was nothing extraordinary about the room. It was a girl's room, the walls a pale shade of pink, a bookcase filled with classics, another with small Madame Alexander dolls, a closet filled with dresses, some of them having belonged to my mother as a girl. On my dresser I had a doll's bureau for hair ties and ribbons and clips. A few pictures hung on the walls: Mother as a small girl in Europe with her parents, my brother and I as babies, an antique mirror in a gilt frame, a painting of Mother Goose. The mirror had belonged to my mother's mother. In the closet as well was a doll's pram that had been my mother's. There were riding boots and hat, a tennis racket, ice skates, a soccer ball, a couple of lacrosse sticks. I did not know true discomfort. I did not know true longing. At that point in my life I longed for little, and I understood, lying on my bed, that this stuff passed down to me by a few generations was a form of wealth. I understood that I, in a centrally air-conditioned ranch house in suburban Maryland, not far from horse farms where I had ridden as a younger girl, had so very much.

I lay on the bed for a long time, staring into the concentric pattern as my great-grandmother's hands grew old, a bit knotty, riddled with arthritis. The canopy cover had been made to outlast her, made of the finest Italian cotton thread reinforced with

Como silk. The canopy cover had been folded neatly and stored in plastic, protected by mothballs, and had moved with my grandmother to Baltimore when she married—a financier too, invested heavily in telephones and automobiles. The window of my room looked out on a garden cared for by my mother and that bloomed from May through September. It was February now and snow covered the garden bed, a fine, thin white layer.

Studying the room it occurred to me that something fundamental about who I am was missing: my father. He was not present in the room at all, and thus, like an equation, there was a missing factor that, once known, would complete the story of who I am: $x + ? = y$. There was nothing of him as a child, no picture, no toy. He was absent entirely, as if he did not exist, or as if he were irrelevant. My mother and her fancy past were all that mattered here, as if they wanted to wipe his struggle clean from the slate. He was always who he is now: the hard-working, well-paid doctor.

My mother and father met at university when he was in medical school and she an undergraduate studying the history of art. He was a strong man, and she liked that he told her what to do. She had always been told just what to do. She wanted a man to complete what her father had begun, and so when my father saw her for the first time, sitting on a bench reading about Michelangelo, studying for an exam, her hair pulled back with a black velvet bandeau, her blue eyes round and hopeful and ready for adventure, he sat down beside her and said, "I'm taking you for lunch. You need a break and I'm taking you for lunch." She smiled ever so slightly, stood up and followed him. She did not bother to ask his name until they were halfway through their meal.

My father's past had nothing to do with hers. He was the son of an alcoholic from Scotland who came to this country at the turn of the last century because there was nothing left for him there. My grandfather was poor and close to illiterate. He used an *X* to sign his name. Even so, he was a dreamer, and dreamed of becoming a poet. In the evenings when his children were little, they sat around the kitchen table and my father listened to his father spin tales about the Hebrides and the Mull of Kintyre and the Irish Sea, sing achingly beautiful ballads. My father's mother dutifully cleaned as her husband sang, wiped down the counters, her hair pushed back with a kerchief, her housedress and thin frame wrapped in an apron.

As my father grew up, watching the alcoholic nose of his father become redder and more bulbous, watching his mother weighed down by his father's life, he formed a decided opinion about art and its creators. He studied to become a medical doctor, something practical and sound. And here is where tragedy intersected his life, as it will, it seems, all lives. As an intern in a local hospital, he was invited to observe as a more seasoned doctor operated on his mother, a procedure my own mother was too embarrassed to name: "a female concern." It was my grandmother's uterus that was in question, I later came to understand. A hysterectomy. My father sat in the operating theater with a group of other young doctors in training, dressed in their sterile suits, hands covered, mouths covered. Observe he did, as the surgeon made a small mistake.

The procedure went terribly wrong, simple as that, because of the incompetence of the surgeon, who cut an artery that did not need to be cut, and my father's mother bled to death before his eyes. The nurse and the anesthesiologist and the others in attendance tried valiantly to right what could not be righted. Blood poured from the wound, absorbed by the cotton covers, towels stuffed against her side to try to stanch the flow. He could feel her kisses on the crown of his head, her king, a shower of kisses. There was nothing he could do; helplessly he watched. The other students filed out, urging my father to come with them, but he became a stone. Once, for a moment, his eyes met those of the surgeon. My father would never forget the look they held. Not a look of culpability, of sorrow, of desperation, or of guilt. Rather, the eyes held blame. The eyes said to my father, big brown eyes edged with red rims, tired, overworked, defiant eyes, they said to him: Had you not been seated there, this would not have happened. The surgeon took off his gloves and tossed them on the table and with the same defiance walked from the operating room.

My father's father drank himself to death soon thereafter. My father had to rise from this, a slum somewhere in Baltimore, a little sister now in his care. Or does the story begin with the birth of my grandfather on a small Scottish island, very cold, where even potatoes were hard to come by and the idea of writing a word, one's own name, was reserved for people of more fortunate means and the only hope was that ship to America?

This was the story my room told. I gave the essay to Miss Fine. The next day she read it aloud to the class. Adjusting her bifocals on the bridge of her nose, she stood before the class with my typed pages in her hand and read the words slowly, patiently, emphatically. It was magic, a swirl in my chest. She asked me to write other stories, and I did. I received an A in the class and the confidence to know that my stories, my words, the effort that went into them, were admirable. I understood something specific, elemental, looking into the canopy cover—the painstaking quality with which those circles were made, a thousand of them, eighty thousand balls, so precise it seemed a machine had to have made them, each one looking like the others, woven together with a needle to turn an ordinary bed into a fantasy for a girl, the cotton reinforced with silk, a smooth and creamy cream, draping the mahogany posts of the four-poster bed—I understood something about patience, and that I would pursue it at the expense of all else. Miss Fine read my essay to the class, and the class was impressed, and the class and Miss Fine thought they learned something more about me and where I came from. They were heartbroken for my father, the stern man they saw only on occasion—if Mother was sick—dropping me off at school. They were heartbroken for me too.

What I did not tell them was that the story was a lie. The Palmers were English, not Scottish; the canopy cover was a bedspread bought by my mother at a flea market. My paternal grandmother lived to be 104. Shall I go on?

That facts were malleable—not irreducible finished goods, but a kind of originating ore, to be shaped and spun and even discarded wholesale for the sake of the story—was a new and powerful discovery. It made me feel powerful, because I understood that people wanted to believe that what they were reading had actually happened, and I believed I could make them feel that even if I was "lying."

I went to a college famous for its undergraduate creative writing program and then went to New York City to graduate school. I read all the young American writers I could find who I believed had talent. I studied them to see what they were doing, if they had the ability to get inside me and move me, and if they did, I studied every word, every comma, to see how they managed the feat. I wanted to do what they did. I studied their careers too, used them as models for my own. I applied for grants and prizes they'd won. I went to writers' colonies they'd gone to. I was calculating. I saw where they were ten, fifteen years down the line from me, imagined myself there, became competitive, imagined I could and should do better. I locked myself in the bedroom of my first small apartment and stayed there until a chapter was finished. I worked until all hours of the night. I rose early, tore my hair out. I wanted this. I did not notice the days slip by. I did not notice the seasons. I went inside myself and in two and a half years pulled out my first novel—the story of a young doctor whose father is an immigrant from Scotland, an illiterate drunk who wanted to be a poet, the story of a young doctor whose mother dies before his eyes during a simple operation, the story of how this young doctor raises his younger sister after the death of both parents—*The Way We Do Things Here.* I met Theodor and together we began to dream.

The novel was sold to Deutsch for a ridiculous amount of money, the publisher and editor in chief promising me the moon. A few months after publication it was nominated for the Washington Award, and I believed myself firmly on the right and inevitable path even if the book sold fewer than five thousand copies. I was twenty-six years old. Theodor got his first big commission. We had money in the bank, more than most of our friends. We were in our twenties and succeeding as artists. By thirty we had a baby, and by thirty-two, two babies, three novels, a fourth on the way. We were rising, rising while at the same time I was being pushed quietly, with a little, subtle force, away from the solitude of the desk toward the playground and beyond. Beyond its perimeter lay the rest of the park and the world. But in this tug of war the desk won in the end.

I needed the money. We needed the money. Only a fool wrote a book for anything else, said Samuel Johnson. It did not faze me when I had to move from one publisher to another. I did not believe in that sort of loyalty. I'd followed the careers of too many writers. If you didn't have the money, you wouldn't be able to afford to write. So I moved, easily. And each time, with the publisher's enthusiastic support, I believed this could be *the* book! But belief and "having a marketing plan" don't mean you have control over the fickle beast that is the reading public. I believed irrefutably in myself and my talent and my own ability to succeed. I knew someday I would make enough money to keep doing what I loved. I believed that as one believes some things sometimes. I just didn't know when. I waited, like a passenger in an airport waiting for a delayed flight to somewhere fabulous—Tahiti, Bora Bora—waiting for things to get easier, waiting for our lives to begin. We were surrounded by artists in the same position, all eager, all hopeful, all waiting, all of us removed from those we had known in college who had taken responsible jobs and were living their lives responsibly in the world in real time. In the meantime, while we waited, I continued to sell novels, and Theodor got his commissions. Like this we could keep going. We could. If we scaled back, we could.

Instead, the girls began private nursery school, which led to private grade school with fancy East Side friends and expensive camps (not to mention birthday parties—rowboats in the Boat Basin, circuses in the park) and country houses on the moon! One goes broke in a thousand small ways: birthday presents, the ticket of admission to those fancy birthday parties; house presents; ballet classes, lessons in general; theater subscriptions, for us and for the children; dinners out with the mothers, with the parents who want to get to know you better; fundraisers (God forbid you don't have your name on the donor list); contributions; dinner parties; out-of-network doctors for my asthmatic daughter, the pulmonologist, the allergist, well-child care not covered, the dentist; bills (electricity, cable, telephone); clothes for the kids, uniforms; taxis, when too tired to take the bus; haircuts even for Theodor, the girls, myself (Do you really need one? I'd find myself thinking); movie theater tickets and the requisite popcorn and soda—all of it adding up constantly in my mind, a spinning calculator, accumulating numbers with astonishing and frightening speed. A taste for small luxuries swells: hair coloring four times a year, eyebrow sculpting by the Eyebrow Man at Barney's, a massage. Who buys those $1,800 bags and $1,000 pairs of shoes?

An excursion to the reflexologist with another mother—an outing I had no business being on: "Sarah Jessica Parker comes here," the mother exclaims. Afterward we stop in a cosmetics shop and the mother buys herself a small jar of face cream for $250 (the size of my grandmother's tiny silver smelling-salts box) that contains an ancient serum, a mixture of mummy dust and some other such nonsense, and that claims to return you to your former self. Indeed. "You must get yourself a jar," she insists, plopping down her credit card, and I understand that she just does not get it, she just does not know who I am, she has no clue, no idea, and the fault is mine. The white glass vial, its sage-green label holding the vivid description of the rectifying powers of the mummy serum, resting so invitingly in the saleslady's creamy palm as she promises that yes, the jar is small, but you need only a speck for the magic to work, that the jar will last a year, that luxury can buy youth. At this point, you will know what I did.

Along this way one is forgiven, perhaps, if one takes a wrong turn, if one gets distracted from the pursuit of art. What did truth matter when money was the only truth capable of speaking its mind, when the amount of money one made was the only measure of success? Perhaps I can pinpoint our fall to the beginning of preschool. Not because of the school or the friends, but because I was not good at being the poor one, and in this new stratosphere, even by the standards of a good year for us, we would be the poor ones. Perhaps it begins earlier than that, with the sale of my first novel, with believing on the flimsiest evidence that a first enormous advance would lead to others, and that with them I'd be able to prove to my father that I could afford the life he intended for me, that the artist didn't always need to starve. Or perhaps earlier still, perhaps our fall boils down to my mother's impeccable taste, she who always wanted the finest quality for her children; she cared not so much about brands but that the clothes we wore were exceptionally made, that the lessons we took would teach us the most, that the school we attended would expand our minds. She was a simple woman in many ways, but her eye for detail was acute and demanding. Or perhaps my desire and its ever-expanding circumference were fueled by the very air of New York.

Here now, home from our visit to England and my brother and his wife and expensive life, it was not a good year, and I was very much the poor one, with debt like a stone slab, with the publication of *Generation of Fire* not having such a promising outlook anymore—none of the glossies were covering it, no reviews had been assigned yet. ("It's still early," my editor would say, though the long silence that I was so familiar with, the post-publication oceanic silence from all involved in the happy occasion was already well under way, the calls to agent and editor returned with more and more delay—after all, what was the urgency? The urgency was mine alone. Their job was done.) The article for *Woman* magazine was on the verge of being killed. Theodor's commission was far from complete, his patron and the museum threatening to withdraw support if he didn't show them something soon. Tuition for the children was due and I had no idea how we'd pay it. Credit card payments were due and I had no idea how we'd pay them, next to nothing left in the once big savings account, notice needing to be given to the cleaning lady and the babysitter. The fights starting with Theodor:

I—*We need to make more money.*
T—*You need to stop spending so much.*
I—*It's my fault? What about the commission? When's it going to be finished? I've never seen a person work so slowly.*
T—*Come on now, darling, have faith.*
I—*Faith? Faith? How about reality? Tuition? How about you get a real job?*
T—*It always works out. Don't let me lose you just because it's a little tight now. It's going to work out.*

This was where we were now, floating on our own little barque of ruin, surrounded by the gorgeous sea of wealth so flamboyantly on display in the early morning hours as the city's parents awoke to take their lovely children to school in their Ferragamo shoes and their shiny black SUVs, juggling $5 cappuccinos and buttery croissants that would both, unfinished, end up in the garbage. That was the only truth I was capable of absorbing. Indeed, I did not like to be the poor one. I, simply, was sick of waiting. I wanted to be among the grown-ups, the responsible, the living. So yes, you could say I was giving up on art. That is what happens when you grow up. Art finds its rightful place as a child's plaything, the preoccupation of damaged souls, hapless academics, tenured nincompoops and exhibitionists, whom we strangely entrust with the education of our children, the way the wealthy aristocrats of an earlier age hired governesses. Art: child's play, nothing more.

A cool, crisp September morning. The sky so blue, ethereal in its majesty. "Severe clear" is the aeronautical term. The summer behind us, the children in school again. I rode the subway downtown to Tribeca to have breakfast with Will Chapman, Perfect Boy, the Renaissance man of the investment house Paul, Smart & Smith: PSS, he called it, or Piss, depending on his mood. His invitation. As I came out of the subway, the buildings of Wall Street, to the south, rose in front of me, awake in the morning sun. Men and women, dressed in their suits, made their way to work, tanned, relaxed, ready to start again, take on the world—a whole army of people. It was 8:30. I was early. Cabs zoomed by, town cars. I walked south.

It was an odd invitation. I'd never met with Will before on my own, but it was just like him, if he wanted to meet with me, to do it in a completely safe way—breakfast. Nothing untoward or to be misinterpreted about breakfast. I figured he wanted to plan a surprise party for Emma or arrange some fabulous adventure (that we could not afford and that I'd have to lie my way out of) for us as couples or for our girls. In any case, I was intrigued. I strolled slowly, killing the half hour before our breakfast at nine. I paused at a newsstand to flip through the glossies to see if Lily Starr had made it that far.

A plane flew by overhead. My cell phone beeped, indicating a message. The screen announced that the caller had been private, offering no revealing number or name. I lifted a copy of *Woman* and flipped to the book page, phone pressed to ear. Lily Starr once told me of a friend of hers who bought a pair of roller skates when her novel was published so that she could skate from bookstore to bookstore to sign copies of her book. Oddly, she thought that a signed copy of a book could not be returned by the store to the publisher. How pathetic, I thought, as if those roller skates would make the difference, and I thought of my ridiculous self, standing here ready to open every magazine to see how much press Lily Starr had received so I could scratch at what seemed to be the writer's perpetual wound. "Hello, my darling novelist." And there was his determined voice. "You're having breakfast with Will to hear his silly news." There was an inflection on the word "breakfast," indicating that he too thought breakfast an absurd time of day to meet a lovely woman, no matter the circumstances. "I'd like to make my own invitation—champagne sometime soon?" He did not leave a date, a time, a place. He did not even mention his name.

Yes, I'd have a drink with Win. I dropped *Woman* magazine back in its stack. I liked this man. He went after what he wanted without a care for convention. I liked his bold determination, the fact that he seemed to know inherently that it does not matter a whit what others think. The art of his confidence lay in making people think what he wanted them to think, in knowing that the opinion of others did not make a person's life. My heart beat a bit faster. I did not need to know what Lily Starr had achieved. Who cared what small successes happened for her? Those successes: here for a nanosecond, then gone. I knew this better than most. I had a message from Win and I wanted to know what it was he wanted from me.

Later, though, at another newsstand on another pee-stained and -scented New York street, I would scan the magazines to find Lily Starr right where I expected her to be, her light scintillating from every glossy out there, heralding the greatest voice in fiction *written by a woman* since Carson McCullers. "Old-school brilliance." "Irresistible." "Sensational." "A tour de force." "A modern master." Shall I go on? Her smile captured in a $5,000 publicity shot brightening all of those pages, the PR machine scooping her up like arms from heaven to lift her high above the rest of us mortal souls. After I set the last magazine back in its place, I'd look to the sky, expecting to see a billboard with her picture, right up there with the clouds, smiling down upon me. Perhaps she would even speak: "Gee, this is great. Isn't this great, India? *Isn't it?*"

But that was later. For now I did not care. I'd have champagne with Win. A married woman, mother of two, with no intention of ever being unfaithful, I'd buy a new dress to have champagne with Win, trying to cultivate for my own the indomitable self-interest that guided him to think first of himself and of all that he wanted. I craved to live fully, richly, to care not a bit for the opinion of others, to do exactly as I pleased, to be far removed from the distasteful pastime of worry and debt. I was a bit lighter on my feet, my cheeks a bit rosier. I loved thinking about the fact that Will Chapman and Win Johns had discussed me. And then I wondered: What could possibly be Will's news, and why did he want to share it with me?

The restaurant was where the titans of industry and finance breakfasted. Expensive flower arrangements. White tablecloths. Silver cutlery. Stemware. Cloth napkins. Butter pressed into the shapes of shells and starfish and sand dollars and sea horses. Male waiters in black suits and white shirts. Businessmen in pairs leaned into each other, making morning-time deals. They'd all been up before dawn, running in the park.

Will sat, tall and elegant, reading the paper. He looked up as I approached and then stood, placed a soft kiss on either cheek. Will is a handsome man with his dark, full hair and green eyes, his strong jaw. He is slender and likes to run, and you can see from his body that his health and what he eats are important to him. As a pair, he and Emma do make an attractive couple. But there was something else about Will Chapman that I always admired: his ability, in spite of being one who liked to know so much about everything, to be shy, to bow his head and avert his eye, somewhat like a woman being flirted with by a dangerous man. She likes it, wants it, but at the same time wants to pretend that she does not. About Will, some might just call it bashful, but for me, his look and general demeanor, when his eyes sort of quivered a little, were more complex, hinted at vulnerability. And I liked that. I thought I had the ability to throw him off balance, and I liked that too.

We sat down, the waiter gently adjusting the chairs for us, and he thanked me for coming. And then with that look, his jaw inclining to the left and then to his chest, as if to pause and think how to say something uncomfortable (which made me infinitely curious), and then, as if coming up out of the water for air, Will lifted his head, looked me squarely in the eye and said, "I've quit my job. I'm leaving Wall Street."

"No, you're not," I said without pause, surprising myself. I said it as though he were my husband and this were news I had anticipated, with fear, for a while. All in one long instant I saw the following: on the table, a pouch-like envelope, big enough to hold a manuscript, and indeed the dimensions of the contents were alarmingly manuscript-like, an 8½-by-11-inch brick. More alarming, the brick was not small. In fact, it was very large. But most alarmingly, my name was written on the label. I sighed to myself; he was going to ask me to read this thing. That's why I was here. It would be terrible. He had quit his job. Before long the Chapmans would have to sell their apartment. They'd never be able to afford the Victorian shack (fleas and all) in Maine. Emma would have to adjust to a way of life that she was decidedly not accustomed to. (And, sweet Jesus, nectar of Schadenfreude, she might even have to get a job.)

"No, you're not," I said again, with an emphasis that indicated I'd read the future and had seen that this was not a prudent decision. It amused me a little that my first and thus most honest response was to save him.

"Is it that bad?" he asked, smiling, showing me that he'd understood my concern. His face had regained its general and more familiar air of confidence.

"You mean the life of the ungainfully employed?"

"I suppose you could put it that way."

"Does Emma know?"

"Of course," he said. Of course she knew. Of course he would not check with me first. And I knew too that she would fill the role in her way much better than I ever would have been able to, and I knew as well that that resilience of hers was what Will loved and what Theodor and I had always admired—to make the best of every situation. Not to complain, but to turn a challenge into a sport. I thought again of the shack on Pond Point. Will wore a light gray suit with a faint green pinstripe. He wore a shirt of the same green, which picked up his eyes and the pinstripe and the tie, all very quietly and yet perfectly upholstered. He's completely crazy, I thought. He's gone out of his mind. He makes something like one and a half million dollars a year, minimum. Any way you slice it, there is no way to bet on that as a writer. "She's supportive," he said.

"Have you already done this? You've already told them at work?"

"Yes, but India, I've not asked you here for your opinion of this decision."

"Then why are you telling me?" I asked. "Silly news" ran through my mind. The waiter brought me a cappuccino, frothy and splashed with cinnamon, the foam like a billowy cloud. Why did he meet me at this restaurant and not a place more appropriate to a writer? Why not a diner, the Cuban restaurant in my neighborhood? Why did he bring me into the mouth of the beast to tell me this news? "You're brave," I said.

"I've wanted this since I was a child. If not now, when?"

"Have you shared your work with anyone to get a sense of whether you could sell the book?" I asked.

"Pragmatic," he said and then answered in the negative. Was he a fool? I looked at the envelope. He was going to assign me the responsibility of judging his work. I was going to have to be the one to tell him that he was no good, which of course I would never do. A job like his wasn't so easy to go back to after time away. At best he'd need a few years to understand the lay of the land as a writer. I knew enough to know that a few years on Wall Street was an eternity. I looked again at the envelope. There had to be a good five hundred pages in there. It was going to be an awful slog. A waiter brought eggs Benedict. In the center of the table he placed a silver basket of croissants, flaky and soft.

"Were you fired?" I asked, showing an intimacy with Will that had never been articulated, though we were both aware of our unspoken mutual affection and admiration.

He laughed. "Would that make my decision easier for you?" He pierced me with his green eyes. This was the Will who knew and understood everything. He knew just now that he was leveling something for me, that his decision made me uncomfortable, perhaps as uncomfortable as it would make him if I were to have told him I was quitting my job as a writer to become a banker. We'd spent the past six years creating myths about each other, never mentioned, never stated, but in these myths we'd invested so much of ourselves that they lived vividly in our minds, palpable and real to the other. I was the successful, award-winning novelist and he was the smart, well-read, big-earning banker with a lovely wife and life, the epitome of the college friend who had gotten a responsible job and was thus able to afford to be a part of the world.

"You don't want my opinion, but I am curious to know how much thought you have given to this," I said.

"Pragmatic again."

"If you want to succeed at writing, you must have a certain amount of pragmatism."

"I have an appointment with Lucinda Blankman," he said, pulling out his trump card but bungling the name. Everyone in the business called her Sig, because her signature had come to mean everything. Sig was the most prized literary agent in New York City. Regularly she made million-dollar deals for unknowns. A flash like a shooting star streaked across my mind: he'd hit the jackpot. I reassured myself by resting my eye on the bulk of his manuscript.

"That's wonderful," I said, which fell a bit flat, because an appointment with Sig Blankman was, well, beyond wonderful, was as close to the jackpot as one can get without owning the jackpot, and he'd learned enough already to know that. It was just like Will to seek the best immediately. When he bought a Mogul miniature there was no learning curve. His first choice always included the rarest, the oldest, the one with the most colors, that depicted the most complex scene, and was always bought for a song. Though his song and my song had very different notes. He didn't give me any more information on Sig, on how he'd arranged the meeting, who had helped make it possible. And I didn't ask.

"I've rented an office not far from here. It's small, in an old cold-storage building, and I've been working with a friend on an Internet marketing campaign for the book. I realize I'm ahead of myself, but if I know one thing about business, it is that it's all about marketing. I've sold junk on the Street that people thought was gold . . ."

As he carried on about his office and the marketing schemes and plans to reach millions on the Internet, all I could think about was my desk, facing a brick parapet out the window of my tiny rooftop maid's room, not even the size of our big bathroom, the bookcases crawling up to the ceiling, so as I sat at my desk it seemed I was smothered by books, reminding me of all the books out there. So many books, a ridiculous sum, about two thousand published per week. Then I remembered that my office would soon have to go. We could no longer afford it. Will Chapman, on a whim, it seemed to me, decided to become a writer, got himself a fancy office overlooking the Hudson and all those beautiful sailboats and the Statue of Liberty, plunked down a few grand, bought himself a laptop, set up shop, and he thinks he's Balzac.

"Where do you go when we finish?" I asked.

"To my new office," he said.

"In that suit?" I asked, and I couldn't help laughing. It was a warm, endearing laugh, though, and he laughed too, explaining that he'd dressed for me and that later he would be meeting with the man who was helping him with his website and marketing campaign. He went on to explain more about this man, Jack. Jack was excellent at publicity strategies, that was really his forte (he pronounced it *for-tay*, with two syllables—not as the French do). He, Perfect Boy, knew better, so I corrected him.

"*Forte,*" I said.

"You've spent too much time in European novels. But that's what I like about you, India, you eat your salad after the meal. Elegance and sophistication grace each step. You crave only the finest." He took a sip of his cappuccino, almost daintily. "In any case, Jack believes we can get a lot of mileage out of the fact that I left a high-paying job to pursue art. A ploy to get people interested in me, and then, with hope, the book. A riches-to-rags story, if you will, which I find very clever. And we'll create a fan base on the Internet. What do you think? I hadn't realized how much one had to think about these things. It seems more must go into the marketing than the actual writing. Is that how it works for you? What do you think—Wall Street to art?"

"Art," I said in a small voice. The eggs Benedict looked at

me like two sorry eyes. I punctured the yolks. The only capital Theodor and I had was the time we had put into our art. We'd paid in blood to be where we were, for our art. And where were we? Now I found myself sitting across from a friend, Will Chapman, heir to a noted New England family name and legacy, if not a lot of family money (but he'd made up for that, in spades), a man with an excellent job (doing I'm not sure what, but excellent nonetheless in terms of remuneration), and he decides he's had enough; he's tired of having merely everything and wants to give it up for the incalculable luxury of talking shop with me. I'd seen enough of the people who populated Will's world to know that when they got bored, they concocted deep-pocketed adventures to show each other up.

I knew that people like Will had to come up with an original act that would distinguish themselves from each other, save them from being simply, predictably wealthy. Richard Branson, for example, sailed around the world in his hot-air balloon. And here was Will's version of that deep-pocketed adventure. To boot, he'd figured out the marketing angle, *From Riches to "Rags,"* always in quotation marks, for here was a man who would never know anything about rags. (I didn't know that much either, but I felt I did in this city.) And now he wanted to speak about *art!* Next he would be discussing "process" with me, telling me about his dreams and how he discovers in his unconscious the themes he finds worthy of pursuit, the depths of truth, of the struggle to rip the words from the mind, talking as if he'd been doing this for decades.

"It's not easy," I said at last.

"I know that," he said. "Wall Street isn't easy either."

The waiter brought a bowl of fruit—kumquats and kiwis and mangosteens and passion fruit and mangoes and champagne grapes dangling over it all—flown in from the tropics that morning. Were they ever going to stop bringing food? Our glasses were repeatedly refilled with freshly squeezed orange juice and sparkling water from Austria. The water was presented to Will like a bottle of fine wine.

"Any fool can make money, India. I don't care about money. I've made money, enough anyway. For two years or so we won't need to think about it. Emma is supportive. Children are chameleons. They adjust."

I thought of my own children, thought of the many times we considered pulling them from their fancy school. It never occurred to us they would be chameleon-like. We could only imagine their questioning eyes: *Why do we have to change schools? What about our friends?* Was this another difference between the haves and the have-nots? By this fear of letting our daughters down, we were propelled forward, to seek other ways to keep this fantasy of the good life we'd imposed on them, promised them simply by serving it up as an option, alive.

"India, you and Theodor are our models. You don't seem to need very much."

"I must stop you now," I said. I realized that he had bought my act hook, line and sinker. He had no idea how fast I was headed down.

"Stop me, then," he said. "But you are my model. I admire you profoundly." I looked around at all the other pairs concluding their morning business. How many of them were selling air? I was air. I was Enron just before the fall, and savvy Will Chapman was an investor late to the party, begging to be let in so that he too could own a part of the magic. Fool, foolish hope. Picking up the large envelope holding the manuscript, he handed it to me. "Will you read this for me?" he asked simply, but again with that vulnerable look, and I wondered if that was what he wanted, what he loved about Maine: the vulnerability of simplicity.

"Of course I'll read it," I said, accepting the manuscript. It was heavier than I had imagined, weighing my arms down. "Is it finished?" I certainly hoped so.

"I think I'm halfway there," he said.

"Halfway?" I asked, trying not to sound shocked. "This feels to be about five hundred pages."

"Long?" he said, posed more as a question he knew he didn't need to ask.

"I don't know where to begin with you," I said. Didn't he know that people don't like to read much anymore? When they do, they want short, clever books that make them feel smart. I thought of Sig Blankman with Will's thousand pages on her desk, how fast they'd end up in the garbage can. "What was the last book you read that was a thousand pages long?"

"Remembrance of Things Past."

"Are you Proust?"

He smiled.

"A *Suitable Boy, Lonesome Dove, War and Peace,* the Forsyte Saga, *Tom Jones."*

"You were fired, weren't you?"

"Just read the first chapter. If you hate it, don't worry. If you hate it, throw it in the trash and tell me the truth. I won't be offended. In fact, I'll be offended if you don't tell me the truth." He wiped his lips with his napkin and replaced it in his lap. He took a kumquat from the basket, rinsed it in a bowl of water, then popped it into his mouth. Two years, I thought. How fast it passes when you subtract vacation, time with the children, weekends, holidays, doctor visits; it becomes a year, and a year is squandered in a blink. I saw Emma standing before me, her face fractured with worry as she learned what it meant to want.

"I will do that for you, of course," I said. Art, the great leveler, I thought. Go ahead and try.

"India Palmer," a familiar voice called as I stepped from the restaurant into the street. The voice belonged to Darwin Smith, who was married to Theodor's tall and plump cousin Sally. He was a small, deliberate, bespectacled man who enjoyed telling people how to do things better in their lives. Only in New York, a city of eight million people, do you run into your cousin's husband by accident.

I loved to listen to Darwin when he'd go on to Theodor and me about how our lives would be so much better if we lived in the country. He could paint such an inviting picture that I really could envision us in Vermont, in a sweet antique farmhouse, the kids in public school, a barn for Theodor's studio, the attic for mine. I found it entertaining because it seemed Darwin wanted to be a savior, as if by saving just one person, he would consider his life worthwhile. Darwin spoke slowly, he walked slowly. He had a gimpy leg, partially paralyzed by a childhood illness. Actually, he was forced to drag his leg, but over the years he had done a good job of masking the effort so that it seemed only a slight limp.

"Darwin Deals," I said and kissed and hugged him, swallowing him whole he was such a petit man. "How are you?" Somewhere along the route to adulthood (at one time selling Italian sandwiches for a hefty price in his college dorm and other entrepreneurial escapades) he'd picked up the nickname Deals and was now so known to most of his friends.

"You get an early start," he said and examined his watch.

"Breakfast with a friend," I said.

"I didn't think writers did breakfast."

"This writer does. How's Sally?"

"She's well." Sally was a lawyer who defended white-collar felons, perps of hideous scandals usually involving enormous sums of money, and on occasion prostitutes from exotic countries, paid extravagantly with company cash.

"Any good cases?"

"Nothing too exciting. Your book? Is it out yet?"

"October sixteenth is the publication date."

"Reviews?"

"Too early for that," I lied. The prepubs should have been in by now.

"I look forward to reading it. I've been meaning to call you. I wanted to ask if you had a thousand dollars."

"Are you kidding me?"

"I'm not." He had to look up at me, since I towered over him. "You look beautiful. You've done something new."

"Just the hair. The older I get, the lighter it gets. A thousand bucks for what?"

"I want to help you," he said. Gold flecked his brown eyes, which were set a little too close together and made bigger and bug-like by the glasses. He kept his reddish hair slicked back in ripples with gel so it looked pasted to his scalp. His suit was light and a little too big for him. "Coffee is going to burst," he continued. "We've got an opportunity and I want you and Theodor to take advantage of it. There's going to be an eruption in the coffee futures market and we're going to get in on the ground floor with an option. It's going to explode. The price pressure is completely on target. I haven't seen anything like this since the early 1980s."

"You want me to trade coffee?"

"Buy a futures option. You're going to buy it for less than it will be worth, then sell. Simple. I'm telling you, it's about to shoot to the moon. I want you to come for the ride." Then he whispered. "I'm speaking about a good old-fashioned Wall Street tip. Coffee's where it's at. Explode," he said again and went on to explain the simplicity of the situation, of coffee calls and coffee futures and options and the right to buy 37,500 pounds of coffee without the requirement of margin deposits of cash, how together we, like surfers, were going to ride the wave and keep riding it all the way up to the moon. And just then he pointed upward into the September sky, to the pale and very full moon. "We're headed there. Coffee's going two hundred and fifty thousand miles high. Six weeks and a thousand dollars will become a quarter to half a million. I've worked out the numbers. It's a no-brainer."

He spoke with that passion of his, his desire to be the savior, and I felt then as I did about the farm in Vermont. I could see it as clearly as I could see the moon. But I did not understand the nuances he offered, that he carried on about at length, the simplicity or the complexity of how one thousand would become half a million. And yet I believed him, and it made me warm to his idea. Indeed, his enthusiasm seemed to make him grow. He had made plenty of money in the past in the commodities market, so I'd been told by Sally, usually when everyone else was losing money. "There are always one or two making money in a down market," he was fond of saying. In times when I'd been more concerned with art, he'd bored Theodor and me about corn and soy and sugar and pork bellies. He was married to a sane, smart woman. Sally was always proud of him and his accomplishments, always regaling us with his financial savvy. Somehow I did believe irrefutably in answers dropping from the clear blue sky to change one's fortune. And here was the preposterous Darwin Deals in the nick of time. And indeed, the moon was gorgeous up there, my empyrean of security. No creditors up there. Even Will's manuscript didn't feel so heavy in my arms.

In our Vanguard money market account, our savings, used for the big expenses, we had $1,927.58 left. Theodor had no idea. He also had no idea that the bills had gotten out of hand, that I was having a hard time juggling Peter to pay off Paul. He didn't know that the tuition was overdue, that American Express had not been paid this month, that the 0 percent promotion on the credit card that held our debt was coming to an end and the balance would need to be paid (or transferred again), that I hadn't paid the IRS estimated taxes for the entire year, not to mention New York State. I did not tell him that I had used just under $300 from my university paycheck (the income we drew on for our day-to-day expenses) to buy tickets to the new production of *Madame Butterfly*—heavily publicized as a sensation, not just of the season or the decade, but of opera history—even though

Theodor had asked me not to. I loved opera. I could always find ways to justify theater tickets. For example, they could be a tax deduction, listed under the "professional viewings" category. And, I figured, if I canceled the cleaning lady twice, the tickets would be almost paid for.

I didn't tell Theodor any of this; I had not wanted to bother him with more fights. I had not wanted him to lose his focus. The sooner he finished the commission, the better off we'd be. But now another hope began to dawn, creeping in around the edges, taking me over slowly but completely. And it smelled like coffee, of all those beans, the rich, delicious smell, the oily beetle-like shape, the sheer quantity, the amassing of so many beans. Did he say 37,500 pounds? I would have them. I would be buying them for a low price and would have them, and once I had them, others would want them, want them badly enough that they would pay me a good deal more for them than I had paid. I thought of how many people loved to drink, needed to drink, coffee. Though I understood nothing, it seemed to make such perfect sense.

In this way I would make a handsome profit. In this way I would be able to work unburdened. In this way perhaps I would find my way back to storytelling. I wanted to find my way back. I understood that now. At all costs I wanted to find my way back to writing. I was a writer. I wanted to be writing. "Dreamers dream," my dear old professor Roger Salter once said, "and writers write." I wanted to make this work. I had fought for this. I will do this. And I realized just then how jealous I was of Will, terribly jealous—the ease with which he had let go.

The coffee, it did make sense. Indeed, the fates were with me. Will Chapman chose that restaurant so that I would be here at this exact time to run into Darwin Deals. I linked my arm happily in his and for a bit we strolled. Later, when I got home, I sent him a check, leaving us with $927.58, just a stick of wood floating up from the wreck of the family franchise.

Eight

OCTOBER 16, A DAY CHOSEN by the marketing gurus at Leader Inc. Books. My publication day. On the proposed jacket, two sisters kissing. This, I am told by marketing, is alluring. Later, a man is added to the design. He sits in an armchair and appraises the sisters. "Sexy," I am told. "Sales are all about the jacket." On the back, blurbs from five best-selling female authors of women's fiction—commercial, less than literary but with that aspiration—sing the novel's praises. The pages of the book will have a rough-cut front edge.

It's been unseasonably cold. I'm wrapped in wool and white corduroys. I spend the morning at the university, teaching. In my first class a student comes late. Her story is due for submission. She's a pretty girl with long black curly hair and sharp features. She's been crying. Her dark brown eyes are puffy. The class stares at her. I don't interrupt what we are doing. She does. "I can't read my story to the class today," she says quietly, but nonetheless sucking the attention of the class to her.

The sense of privilege of these students always reminds me of my age. What they take for granted, my generation of students never would have—the display of personal drama, grubbing for grades, cell phones ringing during class, texting. "But you're due to read today," I say. "Please," she says, her mouth long and slack. "Why?" I ask. "It embarrasses me," she answers. I hold her with my eyes. She has already confessed to me in private that she's been having "psychological problems." All semester, my students have eyed me doubtfully as I have tried to find new ways to address certain irreducible laws of the writer's craft—that art is not random, that conflict and mayhem are not synonymous, for instance—but often they seem to stare blankly, as if to say, You're not John Grisham—what do you know?

Today's my publication day, I think. I want the kids to know it, to know they have a real writer teaching them. I get a jolt of joy, a high, because I've done it again. I've sent another book out into the world—the book, glossy and smooth and mine. Just looking at it, holding it, ignites the butterflies in my stomach. Yippee for me. Tonight Theodor is cooking me dinner at his Williamsburg studio to celebrate, the book party having transformed into a wine-and-cheese event at the Chapmans' after a reading in Tribeca on a later date. I have not yet seen Theodor's commission, the progress of it. "Dinner on the roof," he'd said to me, kissing me on the lips, holding me tightly in his arms. "No matter the temperature. Congratulations, my girl." The way he said "my girl" always made me feel sixteen.

The troubled student's eyes are laser-like, trained on me, awaiting my response. "We can talk after class," I say to her, and the class carries on. Another student reads a story. This one is about a dentist who suddenly realizes that the patient in his chair is a former girlfriend who dumped him back in high school. She is unaware of the connection, doesn't recognize the doctor behind his surgical mask. With his drill he takes his revenge on her face. I only half listen, like a shrink, I imagine, sitting across from her patients as they rattle off their endless tales of abuse. I don't need to listen; I know my comments—gratuitous violence and the implications, violence as pornography, not interesting, no complexity, who cares? Your job is to make us care.

My mind flits to a doorman in our building. A week ago, at forty-nine, he dropped dead of a heart attack. He loved to draw cartoons, cartoons worthy of *The Literary Review,* and I always thought how wonderful it would be if the magazine ran one of them: Doorman Becomes Famous Cartoonist. I had wanted to be his savior.

Today is my publication day! Fall light slants beautifully into the classroom while the drill does its business on the patient's face. I'm thinking, I'll send the doorman's family $1,000 if my book does well. I'm thinking, I'll ask the family for his cartoons, and I'll submit them myself to *The Literary Review.* I'm thinking, I'll get him an agent. I'm thinking of all the good I'll do with my money. I'll give April, the babysitter, permanent employment, guarantee her job for life. Such pondering was a favorite pastime. Ah, I would be good and generous at the task. The cleaning lady too, I would save her: employment for life. She's been with us since before the children were born. I'm loyal, I think to myself, brightening. I love being loyal. It's a fine quality. Karma, the world should be good to me.

Today is my publication day! The drill tears from the nostril to the lip, then up the cheek toward bone. *She had beautiful bone structure and he loved defiling it. He loved how easy it was to wreck beauty. Blood spurted everywhere, coagulating as it met the air.* The student reads with vivacity, a real sense of himself and the power of his work. He's a solid boy, like a football player, with fat eyes and a buzz cut. The woman is anesthetized but conscious, aware of what is happening to her but unable to do a thing about it. The coffee option is looking good. Darwin Deals has been phoning almost daily. "Up, up, up," he says. "A blight in Brazil. We're reaching the strike mark and we're going to keep surfing until . . . India Palmer, you're going to be glad you know me." *Blood spurts like a fountain, oozy, from the once pretty chick's face. She's flailing her arms as if she could reverse the horror. The horror!* If the book fails, there is always the coffee. It's a pretty day outside, if cold, the clouds booming across the sky. In this fashion, the class proceeds.

My students are serious, sweet, young, impossibly young. The strange boy reading with those fat eyes of his, I'm not sure he qualifies as sweet. To them, I am an old lady. They are pierced everywhere. One is stoned, eyes rimmed red. They wear clothes that look like pajamas. "The violence is well rendered," a student begins the critique. "You grossed me out," he offers as evidence of the writer's success. His name is Bob. On the first day of class he declared that Bob was his new name when he introduced himself: "My name is Bob. It used to be Malcolm Bennett Johnston VIII, but I think that's one too many Malcolm Bennett Johnstons. And I'm taking this class not because I want to write novels or fiction or stories—there's no future in that—but to learn how to write a good plot so I can make video games. That's where the money is." He looked me in the eye as if challenging me. "How long have you gone by 'Bob,' Bob?" I asked finally. He checked his watch and said, "Three minutes." Now he adds, "I love being grossed out." Hands shoot up, waving eagerly, stems in a breeze, and then all the students are a-chatter about what's wrong and right with the story: point of view and conflict and characterization, and is "the horror" referencing Conrad? They take the story and their responsibility to point out strengths and weaknesses quite seriously. The girl with psychological problems sinks in her chair.

After class, the girl and I sit on a bench outside in the sun, wrapped in our coats. She explains that her piece is about her boyfriend doing something very unpleasant to her. She apologizes, says she *had* to write the story. "It *had* to come out," she says. "But I just couldn't bear to read it in front of the class."

It's very short. I skim it. Today's my publication day. Yippee. The story is not clear, skates by on allusive images. Apparently the couple is having sex. He's entering from behind, his front to her back. The story is not very good. The woman is hostile afterward, not sure how to talk to the man. I don't understand the predicament or why this would trouble her so, and I explain myself. She says this approach to intercourse was new for her. I think, How naïve, how young. She seems, with all her curly hair and her lovely face with sharp planes, to have a bit more experience than she is revealing. She lights a cigarette. I hate the fact that part of my job entails reading about the sex lives of my students—worse, having to critique them. A helicopter flies low overhead. Today is my publication day and I'm talking to a student about sex.

"I just couldn't read this out loud," she says, her hands trembling as they hold on to the story and the cigarette. "Do you understand?"

Do I understand what? Having a man come in from behind? Doggy style, as they say? And this is so troubling to her that she finds it worthy of fiction? I study her for a minute, the intensity of her face, filled with concern. None of this matters, I want to say to her. Just breathe. A colleague passes and congratulates me because he's seen my book in a bookstore. Yippee. I'm glad the student now knows I have a book out. Her face remains fractured with her own concerns. "It's not that unusual," I say to her, regarding the position—that is, wanting to snap her into a more perceptive self-awareness. Then I get down to other points of artistry and characterization, and she, hanging on to my last comment, stares at me dumbly, blankly, holding me with her eyes for a moment as if in disbelief. She turns away. I quickly finish commenting and am off to the next class.

In the afternoon, I take the subway downtown to the West Village to meet a college friend, Kathy Park, who is taking me to Queen's Spa Sauna for a jjimjilbang treatment. This is Kathy's surprise, and surprise it is—a way to celebrate the publication of *Generation of Fire.*

Kathy, tall, with a dark bob and large, arching, humorous eyes, kisses me at the golden dragon front gates. Inside, the décor is bright red with more gold. Sculptures of lions stand guard, and a flurry of women in black bras and panties speak among themselves as naked women saunter by on their way to the sauna or steam room or the heated mugwort room. Kathy says something to the receptionist in Korean. She came to America when she was fifteen and retains a slight accent. She's tough and strong-willed and always the boss. It's one of the many things I love about her: she takes charge and gets her way with a firm and commanding pursing of the lips. She's an attorney, a litigation partner specializing in white-collar-criminal matters (like Sally), an avid reader, a fabulous dresser, a divine cook, a mother of three. Her husband is a thoracic surgeon. As a friend, she never had sympathy for any stories of my financial woes. And she certainly had no answers, or not the kind I wanted to hear. She yearned to be a pianist but gave that up when she had children, because that is the way things are done. "When you have children you have got to be responsible, and that means doing things you don't want to do."

Now Kathy's carrying on with the Korean ladies, fluently in her mother tongue. When she came from Korea, her father had been here six years, working nights so that he could bring his wife, Kathy, and her two older sisters to New York. He'd lived in Central Harlem and started a well-respected business creating wigs in all styles and shapes for African-American women. Kathy spent her high school years forking wig hair into afros, combing it, teasing it, until it was wiry and firm and perfectly oiled. The time I shared my money concerns with her—the only friend with whom I would ever do so—she said impatiently, "You have to sit down with someone who can show you the numbers." She gave the phrase the special emphasis it has in the business world, a cult-like Pythagorean regard for *the numbers,* and for the doing of them, the way that the numbers, once done, can crack through fortresses of rhetoric and blarney to reveal the truth of a given situation, like a scrawny, wet dog. "The numbers," she continued, "will show you what you need to put away each year. You'll be frightened. It's scary. But if you don't, then I don't want to hear any complaints about your lives. Look at how you live. We are all working and you are running off to Europe for extended vacations." "We" included the entire rest of the world.

If I had dared to explain myself, dared to say "But I don't have a choice in the matter," or "I'm not trained to do anything else," or simply "But I'm an artist," Kathy, with love, would have scoffed: "Artist? Don't hide behind that excuse. If you're an artist, live like an artist. Don't live like a rich woman. Move to a town you can afford. Put your daughters in public school." She'd worked sixteen-hour days since she came to this country. She'd left behind a dozen servants, a maid who followed her everywhere, a baby-grand piano. If the sinew of her life in Korea had been whimsical musical dreams, in America, land of dreams, she'd evolved into a person of solid, practical ambition—defending, for instance, major pharmaceutical companies in criminal investigations into fraudulent marketing and pricing practices. I stopped sharing my financial predicament with her a while back and always pretended that everything was wonderful. And today we were celebrating. Yippee!

"I'm proud of you," she says. "Congratulations. And I adored the book." I don't realize until she says it how much her opinion means to me.

She smiles at the ladies and then at me and says, "The works." We take off our clothes and enter a big room with cushioned tables and are asked to lie down. In all our years of friendship, I believe this is the first time I've seen Kathy naked. Slender and tall, even naked she walks with that determination. I can imagine her in the buff, running into a client and holding forth without a second thought.

The works: a Korean woman in her black bra and panties rubs me down for a good forty-five minutes with a Brillo-like scrub pad. This is supposed to rejuvenate the skin, remove the dead so the new can shine. At some point I wonder what the gritty substance is that she is using with the Brillo, then realize it is my own dead skin. I am covered in fine balls, like sweater pills, of my own sloughed gray skin. After a while she heaves a bucket of water on me and the dead skin floats off to the floor and drains away. When I've been thoroughly sanded, the massage begins. The woman gets on top of me, knees pressed into and along my spine, thumbs up under my ribs as if she could penetrate all the way to my lungs and heart. She does not speak a word of English, flips me over as if I'm a fish, all five feet nine inches of me, all 145 pounds of me. She pummels my calves, stretches my arms, bends the joints in awkward ways. I've been sanded and kneaded and washed down, flushed and flexed, reborn. Today is my publication day!

Kisses goodbye on either cheek. Thanks and love and good luck and congratulations and "When will I see it reviewed in the paper?" I say, "Soon, soon," though I have no idea. Nothing is scheduled. I'm not sure if the book has been assigned. But I don't share my woe with Kathy. "Soon." I hail a cab. Jump in. Blow more kisses and zip off uptown. Hop out at the next traffic light because I realize I have no cash. Check to make sure Kathy's vanished. Descend into the subway. Zip up to Citarella to food-shop. Steak and ravioli and baby bok choy and mâche and bread and macaroons and olive oil and Humboldt Fog. Flowers (because they look so pretty). Total: $113.87. Today's my publication day. Cash from an ATM, am overdrawn (thank God for Checking Plus), a taxi the rest of the way home. Lug the bags into the building, up to the apartment.

Where it's bright and sunny and sparkling. The cleaning lady, Janine, is there. Janine never says a word. But she is loyal to us and we to her. She insists on wearing a white apron. I give her cash, $120 (note, as I have of late, that she's paid more for her time than I am for mine; note, as I have of late, that I really must tell her I can't afford her anymore). She has long hair that she wears in braids. Her white apron is pulled taut over blue jeans and a T-shirt as she irons the children's shirts and our sheets and napkins from a dinner party we had last week. She smiles when I hand her the cash, as she always does. Her two front teeth, encircled with gold, shine. I must give her notice, I think, one more month. I hear the children in their room. "See you next week, Janine," I say and disappear into the children's room.

The girls jump all over me. April, the babysitter, is sitting on her duff, reading the discounts offered at the pharmacy this week. She's always trying to get a deal for us on toilet paper and paper towels and cleaning supplies. She tells me about the specials and hands me rebate forms I need to fill out and send to a rebate center somewhere in South Dakota. In a month or two a check for a dollar will arrive in the mail. I do the task faithfully and as instructed by April. You do not cross April. "Did you read in the paper?" she says to me. She reads the paper from cover to cover, is up on world politics and the presidency and interest rates and the housing market and the wars. Today it's worms in someone's apartment. Some man and his family are going green in New York City. "They've given up toilet paper," she declares in her lilting Caribbean accent. She's a tall woman with bulk. She's from "the islands," as she puts it, where she has a husband and two grown children.

April condemns the practice of going without toilet paper as grotesque, taking the gimmick "just too far." I hear the rumors, other mothers complaining about her because she "reads so much, almost as much as she disciplines the kids." Discipline is passé, alas. Kids rule. Not mine. Not with April. Sun streams through the windows. The girls are all over me with hugs and kisses. Gwen has made a card for me: CONGRATULATIONS. "I helped make it," says the little one, Ruby. "You did not," says Gwen. "Did too." "Did not."

"It's beautiful," I say.

"We're proud of you, Mom," they say together. "My teacher saw your book in the store."

I'm still in my coat and quite hot with the girls hanging from me. I kiss them on their heads and April scoops them away so I can complete my day of work. She knows my rhythms. The girls march off in their dresses, ironed and selected by April. She is proud of their appearance, as if they are an extension of her, a queen bee with her own elegant wardrobe. They sometimes seem to me to be her children as much as they are my own, a bond we first learned to accept and then came to cherish. The girls' hair is neatly brushed and pulled back, fingernails and toenails manicured. Their little heads are held high. They have no idea what I'm thinking: that April needs notice too. And April, striding out, poor thing, has no idea how much I need to give her notice. Has no idea that we here on the thirteenth floor (it's called the fourteenth, but let's call a spade a spade) are perched on a house of cards. Dear me. Tomorrow I'll take care of all that; today is my publication day!

Gwen catches me with her eyes and holds on for a moment, going inside me, reading me—my quizzical girl. She knows; she knows everything—that there is a large difference between her and her friends.

I disappear into our bedroom to check the phone messages, hoping for one from Darwin. I need to hear his enthusiasm, need to hear how we're going to surf coffee to the top. My troubled student comes to mind, the way she looked at me, as if shocked by my revelation, as if I had revealed something atrocious about myself. They are so young, I think. I forget how young they are. No messages. Turn on the computer. Throw coat on bed. Take off shoes. Look in closet. Pull out pretty dress, a pair of tall black leather boots. Draw a bath. The phone rings.

"Congratulations." It's Win. I know the voice. It's a singular voice. I shiver, feel guilty everywhere. I've not seen him since Maine.

"Win?" I ask.

"You know it's me."

"I do?"

"Don't pretend you don't."

"When are we having that champagne you promised?"

"Tonight."

"Tonight? But—"

"No buts. There's this little bar on top of the . . ."

The girls bound into the room, stumbling over themselves, clamoring, fighting over something or other. April is close on their heels. Win is talking but I don't hear him. I hear the girls and April's reprimands. The room is sparkling, bed freshly made with ironed sheets. All the surfaces dusted. In the corner is a chair I had re-covered recently, elegant and decadent, in Scalamandré chenille, picturing prancing tigers—the fancy fabric bought deeply discounted on the Internet (to upgrade the hauled-off-the-street aesthetic). The cushions are fluffed and a throw drapes the arm, as if the chair is a refined lady, languishing. Janine can never be given notice. Money, all of this was made by money. Out the window: New York City, buildings rising, shooting into the sky, money's creation. Theodor refused to care about money; for him money was a cancer, eating the individual alive. It seemed life offered little apart from the care of money. Are we all money's prisoners? I'll call Theodor and explain that something's come up. How far would I go for it?

"I'll have to call you back," I say.

"I'll see you there," Win says and clicks off.

I would find it unattractive if a friend described a man to me in this way, his presumption, his hubris, but all I want to do is meet him. I want to be a poor girl in a Dreiser novel, hear the rich man claim me: "You're my girl now. Come with me. You're mine." I want the decisions to be made for me.

I shut the bath faucet. April takes the girls to the store. Peace for a moment. I notice Will's manuscript on my bedside table.

It's been there for a month, uncracked. I've been giving him excuses, but he always tells me not to worry, when I'm ready for it that will be the time to read it. To the kitchen for water. Pass through the dining room. A gigantic bouquet of lilies—twenty different kinds and colors of lilies, shooting from a vase every which way like fireworks, calla and tiger and trumpet and Easter and Nile and kinds I can't name—casual yet clearly carefully designed. A crushing sensation pushes into my chest. Theodor just doesn't get it, that we're nearly ruined. Their scent fills the room. I open the card: *Nirvana at 8.* No signature.

I light candles and a stick of incense, sprinkle the bath water with oils and slip into the tub along with the first chapter of Will's manuscript. Title page: *Never Say Die by William Banes Chapman.* Dedication page: *To Emma Billings Chapman and our daughters, Elisabeth Chapman and Catherine Chapman, my trifecta.* My goodness, how many times does he need to print his last name!

The story is a family saga that opens on a train heading west from Ohio at the turn of the last century—two girls and their mother, impossibly poor, with a trunk filled with beautiful linen dresses. The mother carries a violin and charms their way from third class to first, where the cars are heated and the rich pioneers are plentiful. They are fleeing the girls' father, the mother determined to make it on her own as a schoolteacher in Montana. It is winter, and snowdrifts bring the train to a halt, and the older daughter, Thelma, named for the heroine of a Marie Corelli novel popular at that time, wonders what will become of them. Will paints the cold of the third-class coach, the coal stove in the center of the car. He paints the black trunk with the white linen dresses stiffly pressed, the iron packed in the trunk, the inappropriateness of the clothes for this time of year but the bounty of their promise. You can see the cold feet of the little girls, their shoes worn. Though in third person, the story is Thelma's, and you want to know what becomes of her, of them.

Before I realize it, I've read the thirty-page chapter, which ends with Thelma's mother in the arms of a stranger in first class, kissing him. The train is stuck in a drift, but in first class no one seems to mind. Thelma's mother plays the violin, and all the men's eyes are on her, on her thin dress, too light for this weather; her auburn hair is held in a twist by two carved ivory combs.

A bit overwritten as it is, too many adverbs and adjectives (nothing a good editor couldn't help fix), Will's story has engaged me. I want to read on. I read the pages fast. His style is big and generous and specific all at once. He can't sustain it, I think. He's a banker, I think. He can't be a good writer. It's not possible. Today is my day. I feel selfish. Terribly, cruelly selfish. I drop the pages aside, get out of the tub and call Darwin, hoping for my own good news.

"We've hit a bump in the road," he says.

"A what?" I snap, dripping from the bath.

"A bump," he says. "I made a very amateurish mistake."

"A what?"

"A mistake."

"How?" On a table in a little nook in our bedroom, next to the computer, sits a stack of unpaid bills, rising, like so much water, at the neck, the chin, etc. "How?" I ask again, softly.

"I failed to consider the impact of China. They are world-class producers of coffee now too." I think of all the children, three-year-olds even, at the Chapman girls' school learning Mandarin. They do not drink coffee in China. They drink tea. Calls and strikes and futures and I hadn't understood what we were getting into. I hadn't wanted to understand. The idea was too attractive. Take a thousand dollars and turn it into half a million by "riding the wave."

"What the hell does China have to do with the price of coffee?" I ask. He explains it all to me again, betting on the future price, which is supposed to soar. Various factors position the commodity to rise in value, meaning the supply was to be diminished in record quantities, in a way Deals hasn't seen since the last price explosion for coffee. I'll confess, hearing his calls, the thrill in his voice, the power of possibility, I'd been struck, not by all the money I could have made, but by how vital I had felt at being involved in stakes so entirely outside myself and my imagination. I understood enough to know that I was betting on a disaster that would create an imbalance in supply and demand, and that it was this that would allow us to win. Now I simply feel depleted.

"We can still make it," he offers. "We still have ten days before the option expires. This can turn around yet. Keep your head up."

"Does a turnaround mean a blight in China?" I ask.

"Well," he begins. But I don't want to hear it. He prattles on for a bit, but I don't hear him. I absorb the bills with my eyes. I'll deal with them tomorrow. More balance transfers, more speaking with the operators. "Are there any other balance transfers you'd like to make while you still have the promotional rate?" they'll ask. They're offering money to suckers at 0 percent, betting that they'll default eventually and then be forced to pay the astronomical fees, up to 30 percent, betting as I do on disaster, on unsuspected illness, the desire to keep up with one's neighbors, that irrefutable belief in our own selves to bring in better futures. "Yes," I will respond, joining the crowd.

Deals is mentioning another trick. Corn comes up, $5.545 a bushel. Record high. We're cruising there. (Note: cruising replaces surfing.) "I'll make it up to you. Don't you worry." Bills swamp my mind, surrounded by bushels of corn and a world paved with coffee beans. Novel? Where are all the novels in this picture? I haven't written a word since I put the last to *Generation of Fire.* Don't think about it. Don't think about it. We'll pay off the bills with the money from Theodor's commission, like a ship come in after years at sea. Believe like Theodor. Perhaps I could ask my father for a loan to tide us over. I'll ask Theodor what to do. I walk to the dining room with the phone pressed to my ear, admire the flowers, the callas like great trumpets in so many colors, how gorgeous they look on my table. How will I explain them to Theodor? I'll think of something. "I promise, India," Deals says. "If this doesn't work out, another one will. Corn, darling, ethanol! I'll win for you yet. Don't despair."

"Ethanol, the big joke," I say.

"Jokes don't matter if there's money to be made," he says before ringing off.

Today, October 16. My publication day. My book with its rough-cut pages, stacked one on top of the other in a crate sent from the publisher, gleaming and glossy and new, repeating the title and my name—*Generation of Fire, India Palmer*—heralding and offering as support the unassailable fact of themselves, with their heft and their sheen and their substance. But the fact is, as I've known all along, none of this works. None of it will suffice. This was a shipment, a ship of sorts, that had returned too late to a city that had burned to the ground. No survivors. The books, with their perky blurbs and advance praise, were the unredeemable currency of a country gone bust, an enterprise that had packed up and moved in the night. Sorry. Wrong address.

In the elevator, headed for the street, a woman from the tenth floor enters, laden with bags—in her hands, on her back, on her shoulder, under her eyes. She's a schoolteacher, divorced, her children grown. She looks depleted. "India Palmer," she declares, and I smile as if all is well, couldn't be better. "I cannot put it down. A magnificent read. Thank you."

I thought about it. I thought about picking up the phone, dialing the number that has not changed since I was a girl, my mother responding. The veins of her hand bulging as they do, grasping the receiver, her graying hair in a net, her prim dress neatly arranged. "Oh, India," she'd say, as she always does, as if I am a surprise. "How are the children? I miss my little granddaughters. When are you coming for a visit?" She'd be in the kitchen, a pot of something on the stove. She is always making a stew or a soup. My father, retired now, would be in the living room, in his chair, compounding interest—the same chair where he has always read the paper. The furnishings just as they were when I was a girl—delicate antiques that had no need to be replaced. Never would they waste money on a renovation. My mother prided herself on her timeless style.

"Is Dad there?" I knew better than to go through her. When it came to doling out money, he was the ruler of that household.

"Why certainly, sweetheart. Is everything all right? He's reading the paper and having an afternoon tea." Her voice quavered a bit, knowing that something was wrong. She always knew.

"Everything's fine, Mom."

"Daddy," I'd hear her call. "It's India, for you."

"What does she want?" he'd respond, not in a mean way, rather with curiosity.

"It's her publication day." And then all the words would become muffled as Mom covered the receiver with her hand.

"Hello, India," he'd say in that way of his that had the singular ability to conjure the entire subcontinent and then, too, to conquer it.

Be bold: "I have to pay the tuition for the girls," I'd say directly, without camouflage. "We'll have the money soon, as soon as Theodor is paid for his commission. This is just a loan. I'll pay you interest." A pause. The inevitable and enormous pause into which would fall all of my father's concern for me, the fear of what it meant to be an artist, the inevitable reckoning that he always knew would come.

"I warned you about this," he would respond. I could see that temple vein of his, flaring as it does. His receding hairline making his face appear much bigger and more imposing.

"Daddy," Mom would call. She always called him Daddy. I'd

hear her in the background, her feeble attempt to interject herself.

"You got yourself into this mess, you can get yourself out. If there is one thing I know about my daughter, it is that she is smart. And I know I'd be doing you no favors if I came and scooped you out of a mess. You're smart. Smart. S.M.A.R.T. And I paid for you to attend one of the country's finest universities. You can do it." Pause. "I do believe in you, India." Thrown in with a warmth, particular to him, that always managed to soften the blow. He'd never tire of his lessons. Yes, I knew the answer, and so there was no need to call.

I fell in love with Theodor because he was a dreamer, and a dreamer, it almost goes without saying, was one who believed. He believed in himself, in his art, in me, my art. He believed in the artistic life, the sacrifices that choice entailed. He believed in them still. It was I, of course, who had changed. I had moved and left no forwarding address. I was the one who had fallen and left Theodor behind. As I rode the subway downtown toward 59th Street, I was eager to get off and meet a man I hardly knew. I wondered what would happen if I did get off; if I walked along Central Park South, dark now at 7:30 P.M.; if I rode the elevator up to the restaurant perched above the park like an aerie. At night the restaurant wasn't nearly as romantic as at dusk, the park a black void fringed by the lights of so many buildings. But romance was unequivocally in the invitation, in the flowers: bold, treacherous, daring romance. Would he be sitting there waiting for me? Would he kiss my hand, my cheek, my lips? What would he do with me if I were to come? Would he marry me?

Yes, I did think that, like a schoolgirl I thought that, the natural consequence of a date with a boy. If I got off the subway, we'd have a first date. We'd ask all those questions you ask when getting to know each other, about college and books and food and trips around the world. The stories making people of us. He'd be the kind to take me on a carriage ride through the park, slipping the driver extra money, lots and lots of it, so the driver would go off course, deeper into the dark park, farther away from ordinary souls. I wanted to get off the subway. I wanted to feel what it was like to have worry lifted, stripped away like so much old varnish. It would be so easy. One foot in front of the other. 79th Street, 72nd Street, 66th Street, 59th Street. The intoxication of the new, the blank slate, the tabula rasa that I love so well. The new dress, the new page, 50th Street, 42nd, there was still time to change my mind, 34th. At 14th Street I switched to the Canarsie Line for Williamsburg, aching at my lack of daring, knowing that if Win was there he'd have enough ego to handle my standing him up.

Walking from the subway to Theodor's studio, I passed a few young hipsters in their skinny dark jeans, a young woman carrying a guitar case, still somehow pioneers, though I knew the real estate had skyrocketed here too. Otherwise it was quiet and cold. Leaves swirled about with plastic bags, catching in the branches of trees. Telephone and electrical wires webbed a canopy overhead. At the end of the street the East River lapped at the pavement. A boat, lit up, floated by. The darkened Domino sugar factory hogged the sky.

Theodor, his hair flying this way and that, dressed in a T-shirt, black jeans and black boots, wearing a leather apron, held daisies at the door of his building: industrial, red brick. How did he find daisies in October? Our wedding bouquet. We'd been married thirteen years. Suddenly I wanted to tell him everything about the day. He scooped me into his arms, and even though he was in short sleeves I felt warm.

"Daisies?"

"Congratulations," he said, and we slipped inside. A long bright corridor led to stairs, which we climbed for three flights. I had not been here in a while. On each floor there was only one studio. This was the kind of building that was fast being converted into condominiums. Paint chipped from the walls in big patches, bare bulbs dangled from the ceilings, Art School Redux. I could hear other people at work in the building. A hammer, a table saw, the shuffling of feet, furniture being moved. No windows graced the stairwell.

"Your book is brilliant. You're brilliant. I read it again today."

"Really?" My voice undisguised and a bit squeaky. Praise from this man, who was still slogging away on the margins, meant everything to me. As long as he believed in me I'd be able to keep going. I told him about the schoolteacher's compliment.

"That's what it's all about," he said. "One person at a time."

I told him about my day, seeing Kathy Park, the bikini-clad skin sanders. I wanted to tell him about Win.

We were at the door now. It was slightly ajar, well lit inside. The light cast shadows on Theodor's face, making him look older and more worn than he actually was. "You're worried," he said, studying me.

Theodor had no idea how intricate the web of bills and debts and desires and gambles really was. If I explained it to him, I'd exhaust him with the complexities. Often I wondered what he'd do if I died, how he'd reckon with the mess I left behind. He never knew when his checks came in, went out, and for what. I'd built a protective wall for him. We were in this together, yet I didn't want to trouble him with the mess because I didn't want to lose control. His solution would be to move. Like Kathy, he'd suggest we live somewhere we could afford. I didn't want to hear that the children had to be taken out of private school. I didn't want to hear that I couldn't buy that dress or these shoes, afford Gwyneth's doctors whom we'd come to love. And what neighborhood could we afford in this city—or beyond? Our rent-stabilized apartment made it impossible to move—not to mention my teaching job. A good teaching position was hard to replace, here or elsewhere. I was trapped. But if I told Theodor all this, he would not worry; he'd find a way to adjust so that we could afford our lives as artists. Never would I be able to engage him in the worry it seemed to take to maintain our lives as I wanted them to be.

"What's wrong?" he asked. He held me at arm's length and looked at me closely. I wanted to confess to him, something. It felt urgent, about to spill out of me. "It isn't the unveiling you're worried about."

"Is it finished?" I pushed open the door to his studio, half expecting to see the chalice right there, fully formed, transformative, on the steel table in the foyer. Instead, on the table was a vase filled with more daisies, two fluted glasses and a bottle of champagne in an ice bucket. I always loved going to Theodor's studio. It was like stepping inside his mind. The downstairs was tidy, a contrast to the upstairs workspace. Off the foyer was a tiny room with a bed in it, neatly made. In another room was his desk and books. There was also a bathroom (tidy too) and a small kitchen with a bathtub in it. On the other side of the kitchen a spiral staircase led to the studio itself and continued up to the roof.

It was a delightful space, surprising. Pots boiled and bubbled on the stove. He poured us champagne and toasted me, took my hand and led me through the kitchen and up the stairs to the studio, a big room, at the far end a wall of arched, lead-mullioned windows. Beneath the windows stood a set of antique brass scales we had bought years before in Nuwara Eliya, in Sri Lanka's hill country. It had cost far more to have them shipped home than it had to buy them, but they were beautiful and still perfectly weighted. Even then he'd had a vision of the studio he wanted someday to create. In the center of the room stood the long wooden workbench covered with tools and parts of chalices and goblets, a child's spoon with an elephant on the handle; little wooden drawers were filled with sheets of gold leaf and blown glass beads, and some had colored jewels. Sheets of copper and rolled gold and fragments of silver, a hacksaw, welders big and small. An overhead lamp shed a bright light on it all. The brick wall was covered with tools that dangled from hooks Theodor had drilled into the bricks. Amid the hanging tools was the Étienne Delaune engraving we'd bought of a goldsmith's workshop dating from 1576. We'd bought it in London when I was there on tour for my first novel, in a print gallery in South Kensington. Theodor's dream was to re-create the workshop in the print. He had. The tools hadn't changed much, nor had the needs of the goldsmith—the fire, the gold, the big windows for natural light, the placement of the table to avoid shadow. All I could think of was our debts could be repaid with the sale of some of the metals, the jewels—little amethyst beads, jade balls, turquoise, jet, emerald, sapphire. All the smallest suggestion of the gem, but gem all the same. Eighteen hundred per month, too, for the space—that would free us up (though it was being paid for right now by the patron). I chastised myself for thinking like this. I should love being here. I did love being here. Where was the commission? My eyes shot to the Delaune. We could sell the Delaune.

"You need to take a break," he said. "Fill up again."

"How could I do that?" I said.

"So you *are* worried."

"Was that a trap?"

"I can't stop you from this," he said.

"I've been gambling," I said dramatically.

He laughed but gave me an inquisitive look.

"A thousand dollars blown to the wind," I said and swept my hand out to indicate wind, blew a little zephyr.

"What have you been gambling on?"

"On coffee."

He laughed some more.

"I'm being serious," I said loudly. "Won't you listen for once? Please." And then I spilled all: Deals and coffee options and calls and futures and tells and terms I did not understand. A blight in Brazil, excess in China, 37,500 pounds of coffee beans aswirl in my head.

"Thank God you didn't win a quarter million dollars' worth of coffee," Theodor said. "Where would we have put it all?"

"It all boils down to a joke. Everything's a joke."

"You don't have to do this. We don't have to get into a fight."

"Why are you always so calm?"

"Because I knew what I was getting into. Sometimes it'll be good, sometimes bad. End of story. You need to remember."

I picked up the spoon with the elephant on the handle. It was made of silver. The trunk lifting, curling upward with joy. A child's spoon. I imagined he'd made it for one of the girls as a birthday present. He was always making them whimsical objects, mobiles when they were babies, rattles. He loved the elephant, that the shape of its mouth made it appear to be happy. Why couldn't he sell objects, fancy work like this at a reasonable price, in the trendy Williamsburg stores that sprouted up like wildflowers?

Every piece in this room had been created by his hand. I remembered Theodor's tiny studio, the one he'd had when I'd first met him. I'd found it intoxicating—the smell of the hot metal, the heavy leather apron, his burned fingers, fragments of gold in his hair. Terms and names came spilling back to me: bosses and frieze-like and bacchant-erotic and maskarons and bucrania and vitreous enamel and granulation in the manner of the Castellani goldsmiths who worked in the manner of Etruscan goldsmiths, chryselephantine. I had cared. Styles and aesthetics descended from Magna Graecia. It had seemed that a life could be made entirely of art. It had been for centuries. It still could be. He was right: I was afraid to see the commission. I saw it now at the end of the table, covered in a velvet cloth.

"Here now. Let's not get grim tonight. I promise. All day tomorrow we can do that." He poured more champagne and I swallowed it fast. "That's right. Now let me show you what I've been up to."

He covered my eyes and led me down the table. "Open," he said. I lifted the velvet cloth and there it was—commanding in the overhead light, golden with pools of the vitreous enamel and mother of pearl used to render the illusion of water. It stood a foot and a half high. A pedestal worked to look like a tree trunk, unpolished, striations in the metal—alloyed with copper. At the foot of the pedestal roamed an assortment of animals, familiar, North American: a bear, a rabbit, a moose, a wolf, a horse, birds on branches stemming from the trunk, a squirrel. Where the cup met the trunk, the trunk appeared to be cut ever so slightly, as if it could break or were about to break, as if too much liquid in the cup might cause it to topple. A question of balance, perhaps of fate. The inside of the cup was engraved with fish. On the lid roamed exotic animals: an elephant, a tiger, a giraffe, a zebra, all delicately chiseled. Inlaid jet created the zebra's stripes. The zebra wasn't yet finished, but the intent was clear. The animals fed on garnet pomegranates and lapis blueberries. The eyes of the animals were holes waiting to be filled. The cup with its lid on was an orb. Upon closer inspection, it was the world—the continents, the seas, delineated with the finest hint of filigree. It was spectacular. Unfinished, but spectacular.

"No wonder it's taken so long," I said. "They are going to love it. The break, it's wicked."

"It's just a little thing I've been working on." He wrapped his arms around me from behind, the real deal. It would work out. I understood that this was how it was and would always be. The animals just needed their little eyes. My student came to me, her doe-like crying eyes looking at me, all that curly hair and seriousness, and I began to laugh—far more than the revelation I was having warranted. But that's what was happening: I was having a revelation. Theodor kissed my neck, pulling my back against him, my butt to his pelvis.

"I didn't intend for the chalice to be funny," he said. "But keep laughing." He was laughing too, at the sheer fact that I was laughing. He had no idea what was making me laugh. He asked me to let him in on it. It was a relief, a release, the laughter pouring out of me as if rendering the day as just that, a day, and irrelevant—one of many stacked up against all the others to create a life, inconsequential, made consequential by me, my silliness, my propensity to worry. I told the student that the position she had her character engaged in was not that unusual. The shock of her dark eyes, holding me, staring at me as if I were there before her in the compromised position. I laughed some more.

"Oh, Theodor," I said and told him about my student and her story. "I said to her in my most professorial voice that it's not that unusual. She gave me the queerest look, as if she were staring at me naked. But Theodor, I just get it now: the boyfriend in the story was having anal sex with her."

Theodor said in his most professorial voice, "It's not that unusual." Then we were both laughing before the chalice of the toppling world, caught, snapshot-like, just before it falls—or not. The big question, raised. But for now the world was ours and the worries of a day were lifted. It would be all right, and it was my husband, my husband, who was going to save the day.

Nine

THE BOOK TOUR. We've all heard about them: the author reading for an audience of three, two, one, none. You fly across the country to San Francisco, feeling important. You are chauffeured to the bookstore, attended by a literary escort. Signs all over the store announce your event at 7 P.M. A voice comes over the intercom: *You'll find India Palmer in the children's section. She'll be reading from her new book,* Generation of Fire, *and signing copies. Five minutes till show time.* There, squeezed into the children's section, between rows of *Mazy* and *Olivia* and *Lilo and Stitch* and *Goodnight Moon*, are a couple of dozen chairs in front of which stands a microphone and a table with your books neatly stacked, several standing prominently on display.

In the back row sits one old lady. It took six years to write *Generation of Fire*! Oh well, you think gamely, the show must go on. You notice the old lady is unwrapping something from a paper bag. She takes out a small tin and rests it in her gnarled, arthritic hand, and with her other hand she pries off the lid. Her hair is long and white and unbrushed. The can she has opened, you realize, though she is a good many rows removed from you, is tuna fish. The oily smell wafts toward you. She proceeds to eat it with a plastic fork pulled from the folds of her dress.

Onward! You read for her. With all the emotion you can muster. There is someone else in the audience: a young girl, who arrives late. When you're finished, she raises her hand earnestly. "Yes?" you ask. Her eyes are bright and her skin is aglow with teenage youth. She has an athletic build and an innocence that makes you ache for her. "I have an assignment I need to do for my English class," she says. "I'm supposed to interview an author. Can I interview you?"

Next stop, Memphis! Festival of the Book. Writers, so very many writers, marching around with their chins held high. Writers from everywhere, in all sizes and shapes. The famous ones are hidden away at the invitation-only events, in special ballroom-sized auditoriums, escorted in through back doors like rock stars. Except for the It Girl of the literary world. A fifty-year-old woman (there's still hope for us) dressed entirely in green — tights, dress, necklace, sweater, reading glasses, barrette — she escapes to waltz and shine among the masses. She wants to be admired. Fame has not yet had its way with her. The rest are ordinary, everyday writers, dazed, frumpy, dressed up with a chic flair, long hair, a proud mane, coiffed, uncoiffed, ponytails on aging men, artists looking like shit, or about to look like shit, others clean-shaven, or that alluring five o'clock shadow on the young buck from Dallas, goatees, sideburns, hipster skinny-legged pants, the drunken swagger, the tart with the overexposed cleavage (*it's working!*). They are for the most part enthusiastic, grateful to have been invited. The writers are legion, too many to have never been heard of. Writers everywhere, carrying copies of their books, marked with notes and Post-its indicating how to read passages effectively.

Did you know that in the United States one in eight adults claims to be a professional writer, and that it has been estimated that the average annual income of this group is $800 per year?

Here they converge, on display in Memphis, walking the halls of the stucco-walled convention center, the Marriott hotel, writers riding glass elevators to the rooftop lounge to sip another vodka martini while awaiting their allotted times to perform. There in the corner is the Latvian performance poet whose subject is standup misery. The drunk from Kentucky is carrying on with the pretty young thing from Manhattan who has just written her first novel. He bends in close to her, telling her she's going to be a smashing success; he saw the reviews in *The Month* and *Punch.* She gives a sweet, flirtatious chirp and looks earnestly at him. He's glutted the market with his books, one a year, the same story, the same low sales. Onward! Here the writer is king, here the writer rules, here the writer will be heard, here book lovers come by the hundreds from all over the state. They volunteer, they sell books, they buy books, they introduce authors, ferry authors from airport to hotel to airport.

Your big event is a panel discussion, "Crafting Betrayal in the American Dreamscape of Fiction." The other panelists do not show. The host does not show. There are three people in the "audience." They are resting, using the chairs to take a load off between events. You read, of course. A passage that addresses betrayal, of course. Your voice bounces off the walls, echoes in the chamber of the empty room. The audience seems to be listening attentively. They are a good audience. A man in the corner takes notes.

The Q&A: "Any questions?" you hear your voice say, as if from across a canyon. And for a moment you think you should raise your own hand.

The man taking notes in the corner (the three people are each in different rows) raises his hand.

"Is this 'fiction nonfiction'?" he asks, gray eyes, hair, face with its sharp provocative features—features designed to irritate, you realize. "Did your husband marry you and then your sister, or did he marry your sister and then you?"

Taken aback, but you keep your literary cool. "Do you mean, is the book autobiographical?" you ask.

"Well, in short, to put it bluntly. Well, yes, yes, I'd like to know. I like to know those sorts of things. It makes the reading of the book more interesting, in a way."

"Since you put it that way," you respond, "let me ask you which sister you think I am?"

"The betrayer, of course," he says, stroking his chin.

"In the nonfiction version of the fiction, you nailed it," you say and begin clapping, and the three follow suit.

On the ride back to the airport, an elderly woman who has written a self-help book on her relationship with her cat tells of how she forgot to bring her book to her event, so she had to invent a reading on the spot. "It was just so hard. I'm just so tired. It's a performance. They want so much out of you. I'm destroyed."

Who, you wonder. Who wants so much out of her?

"I would have liked to talk about my cat," you say.

The first review of *Generation of Fire* appears six weeks after publication day. It appears in *Free Moment*, written by some poor, underpaid, overworked creature who uses the first three chapters of the book (which also seems to be where she stopped reading) as a launching pad for a tirade against her boyfriend. It is a performance of the sort I see every other week, it seems, in at least one or two of my undergraduate student papers, a kind of lofty opening that addresses something big: "the beginning of time," for instance, or in this case, "American letters," and then hauls in the hapless author as Exhibit A of All That Is Wrong. There is a classic, three-paragraph "middle" of willful misreading, followed by a paragraph in which the reviewer holds up sentences that are better than anything I've ever written—lines that kept coming back to me, haunting me, that were literally beyond me, beyond my natural powers, that had, nevertheless, by dint of my persistence, rewarded me by taking up residence here and there in my book. These same sentences, which knocked Theodor out of his chair, are given a pistol-whipping by the reviewer.

"Ponder the career of India Palmer if you want to know what's gone wrong with American fiction. Grade: D-minus."

I can take a D, but a D-minus?

A sweet, small bookstore in Chicago. All the books hand-selected, personally and thoughtfully read by the owner and her assistant. A jolly pair: one old, one young; one stout, the other thin; one a big laugher, the other sardonic. A book group of five attends the reading. They are deciding if they will read *Generation of Fire.* Their decision will be based on the passage I read. "Not to put pressure on you," one of them says with a giggly smile.

"Lily Starr was here last week," the owner says boisterously. "She mentioned she was a friend of yours. She was so delightful. So talented. The place was packed! If we get her back for the paperback, we're selling tickets."

Washington, D.C.: My parents are the audience. My mother, a flurry of positive comments about the bookstore, how important it is to be asked to read here. Too bad about the weather—such a beautiful evening keeps people outdoors.

New York City: The store is packed. Theodor brings out all our friends, cousins, parents from the girls' school. The Chapmans invite everyone over afterward for drinks.

At the girls' school, a mother asks, "Have I missed the reviews?" In the paper that same day: Lily Starr is the winner of this year's Washington Award. Three days later the paper will announce her nomination for the biggest prize, the Golden Fleece: the Eiseman.

Midnight. I am on a high-speed ferry home from a reading in Little Silver, New Jersey. Alone. All the commuters safely in bed.

It is so black outside we could be high in the air above the Atlantic. It is raining, but I cannot see the rain for the dark. I can see nothing out the window. Inside the cabin the lights are bright. The reading was a good one. Thirty women in the audience. So many questions. This is the way it goes: a sudden high to give you that bit of hope. "Your masterpiece," one woman said. "I've read all your work and this is it. This is the hit. Trust me. I'm a reader. You've captured perfectly the personal disconnection one feels against the backdrop of the hedonism of the late twentieth century." Appreciated, understood and feted in Little Silver. Well, that was something, anyway.

I cross the black water of the Narrows. Somewhere the Verrazano Bridge looms. Other boats are out there, but I cannot see them. I'm alone on a high-speed ferry with my face pressed to the glass. I could vanish easily, without a trace. Would I attract attention then? In my lap Will Chapman's manuscript languishes. It is good, very good, if long. So fine it has been taking me a long time to read it—in part because I savor it, in part because I am jealous. He will sell the book, and well.

A young man appears. I can see him standing before me, reflected in the window glass. Out of nowhere, he tells me he's nineteen years old. He says it's raining outside and that I'll need an umbrella. He says, "Funny, on nights like these, how you can't see anything." Tells me he's working the ferry while in college, to see him through. "Can I talk to you?" he says eventually.

"Aren't you already?" I ask.

He chuckles, says "Funny." Then, "You're all alone."

"Observant," I say. He laughs again. We're in a bubble of light, just the two of us, in a vast darkness. He pops open a broken umbrella and tells me I can have it.

"Thank you," I say. "Where's the bridge?"

"Out there," he says.

"Oh, really?" Again I press my face to the window, and again I see nothing.

"I figured you might want some company." He wants to talk, so I let him. "This is the last shift of the night. Manhattan means quittin' time. I love this ferry. Do you ride it often?" He looks me in the eye. He's an adorable boy, not too tall, fit, filled with enthusiasm for life that seems to buck from his face, that cocksure innocence that seems to know already how the whole world works, as if on a formula, a recipe. "This boat teaches me everything I need to know. You know that? It does. Amazing how a boat can teach what you need to know. The people that ride this boat, they're the bosses of all those people who take the subways, the buses, the trains. The people here are the rich cats. It costs them seven hundred a month just to ride this boat to work. They come in here looking all tired and frazzled and worn out. And they're impatient and touchy and jumpy. I look at them and I feel sorry for them. And for all their money, they're still like lemmings." He stops and looks at me. "You mind?"

"Of course not."

"Why are you on this ferry, anyway?"

"I gave a reading in Little Silver tonight."

"A reading?"

"I'm a writer."

"You are, are you? Cool. Just like fate," he says with genuine astonishment. He is not an ironic boy. "I've got an idea for a novel, you know? You want to hear it?"

"Sure," I say politely.

"It's about an artist, an artist who's sick of all the posers, really sick of the fraud. You know, the guy who says he's an artist but isn't really, just wants to make a buck. The kind who makes the buck, many bucks, because people believe he's the real thing because as a fraud he has the routine down, knows how to sell himself? Well, the real artist can't stand this type. The real artist is a Pollock or a Johns or damn, a Picasso. The real McCoy. Well, he beats up the frauds, really messes them up—at bars and art parties, in galleries. Anywhere he can. And then he uses their blood to paint his pictures, really beautiful pictures made of fraudulent blood. What do you think?"

"Does he kill the frauds?" I ask.

"Oh, no. No, he definitely doesn't kill them. Not at all. Just their blood he wants. Rips them up a bit, but he doesn't kill them."

"So you're a writer," I say. "Write by day, work the boat by night?"

"No."

That makes me curious. "A painter?"

"I just work the ferry," he says, "to get me through college. I'm going to be a bridge builder someday. I want to build little bridges. Not the big ones. The little ones that get you over streams and such. I'm learning how in college. I want to really know how to make something, something with my hands. Not like all these people riding this ferry. Not like them. The people who ride this thing, they're like cattle at the gate, jostling to be let in. No dignity. Pushing up against the gate, rushing in to get their seats, waiting to do it all over in the morning. Day in, day out. They don't look happy. No smiles on their faces. You know who their bosses are? Their bosses are the ones who get to work in helicopters. That's the top of the crop. These cats think if only they could fly to work in a helicopter, then they'd have arrived. That's what they want. Imagine that." He brushes his hair back with his hand, using the window's reflection as his mirror. He unzips his fly and loosens his pants to tuck his shirt in. "Cattle," he says, and then asks again, "Do you like my idea?"

Ten

IN THE OLDEN DAYS, as my daughters like to say, fifty, sixty years ago, just after the Second World War, a mortgage was a relatively simple thing. People deposited money in their local banks and accrued a little interest. The banks in turn loaned that money at a higher rate, most commonly for home mortgages. The profit, of course, belonged to the bank. Before the war, mortgages were a bit more complicated. Panic-driven runs on banks caused the banks to create callable loans, meaning that if a bank needed to, it had the right to ask for the loan back for any reason, at any time. This made loans nearly impossible for the working-class family. After the war, all of this changed. The government stepped in with greater force and a housing policy that subsidized a vast portion of home mortgages, making them affordable for almost everyone (except African Americans, because it was believed they would bring down neighborhood property values, thus making loans riskier).

A young couple visits the local savings and loan and presents their financial picture to the loan officer. The husband works in the city, a commuter. The wife stays at home. Yes, they want a family. Oh, they'll be in the house for a while. Three bedrooms, plenty big. The local school district, excellent. Tree-lined street, house after house, mailbox after mailbox, driveway after driveway—the great American suburb. Hedges and emerald lawns, fanning sprinklers, perhaps a basketball hoop in the blacktop driveway, a pool, white clapboard Cape or ranch, picket fence, a pink dogwood, certainly the dream. They are a handsome couple, they will have beautiful children, they'll grow into the house, then out of the house. They'll upgrade—use the equity to get a four-bedroom, perhaps a five-. Then one day the children will be gone. The house in that little suburb, on that dandy street, is too big and worth so much more than they bought it for. Husband and wife smile at each other as if thirty years hadn't just passed—all of those memories and then all of that profit.

Go back thirty years. In front of the loan officer, a little nervous, a little scared (she with her kidskin gloves, he in his fedora), the couple is given the 10.8 percent fixed-rate for thirty years on their $30,000 loan. Husband and loan officer discuss the particulars. Wife quietly feels that she, they, have just made one giant leap up the social ladder. She has always believed in the best.

The best: social and economic capital, generous tax deductions that would allow them to amass wealth, have access to a better education for their children, accrue equity so that they could send their kids to private colleges, allow them to save for retirement, and pass some of the wealth on to their kids. The best: this house would allow them to better their lot in life, thus their children's and their children's children's. And so the cycle went. No wonder the wife perspired as the loan officer studied the documents, asked questions about her husband's salary. Thirty thousand was a stretch. Nervously, she flapped her gloves against her thigh, caught herself, stopped and then caught herself again. This was freedom, their right to own land—a little tract of America. Approved!

The savings and loan held the mortgage. The couple paid their monthly bill to them. They accrued interest, reaped government subsidies, grew wealth—an acceptable form of lending and financial growth. The couple built equity, had a voice in the community, a say in the direction of the local schools. On Saturdays they all converged at the country club—husband and loan officer playing a round of golf. If the husband got in trouble, lost his job, say, he knew where to go, knew the flaws in the loan officer's angle of attack, knew his frustrations with repeated fat shots. Always the husband encouraged and praised the loan officer, because this was the way it worked: someday the husband might need help, and if he and the banker were friends . . . On Sundays they congregated at church. They prayed together, week in week out, and so it went. They both grew older, the late seventies arrived, and then everything changed.

Let's be more personal. Remember the Hovs? "Chekhov without the *chek*," the elderly couple who owned the Victorian cottage in Maine, the one Emma Chapman coveted in order to complete her dreams? In 1951 the Hovs bought a three-bedroom ranch in Realville, New Jersey. Mr. Hov had a tenure-track job at Rutgers—a renowned Swift scholar. They were hoping to start a family. The house cost $24,000. With 20 percent down, they got a thirty-year fixed-rate mortgage of $19,200.

By 1958, the value of the house had risen, giving them considerable equity. So when the cottage in Maine became available that year (Mrs. Hov had been vacationing at Pond Point since childhood) for $20,000, they easily qualified for a second mortgage. By the time Mr. Hov retired, both houses had been paid off in full, owned outright. His Rutgers salary would never have made him rich, but in essence his real estate decisions did. In the fall of 2003, Mrs. and Mr. Hov, together on the phone, called Emma and Will, not long after Will let go of his job to become a full-time novelist, and not long before I saw them again at the fundraiser at the Metropolitan Museum of Art. "Make us an offer we can't refuse," the Hovs said in unison, the pitch of Mr. Hov's voice a bit deeper than his wife's.

"You're selling!" Emma nearly screeched. Standing in her

Tribeca kitchen, with its view of the sailboats on the Hudson, everything chrome and Sub-Zero, she covered the receiver with her hand and screamed with joy and surprise and did a little dance and mouthed to Will, who was also on a phone, their unbelievable good fortune. How was it that everything, *everything*, always worked out so well for them? The house would be hers. Will loved seeing her like this, electricity lighting her up with joy. And now he too would have the time. They could spend entire summers at Pond Point, do a few renovations, make the house more comfortable, sand the floors, change the windows, upgrade the kitchen.

"We'll get back to you," Will said. "This is exciting news." He used his most professional deal-making voice to temper his enthusiasm. He thought. He went into the library and drew the doors, told Emma to give him some time. "But can we? Is this prudent?" And again he asked her for just a little time.

He sat at the desk with a pad of paper and a pen before him. He felt as if he were back at work. He liked the feel of strategy, the taut tendons of the deal's structure. He missed that most in his new life, the physical feel of the deal. He thought some more. He could juggle things. His accounts were solid. His credit was impeccable. They owned the Tribeca loft. They'd bought low and real estate now soared. Their equity had accrued, as it does. Real estate never goes down—not in the long term. Given his new circumstances, the budget was tighter, but that house couldn't be worth much. It sat on a quarter of an acre. To Emma, back in the kitchen, he said, "What unbelievable luck." This was his first mistake.

Research revealed that in this market the property (you really couldn't say the house, because it was not the house they were buying, but the view) would sell for a lot. An offer the Hovs couldn't refuse was $1 million, at a minimum, but even that was not a guarantee. "A million?" Emma asked, astonished, her blue eyes actually becoming a prettier shade with fear. A million was out of their reach, certainly, given that Will did not have a job, given that they could use the house only four months of the year at best—it was not winterized and could never be, unless it was knocked down and rebuilt, which they would never do.

She studied her husband as he pondered this, his beautiful jaw, his green eyes and thick dark hair. He was so familiar to her, his looks no longer had that searing appeal. In studying him she hoped to understand whether this plan of theirs was viable or foolish. Instead, he made the call to the Hovs, proposing $1 million. The offer was contemplated. Several days of anticipation, nail biting, hair twirling, pacing, fantasizing, lying in bed late into the night and drawing pictures with their words of all they would do to their house. Emma lay in her silk nightgown, promising the stars that she would never take fortune for granted again. Will, on his side, worried, of course, but he was a banker, after all. If he couldn't swing this deal, then what had all those years taught him? He knew how to borrow from Peter to pay Paul and make a killing in the process. That's what credit markets were for, and paper was cheap these days.

Finally the Hovs accepted. The Victorian shack would belong to the Chapmans, and in turn the Hovs would officially be millionaires. Real estate had done what it was intended to do.

Borrowing from Peter to pay Paul was an easy task. With interest rates at historic lows, Will refinanced the Tribeca loft. Bought for $1.3 million in 1998, it was now worth $2.1 million. He took equity out to use as a down payment, and while he was at it, to shore up his ability to pay the girls' tuition and the family's expenses for the next several years. As a banker they'd lived on 45 a month—that is, $45,000, after taxes. The marquee loan of this year, 2003, was the interest-only loan. This would allow Will to make lower monthly payments for the first few years, thus ensuring their ability to keep up with the payments while they adjusted to the new circumstances.

For the house in Maine he used a different mortgage structure. Instead of putting down 20 percent, he put down 0 percent and took out a 2/28 mortgage—that is, a mortgage with an initial two-year teaser rate of 3.5 percent, which would (he was well aware) be adjusted in two years to a market-dependent rate, usually higher. In this way, he'd have more time to figure out his new financial picture.

Given the market, the Maine house and the Tribeca apartment would continue to rise in value. He could refinance or, worst-case scenario, he'd have to sell Maine. But he knew enough to know that you had to take risks in order to win, and he had both money and wits to risk, and the horizon looked clear and long. In fact, his greatest concern involved storms wreaking havoc with the house. But even that bothered him little. Insurance, though expensive, would take care of it. The house had been there since the 1880s and nothing had knocked it down yet, and if it came down, they'd be free to rebuild.

Maine was theirs.

When I saw Emma again at the Met, in her red velvet gown, her black hair pulled back in a French knot, she was bursting with excitement. The evening well lit with votive candles, drenched in champagne, Emma took my hands, kissing me on the cheek, and flooded me with news of her new house. "You'll have to come stay with us, continue that novel of yours . . ." Smiling her nuthatch smile.

"The plot has just made a turn," I said.

"Indeed," she said.

"How did you kill them?" I asked. I couldn't help myself. She looked at me, confused, a smile quivering on her lips as if it could rise and fly away. But she wouldn't let it. The smile turned to laughter, bubbles bursting forth as she recalled the reference.

"Actually, I think the Hovs killed us," she said, standing before me regally with all the confidence of someone who can frame financial ruin in a joke.

Money could always be had, more made. It would not run out. This room in a grand museum, filling as it was, was a testament to that. And I wondered too if she had more news, news of the sale of Will's book. Failure was not in the Chapmans' vocabulary. He'd sell the book for a million, part one of a series. It was clear to me after having finished the book (he'd also given me part two) that it would be published in two volumes—a woman's life as it spans the twentieth century, Laura Ingalls Wilder for the new world, written by a man, a banker turned novelist, riches to "rags." Perhaps it was already sold, his marketing scheme the icing on the deal. Of course Emma did not explain the fancy mortgages, the subtleties of Will's financial prowess. I'm not certain she knew the details or understood the risks, what it meant to be completely leveraged. And if she had tried to explain these complexities to me (which she never would have, because she knew that it smelled a bit too much like a scheme, a way for someone with not enough to afford more, like those 0 percent credit card loans I was so fond of), I would not have understood much. The house in Maine belonged to them—it was that simple from my point of view—not to the bank, not to a complicated compilation of fancy mortgages. I congratulated her.

Theodor, handsome in his tuxedo, appeared at my side with Sally and Darwin Deals. Sally wore a cream lace dress that hugged her neck yet hung loosely everywhere else, trying (unsuccessfully) to hide the bulk of her body. Deals wore a tuxedo that was too big, the way he seemed to like his suits, as if the larger size were a promise of what he could become. Introductions all around, hellos and kisses on the cheek. Will too joined the cluster. He wore a red plaid bow tie with a matching cummerbund. He kissed me and thanked me for the call and e-mail about his novel. "It's terrific," I said. I could have been jealous, but the truth of Will's talent took the sting out.

"You think it will sell, then?"

"No question," I said.

"So you're no longer mad at me for leaving Wall Street?"

"I still think you're a fool."

"I'm glad you're consistent."

"He's written a fantastic novel," I said boisterously to Sally and Deals, and then explained how crazy he'd been, leaving his job. I was a little giddy and overly familiar with Will because of the champagne. Just looking at Deals I thought about the fiasco with China and the coffee contract, but Deals didn't dare mention it, or corn or soy or any other commodity. He carried on about the bond market and mortgages, engaging Will in the topic, with Sally chiming in here and there. Coffee had tanked, of course, because luck does not fall from the sky, and corn was just a maneuver to make the loss of coffee more palatable.

Canapés all around, and the music began. Emma's news burst forth again—smiles and toasts—and then the conversation divided and subdivided, like a large group of birds into separate flocks, soaring and darting and weaving together, then splitting—private schools, public schools, doormen, supers, plays opening, plays closing, the cost of babysitting, neighborhood bakeries, the virtues of having a mini-tractor in the country. When you are part of the repartee it is impossible to see that your voice—the flight of your conversation, the particular direction you take, the strange dives and offbeat vectors you deploy to assert your point of view—is still governed and sustained in some measure by the air through which you move—together. You are part of a group of birds—pigeons, say—each one flying separately but together. In the end, the whole dazzling lot is swirling around an apartment building. Real estate, again. Special subcategory: Manhattan, a market universally acknowledged to be unique, a story unto itself, a story that could logically go in only one direction, up.

Just so: one found oneself saying "$2.2 million" or "$3.5 million," the asking price for apartments no bigger than our own rental, and one found oneself at realtors' open houses, walking through buildings in Harlem, with other earnest buyers strolling the place, inspecting the stoves and the views, and one found oneself deploying a calculus under one's breath by which one could arrive at a smaller monthly figure, which would be the hypothetical maintenance fee, and one saw that this number was not insurmountably higher than the going rate for rental apartments (never mind that Theodor and I paid a quarter of the market rate for rentals). And of course there were the stories of people getting in a little earlier, say ten years ago, people who bought apartments for what seemed at the time a preposterous price, $800,000, which were now worth more than $2.5 million.

These were people you knew, parents of the friends of your children, sober, responsible, welcome dinner guests, people who were in charge of large corporations, who knew firsthand the ways of the world and who looked you in the eye when asked what they thought about the asking price of a townhouse in Harlem: "One-point-nine is a steal for that part of town." Real estate in Manhattan was the exception to every law in the universe. That was the way it was, and only a bumpkin thought otherwise.

Emma held forth with her plans for renovating Pond Point, modernizing the appliances, retiling, re-laying the pine floors. How many kitchens were there across America in stainless and chrome—the deep wells of Wolf and Viking and Sub-Zero. Five, ten thousand dollars a pop. Chump change! Others offer their views of the Viking: the oven and burners run too hot but they're fabulous; the gorgeous Wolf, with the red knobs, just too expensive. Deep into the granular specifics of kitchen appointments, Emma and her new friend Sally bonded over their too hot but wonderful high-performance kitchen stoves (which they never used). Sally was the sort of woman who latches on at a party because she's too shy to circulate. She had Emma's ear and interest and she would not let it go, and Emma, who was well cultivated in the skills of circulation, delighted by this conversation about Viking stoves there by the Temple of Dendur.

All of us soaked up in a private evening at the Metropolitan, in the heart of New York. Nile lilies, bread stacked in pyramids in the center of the cloth-covered tables, the female wait staff with Cleopatra wigs and kohl-encircled eyes offering Egyptian delights: canapés of goat cheese and barberries, and saffron-infused chicken with pine nuts, and platters of dill to be dipped in hummus, and walnuts glazed with honey. Sally and Emma were absorbed in the specifics of how best to vent the Viking range. And I, on the periphery, stood with a novelist's eye and a pauper's purse, dazzled before the spectacle of it all.

"Have you seen Win?" Emma asked. "He was to have brought his new girl, Beatrix, but she's sick." I flinched, a prick of jealousy. Beatrix, what an unlikely name. I pictured the woman behind the name; somehow it didn't add up to Win. "Apparently she's a knockout, but his girls always are." And she drifted off to something else. Of course he'd have a girl. Hadn't Emma described him as a notorious Casanova? I looked around the room but didn't see him.

The room thickened with arriving guests. Photographers snapped pictures, a flurry of lights—famous personages here to celebrate and preserve the arts. Amid the swirl of party chaos, Kathy Park, in a black lace gown and a strand of South Sea pearls, took me in her arms. "How wonderful to see you," she said. A kiss and a pat on the arm and the crowd absorbed Kathy, spitting out a mother from Ruby's class, Mila Ferragamo (no relation), the one who took me to Sarah Jessica Parker's reflexologist and who bought the $250 mummy-dust-enhanced face cream with its ancient recipe for preservation. "I saw your book, darling. Sexy cover." Her big black eyes flashed with mischief, and she went on to talk about herself: her husband had a job offer in Singapore, "and we're thinking seriously about taking it. Singapore's the new Upper East Side. No different, really. All the women dress the same."

Our constellation was still active, a dividing cell. Theodor discussed his chalice commission with Deals. Will swooped away to greet friends and soon came back, holding court with his old colleagues. More flashes, a sudden frenzy of them that drew all eyes to the entrance, cameras madly working. The subject: Carlyle P. Smedes, with his Prada clothes, looking charming—all the accoutrements of his style and position adding to his already significant height. A warm smile on his contented face. On his arm was the Dashing Cavelli (ascot at his neck, offering a stream of comments to the eager press). He'd been my publisher once. I thought wistfully of what could have been. Then I had to look twice, clear my eyes and look again. Lily Starr entered, ravishing and slender (though she had not been a slender girl a few months before) in a sage gown, a single but significant diamond around her neck—how sudden and complete the transformation from no one to someone can be! The triad, Cavelli with his two successes, both authors on the bestseller list, literary rock stars. The goddess Sakhmet, four repetitions of her in stone, served as their backdrop—goddess of war, violent storms and pestilence—as they briefly posed for the paparazzi, triumphing, it seemed, if we were to read the visual cues, over Sakhmet. How easily Lily wore fame, walking, slowing, smiling, aloof. Trailing behind her in black velvet, star of her own show, was Lily's new agent, agent to Smedes too, the fair-skinned and lightly freckled auburn beauty Sig Blankman. Lithe and swan-like she drifted into the room.

I turned away. Here was the brick wall that I had been speeding toward. I looked for an exit, but the escape I longed for was of a different sort.

We could have done things differently. We could have packed up, moved out, headed to the Vermont that Deals imagined as our answer, sent the kids to a good public school, bought ourselves a $300,000 house, watched the equity grow over time, continued writing, sculpting, affording our life on Theodor's commissions, on magazine assignments, on the occasional sale of a novel. We could have chosen simplicity, had a yard with a swing set, perhaps a garden we'd plant in the spring, harvest in the fall. We could have eliminated the high overhead: tuition, babysitters, housecleaners, offices, the ludicrous price tags for all the lessons, contributions, birthdays, the basic expense of trying to keep up in the city. There was an alternative. But being here, looking out over this sea of people, admiring the votives and the string quartet and the Egyptian motif, stepping lightly in the empty corridors of the Met, passing the mummies and their divine offerings, I understood unequivocally that I could not leave New York. I had been here for fifteen years. I would not be forced out. To leave now, to scale back, to compromise would be to live within a shadow of regret, of second-guessing, of exile.

The sinew of life is made of dreams, passion, hope—ethereal and misty as a veil, a scrim, the Milky Way, but strong threads all the same. Without that quality I'd have led a quiet, cautious life, a humble suburban life. Would I have dared to be a novelist? Would I have dared to defy my father? No, I would not be exiled. That was not the stuff that I was made of. A famous lecturer with pancreatic cancer said to his audience in the last speech he gave before his death that life's brick walls are there to show you just how ferocious your desire is to get what you want. I scanned the room for Win. I had come for Win and I wanted him now.

And then he was before me, smoking jacket and pale pink cravat, leaning in to greet me. "Ah, my protégée," he said and kissed my forehead. His embrace was solid and reassuring. He was just as I remembered: not one bit attractive but beguiling all the same, with his big brown eyes and confidence. He turned me around slowly in a proprietary way. "Smashing," he said. Beatrix became irrelevant, blotted from my mind. "I have missed you." An isolated moment, when the crowd faded away and it was just the two of us, just before my fall, if you could call it that.

What is it that Socrates says to Adeimantus? There seem to be two causes for the deterioration of the arts—wealth and poverty. I felt finished, and the sensation dazzled me. I could change my life; I could become someone else. The pool simulating the Nile, surrounding the temple, sparkled with wishers' coins.

"Thank you for all the messages, the flowers," I said. I apologized for standing him up. I felt like a girl on a first date, uncertain what to say, awkward in that way, looking to Theodor, who was caught up with Emma and Deals.

"Have I won?" he asked.

I said nothing. He knew he had. There was nothing to say.

"It's your best," he said.

I looked at him blankly. He was talking about something that had fallen as if from a great height. I had watched it vanish and now, in this hall of echoes, I could no longer remember what it was that I had finally, gratefully let go of.

He regarded me for a moment. He understood everything. A man like Win didn't dwell or linger in emotional terrain. "I want you to meet the Radalpienos, Ralph and Pretty, my boss and his wife, our hosts," he said. Without bothering to wait for my reply, he linked his arm in mine and led me to the Radalpienos. She was quite simple actually, not especially pretty, in her sixties I guessed, a kind demeanor. Her arms glittered in serpentine spangles. Some ten years before, she had changed Win's life because she liked his smile, his banter. She had loved her power, feeling its strength. Ralph was about the same age, large, portly, thin silver hair. His tuxedo was one from fitter days. It seemed he had stuffed himself into it, or perhaps he'd just been hopeful.

"Ah, Ms. Palmer, we've heard about you," Ralph said, offering me his hand. No small talk, direct, but he offered no more. What had he heard? What had Win said?

"You're just as I pictured, given Win's description," Pretty said, looking me over. "He says you're a novelist. How brave."

"How do you make a living?" Ralph asked.

"He cuts to the chase," Pretty said. We were standing near the windows, snow coming down now, falling softly, gently into the glass. How I envied women like Pretty, for whom questions like the one Ralph asked were mere sport, of absolutely no significance or consequence.

"On her writing," Win answered and explained no more. Ralph too looked me over, as if I were a painting or a work of art, evaluating its worth.

"Oh, for the life of an artist!" Pretty said.

"A pleasure," Ralph said, excusing themselves, as dinner had been announced.

I offered them my hand. "How kind of you to let me come," I said slowly, enunciating each word.

"Clever," Win said when they were gone.

"I was being appraised," I said.

"I saw you earlier. You're tired."

"Spying on me?"

A tap on the shoulder. Big kisses on either cheek. Lily Starr, alone, without her entourage and snapping paparazzi, in front of me, interrupted, "You're in a very serious conversation. Excuse me." She thrust her hand into Win's and introduced herself. "I'm Lily Starr," she said, showing all her nicely aligned teeth. "It's so amazing to see you here, India." She splayed her arm to take in the two of us.

"She's my date," Win said protectively.

"Intriguing," Lily said and offered me a private wink. "Well, have fun then. I'm here for work, alas. But you know how it is!" She waved her arms as if to shovel coal into a furnace. "Throw the artists in with the high rollers!" She fiddled with her curls, adjusted her dress at the chest. She was high on champagne, or her own good fortune. "Ah, if these were the only hazards! Wish me luck."

"Enjoy it," I said.

"I've got to," she said over her shoulder. "You know how it is," and she fluttered off. The room by now was packed, the temple looming above us all.

"Call me in the morning," Win said, and then he too was swallowed up by the crowd.

At our table, I sat between Emma and Will. Theodor sat across from me, next to Win, and the two men were between the Radalpienos. We settled into dinner and the ensuing auction. The auctioneer, a stub of a man with a belly and suspenders and the requisite handlebar mustache, stood before a movie screen that displayed in Technicolor the goods he offered. In the droll, cajoling manner of his trade he built a tower of figures, a Babel of another sort, conducted by so many bejeweled arms waving paddles. A chorus really. A finale to the evening. Gstaad, going, going, gone. Aspen. A private island in the Tuamotu archipelago. A tour of the Valley of the Kings. The world for sale before our wondrous eyes, followed by its treasures. A Kelly bag. Rejuvenating treatments at Exhale. A Harry Winston diamond. A Mikimoto pearl. A portrait by Sasha McDermott. All of it going, going, gone. "Thank you very much, sir!" More wine poured. The MC, tall, thin, the auctioneer's counterpart, encouraging all to drink, the MC, curator of the evening, lord of the fundraiser: "Drink and be reckless and forgive yourselves in the morning. This is all for a good cause. For the sake of *art*."

I became finished with art—the giving of one's flesh to try to make something live, to achieve the truth, of having it follow me around like a shadow, to lunch, to dinner, to the food I'm chewing—not food but an idea, an idea that I might polish and revise as much as I like, but that in the end I would always despise because it would be untrue to the original conceit, the one I had pictured perfectly before beginning, the one that mimicked life unflinchingly. All these lovely people, with their present concerns of new homes and stoves and auctions, were free of that, of the sovereignty of art.

Outside, the late November snow draped the city in white and it was very cold. Theodor and I walked home through the midnight park, stopping now and again to admire the formations the snow made in the branches of the trees, the beauty in the design. He examined it closely for patterns. The snow came down heavily, wrapping us in a cocoon, alone, the park ours. A little drunk, flushed. I was eager, hungry. I loved that the park was ours, that it was white and clean and fresh, the blank slate.

Theodor held a branch for me and I peered at the miniature drifts of snow on it, snow making art of the barren branch. On the question of art, I thought, he does not fight with himself about the pursuit. That was the difference between us: I struggled while he did not.

"What a bunch of jokers this evening," I tried.

"You didn't have fun either?" Theodor asked, relief palpable on his handsome face. My nose pricked, my throat felt tight.

"Oh, please," I said. "They pronounced the *G* in Gstaad." I lied quite easily, my first betrayal. Guilt would come later.

Theodor let the branch go and it sprang up, throwing off the snow. And in the suddenness of the gesture, it was as though I too were set free.

"Let's agree not to go to one of those again," he said.

"Never," I concurred.

In the morning, I called Win.

Intermezzo

Instant Messages

TO RALPH: Got a minute?

TO WIN: All the time in the world. I'm just sitting up here twiddling my thumbs. Do YOU have a minute? That's the question. The answer should be NO. Or did you knock back one too many last night with that lovely married woman with the exotic name? A belly dancer perhaps? Remind me where you found her.

TO RALPH: I see you do have time to spare. Thought you'd like her. Actually, I'm writing to notify: we're moving forward with Pygmalion Ltd.

TO WIN: So you ARE still drunk!

TO RALPH: No, sir.

TO WIN: Atta boy. I do like it when you remember to doff your cap to me.

TO RALPH: Yes, sir. She's on board, sir. She called for a meeting. She's gonna be smashing. A tour de force, sir.

TO WIN: I don't get it. Things too slow for you on the floor?

TO RALPH: Good teams in the trenches, is all.

TO WIN: How's Snake holding up?

TO RALPH: We've got to let him run with it. But this is either the stupidest plan or the boldest. We'll see.

TO WIN: It's only money. The trace is intriguing nonetheless. He's finding mean revert.

TO RALPH: Some of the rolls are doing well late in the cycle, the usual bullshit. Maybe forgoing the upside will lock in the better ROE on the 30bln.

TO WIN: There's an 80% chance of 50bp cut.

TO RALPH: Then say a prayer.

TO WIN: On the other score, I'm not a fan of the hi-jinx spilling over into the business. Why don't you stick to practical jokes, pushup competitions, hamburger-eating contests? And don't tell me you've outgrown them.

TO RALPH: Too late, Ralph. I've gone long. She's already commandeering the trading floor, whipping the boys into shape.

TO WIN: I'm ringing the bell here—once for myself: she's got nice tits. Pretty took note. By the way, she likes your little scheme.

TO RALPH: Watch your hands, old man.

TO WIN: It takes my being away a few weeks to forget what an incredible ass you are.

TO RALPH: Sorry to hear Europe isn't panning out. But I told you it wouldn't. Archaic laws. The story remains here and it's getting big and the big here is gonna be eaten up over there. They'll be bringing a lot of dough here. The American dream is strong and well. You're paying attention to the sand states? Might be a problem in the end.

TO WIN: That's why we pay you.

TO RALPH: Three months. Three months and she'll be pricing pass-throughs with the best, six months she'll be making dough, eighteen she'll be trading with ease, after that the press'll take note, job offers.

TO WIN: I repeat: eighteen months?

TO RALPH: I'm talking big, Radalpieno. She'll have my training and the story. It's all about story, isn't it?

TO WIN: I prefer sir.

TO RALPH: Sir!

TO WIN: Watch yourself, boy. If you're going to play Pygmalion on my dime, don't lose.

TO RALPH: *What is life but a series of inspired follies?* I've earned this folly.

TO WIN: Fair enough. Since I lost the last one I'm allowed to call double or nothing. So, double or nothing, baby.

TO RALPH: Now you're talking. Deal, sir.

TO WIN: Don't forget she's married.

TO RALPH: To an artist.

TO WIN: Another form of flower girl?

TO RALPH: And she is too. What rhymes with "pluck," Colonel Pickering?

TO WIN: I'm ringing the bell. Full steam ahead!

PART II

Our Times

Eleven

I DIDN'T TELL THEODOR that I was seeing Win. I wanted to feel the sensation for myself, wanted to know how it informed the way I dressed, the choice of makeup, the coat I wore. I was on my way to Park Avenue and it felt like a bold adventure to an unfamiliar land. This was a lark, but the possibility of changing the course of one's own fate was a heady drug.

After the fundraiser at the Met, I had called Win and he'd invited me to come speak with him and Ralph Radalpieno. And now I was in a cab on my way to them, on the verge of a kind of affair. It was midmorning, the time when respectable people are at work, well into their third coffee, anticipating lunch, the break that issues them again into the world. The cab was driven by Akbar Ahmed from Pakistan. Nimble Akbar wove his car through the traffic, the buildings seeming to part for us beneath the heavy gray sky, becoming denser and taller, the light darkening as we entered the forest of midtown, until he pulled over to the curb beneath the glass tower that held the Bond & Bond Brothers investment house, the exterior adorned with reminders of Christmas: outsized poinsettias and wreaths with giant golden bows. A little sad, however, their time already up.

Theodor would assume I was in the maid's garret beneath

the shelves of so many books—the dictionary, Shakespeare, even the Bible open on my desk as I searched desperately for something to say. Instead I was here. I knew what I was doing, what I wanted. Later, I would come to learn how the perceptions of others could have a tight grip, but I didn't feel that now. On Wall Street so many people stay long after they've made their millions, not because they want to, but because they are afraid of the perception of others if they leave—fear they couldn't hack it, fear they didn't have the stamina, fear they didn't have the drive, fear of releasing their spot—like the prized Manhattan parking space that you don't want to surrender even if you have no need for it. (Understanding this later, I would realize just how brave Will Chapman had been to let it all go, because you do not get it back.) The perception of me now, in my realm, would be that I had failed as a writer. I could see Lily Starr leaning into the ear of one of our graduate school friends: *Have you heard about India Palmer?*

But I didn't care, for the first time I didn't care about the writing. I thought of my desk again, alone on the top floor beneath so many books. How I'd sat there for hours, days, weeks, trying to understand what was next. The blank page in front of me no longer held me—the hours of staring out the window—the joy of an e-mail, the daily mail—the lingering over the newspaper—the calls to the agent to complain about the lack of reviews, to complain about anything so I could feel productive—the dull spark of a vague idea that wishes to be much more—the relief of the day's end—racing home to the girls—the hope, indelible, that the rush and urgency of desire would come again.

Beneath the glass tower of Bond & Bond, I felt a new kind of hope. And I understood that I hadn't told Theodor, just as the lover doesn't tell the one she is betraying, because he would turn my new hope into something sordid. He, with his faith, his vow of artistic chastity, would be the one to turn hope to guilt. I paid the driver and stepped into the cold. It was Friday, January 2,

2004. Fairy lights dressed the trees running the length of Park Avenue.

Bond & Bond occupied six floors and the building's penthouse, on the forty-third floor. On the ground floor, the company had security guards stationed in front of its own bank of elevators; one elevator shot straight to the top, no stops. A guard called up to Win to announce my arrival. "A Miss Palmer to see you, sir," he said, giving me the once-over. I took the express elevator to the penthouse.

I was greeted by Miss Lane, a late-middle-aged woman who had been a beauty and was trying to hang on to the quality that had once best defined her—Botox smoothing out wrinkles, sort of, the way an iron that is not hot enough makes only slight progress with a fabric's creases. Her blond hair was piled regally on the crown of her head, and her blue eyes held an alluring twinkle as she informed me that "the boys" were waiting for me in Mr. Radalpicno's office. She swiped a plastic ID card to open a set of glass doors, and we entered a sanctuary of glass and white walls upon which hung a spectacular collection of investment-grade photographs—a large space, high ceilings, like a gallery. This, I would learn, was a kind of fad in the world of investment banks, especially of those that were doing extremely well, a white-walled corporate Paradiso in which only a very few were allowed entrance, ever.

I followed Miss Lane to the outer reaches of the penthouse, past photographs by Ansel Adams, Dorothea Lange, Cindy Sherman, Alfred Stieglitz, Arthur Leipzig and countless others—obscure, rising, renowned—our heels clacking on the marble floors. There was nowhere to sit. Even on this gray day the room was flooded with natural light. I could appreciate the different tones of white the farther into the space we ventured.

Miss Lane, in front of me in her white suit, guided me like a celestial being. Edward Steichen's picture of Gloria Swanson, her face veiled by a floral scrim, seemed to watch over the room. I knew the lives of these artists. In my own small way I understood them. I knew the sour admixture of cabbage soup and film developer and body odor that went into the making of these prints, but they had been lifted out of their lives, beyond their lives, and landed here in the rooms of Apollo, the blinding albedo of the corporate divine.

At another set of glass doors, again Miss Lane swiped her card and we entered a waiting room, also spare, with a glass coffee table and a chaise, love seat and armchair upholstered in a cream chenille that contrasted, just, with a woven wool rug in various tones (yes) of white. A smoked-glass door apparently led to Ralph Radalpieno's office. Miss Lane offered me a seat, took my coat and asked if I'd like anything to drink. A photograph by Sally Mann, of her young daughter holding a cigarette, hung to the left of the office's entrance. To the right of the entrance hung a photograph by Gertrude Käsebier of the early-1900s showgirl Evelyn Nesbit in a white dress, off the shoulders. She leans forward with half-parted eyes and lips. In her right hand she holds a small ceramic pitcher. The idea that all of this, which I felt in my chest like an old injury, had become the private reserve of a titan of finance made my knees buckle.

I sat down and took in the scene again. I was at a threshold, Dante notwithstanding, and this was its odd whitewashed portico. It was a test. Not of Radalpieno's devising, but mine. I had always been one for detail. It had been my life's blood. But I was entering a world in which, in order to succeed, such detail needed to be purged. That would be what I imagined bond traders called "noise." Theirs was the Apollonian quest for the purest signal, to filter out the noise (the cabbage soup) and its associated moral quandaries and grasp from all the distracting bits that I once used in my daily life—to jettison all that, and to seize the signal, the trend, the very flow of history itself.

I told Miss Lane that I didn't need a drink, at least not of the sort she was offering that morning. "All right, then. Good luck with them," she said, giving me a knowing wink but nothing more. I imagined she'd been with Mr. Radalpieno from the beginning. I waited there for some time. A peaceful silence; the low din of the building's circuitry. Then Miss Lane returned. She now had a yellow silk scarf wrapped around her neck, and on a silver tray she carried three cappuccinos. "Do you like cappuccino?" she asked. She had no identifiable accent. Deftly she held the tray with her left hand, and with her right she opened the door. I followed her. She smelled of lemons. There was a veneer to her that, I later realized, didn't allow me to look beyond the surface. There was no life for her outside the office. This was where she existed, within the glass walls. Somehow it seemed almost strange to me that we spoke the same language.

Ralph Radalpieno sat behind a large steel-and-glass desk, and behind him lay the East Side, the East River, lurking like a fat snake beneath the leaden sky, Brooklyn and beyond. From here you could see the clear demarcations of class, rippling from the epicenter of Park Avenue wealth to the outer reaches of Canarsie and East New York. A few planes lined up to land at La Guardia. Win sat in a highly designed but uncomfortable-looking leather chair, but hopped up as I entered. He extended his hand to me and, taking hold of mine, he pulled me in for a kiss. "At last," he said. I smiled. Seven computer screens, in two tiers, sat on one side of Radalpieno's desk, a blur of green lines, graphs and figures.

"Sorry we kept you waiting." His desk was vast and so was his desk chair, but his imposing size dwarfed both, not to mention Win. Had I not been a novelist, had this not been a lark, had I not had my teaching job (simple as that), I think I would have been afraid. "One of the traders had quite a show going in subprime," Radalpieno said. "We've been riveted by the trace."

Miss Lane set down the cappuccinos on his desk. Next to the phone, an old-fashioned black rotary model, stood a polished bell—like a bellhop's bell but sterling silver. Otherwise the desk was as spare as the rest of the floor. Miss Lane left, shutting the door behind her. The figures on the screens moved about, a dance that I didn't think I would ever understand. One screen, I noticed, simply offered the business news, on mute.

"This is some bank," I said to him. Radalpieno, thick of girth, had short silver hair that accented his steel-blue, secretive eyes, though dimples softened him when he smiled. He gave me a quizzical, confused look, marked by a little impatience. "I didn't know banks looked like this," I added, in explanation. He wore a blue suit with a subtle pinstripe. His wedding band pressed into the flesh of his ring finger. "Where's all the mess? Isn't mess what makes everything happen?"

"There's mess," he said, "but not here. This is the brain. The mess is downstairs with the guts and gore."

"I'm honored, then," I said.

"As you should be. Not everyone gets to come up here. You probably won't be up here again."

"He's direct," Win said.

"I can see."

"I'm intrigued that you've come," Radalpieno said, staring me squarely in the eye, a kindly challenge. Again I realized I would have been afraid of him if . . . if he were the Dashing Cavelli, say, with a book deal for me that hinged on his opinion.

"I wanted to hear Win out," I said.

"We like bets," Radalpieno said. "We're probably a little—how shall I say it, Win?—overfond? Yes, we're overfond of betting. It's a kind of occupational hazard, as you'll see if you stick around. Win's made a bet with me. He's bet he can take you and turn you into a trader, a good one."

"I'm familiar with the terms," I said.

"But I'd say that, among other things, you're too old."

"Thank you," I said.

"What are you? Thirty-three or so?"

"Or so."

"More?" Radalpieno asked, alarmed, not for himself but for Win.

"You know better than to ask a lady her age," I responded.

"She's direct too, with her evasions," Win offered.

"Good raw material," Radalpieno said, as if I weren't in the room.

Then, to me again, "Most of our boys are boys."

"It's all part of the challenge," I said.

"What do you know about battles, fighting? Do you like blood?"

"I don't think so," I said.

"Then why are you here?"

"Does there have to be blood?"

"The people who work for me, they bleed green. Win, who've you brought me?"

"Green?" I almost laughed.

"Green!" he boomed.

"Hear her out," Win said. He smiled at me encouragingly. None of this worried him. He wore the air of confidence that I'd admired, grudgingly, when I first set eyes on him, with his goggles and his leather jacket, trudging through the sand. That seemed like a very long time ago. Yet against the backdrop of these offices, humility seemed part of his demeanor too.

"What do you know about finance? Do you have a mathematical background? Do you have any idea about bonds, how they're priced, why people want them, how to predict prepayments, what LTVs mean, FICO scores, the basics?" Radalpieno paused and studied the back of his hand. "What about mortgages? What can you tell me about their design? Why would anyone want mortgages? Why would an investor want a pool of subprime originating in the sand states? Mortgages are math."

He spoke as if everyone were an investor of some sort. He had a large appetite for everything, I could tell, and he burned it off, most of it, simply by existing. "You, as a pretty little woman" —he appraised me, his eyes lingering at my chest as if to draw an exclamation point—"why in the world would you want to try on this? Shouldn't you be at home with the kids, redecorating?" Win leaned past me (I was still standing) and lifted the bell from the desk and shook it, to ring it once. I thought that very odd. "Might as well keep that in your hand, Johns, because it'll get a workout this morning." Then to me again: "Bonds, blondie? And that suit'll get you laid." (A black velvet suit cut with eyelets, the skirt form-fitting, patent leather heels.) The bell rang again. (I noted the detail. Had I been studying the scene for fiction, I would have written it down in my book: an odd pair with a bell between them and all the money in the world.)

"I'm not claiming to know much of anything," I said. "I believe the fact that I know so little is Win's point."

"Won't you sit down?" Radalpieno asked, standing and gesturing to the couch and armchairs. He lumbered his heft to the couch. Win and I sat in the chairs. Miss Lane entered with sparkling water and three glasses, set them on the glass table, and as she was leaving Radalpieno asked her if she thought I'd make a good trader. "But mum's the word," he said to her, putting a finger over his lips. "Can women be good traders?" he asked her. "I can count on one hand the lady traders on the Street who are worth a cent." Win rang the bell, a little smile alighting on his face.

With Radalpieno's eyes on Miss Lane, I took in Win. Dressed in a brown suit that illuminated his lovely eyes, he was adorable in that boyish, privileged way that I would come to recognize as a characteristic of the trader type—from home to college to making millions, they were a cocooned lot. Company cars ferried them about the city; they flew to Paris because they liked the way a particular hotel did their laundry; savoring hundred-dollar cigars and thousand-dollar bottles of wine was part of the job description. For all the calm this floor's furnishings were supposed to instill, Win did not seem perfectly calm. Almost calm, perhaps, someone trying to be calm, knowing that to appear calm was the goal. But beneath the surface I could sense that he was excited, ready to get started—someone at a roulette table, feeling lucky, ringing a strange bell. It was also clear that Radalpieno sat firmly in the center of Win's palm, though completely obliviously. "Miss Lane has been with Radalpieno for thirty years," Win offered, glancing at me and then quickly toward her. In that darting of his eye, I wondered if I detected a little nervousness on his part. We had never seen each other without a healthy dose of champagne. Or was I flattering myself?

"She's never ventured too far into the business of what we do," Radalpieno added. "As a lady, she knows better." (The bell tolled.) "So, Miss Lane?" he persisted.

"These modern women seem confident of their abilities to do anything," she said kindly, almost proudly, longing to be more closely related to the species she was speaking of.

"So why are you here? What's in this for you?" Radalpieno turned the spotlight back on me, emphasizing *why* and *what*, leaving Miss Lane behind, an afterthought now and not perturbed—used to being an afterthought. "Can't your husband take care of you?" Again Win sounded the bell.

"I'm here to make money," I said simply, while also trying to make sense of the bell. "All of you make so much of it and I'm curious to find out how and why. I'm just as curious as Win to see if he's right, to understand if I could do what you do here—take the road not taken. That's the idea, I suppose."

"Suppose? We don't suppose," he said. Again his impressive size inflated. "I rip the throats out of those who tell me they suppose."

"I've done a little research," I said. He wasn't scaring me with his war talk. "I understand what Win does to a certain degree. He manages the trading floor that handles all forms of mortgages and rates." I continued to explain all that I knew; I'd prepared for this moment. I spoke of pools and tranches, making mortgage bonds a viable investment option for big investors, insurance companies and pension funds—structures that offered a variety of risk possibilities. I knew too, and let him know that I did, that in the 1980s he was among the original architects of collateralized mortgage obligations (I referred to them as CMOs) and thus opened the mortgage-backed-security (MBS) frontier that thrived today. He let me talk the way you might let a fish run. "You had the mathematical mind that could understand how to turn vast mortgage pools into bonds that would appeal to investors of all sorts."

I spoke evenly but felt that I was falling down a rabbit hole. I'd read about Radalpieno in the paper and online. There was plenty to read. He lived in a twenty-room mansion in the East Eighties, with a skating rink on the roof in winter and a pool in summer. The most prized piece in his wife's collection of contemporary art was by Damien Hirst, of a tiger shark in formaldehyde. But the house and the shark were details, the accoutrements that described what he and Pretty did with his excess. It was all hard won, and his to claim unequivocally. He'd taken B&B from a slide into a one-trick bond shop, left for dead by the industry, and turned it into one of the most profitable pure-play boutique firms on Wall Street. I used the term "pure play" for effect. I let him know all that I knew, though not about his house and his shark.

He clasped his hands and studied me, working his thumbs. I think he would have enjoyed hearing what I had to say about his mansion and his shark, if only because he seemed to like the notion of a stranger caring to know the details of what made him the man he was.

"Because of you and your colleagues, mortgage securities are an eight-trillion-dollar market today," I added for punctuation, and not a little flattery. "You've taken the puny debts of individual mortgages and turned them into the largest capital market in the world, exceeding by a long shot the combined U.S. stock market. I like stories, and that's a pretty nifty one."

"And you love money," he said. "I like that you love money. You have to love money. That raw impulse is the heart. So tell me about money. What stories can you tell?"

Before I had a chance to look confused, Win stepped in. "He wants to know the schemes you were involved with as a kid, early signs of your entrepreneurial nature. This is his favorite interview question. Once the math checks out, he wants the stories that describe the passion."

"What's your story?" I asked Win.

"Fireworks," he said. "They were illegal in my town but not in the town next door. So I'd go over there on my bike and get them and bring them back and sell them for a profit. I'd buy bricks of them, divide them up—"

"Into tranches," Radalpieno said. I laughed.

"She gets the joke."

"I do," I offered, smiling, imagining Win as a kid, riding his bike between towns with bricks of fireworks. But I was trying to come up with my own story. I didn't have one at hand. Mine had been an easy, safe childhood. I kept thinking, though, of a friend who had a sort of colorful childhood, lots of kids, a crazy stepfather. They lived in a sprawling house in a commune. A friend from grad school, she'd written a novel about this childhood, and I remembered a scene in which her ten-year-old narrator rented out her bedroom for ten bucks to a friend of her older brother so he could have a place to take his girl. "I rented out my room," I said, and told them the story. Dirk Vandewater and his girlfriend, Sunshine. It was the 1970s—the names, the dates, straight from Kali Krane's novel *The Tiger's Mouth.* I knew they'd never have read it: two thousand copies sold, at best. "I used the money earned on the room-letting to buy Avon products that I peddled door to door. By the time I was sixteen I had over five thousand dollars in the bank."

"So you were a pimp."

"A madam," I said, lifting my chin.

"And what did you do with the cash?"

"I went to Europe, learned Italian, fell in love."

"You spent it all?"

"I like money because I like to spend it."

"*Like?*"

He was right. I didn't feel comfortable saying "love" when it came to money. I wasn't brought up that way. But I said it now. I said, "Love money," because suddenly I got it, and I wanted this. I wanted it very, very much.

"How much are you putting on her?" Win asked Radalpieno. The planes kept lining up, one after the next, cruising in low over Brooklyn and Queens. From up here, the East River looked inviting and the city seemed almost as calm as these rooms pretended to be.

"Am I a racehorse?" I asked.

"Yes you are, darling," Win said, "and this is Saratoga."

Radalpieno took the bell and started ringing it.

"Really, that too?" Win asked Radalpieno, and Radalpieno smiled and shook the bell again.

"That too," he confirmed.

"As you like," Win said.

"What are you making now?" Radalpieno asked me.

"What do you mean?" I said.

"You know what I mean," he responded, almost curtly, joviality fading from his face with the speed of a flicked switch.

"Salary," offered Win.

"I'm not so sure I want to be Eliza Doolittle," I lied. They moved so fast.

"Don't be coy. That's why you're here. You said so yourself," Radalpieno said. He paused to study his thumbs again. "It'll be fun," he added, the curt tone giving way to joy once again—though I noted that the joy took its time seeping across his face.

This was all a joke, a game. I was just another shark in formaldehyde, a performance piece for the office, a living photograph to prance the halls. I thought of Gloria Swanson's eyes. Anything could be bought. If this were an affair, it would have been the point of no return.

"I'll bet her salary and give her one to boot, a bonus in a year if she performs. Guaranteed contractually. She's a writer. How much can it be?" He pressed a button somewhere beneath his desk and spoke to Miss Lane, telling her to inform HR. "I'll be rooting for her even if I'm betting against her. A hedge. Does that satisfy your requirements, Johns? Your *folly,* as you said."

"When I was younger I imagined a different future," I said.

"Ring the bell," Radalpieno said. "She's getting philosophical. We don't want philosophy, Miss Palmer, we want fast brains."

"What is this bell you keep ringing?" I asked.

"In the fullness of time, Miss Palmer," he said.

"Fast brains," Win offered and winked. Though clearly in control, Win seemed to be a different man in the presence of Radalpieno, more aware of the effort it took to control the likes of him, the effort, as if that power could vanish in an instant and become a puddle of illusion at his feet, the chimera of what had been.

"Your salary?"

"I make some money. I contribute to magazines. The books pay a bit. My teaching job."

"A good year?" Win asked. "Don't be shy. It's just money." *Just money:* to those who have plenty of it.

"A good year?" I shrugged. "One hundred and fifty, perhaps." I felt I was undressing in front of strangers. Once I would have been proud of that sum. If I'd known at twenty that by the time I was thirty-eight I'd be making that amount of money, I'd have thought I'd become a great success, even if just now I'd padded the figure a bit.

"That bad?" Radalpieno asked. Then to Win, "Why don't you put her in sales? Give her something certain. She has a pretty smile, a charming manner. The Japanese would love her."

Win rang the bell and said, "Because I intend to make her a star, and you know stars aren't found in sales."

I thought of Lily Starr gossiping about me, whispering my exploits from ear to ear. I wanted to be a star. I wanted to work hard. I was seized again with that wonderful sensation, the gambler's blood. I was gambling everything and nothing.

"I see," Radalpieno said, stretching out the two words so they seemed to say much more. "It's our policy to pay top salaries. You should know that. Win can tell you. He'll fill you in on the details. This is a good opportunity. Such chances don't fall in the laps of just anyone. Win's word is *the* word," he said and added, "Your life will be your own, I imagine, at last. Free." I'd thought freedom was writing's currency. "Don't ever underestimate the ability of money."

"What's in this for you?" I asked. His gruff manner did not deter me. Today he was a man whose empire, his universe of white rooms and light, did not have sovereignty over me. Not yet. This was still, in part, just a fabulous procrastination technique—an escape from the blank white page and the lonely desk. My old life still awaited me, though the idea of earning $150,000 and a guaranteed bonus, ditching the scramble, had taken a firm hold of my imagination. Ease, like stepping into a hot tub.

Radalpieno said, "I'm here to make Win Johns happy. He makes me happy, I make him happy." He spoke with a little exasperation, but it felt more forced than genuine. It was clear he enjoyed playing—anything, everything—immensely.

"Then what's in it for you?" I asked Win. I knew that my

salary would make no difference to the business, could be deducted from Win's bonus or salary without his noticing.

Win held me with his big chocolate eyes. "You," he said. He let the bold declaration hang in the air for a moment—the desire to unsettle. "You showed a willingness to play. I liked that. It motivates me." He paused, then added, "And you're an artist, a talented writer whose work I admire, and it seems the arts are in need of a bit of saving these days." With that, the challenge became much more complicated. Did he want to save the arts or squash the arts? "And also the knowledge that I can."

"He believes there is nothing magical about what we do. He believes it is not pure innate talent and financial acumen, so therefore anyone can do it," Radalpieno said.

"We're used-car salesmen," Win said. "That's all we are, really."

"Oh yes, he likes that metaphor. You'll be trading a lot of Toyotas and Hondas. Watch out if you ever get a Model T."

"If you fail, which you won't," Win said, "I may become a character in one of your novels—like Emma Chapman, right? So you see, I win even if I lose. But I won't lose. I don't lose."

"He's doing it, Johns. Your boy is pulling it off yet again." They both hopped up and went closer to the screens—the green lines and gibberish. "Snake's moving the whole market. He was right about the curve on the 6s. It's an ambush. The carnage won't be small. 'A good plan violently executed *now* is better than a perfect plan next week.' Patton," he said to me, radiant in the screen's green glow. "I love this," Radalpieno nearly sang, clenching his fists and shaking them to the sky, which seemed to bring down the snow that was gently beginning to fall outside the windows, as if calling forth so many specks of light to add to his luminous collection—the specks like all those dollars my father tried to save, simply fluttering to the ground for the sake of extravagance and nothing more.

"We're moving him to subprime, Johns. He'll head the desk.

Get your little beauty to do this and you're the star magician, Johns."

From the glass palace Win took me to the pit. His office, the mess I imagined I'd find at a place like this, of papers and books and computers, also had a glass wall, but this one was transparent, not smoked, offering a clear view onto the trading floor—an empire in itself, as large as an ice rink or basketball court, with a high ceiling beneath which were rows upon rows of desks, open to allow for the easy flow of information. Each desk was occupied by a man (there were few women) busily working phones and monitoring computer screens, tapping away on wireless keyboards, the steady hum of electricity, the ring of phones. In the center of the room was an empty space above which, suspended from the ceiling, was an enormous box of screens showing the same figures and graphs and charts and information that had been on display in Radalpieno's office. Also the news—in case disaster strikes, I was told. On the morning of September 11, 2001, for example, the instant news on these screens was how all the traders understood to freeze trades immediately. The noise was constant but not loud, the steady rhythm of money being generated. The overhead lights were bright and seemed to extinguish any natural light that forced its way onto the floor.

"It's fascinating," I said, "like a machine." When Win shut his office door, the sounds of the dealing room vanished, but he could see everything. Win's office overlooked the East Side as well, and though it was only ten stories below Radalpieno's, the view seemed less spectacular, more chaotic. Helicopters that I had not noticed zipped about like flies. From here the city was not as calm, and it seemed the powers above wanted it just that way—energy igniting energy. I opened the door fast just to hear the sound again. Then shut it swiftly. Win looked at me, amused. A big old-fashioned gumball machine stood guard outside the door, filled with the colorful balls.

"I have no idea what you do," I said to him. "We're in a fine mess. Or I should say, you are. Either this is an enormous joke or you're a complete fool." I opened the door again. "It's a beehive, all those busy bees making so much delicious honey." I closed the door.

"That's a workable metaphor. You'll learn what we do. The good news is, you don't have to understand the whole picture—just what you do specifically. No one understands the whole picture, not really, not these days. Not even Radalpieno, upstairs in his sanctuary. Actually, he probably knows less than anyone down here, and for that reason he has time on his hands, can play a fine game of golf for all his practice. But it doesn't seem to matter too much."

He told me to sit down—an old leather chair, comfortable. "The business is simple. There's only one equation. Profit and loss is what the trader is all about. See those guys?" He lifted his head to look onto the floor, but he did not point. "They come into Manhattan every day, crossing the bridges, the skyline active in that light, and they want it. The whole entire city. They think, each and every one of them, 'This could be the day I win.' I want it that way. Radalpieno insists on it being that way. 'Bleed green, bleed green,' he says."

Then came his used-car-salesman analogy, his humbling way of illustrating how basic and simple the business is, knocking all of them off the pedestal. There are a few dealerships on a block. They have a bunch of different kinds of cars. One guy gets a lot of Pacers—remember those enormous ugly bubbles? And this guy knows that the Pacer gets really good gas mileage for a used car, and he knows that the price of oil is about to go up. He knows too that the economy isn't so good, and the bad news will soon be catching up with the consumer. He knows that the Pacer drives well in wet weather, and big rains are predicted for the coming year. He figures he can make a market. He knows where to get Pacers, knows that another dealer needs to unload them, then decides that he can do something really spectacular with them, so he starts to stockpile, purchasing Pacers with the company's capital. Now he has so many Pacers coming in that he starts offering them low, to see where they'll price, and as people catch on to all the good reasons for owning a used Pacer, and simply because there's so much desire (we all know about lemmings), he creates more demand, starts selling them at a higher and higher price while all the other used-car dealers are scratching their heads as he's poised, making the killing. Now those other guys want the Pacers too. Everyone wants the Pacers. So our guy, he's moving on to the Opel, the Escort, the Aspire, and doing the same thing all over again.

He spoke quickly, with assurance, sort of mumbling his words, though more from fluency than bad elocution—the manner of a native speaker speaking his language fast. Another tool the car dealer had was a reference listing car values, like the Kelley Blue Book. "So our dealer has a hundred Toyotas, and one day some guy with a car rental agency walks in and wants to buy the whole lot. Our dealer knows the cars are worth ten thousand each, based on the book value. He wants to sell with some spread, so he offers the lot for a million-fifty. Sold. Now he has no cars. Is he going to sit around and wait or go out and get some more?"

"He's going to get some more."

"Exactly. But this time it might not be Toyotas. It might be Hondas. Or maybe he comes across a Model T. Very rare. Maybe he has a customer who wants two Model T's, and our guy's pretty sure he can get another one at the same price, so he says he'll sell two at twenty K apiece. Only problem is, he can't find another one. Look as hard as he might, he's not turning up the other Model T. Well, let's say the customer turns it up at twenty-five K. The rule is, our guy's got to pay the coupon on the bond at the price the customer found. That's the penalty."

"Oooh," I said. I was sort of getting it. He sold what he didn't have and couldn't get. "He failed."

"Indeed. Happened this morning with my Chilean. He lost a million over Model T's."

"Did you yell at him?"

Win laughed. "I don't yell. I've got to get the best out of my traders. Yelling won't do that. Yelling will shut them down. If he doesn't keep up, he'll go. They all know the consequences."

I didn't quite believe he didn't yell.

"Who'd ever want a Pacer?" I asked, teasing, but quickly noticed that any flirtation that had existed between us was dissipating. This was business for him.

"Anyone can be convinced of anything. Look at you, here."

"Why?" I asked, suddenly serious, meaning, *Why am I here?*

He understood. "Luck played for me" was all he said, explanation enough. If he hadn't run into Pretty Radalpicno, where would he be today? "I'll be taking this very seriously," he said. "You'll need to do something about the teaching job. It will be a lot of work, you know. Long hours. We'll be rolling up our sleeves."

"I understand."

"Are you sure about this?"

"I'm scared—if I can be honest."

"For today, that's all right. But Monday, fear stays at home. Fear and the trader are incompatible. A little fear is all right; it keeps you on your toes. But too much and you're ruined. We'll begin with rolls."

"You're a star at what you do."

"How do you know?" he asked. I wasn't sure if it was a challenge or if he wanted to see himself reflected off me.

"Talking to you. Your passion. It's clear."

"I love the system. Showing it to you makes it new."

"The guy with the Pacers," I said, "he has the ability not only to perceive opportunities before others do but to convince a whole group of people that that opportunity is something it wants and needs."

"You're a storyteller—that's why I wanted you. Most people are driven by consensus, but while they're following that line you're going to be reading, perceiving the larger story, and that's why we're going to win this bet. Then, if you like the business, you'll go deep, to a place where the story will seem irrelevant." He looked through the glass to the trading floor. "There are a whole bunch of guys out there speculating on who this chick is in here with me, asking questions."

Before I left, Win gave me a quick tour of the floor. What struck me most was how young the traders were. Of course that is a well-known description of them, but their collective youth made them seem impossibly young, and being confronted with it, as familiar as it may be to a person who knows about this world, was at first startling. Kids you wouldn't want to leave in charge of your house were in charge of billions upon billions of dollars. In fact, they *were* in charge of your house—you just didn't know it.

No gray hair, kids from everywhere. Indians and Koreans and Chinese and Japanese—they all dressed in uniform: short haircuts, dark suits, light shirts, sleeves rolled up, jackets hanging over the backs of their chairs. They sat at their four-foot desks, eyes intensely focused on the screens before them, each desk space personalized with photographs and decals of sports teams, Yankees and the like, hot-chili sauces. One guy had a signed photograph of Dick Cheney, another one of his newborn. Well over five hundred traders and salespeople and their staff. An all-consuming concentration, each trader driven by the immediate transaction, deals beginning and finishing in less than a minute while holding conversations on the phone and with a nearby salesperson or clerk or another trader.

It seemed the energy of the market infused the room, the traders, the air vibrating with the low hum of voices, punctuated by an occasional effort of one to be heard above the din. Proximity clearly facilitating transaction. Money, though invisible, was in constant motion, and I found the pulse infectious. They all seemed to find it so—the sheer raw enjoyment of winning . . . or striving to win. *Today could be the day.* They were a collective lot, a whole. If, to Miss Lane, I were another species, then they too were their own species—these, oddly, her own children: well trained, emotionless, eager for yield and blessed with an aptitude for bleeding green. "You'll never find anything like it in any other business," Win said.

He led me across the floor to a group of traders who worked in the pass-through market, as it is called, a subset of the mortgage universe that handled three trillion of the eight-trillion-dollar market and the safest of the mortgage securities—those backed, or quasi-backed, by the government, known as GSEs, or government-sponsored entities: Fannie, Freddie, Ginnie. Win introduced me to the six in the group, all of them in their twenties, from the top universities, all nimble with numbers, their desks decorated with personal effects. What best described them, as a group, was a perfect rationality and an unambiguous self-interest. Or that is what I recall believing at that moment, before I came to know them, before they became human to me. How does one go back to the moment before, remember those first impressions (often accurate in the end)?

Who were they on that day? Snake, from Calcutta, wearing a starched white shirt without the sleeves rolled, very trim and tucked and neat for a man named Snake, a smooth and handsome face with long bangs swept to the right of his forehead; Tiger, a white boy with a broad, chummy face and a photograph of a slender girl in a bikini on a beach with palm trees, and next to her picture stood six different brands of exotic bottled water; Sam, more of the same, a kid who would have starred on the college lacrosse team, didn't seem to want to be in his shirt; Josh, an African American who had a small framed postcard on his desk of Winona Ryder, the caption reading FREE WINONA, next to her a lassoed Clint Eastwood; Gus, an earnest Korean, eyes hard on the screen, on doing the job, not too interested in my intrusion; and Maxi, the Chilean who just lost a million because he sold a Model T he didn't have and couldn't get, a determined and self-centered-looking individual.

When Win introduced me, he offered no explanation of who I was or why I was there. They smiled, collectively, kindly. I tried to remember where I'd been at their age. How had they understood to come here? What was the inspiration or the motivation? Money, of course, but how did they understand that so young? I imagined them flying to Paris to have their shirts pressed. It seemed even that would take more know-how than their age allowed. Up close, they lost their edge. They seemed like boys on a team of some sort—like swimmers competing individually yet for the greater good of the team. You could sense it in the focus of their eyes.

"A pleasure," Snake said.

"Good moves today," Win responded.

"Almighty," Snake answered.

"You impressed Radalpieno. He's making jokes about moving you to head subprime."

"The Wild West," Snake said. "I'll take a pass for now."

"Bold," Win answered.

Snake was the handsomest, with his dark skin and light brown eyes and thick lashes. I imagined his parents were immigrants, unsure what to make of this American kid they had created. He offered me his hand, and the others followed. They were working their screens and phones and e-mails while also absorbing me.

Then we drifted away. I smiled farewell over my shoulder as Win escorted me to the elevator, swiping his card once to get us out of the room and again to call for the elevator.

"They're already making bets on you," he said, wrinkling his lips in that all-knowing way. He knew what they were doing even when he wasn't watching them, standing behind their chairs. He made them. He understood them.

"And who will win?" I asked.

"Snake. He's got the instinct. He's telling the boys what my plan is for you. He's telling them that you're raw material that I intend to shape, and he's betting I'll succeed. He's got the willingness to perceive, and that is the key to this trade. That and mastering your emotions."

"How much is he betting?"

"He's going high with this one. I'd say he has four grand riding on you. I'd say he's calling their ideas too, telling them each what he believes they think. He's going to make money all the way around. There will be side bets, derivatives of your success, the over-under, on time, you last. The boy's well trained."

"What do the others think?"

"Maxi thinks you're a girlfriend. He believes in the easiest explanation because he's too busy thinking about racehorses to be bothered. His family owns a few stars in Chile. And it's his desk you'll be filling when the time comes. The others are somewhere in the middle; they want to see a bit more before they commit. But theirs will always be a choice of who is the best person to believe in rather than believing in their own instincts. They'll make good, if slow, choices. But Snake is the star."

The elevator doors opened and I was gone, ushered back into the familiar world.

Outside, the snow still fell, accumulating, abundant, aswirl in strong gusts. "They're forecasting a blizzard," I heard someone say, rushing past me toward the curb with another well-dressed friend, arm out to hail a cab. I looked up. The sky was low and thick with the flakes, a pointillist's point of view. The force of the snow picked up speed, a wonderful New York storm. I imagined Radalpieno above, fists clenched, the architect of it all.

Twelve

REAL ESTATE WAS in the air, like tech stocks in the late 1990s, like all stocks in the late 1920s when even the shoeshine boys offered tips, famously forecasting the end. By January 2004 everyone—cab drivers, policemen patrolling neighborhoods, short-order cooks, bicycle messengers, children playing make-believe, mothers, fathers—on the street, at cocktail parties, at school during morning drop-off—everyone had discovered the golden-egg-laying goose called real estate.

It had, in its very name, a kind of commanding authority that was solid, unsexy, and it rang true: it was real. "I had a dream last night," one mother said to another, quieting the packed elevator ascending to the classrooms at the girls' school, a captive audience. "We were in your new house in Palm Beach, walking from one magnificent room to the next." Theodor bent to me and whispered into my renter's ear, "Real estate porn." We were not immune; we wanted a house; I wanted a house. I wanted to be part of the conversation.

It was good to own. But we didn't have that kind of money. By New York standards, we were poor. We had nothing. Anywhere else we would have been rich. Even so, we were advised to "buy something." So we looked at a studio, a bunker-like dwelling that smelled of cat pee in the hall, had a view onto an air shaft and a hot plate for a stove, an apartment that could be purchased for a price that was best shouted at the top of one's lungs. Anything better than the price of that studio would mean shouldering a debt that started at a million dollars. To Theodor this seemed outside the bounds of sanity, but others were willing. Lily Starr was in the paper for buying a million-dollar house in Amagansett: "New Starr of Literary World Builds Nest Among Long Island's Elite."

Harlem was hot. Queens was hot. Staten Island was hot. Just about anywhere was hot, actually, and everyone had an opinion. The cobbler on the corner was telling a customer about a house he was buying in Crown Heights. I remember a long taxi ride with a driver who wore a cell phone earpiece and spoke to clients about real estate deals in East New York. The airwaves sang of the abiding enterprise: home improvement shows, house-hunting shows, gut-renovation shows, flip-the-house shows. Up, up, up. In rural towns, homes replaced farmland, McMansions shooting up like mushrooms all across this great land.

Mortgages were easier to get than flu shots. They came in every color, every configuration: thirty-year fixed; fifteen-year fixed; jumbo; conforming; two-, three-, four-, five-year teaser rates; ARMs; balloons; no-interest; interest-only; no-doc loans; no-down-payment loans. No closing costs. No middlemen. No points. No processing fees. No credit report necessary. Were you breathing? You could get a mortgage, it seemed. Real estate was the ticket. Mansions were being built on apartment building rooftops on West End Avenue. Multifamily brownstones, SROs, schoolhouses, fire stations, churches, an old cancer hospital—everything was being turned into a home. Those who had primary homes now had second homes. Those with second homes now had third homes. And there were those who bought, not because they wanted the home, but because they knew someone else would—a whole new breed of speculators.

Homeowners comprised 68.6 percent of the American population, the highest percentage ever. In 2004 the real estate market weighed in at $8 trillion, and three years later it would rise to an astonishing $11 trillion. This ascent would never change. The population was growing, and land was a finite resource. It was as simple as that. "It all boils down to real estate," a mother who was reading her daughter the Old Testament (a child's version) said to me in jest, but with the insight of conviction. "The entire story is about real estate. You know, the Promised Land, getting it, keeping it, getting it back, etc., etc."

Remember the Hovs of Maine? Remember their conventional mortgage, how we followed it up to the end of the 1970s when everything changed? Now comes the sequel, an important part of this autobiography, for without it my story would not have happened. Real estate allowed two exceedingly talented financial wizards, a little bored with the monotony of always getting it right, to pluck an artist from the streets of despair and place her in the center of the beautiful, wild storm that was the mortgage securities market. A swirling storm, a wonderful whipping blizzard—the kind that settles over the city like magic.

A family like the Hovs, buying their first home in the 1980s, went to the local savings and loan and took out their $100,000 mortgage, a thirty-year fixed, at 12.5 percent. (Remember those days?) But this time the mortgage did not stay with the bank. Instead it was sold off to a Wall Street investment bank, where it was pooled with other mortgages to form an investment vehicle so large that it would be attractive to the corporate, long-term investor—a pension fund, an insurance company, a foreign government even. The homeowners' monthly payments, interest and principal, became a revenue stream to pay the investors. Selling the mortgages gave the banks more liquidity, and this in turn was used to make more loans, and so the cycle grew.

What would happen, my new mentors would patiently explain, giving me the most basic sort of example, is that they'd take the $100,000 and divide it by ten, each investor then having $10,000 (this example, a microcosm of the pool). That would be the bond, with a thirty-year amortization and the interest at 12 percent (37bps), most going to Fannie/Freddie for the guarantee and 12.5bps going to the servicing company as payment for sending out the monthly bills. But creating bonds out of mortgages wasn't quite so simple. The neat little bundles of debt changed as homeowners paid off a portion of the principal along with the interest, which meant that interest payments to investors diminished over time. And homeowners sometimes did unpredictable things: they sometimes defaulted or, more likely, prepaid the debt, if by chance they got a windfall or if interest rates went down significantly or if they needed to sell their house. This left the investor with sudden capital that couldn't be easily reinvested for returns that were as attractive. Known as pass-through securities, mortgage-backed bonds had been around for quite some time but did not hold wide appeal because of these inherent problems. But this had rapidly changed.

The investment structure that I was swiftly learning about is the foundation of the proliferation of the American dream of homeownership. It became the cornerstone of a new generation of property barons (large and minuscule) and was fueled by an ethos first inscribed in our nation's birth document as the right to life, liberty and "the means of acquiring, possessing and protecting property." "Property" was changed by others to mean "happiness," and no one has looked back since. Owning property meant owning one's tangible share of happiness. And now, some 230 years later, a few roads converged to bestow this right on the American man and woman unequivocally and without bias—such a solid part of who we are as a people that foreigners (governments and businesses) wagered hefty sums on the lucrative American MBS market.

This information I absorbed from Frank J. Fabozzi's *Handbook of Mortgage-Backed Securities* (the bible of the market) and countless other books I read over the next few weeks, in order to understand the history and the finer points of how the system worked.

I developed my understanding of the contribution that Radalpieno, along with others, had made to the MBS market with the creation of the collateralized mortgage obligation, a product that addressed the underlying prepayment risks and thus structured the bonds in a more attractive fashion. The CMO divided the pools of mortgages into two-, five-, and ten-year bonds that would appeal to a broader sweep of investors with various maturity requirements and—a significant factor in the explosion of MBS trading in the late 1980s—by more closely defining those return dates.

In other words, the CMO made it possible to reduce the wildcards for the investor so he'd have a more certain sense of when he'd get his principal back. The so-called tranches pay back principal according to a schedule, with the first tranche taking on the highest level of risk by absorbing the first prepayments. The second tranche absorbs the subsequent losses in case the equity tranche goes under. The third tranche, the least risky, absorbs whatever is left over. This form of CMO came to be known as "sequential pay" or "plain vanilla."

With the restructuring of the mortgage pools came an explosion of other mortgage-backed security products—PACs and TACs and Z bonds and IOs and POs and floating-rate bonds and stripped MBS bonds and countless other derivative products that only the creators truly understood and that politicians had allowed to become deregulated—a proliferation that rivaled any boom but that quietly grew during the 1990s to a mega-scale. Also growing were ways to hedge. Insurance products were created, swap options and calls and puts and the like. With the secondary market, the shadow market, set up and ready to go, with the variety of possibilities for dicing and slicing the bonds (companies in France and in Texas, for example, owning the same mortgages) and for hedging them, the demand and need for mortgages from the primary market (that is, originating mortgages) multiplied exponentially. There was such a demand for mortgages that the primary market couldn't furnish them to the secondary market fast enough. And so with time, mortgage products in all colors, sizes and shapes were created and offered to home buyers. The secondary market soared. And the benefit: those 12.5 percent mortgage rates tumbled.

At first, there were good reasons for the fancy mortgage products, for the teaser loans and the adjustable-rate mortgages, as they were designed to help wealthy people like bankers and lawyers, whose money came in lump sums at bonus time, to buy a house before the bonus arrived. Will Chapman, for example, bought Maine with one of these exotic loans. He put 0 percent down and got an initial teaser rate. He was betting that he'd sell his book to a publisher for a bundle and then be able to refinance the house in a way that created more certainty for the monthly payments. The advance from the book sale was not money he needed to live on. He had budgeted domestic expenses from money he'd made in the refinancing of his apartment and from a mass of accumulated savings from his days as a banker. Since his book was so long, he made a calculated judgment (with the advice of his agent, Sig Blankman—yes, she did become his agent) to divide the book in two. This, therefore, would bring him two hefty advances rather than one. If all else failed, he'd go back to the Street to fill his coffers. He'd been very good at what he did, and well liked. If they wouldn't have him back on the Street, he could sell Tribeca and move to Harlem and he'd be all right. (I loved the way these guys spoke, as though they were buying the whole state, the whole neighborhood: Maine, Tribeca, Harlem.)

So when the housing market exploded, a product designed for the wealthy became an asset for just about anyone, servicing those who dreamed tomorrow would bring more—those who never counted on tomorrow bringing less. A Mexican strawberry picker in Bakersfield earning $14,000 annually is loaned all he needs to buy a $720,000 house. The arithmetic was easy: property values could only go up; our homes only become more valuable; we'd refinance and lower our rates once our home's value rose. Banks were on to this. It was an elaborate design but a simple creed: tomorrow was the great American hope, and today there was money to be made.

And so the lesson continues. I spoke of roads converging. One road was our national belief in homeownership, a notion nurtured since the Declaration of Independence, fortified by President Franklin Roosevelt during the Depression with the creation of the New Deal and the Government National Mortgage Association (or Ginnie Mae) and again after World War II and up to the present. The second road was created by the dot-com bust, followed immediately by the September 11 terrorist attacks and the recession of 2001, which caused the Federal Reserve fund to be reduced from 6 percent to 1.25 percent, an action, Win explained, that led to lower rates or drops in LIBOR (the London interbank offered rate), which is used by banks to set adjustable-rate-mortgage rates.

The third road was the mortgage-backed-security market with its primary and secondary markets waiting and ready to thrive. Since the cost of borrowing money plummeted, money was easy to get. A house worth $600,000 could now be bought with a mortgage that would have the equivalent monthly payment of a $300,000 mortgage taken out only a few years before. Who wouldn't want to own? Why should the strawberry picker forgo such a chance? Why should the banker let him? The banker, after all, could pass off the loan to a financial institution in the shadow market, which could chop it up and ship it off to China and France and Sausalito, say, and in turn those institutions could hedge with swap options and derivatives and . . . And that big, beautiful home with the Viking kitchen and bathrooms so sleek they seemed to belong in expensive hotels—heated chrome towel racks and piping for the shower that looked so elaborate it could steer you to the moon, not to mention the Jacuzzi and the marble bath and the travertine walls imported from quarries outside Rome, quarries once used by Brunelleschi and Michelangelo and Bernini—could be yours.

Demand for houses skyrocketed. Suddenly everyone wanted to buy a house. Suddenly the American right to homeownership was powerfully recalled, and you were not quite American, not quite up there with the prospering class if, like Theodor and I, you rented. Cheap mortgages made expensive houses cheap, and demand kept the prices going up, up, up. Supply and demand—supply low, demand high—the only equation that means anything on the Street.

So the fourth road comes into play, the need for capital—the money to be loaned to finance all these dreams. Where did it come from? It came from those investors in China and France and Germany and Waco. Here the roads begin to intersect, an elaborate freeway with exit ramps and on-ramps and cloverleafs. And there you have it: home values rose, homeowners tapped into their newfound wealth, squeezing every last drop of value from their houses. Houses became ATM machines, allowing us the means to fund our desires. Appliances became fancier, trips more exotic, children more numerous—three was the new two, four the new three, credit the new savings. In 2004, when I went to Wall Street, this was the party I joined.

I lied to Theodor those first weeks at B&B. I told him I was doing research for a story I wanted to write, that I'd be leaving the apartment early every morning for a few weeks, that he couldn't ask me about it. "Mysterious," he said with a big, sincere smile. "A story? About what? You don't write stories." It was Saturday and we were making pancakes for the girls. Behind me was the old life, worn and comfortable and familiar. In front of me was Monday, hard, unfathomable, exhilarating.

"No questions," I said. He continued smiling, his mind filling with relief, I could tell. His smile recalled the old days, the woman I no longer was. He had always been happy when I went from not writing to writing—as if it justified some truth for him about the creative process, about us. In the past, the smile, the dimples, the knowledge that sat on his lips, had been reassuring, a sign that I'd made it back. Now, however, the smile annoyed me. I was tired of where we existed, the soft hope that things wouldn't always be this way. You see, I could no longer equate tomorrow with hope, tomorrow bringing it as surely as a tide brings water. But I did not say anything, of course.

Gwen licked at the pancake batter, cocking her left eyebrow as she could do—double-jointed eyebrows, she liked to say to Ruby, lording the talent (and the drama of the gesture) over her. She knew I was lying, but she wasn't old enough to call me on it. I remember being very present in that moment, the way I could be before a big trip to some distant shore—admiring and appreciating all that I would leave behind, as if I might never return. Theodor poured the batter onto the skillet and Gwyneth stood ready with her spatula. Would I come back to this? Would I fail, fall? Would Theodor, once he knew, have me back? I also felt exhilarated and sullied, the way I imagined an adulterer must feel. What if Win was right and I did succeed? What would it be like to earn, unabashedly, so much money? I thought again of the trading floor, the energy I felt, the buzz and hum of the room as it generated so much cash (or, I should say, revenue), here, the epicenter of finance—rooms like this all around the globe, working in sync to create the world's financial rhythms—never sleeping as time crept from time zone to time zone. Lines formed at the corners of Theodor's eyes. He looked tired. I wondered if he too was aware of the toll.

"You haven't written a story in years," Theodor said. "I'm glad. It always comes again." The *it* was ours. No identifier necessary. The sum of who we were. Gwen continued to haunt me with her penetrating eyes.

The party I joined in 2004 was in the secondary market, the market that was making all the capital to finance homeowners in the North, the East, the West and the South while also generating wealth for large companies and countries alike. It was going full throttle. It was around 11 P.M. and the room was packed, champagne flowing, the supply seemingly endless, everyone high, friendly, giddy, welcoming. Interest rates continued their fall. Pop went the champagne cork, a nice loud burst. The ten-year U.S. Treasury yield dropped below 4 percent. The rate environment added to that confluence of favorable circumstances. Champagne glasses were being stacked, one on top of the other, as high as daring would take them. Up, up, up. Employment peaked. The American Dream Down Payment Initiative Act had been signed into law in December 2003, providing $200 million per year to help people with their down payments and closing costs, fueling the furnace. A stream of tiny golden bubbles poured into the top glass and flowed over the rim, spilling into the glass beneath it—a champagne fountain, cascading from glass to glass. The Zero Down Payment Initiative was also signed into law, allowing the Federal Housing Administration to insure mortgages with no down payment, thus generating more than 250,000 new homeowners that year—more fuel. Twenty-five percent of borrowers put no money down. The subprime volume of $2 billion rose 80 percent.

Have you ever arrived late to a party, a really grand party at which everyone is having a fantastic time, completely wired, knowing that they are on to something? Everyone filled with so much good to say, exuberant with enthusiasm? You want to chug down a few drinks just to catch up.

Monday morning I arrived, swept up quietly and certainly

to the action on the thirty-third floor of B&B and into Win's office, where I sank myself into the mathematical complexities of the mortgage market. For a few weeks I read and listened and learned and observed, watching as my life shifted from the solitary orbit of the writer to the frenetic social universe of the bond trader. I fell into the role like an actress into her part, easily and with confidence. I was a good mimic, wanted to do as they did. I rose at 5 A.M., went for a long jog, donned suits (which I had fun buying), applied makeup, blew out my hair, was in the office by 7 (having kissed my sleeping husband and girls before leaving), paid attention at the 7:30 meeting, shadowed Win while he hovered over his traders at meetings and in his office, gulped down lunch (bought by a lowly—I soon learned the hierarchy—analyst at the command of a trader: "You fly, I buy"), felt the rise at noon, the wind-down at 4, out for drinks with clients at 5:30, home to relieve April, kiss the girls good night, fall into bed by 10, overwhelmed, exhausted, ready to start the whole thing over the next day.

It took a week to settle into this routine, and there was no time to think about the writing I'd left behind, no time to think about the novel I had out there that was just beginning to get reviewed. I was on that trip to a foreign land, learning (or trying to learn) its language, a total-immersion course, English a sister language, similar but largely different in the way that Italian and Spanish are. Acronyms were cast about with mind-boggling frequency: MBS and TBA and CMOs and CMBSs and ABS and Alt-A. And in the division of the mortgage universe that Win wanted me to focus on, there were Fannies and Freddies and Freddie golds and Ginnies and jumbos, "dwarfs" and "nuggets" and "midgets" and "gnomes." Trades were "done" and "subject." You "hit" the bid and "lifted" the offer. "Axed" indicated something you wanted to do.

I loved the terms even if I didn't understand them. It made the world real to me, just as I loved to know how to ask directions or indicate needs and desires in foreign languages while visiting other countries. Referred to as the "mortgage universe," it was indeed vast, not a country but a cosmos with its galaxies, planets and stars. In this universe there were basis points and wider/widening/tighter/tightening, outperforming and underperforming. There were quotes. There was a mid and a bid. People were making markets. People locked markets. People were "going fishing." People were "on the follow" and "throwing the flag." Deals were rinsed, killed, crushed and spun.

I had my own spinning to do. By the end of the week I had called the university, told them I needed to take a leave of absence. That spring I was scheduled to teach only one class anyway. The department could find an adjunct easily. I lied to them, said I was having a private crisis. How much of a lie was it really? A thirty-eight-year-old woman, a writer no less, with little financial experience, goes to Wall Street to become a bond trader; I'd say that qualifies as a personal crisis, a full-blown midlife meltdown.

Though I told the university, I had not told Theodor. "You're working hard," he said. "I am," I said. "Are you having an affair?" he asked. "That question's completely out of character for you," I snapped. I wouldn't dignify it with an answer, but I could feel my cheeks flush in our darkened bedroom. "You're running," he said, as though to explain himself, a signifier of infidelity. "I'm approaching forty," I answered. "It's a new year. A New Year's resolution." We were quiet for a bit, the night sounds of New York City drifting through the closed windows. I wanted to tell him then, but I was afraid. Afraid that he'd be mad that I'd lied, afraid he'd lose respect for me, see the truth of whom he'd married. I remembered the night we first met: he was a thief and I a rich girl. How I'd enjoyed that notion, a rich girl being swept into the arms of a bohemian: it formed our story's originating mythology.

Now I was in love with my proximity to so much money, the staggering sums, small trades in the millions, medium trades in the low billions. "Research?" he asked. "Research," I answered flatly. "Sullivan's coming to town," he said. "Who?" I asked, my eyes closing, sleep pulling me. "From Fort Worth. To see the chalice. I'm ready to show it. He's coming for business." He spoke so casually. Two weeks before, I would have jumped up, turned on the lights, asked a thousand questions, all pointing to when we might see the money to pay that stack of bills. Oh yes, and to congratulate him. I could see that woman, the former me, doing just that, and I did not like her, her desperation, how exhausting it all had been. I would have cared urgently. I tried to care now, in a new way. I did care. I cared enormously. Warren William Sullivan, with his cowboy hat and boots and bolo tie and the money to wipe out our debt and pay the girls' tuition for a year simply by paying Theodor the commission.

Yet I couldn't muster the truthful enthusiasm, and I knew Theodor would know. But I didn't care about that either, about explaining myself, justifying myself. I had mortgages on the brain—all that I'd read, that I wanted to read—so much of it made no sense. Could I do this? How could money be loaned to people who couldn't easily pay it back? That would be like loaning money to Theodor and me. Who in her right mind would do it? *I* wouldn't loan money to me. This was the aspect of the party's wired excitement that I was trying to understand. And why would an investment bank find this mortgage, and mortgages like it, an attractive investment, not to mention entire countries: Iceland, China? The stuff I'd read didn't add up. Why would people want loans that would double their debt within a few years? Didn't they know how fast those years pass? Didn't history inform them that markets change, that up is not the only direction? Why would the government encourage this? Care?

Lying in bed beside Theodor, I was the lie leading her double life. On the machine was a message from my editor, another from my agent. Isn't that how it happens when you travel? A week can seem like a lifetime and everything you've left behind so remote and irrelevant when confronted by the present moment? I recalled a trip to Morocco to write an article for a magazine. Two in the morning beneath a Berber tent on a *riad* rooftop in the Marrakech medina, a North African breeze blowing over me and a fingernail moon suspended in the sky like some kind of punctuation mark. A man on the street below played a song on a horn, a beautiful piercing song, for a long time, a call to wake the people, to remind them to eat before sunrise, as it was Ramadan. I had felt so far away, so happily far away from the girls, from Theodor, the demands. They existed in a different lifetime, though I'd been gone only three days.

I kissed Theodor and told him I wanted to see the chalice as soon as he'd show it to me, and did he want me to come when Sullivan visited the studio?

Then he asked, "Where have you gone?"

Here: to the mortgage universe. I was being trained to trade pass-throughs, agency fixed-rate mortgage-backed securities. This was where Win had started; it was one of his specialties, the universe of Ginnies, Fannies, Freddies—conforming mortgages backed, or quasi-backed, by the government. He was clear and firm in his expectations. Immediately I learned to run a roll; within a month I was writing a daily commentary detailing flows, performance, the desk views on the market:

> The mortgage basis traded notably well into yesterday's uptrade, amid heavy two-way flows. While we did see some profit taking from domestic real money ahead of payrolls (in 5.5s and 6s), there doesn't feel to be a lot of basis longs left in the market. Despite the largest origination day in weeks ($1.25bln, mostly 6s), flows on the day were heavily skewed toward the buy side, easily absorbing the supply.

A far cry from the narrative concerns of *Generation of Fire,* which, by the way, received a daily in the paper three weeks into my stint on the Street. A glowing, if mixed, review with a few excellent pull-quotes, a review that would have made my year, the editor and the agent congratulating me, a call from Lily Starr and Will Chapman, my mother and father, my brother, explanations of a bad pub date for the delay in attention (too much competition with the heavy hitters pre-Christmas), followed by a well-placed Sunday review, questions about what was next, what I was working on, and over me the settling of a tremendous relief, not because of the reviews but because of the new freedom from the urgent concern: my life, my welfare depending on those forces that were designed by the Great Unknown. Radalpieno had been right. I was free. I did not want to do that anymore—pull nothing from nothing to make nothing:

> As expected, another 3bp rally in the 30y mortgage rate caused some heartburn among convexity accounts, and we did see some risk reduction late in the day after the month-end uptrade held . . .

If the days were defined by numbers, yield curves and the rest, the evenings were defined by the clients: middle-aged men with wives, families, expensive homes, daughters who longed for front-row seats to the Hilary Duff concert. The conversations, over drinks, were decidedly not about the numbers. Rather, they were designed to build trust and adoration. You went to the bars for that post-work wind-down so that your personality could shine. "We're all selling the same bacon," Win said to me in his office, the light fading with the day. "I thought we were selling used cars," I said. He smiled. "Today it's bacon we're selling, and it's all the same. Nothing fancy. Nothing organic. Just the same old bacon with nitrites that tastes good, that's consistent. We're all selling it. So why are they going to buy mine instead of yours? Here's why: I talk about the kids, ask how they're doing in school, how's Marjorie, the new addition, the trip to Aspen, did they get into Cache? I pull some strings, get the kids front-row seats to Hilary Duff. And why do I know about her? I'm a single man, interested in women and money and planes. I know about her because I need to know about her, just as I need to know about munis, LIBOR, midgets. Sure, there's some idea generation, market discussion, flow of information. But they also come to me for the bacon because they like me, because I *know*. That's all I've got on the other guy. I've earned their trust, so they believe what I tell them."

He beamed, impeccably dressed but not in a showy way—someone who has a good sense of what works on his stout frame. Sometimes he could seem as elusive as Miss Lane, a product of these walls with no outside life. Sure I knew about the planes, the quick trip to the Chapmans', his childhood, his firecrackers. But in his office there was nothing that indicated a world beyond this one. Women never rang for him or e-mailed him—that he'd let on. There were no calls from Mom, pictures of home. His definition was found in what B&B had made of him.

"On top of all the math, I also have to be well liked?" I asked. "I've got to sell myself?"

"Yep," he said.

"Sounds a lot like publishing."

And drawing the analogy to publishing was what helped me make sense of how this empire worked. The schmoozing between trader and client was similar to what happened between agent and publisher when the agent tried to peddle her authors. The trader was the agent making deals between the author (the originator) and the publisher (the investor). And it seemed that Win, as the strategist, could do this: take a bunch of aspiring writers earning nothing (subprime mortgages), pool them, put them in a nifty package with bells and whistles, offer it up for trade and make money—loads and loads of it.

Win loved what he did. You could see it in the lightness of his step, in the way he talked about the market, the strategies he schemed, making sure his boys were giving him the most they could. As the head of fixed income, he no longer traded, and he missed it (and if he worried about anything, it was that he'd lose his trading touch), and so every one of the traders was his surrogate. He wanted them to perform as he'd performed. In those first weeks I watched as he got it out of them, quietly asking questions about why they did what they did. His calm voice elicited trust, the words coming out of the corner of his mouth, the mumble that was not sloppy but more of a fluency, the speech of someone completely comfortable with the complexities of his language.

In those first days he also seemed to take great joy in my presence, though he felt no need to explain me to anyone. He seemed to like the speculation. He seemed to relish the unease created by me, the pea beneath the many mattresses. *Who is that chick?* The not knowing psyched them out, and Win understood this, understood how he was playing them, wanted to see how they'd play the situation, if only to see if his hunches about them were correct. And I understood my role without being told. He wanted to see how long it would take the boys to boldly ask. A game of dare, really. Who'd break first? I revealed little. It would have been easy for someone to Google me, of course, but that wouldn't have told them why I was here. Instead, I quietly observed, absorbed, the way I'd done as a writer. In the first days I wasn't on the floor much, so my first impression remained: the floor a well-structured organism, all the parts working together to create the business, its skill and efficiency.

Occasionally Win let me know that the boys were all in now; they'd all placed their bets. Snake was the most direct, cornering me on the way to the bathroom, out of sight of the floor and all the traders, who had me under their microscopes. He laid it out: "He's brought you here because you know nothing and he wants to prove he can teach you everything." Snake, the handsome man with dark skin, tall, slender, a swimmer's taut frame that you could see defined beneath his well-tailored shirts, didn't need a response from me. His expression indicated he had a lot riding on this, but he knew he was right, so he didn't solicit confirmation. "I've raised the ante," he continued. "Now they have to tell me what you do and when he's placing you on the desk." He slipped away, turning his head back to me to add, "I'm rooting for you. If you need any help . . ." He took a step forward, paused, pivoted, came back to me. He leaned toward my ear and whispered, his breath warm and sweet, "You know this intuitively but know it now consciously. It's all about the bet here. We're betting on every level. We're hard-wired for it, for the win."

I realized it then, just as Snake wanted me to: the bet that Win and Radalpieno were making of me was no different from all the other bets. It was the foundation of the game, describing the casino that this business is. Math is important, but the nuance of bluff, of poker face, is just as crucial. Here, I was a pebble thrown into a pond, and the rings of water reverberating from me only echoed all the other bets being tossed around. Understanding this was crucial. I was a bet for Radalpieno and Win that was turned into a bet for the boys, all of whom were caught up in the action and volatility of the homeowners' gamble—betting that interest rates would keep coming down and housing prices would keep going up, on easy money that would finance dreams (their own and those of others), placing their confidence in the wisdom of Wall Street. And the Street was betting on the fact that homeowners would behave this way, so that by 2005 the headlines in the paper would read: "The Trillion-Dollar Bet: Homeowners Take Risks in the Bid for Lower Mortgage Payments."

This is what I understood in that encounter with Snake: none of this had anything to do with true value. Rather, it amounted to the market's value of it—"what the market will bear," said Win. For that reason it was silly to try to make sense of the flourishing of nonsensical lending practices. They did not matter, just as the outcome of a novelist turned trader did not matter. As long as the market valued the funny mortgages, they were worth a lot; as long as Win valued me, I was worth a lot. Snake understood this measurement and he passed it along to me: the only big tip I ever got from another trader (aside from Win). Snake was like that, confident enough to be generous in this very entrepreneurial world in which people are not going to help you make money because they're too busy making money themselves. And making money at another's expense is the name of the game. Snake handed me the formula: bets and their market worth, not their true worth. Win had quietly, surreptitiously made a market of me, and I was being traded on the basis of his value from traders to analysts to salespeople. And he'd puppeteered the whole show without uttering a word.

By the time I was seated at the desk, had taken the Series 63 and Series 7 exams (which you need to pass in order to get licensed by the National Association of Securities Dealers so that you can trade—exams that test your knowledge of technical stuff, on settlements, equities, munis and ethics), New York had gone wild on its own bets. (Remember the party?) Firms all over the city, the country, the world, were expanding, multiplying, hiring at an astonishing rate, betting on the money to be made in the housing market. Radalpieno bet that Snake would ignite the already well-ignited subprime, so he wanted to move him to head that desk. Snake refused. He was betting that turning down the chairman and chief executive officer of the company wouldn't matter, that it would prove his mettle: "I don't like what I smell over there."

And Snake was right. He knew his value and stayed put. Instead, to head up subprime Win brought in June Scarpetti from Silver Brothers, betting on her (one of only a handful of women on the Street to trade subprime, the daughter of a New York City policeman, raised in Canarsie, a stylish dresser with a penchant for speaking about her personal shopper) to outpace B&B's stellar record, allowing her to leverage (compounding exponentially both her risk and her reward) in a way the company had not allowed before. Maxi had lost all bets, one too many Model T's, so was out of a seat altogether. He went back to Chile and his racehorses, and I took his seat.

So this is how the desk looked by June 1, 2004: Snake, the boss, twenty-eight years old, on the Street for six years, former Stanford swimming champion, mathematical genius, boyfriend of a woman four years his senior, a trader too, and the talk of the town, not for her considerable talent as a currency trader but because she'd robbed the cradle; Tiger, with his sexy girlfriend who loved to send him photographs of his cat in cute positions (sipping milk from a baby's bottle and the like) and his fondness for exotic waters; Sam, a former lacrosse star, who, I discovered, was more of a renegade than a carbon copy of Tiger, whose parents (both artists) had steered him toward an artistic, bohemian life that he couldn't abide, and he'd let them down by going to Wall Street; Josh, with his FREE WINONA photo and a lot of talk about girls, always a new girl—"I'm shorting Lynette because, you know, there's a lot of overvalue here"; Gus, the Korean, whose intensity served to mask a shyness that he was right to try to disguise, since you could not be shy in this line of business; and me, out of the closet now, shadowing Snake more than Win for firsthand experience with trades, stepping in from time to time for small trades when Snake was too busy with big ones.

After six months I was successfully integrated, like a car merging from an on-ramp onto the main artery. I was in, part of the organism, no looking back, millions, billions being par for the course. But my feat was not accomplished by time alone. Rather, it was showing these people that I could do it, that I could be one of them. Over the six months, the façade of the floor had been lifted, like rolling back a sod field, exposing what's going on below all that grass—the worms and the slugs and the ants and the grubs and all the rest, busy with the routines of their lives and work, the routines that define them individually. To change the metaphor, it was a locker room down in the pit, everyone in various stages of undress, happily revealing his true self, doing that which men do in locker rooms: belching, farting, snapping towels, psyching each other out. That famous coach's line stood as the only truth: Winning isn't everything, it's the only thing.

Betting, at the core, was simply an expression of competition, and so, as Snake had promised, bets were everywhere. I had not quite known how competitive I was until I went to Wall Street. But I wanted to win at all costs and just as much as the other guy. In those first months, I entered every kind of competition you can imagine. It was the way to let off steam, training for the big leagues, the multibillion-dollar deals. I was in a water-tasting test. Twenty-to-one odds that I couldn't blindly taste-test and identify six of Tiger's bottled waters. I did. There were bets on how many home runs a player would hit in a season, on how fast one of us could run a mile, on who could eat Snake's mother's spicy curry without breaking a sweat, on who could dip his head deepest into the tub of melted ice that had held the day's supply of sodas—water that everyone's dirty hands had plunged into all morning long.

A hamburger-eating contest. This was the kind of thing that lurked beneath the surface of the incredible machine. The hamburger challenge had started a few years before I came to B&B. Earlier winners and losers had achieved almost mythic status. The task was to eat more than twenty hamburgers in an hour. A guy in EDM (emerging domestic markets) had eaten twenty-two. The next year a guy from Australia, a rugby star, a six-foot-four blindside flanker, took up the challenge. He ate six and then stopped because he didn't like the taste of the onions—a huge failure in the eyes of those who'd bet on him. "Onions? He gave up because of goddamned onions?" He moved on to Dallas, to work at a firm that handled private wealth; it was widely believed that the burger contest had done him in.

Such were the stories that circulated. There was an actual, bona fide yet unwritten reason for their existence. For the fact was that nothing prepared you for life on the trading floor. No degree however fancy, no amount of advanced training, no IQ test existed that could predict whether you would be any good at this stuff. The only way that Win had discovered to find talented people was, in essence, to cast a wide net. And then winnow. The way was wide, in other words, and I was proof of that to everyone here. And so, as part of that narrowing process, and for other reasons that had to do with teamwork and trust, I knew that if I was ever going to be allowed to make a serious bet on the market, I would one day have to pass through an office door, and behind that door would be a long table, and on that long table would be a stack of hamburgers, around which would be a group of guys grinning from ear to ear.

This is how it happened: A bunch of us from fixed income are at a Memorial Day party at the Boat Basin in Central Park, and someone mentions the hamburger-eating contest, and June Scarpetti starts telling everyone about the time she ate an entire large pizza by herself. It's easy to see how someone falls into this behavior—none of us ever really wants to leave high school, I suppose. Tiny June Scarpetti, her dark hair bobbing at her shoulders, her blue eyes as sharp as a lizard's, a straight-A record and a degree in economics, a designer of prepayment equations and formulas that could beat any index—that was the hope anyway. She's wearing a chiffon dress with water lilies so numerous their image becomes splashes of color. She's young and intelligent, and before me she's boasting about how she was able to eat a whole large pizza.

"I gulped it down," she says. "Four big bites." She takes a sip of beer. Her cheeks are flushed. Everyone knows she's talking shit. "Four bites. Right," someone scoffs. The flowers fill the air with their fragrance. I think of writers at parties—a different breed. But I'm not bored. I'm long past that, though I still note the differences. I look around at this well-dressed crowd and there isn't a person who makes less than $300,000. "It's true," she says. "One large pizza, four bites," she says. The conversation turns to tales of strange things that people have eaten, everyone knocking back drinks and talking about dog in China and cat in India and snake in the swamps and raccoon and bats. It's a warm afternoon. Families out with their kids, drifting about in the boats. Scarpetti has reached a balmy sort of drunkenness, her guard down. Sober, she'd have just let go of the Large Pizza Incident, but now she's insistent and won't let it rest. "You don't know," she says. "A large pizza, that's really something else."

"June," I say, pointedly using her first name. She's about ten years younger than I, but her authority is greater. She's been in the business six years already, makes well over a million a year. She can demand to be called whatever she pleases, and she likes being called Scarpetti. I break a tacit rule in saying her name, but I go ahead and say it again. She's making me nervous. "June," I say, "you're going to talk yourself into something." She looks at me and her face shimmers for a second between an expression of a guileless younger sister in search of a confidante and the mask she usually wears—"the Man-Eater," the boys call her. She wraps her arm around me. "A contest?" she says with a grin.

As if on cue, Snake steps forward, appearing from nowhere, relaxed in jeans but with a white-collared, ironed shirt, tucked in and buttoned at the wrists the way he likes, as if he's hiding some problem with his arms, covering them up. He's going to call for an ante. That's clear in the mischievous smile circling in his eyes. "You know what would be really interesting?" he says, loud enough so a few people can hear, and they stop what they're doing to pay attention to him. "A head-to-head competition: trader versus trader, woman versus woman, Writer Chick versus Man-Eater."

"Ooooooh!" The tables shake and the silverware clatters. More people gather around, attracted by the ruckus. "No way," I say. "I'm out. No bid. Sold to you." But it's no use.

By the time I get to work the next day, there are already a few thousand dollars riding on the bet. There's an enthusiasm to see me that I've not experienced before at B&B. It makes me hungry, makes me want to take on the challenge, makes me game, brings out the scrappy side of me I'd forgotten I'd had, lost somewhere back in high school. "Put your money on me, I'm your man," I say. All afternoon I watch these kids, looking over at me, joshing with Scarpetti, who then pops her head into my row: "You know, fuck these guys, right? Talk about a bunch of cases of arrested development, right? So listen. Just ignore them. They're so ADD, most of them have forgotten about it already."

"You're wrong there, June."

All afternoon I watched these kids. In a different decade they would have become doctors, lawyers, history professors, journalists. I felt an affinity with them. I was no different, just late. I spent the afternoon telling everyone "I'm the man."

On the big day, I take the morning off to prepare. I tell them I'm going to be late for work, a doctor's appointment. (I never use the kids as an excuse.) No problem. They let me. The night before, I eat pasta for dinner, run six miles in the morning, make myself strong and hungry. I go to the office around noon and am met by Scarpetti, who tells me she's taken the morning off too. She's wearing sweat pants and jacket and looks real comfy. I hadn't thought of that. I'm in a suit.

"Ready?" she asks, her blue eyes confident, noting my suit. In the exercise clothes, her black hair pulled back in a ponytail, she looks impossibly young. I smile. "Set," I say. "Been exercising?" she asks. She's moving from foot to foot like a tennis player getting ready to receive a serve. "In fact" is all I say.

There's lots of commotion. We're both led to a conference

room. I think of the Australian flanker, exiled to Dallas because he didn't like the onions. The hamburgers start to arrive, all neatly wrapped like little presents, oozing with onions and pickles. A bottle of ketchup stands before me and Scarpetti. We're seated at a huge oval table facing each other, each with her own stack of hamburgers. Scarpetti is dwarfed by the chair—tiny pert young Man-Eater. Everyone stands around the table, thirty or forty people, mostly male, squeezing themselves into the room, spilling out the doorway. Only one thing matters now, and that's the hamburgers. Snake takes off his watch and places it in the center of the table, identifying himself as the official timekeeper. I shut him out, set my focus on the stack of burgers. "Ready, set"—Snake speaks with a loud, authoritative voice, one that could be commanding a much more deserving event—"go!"

And we're off. The first few are surprisingly delicious. I'm eating one while unwrapping the next, like a teenage date fumbling for a bra strap. I keep count, keep on task. Scarpetti is somewhere in the middle distance, her cheeks like Dizzy Gillespie's, stuffed with masticated burger meat. My kids flash across my mind. What would they think of their mother? I shut them out. Five, six, seven, eight. The count rises, and I realize I've fallen behind the Man-Eater. The score is constantly being announced. I slug a big burger bolus down my throat and try to play catch-up. Nine, ten, eleven. The spectators carry the latest updates to those at their desks. There's clapping. Ketchup is dripping down my chin, down my suit. I keep squirting it on the burgers to lubricate their journey. I could almost tear off the suit. Who gives a shit? This is primal. The burger primeval. Man-Eater is a punk. I've given birth. I know what a body is capable of, and this little shit from Canarsie with her fancy wardrobe is going to have her burger-swallowing butt stomped.

Now I've eased up alongside Scarpetti in the burger count, and everyone cheers. They love a good race. Win announces the progress over the hoot and holler (the loudspeaker) so that people in the outer regions are updated. Somewhere Radalpieno is smiling. Miss Lane is ringing the bell. I keep stuffing the hamburgers in, giving the boys a good show. The wrappers pile up, the burgers fly. Fifteen, sixteen, seventeen. The entire audience watches as I masticate more. Little June Scarpetti just stuffing her mouth. This is what they want, she seems to say. Okay, then. Her pert little ponytail flopping as she crams it all in.

I must shut her out. But I can't. I watch her, fast, formidable, efficient. She's a different breed. She's surrounded by people her age, raised to be all right with this, to look beyond this. People are chanting my name. "India, India." Lumps in my throat, I force the hamburgers down. Hearing my name drives me forward. Okay. I understand now. This is how much I want this. You all get to watch the spectacle, standing there in your pressed trousers as I stuff my mouth. Okay. I understand. Food spilling, mustard on chin, bun stuck to lips.

Then silence as, softly, melodically, Beethoven's *Für Elise* comes from Snake's 18-karat white-gold Patek Philippe watch. "How many for New Chick?" By hour's end I've eaten twenty-one. Man-Eater has eaten only nineteen. The cheer is like a rifle shot in the small conference room. I have won. "Booya, Little Miss Hamburger!" someone shouts. "Fuckin' deadly," someone else says.

Silence again, and suddenly I realize that there is no way around what I'm about to do. I feel it coming on and decide to use it, that there is only one way to punctuate this moment in a manner that is appropriate, that encapsulates it, that encompasses it, surrounds it and triumphs over it on its own terms. No way but through, the Buddha says. And so I stand up as Win enters the room, and I open my mouth as if to speak, but it's not quite a speech I give, though it is, in its own way. Out of my mouth comes an extended belch as I've heard it done a few times on the trading floor after closing, a long, virtuosic and obviously enjoyable low-down eructation, rising in a crescendo like a foulmouthed aria and tied up at the end in a crisp little flourish, eyes closed, finger pointing to the ceiling like Celine Dion hitting a high note, as if to say, You boys don't know who you're dealing with here, do you?

The second roar of approval is different from the first. It is a firm, unguarded and deal-sealing round that rolls through the room and spills out into the office in high-fives and hand slaps and shoulder bounces, with me somewhere in their happy and satisfied midst. I have surprised and bested them (this is one for the history books, epic B&B), and what they love above all else is to be bested in this way. I have outgrossed them all. I am welcome. I am one of them.

I can go home and tell the kids and Theodor I had a good day at work, but there is no way to tell them exactly what I have tried—and failed—to tell you just now. And the fact that I cannot tell you, that nobody can tell you—that you had to be there—is the very purpose of all such ceremony. There is no word for it in this world. You know it when you feel it. You can only point to it, in all its riotous excess, and hope someone understands. There it was, and I was now welcomed into it, and had earned something beyond reckoning. Even with all those hamburgers in my belly, I felt light. I was walking on clouds. Snake looked at me and beamed. "Congratulations," he said. "Your first big win on the Street."

Then, so no one else could hear, June Scarpetti whispered, "That—the belch—a nice touch. This, I hate to say, could make your career."

Thirteen

BUT LET'S GO BACK to the beginning, the day I told Theodor. I'd still wanted to keep the secret, worried that I'd betrayed the code of the artist to stay broke (to roam the earth untethered, unsponsored, free), that I'd become a sellout like so many other of my artist friends, their dreams put on hold, "temporarily" at first, just until they caught up, paid off some debt, got things "squared away" by wandering off into commercial real estate, for instance. Time passed and you saw them at lunch, say, and they seemed to talk more about commercial real estate than you ever thought possible, or more about their children than you remembered, or about where they spent their last vacation. They'd punched the ticket by which one life gets jettisoned to make room for another, perhaps more adult, life. So the shackles fell, light as page-flutter.

And in all the excitement of *la vita nuova,* with its seductive strangeness, I too seemed to have shed the old life. But for me there was no buyer's remorse. I'd somehow jumped the track from the hard-pressed life of the artist to its opposite number, the blessed class amassing wealth, and I discovered that everything I'd ever thought about the world of finance was of a fantastically low order of caricature. The new life was wilder, more potent and more bizarre than anything I could have imagined. I found nothing wanting. As the *über*-boys in my department put it, I was good with that.

At least until the time approached, as it would, when I had to tell Theodor the truth. It would be like telling him I was having an affair. That I was leaving him for another man. Another man who made lots of money. And though I was not having an affair, and I loved him more than anything—and he would know this—he'd look at me and what I'd become and say the truth, which happened to be the worst thing anyone could say to someone who had built her life around the written word, which was that I'd become a living, breathing cliché. And he was very much *not* good with that. So I thought about telling Theodor a partial truth, that I'd taken Win up on the offer because I'd decided it might make a good short story, a novel even. The thought of lying, though, had made the guilt multiply, and now it seemed easier to say nothing, to find ways to justify myself, which I did by believing I was only trying this on, that I could always turn back, that it would be better to know for myself if this was what I really wanted before confessing to Theodor. Mostly, I simply tried not to think about it.

The day started at 5 A.M. with a jog in Riverside Park. Very cold. A thick layer of ice blanketed the Hudson, chopped and cracked into brilliant fissures and floes, the new sun casting sharp light into a quiet hour in which, as a lone runner approached from the other direction, it was hard not to at least nod in recognition of the brief, chummy solidarity of witnessing the world as it was just then—forever lost to all those who had yet to press the snooze button on their alarms.

My running partner, Isabella Power, was another mother from the girls' school, a stay-at-home mom with four children who claimed her only free time was early in the morning. My Ruby was in the same class with her second child. Isabella had once seen me in jogging shorts at the school and had been pursuing me as a running partner ever since. You couldn't run in Riverside Park without a partner at this time of day, even though, with the city's resurgence, crime was down and the parks were cleaned up. When we'd first moved into the neighborhood, the park's paths were strewn with syringes and used condoms and crack vials, but that was long before Isabella's time. She was one of the younger mothers, just turned thirty-two; she'd had her first child when she was twenty-five. Her newest was five months old, at home, asleep, with the live-in nanny awaiting his wake-up cry. Isabella had heard the stories of what the neighborhood was like, and she wouldn't set foot in the park without a chaperone, so when I started running again as part of my training for the new life, I took her up on her long-standing offer.

I loved the city at this hour, hearing only the sounds of our feet thumping the pavement, our breath a cloud of vapor, the world still dark in the west, the in-between of the light. There was nothing finer than this moment, but it all seemed lost to Isabella, who loved to chat. She'd just bought a mansion on Riverside Drive, a former school that had wanted to take advantage of the soaring real estate values and the wealthiest New Yorkers' need for more square footage. When she didn't talk about The House, she talked about The School or The Money they'd donated, or she complained about The Tuition—having four children, sending three of them to private schools in New York, was a unique way of driving a point home, it seemed. As were the dinner parties and fundraisers and art openings, the attendant guest lists—a Who's Who of The School's society. It was all here, the ease with which the moneyed class ascended to an unstated yet higher empyrean of parental citizenship. Other mothers regarded Isabella deferentially, made playdates for their children, their laughter echoing across the city's playgrounds. Isabella's husband, a banker, was not the lingering type at school or anywhere else. He shook hands and generally made quick work of the rituals involving the children—the morning drop-off, attendance at various performances—nodding to fellow dads as if addressing a phalanx of junior officers.

This morning, on our jog together, Isabella was carrying on about an enormous gilded mirror surrounded by crystal that was being delivered in the afternoon. The crate wouldn't fit through the front door. "Can you believe that?" she said, affronted. "They're going to have to uncrate it on the street. It's going to take three big men, and the mirror simply can't touch the ground. The crystal is antique Baccarat, mouth-blown. It cannot touch the ground."

I enjoyed listening to these concerns; they were peaceful in a way, guileless. There was nothing sad or woeful about what preoccupied her. It was like flipping through a decorating magazine—safe and filled with the stories of all the small complications one needed to attend to in the world of home interiors. The other day she told me about a pair of oil portraits that an East Side friend of hers had had commissioned—a portrait of herself and her husband in evening attire to hang in their library, Isabella's friend in a black dress with a plunging neckline. "Very *Madame X*," she'd whispered, not daring to say it out loud even though we were running. The portraitist was the renowned Sasha McDermott, grandson of a well-known Scottish cubist I'd never heard of but assumed I should have. "McDermott has paintings in all the major museums around the world." Indeed, his services had been auctioned off that November evening at the Met, I recalled. "Husband-wife portraits are the rage."

If anything resembling tragedy had ever struck Isabella, it was part of a past that may have occasionally returned, the way memory does, and moved her in her most quiet and private hour—which, need I add, did not include the hour that we jogged together. But for the most part such things had been neatly catalogued and packed off. So she carried on about the mirror. The men were going to have to remove it from the crate and carry it into the house and hang it immediately. "If it's ruined . . ." She paused, allowing the consequences to surround us as our feet thumped the ground. "It was just absurd to spend so much," she said.

"How much?" I asked.

"Oh, India!" She laughed. "You *are* direct."

But she wouldn't tell me. It was unsavory to speak of price tags. She picked up her pace as if to run away from the question, tucking loose strands of hair behind her ears. Isabella had strawberry curls, full cheeks, ribbon lips, a well-defined jaw line. She'd confessed to me on our first run that she'd been eager to know me better because she too wanted to be a writer, had set up an office on the top floor of The House, sliding glass doors leading to a terrace (landscaped by a plant sculptor) with a river view and a chaise with a blanket so that she could lie there to read even on cold days. "Like Hans Castorp," she'd said, "at his sanatorium." She was an educated woman, had been working on a Ph.D. in comparative literature when her first baby arrived—though that feat too seemed neatly shelved.

I wondered what she'd make of me if I told her I had left writing, that I was preoccupied by very different concerns these days. For example, I was certain that already I could explain to her the nuances of her mortgage, chart the arc it would follow across its lifetime. But she would not have cared. One of her primary luxuries was that she did not need to care. She did not know what kind of banking her husband did. "I won't pretend to explain," she'd said. "Something to do with bonds, but really I'm not quite sure what he does."

We ran past the Boat Basin to the pier at 72nd Street and then back to the tennis courts at 120th Street, finishing with a race up the steps out of the park. Some days she'd win; some days I'd win. Today I won. I left her in front of her house and walked briskly to my apartment, showered, dressed and primped and was out the door by 6:45, in the office by 7:10. I swiped the door with my ID badge and walked into the pit, now humming with activity.

Friday, January 16: I'd been at B&B exactly two weeks. The boys had made their bets, each of which in its own way groping for the truth about who or what I was: I was a journalist, perhaps a producer at *Dateline* or *Extra,* or a reporter from *Newsday,* here to observe and develop a story; I was a Method actress preparing for a big Hollywood role; I was an intern; I was a girlfriend to whom Win owed a big favor; I was a distant relative's daughter, an artist, a chef, a heroin addict, a sorry soul whom Win wanted to help; I was never going to be seated on a desk; I'd be seated within six months; I'd be seated in a year, two months, five months. There was real money riding on me, all told the various bets adding up to $4,500. In those first weeks I felt a bit like a gyroscope: just a tap would send me into a completely different orbit.

Win's strategy of saying nothing helped me, as I'm sure he knew it would, to learn without pressure—freed me to absorb in my own natural way, without interference, while preserving me as his to shape and design. Some days I felt like a beginner, the woman that I was, learning a whole new trade. Other days I felt like the old me, a writer, a spy in their country, noting all the ridiculousness of the place: the gargantuan telephones with glowing blue screens and forty lines, all programmed to connect, with one press of a button, to clients; the recourse to male anatomy as a qualitative descriptor—to be "hung like a horse" meant you were a stud trader, someone to be reckoned with, unless you were, sadly, "hung like a field mouse"; the use of sports and military exemplars—Vince Lombardi or George Patton, whose words became company slogans. *Pressure makes diamonds. Perpetual peace is a futile dream. No bastard ever won a war by dying for his country; he won it by making the other poor dumb bastard die for his country.*

Neither horse nor field mouse, I searched for a position of advantage. I liked the notion of myself as a spy, an outsider. Being a spy might give me perspective, though I had no idea how perspective would serve me or what it added up to. When I told Win that so much of what I was reading in the papers and online made no sense, he said that it didn't need to make sense. What had to make sense was valuing the bonds against the market's desire for them. His job was to think about strategy: how far to go, how deep, when to back out. "But it's interesting to me," he said, "that your primary concern is that all of this makes no sense."

I was sitting in Win's office, as I did in those early days, his door open to the trading floor. It seemed that for many days I'd been quietly nodding my head, understanding nothing but marshaling an alert, attentive look on my face. When I spoke, my own voice almost startled me.

"I don't understand why a huge pension fund would find a collection of risky mortgages a reliable investment." Did I have any idea what I was asking? Only in a graduate seminar sort of way. Not in a way that would count out there on the trading floor. A trader from currency was buying a gumball from the machine outside Win's office. Already I was coming to understand who sat where and did what. At best I possessed a knowledge of the firm's seating chart. The gumball kid's name was Jud. He looked in on us, smiled, popped the gumball in his mouth and went back to his seat. "Imagine," I continued, "if you're too leveraged, something's got to give, right?"

I was thinking of myself just then, how I'd been managing the bills for the past six months: borrowing on credit cards, elaborate schemes to buy time, ultimately leaving the bills in their stack beside the computer in our bedroom. Investors were interested in that debt of mine. I had a 0 percent credit card with $10,000 on it. If I kept up with the minimum payment, I wouldn't be charged interest for eighteen months. There was no balance transfer fee. As long as I paid it off on time, the credit card would make nothing on that loan. Even so, that debt had a lot of value to investors, because they assumed I'd make a mistake, miss a payment, that in the end I wouldn't be able to pay it off and the rates would rise drastically. But I intended to stay one step ahead of them, get another 0 percent loan from a different bank with no balance transfer fee and transfer the debt again. Sooner or later, they were betting, I'd get stuck. Hot potato. Something would happen, some life-changing force, and there I'd be exposed. The music would stop and I'd be left holding the potato. They were betting on the actuarial likelihood that misfortune happened to all of us, that I'd be blindsided by some unexpected event that made me unable to pay. But was I any different from a bank? Why couldn't it be a bank that suddenly found itself without cash? Not just one bank but many banks, banks in the same boat as all those sad, wretched debtor people?

"You're right," Win said. "It's a guessing game and an assessing game and like any game it can get out of hand. It always does. And that's my job, to forecast when the game will get out of hand, and to be ready for it with a plan, but to take advantage in the meantime."

"Can I tell you what I see as we go along?"

"You better. Remember, you're the storyteller. But as you begin to trade you're going to become very specialized. You'll think micro instead of macro, deep instead of wide."

The day had sailed by already. The winter evening came on at 4 P.M. From the windows in Win's office I could see the city begin to light up like candles at a table, reminding me that I had to leave early to go to Williamsburg. Sullivan was coming for dinner to see the chalice.

"You're seeing Will and Emma tonight," Win said, more of a declaration, that way he had of wanting you to know he knew much, if not everything.

"That's right," I said. We'd invited them along with Sullivan's wife for dinner, a celebration of the chalice. I hadn't seen the

Chapmans since the fundraiser at the Met. Then a chill shivered through me. "Have you told Will?" I asked sharply. I imagined him making fun of me tonight in front of Theodor.

Win gave me a quizzical look, studying me. "What are you worried about?"

"Am I worried?"

"You tell me." He paused, then said, "Ah-ha!"

I didn't say anything.

He persisted. "You haven't told the husband." This Win said with a devilish flourish. He loved every moment of this. He spoke as if referring to that other sort of scandal, referring to Theodor as "the husband," never by name. "I've committed to you," he whispered. "I need you," he said, letting that phrase develop its own heft, "to commit to me." He smiled. This was his way. I'd become familiar with it: rakish when he was disappointed. He didn't get upset. He simply told you what needed to be done, directing you so that he elicited the best from you. Knowing he'd made his point, he added, "Have you heard Will's good news?" I looked at him, again taken aback. For some reason Isabella's mirror popped into my mind. I hoped getting it through the door and illuminated had been a success.

"I'm looking forward to hearing all about it tonight," I said, revealing nothing, for this was a test too. I could feel his eyes on me as I left, making my way to the elevator. I walked up Park to 57th, over to Fifth, into Bergdorf's, took the elevator to the seventh floor to buy napkins for the dinner party. Theodor had made napkin rings, gold wire entwined with elephants—their eyes jet beads. Will's news could be only one thing, and I was not yet immune to the writer's competitive, desperate nature—the sense that someone else's gain was necessarily your loss.

In Bergdorf's I wavered for a moment, caught between the old and the new life. I was firm in the knowledge that everything here was priced preposterously, but knew that here I would find something special for Theodor's dinner. I knew too that I'd never hear the end of it from him. Indeed, he'd get years of mileage out of the extravagance that I was about to perpetrate, but he and I both also knew that that was part of the gift, an acknowledgment of his first and original snap assessment of me so many years ago at our first meeting. "You're a rich girl," he'd said. He wasn't right then, but he wasn't exactly wrong either, and I was about to help him make his own case. I'd not yet received my first paycheck, but I would soon enough. So the truth was, I was still broke. The first of many big checks, twice the size of my university check, had yet to arrive.

Here among the preposterous things—they used to be called "notions"—lingering, pausing briefly to let fabrics fall between my fingers, I found myself in dinnerware. A woman approached me. I want to say she was middle-aged, but aren't we all? What I mean is, she managed to have assembled, "put together," out of the wreckage that life brings, a valiant sense of order, and one found it among the patterns of plates, whose names read like a catalogue of ships. She asked a few discreet questions, and I answered as if speaking in a confessional. She understood a few things about how the world works and guided me, gently but firmly, to a display table arrayed with napkins. She was a sensible woman. She would not let me wander off course into cookware or appliances or bedding and become dispirited. The napkin table was where I belonged, at least for now. She understood. She would hold my little secret. I felt moved by her discretion.

I chose what I liked best, what might look most appropriate rolled as tight as a fat Cuban cigar inside a golden wire, beneath the elephants of Theodor's opulent and clever design. A cream linen with the thinnest border of silk organza—so pretty and delicate they should have been in a lingerie drawer among the sachets. They were $60 each. I'd like to say I thought nothing of buying six of them, but I can't. The old life was still fresh within me. I felt the desire for them and the rapid beat of my heart.

"Aren't these sumptuous?" the saleslady whispered, taking the napkins from me and counting them gently, as though she were performing an arcane Japanese ceremony. "Is six all you need?"

"Yes, thank you," I croaked, and reached into my purse to pull out the old wallet into which Theodor had long ago stitched, in fine silk thread, ANARCHY. From my anarchy wallet I extracted a credit card. "That will be it for today." I smiled and she took my card.

"India." I heard my name. "Is that you, India?"

Behind me, with her fingers wrapped around a sterling silver fork with carved grapes tumbling down the shaft, was a newer, improved Lily Starr. I hadn't seen her since the fundraiser, and she looked even more becoming now in well-fitting jeans tucked into brown suede boots and a cashmere turtleneck, her hair short. From her wrist dangled a cerulean-blue alligator purse. I wasn't yet learned enough to know the designer. It was beautiful, though. Little silver feet glimmered from the corners of the bag's base. Money had been good to Lily, and she was not hesitating to flaunt the effect. A leather bomber jacket draped her other arm.

"You're in a suit," she gasped, chic girl giving my corporate get-up the once-over. "Why in the world?"

"Fancy running into you here," I said.

"A wedding present," she said, almost apologetically. "My niece has registered for this pattern." She held up the fork with the intricate grapes. "Can you believe this place? Nine-eighty a setting. She's marrying a banker," she added for explanation.

"Smart niece," I said.

"Right! What were *we* thinking?" she said, taking me in with her big infectious smile, knitting us together in camaraderie. I remembered her once saying, after her husband got his first teaching job following a prolonged stint of unemployment, that a salary made her want to have sex with him again. "Note to self," Lily Starr said with a wink into an imaginary tape recorder, "next time around, let him be a banker."

Lordy, she was trying to realign herself with me, with what she thought I still was, perhaps here with what she thought *she* still was, with what she had been before the best-selling publication of her book and the $5,000 invitations to give readings at colleges all over the country. ("I've no time left to write," she confessed.) The past: when there was nothing to lose, when all was driven by the white heat of the page, "the sexy theater of 8½ x 11," as one writer had called it, "the only game in town that ever matters," another had said, the place where one lived and died to make one's audacious mark on the world. Now she was the proud owner of a million-dollar bungalow in the Hamptons, I remembered. Then Lily noticed the suit again, and I could see it jar the nostalgic tableau.

"The suit?" she asked, screwing up her eyes.

"A disguise," I said.

"Who are you hiding from?" She raised her eyebrows and looked around the store, teasing me.

A mother and daughter sauntered by, the daughter apparently a bride-to-be, looking a little bored and tagging along with her mother to register for wedding gifts. They were trailed by a saleslady who held a pad and pen, taking notes as the mother listed the items they'd like: "We'll take two Buccellatis, one small, one large." She held up a wine glass for her daughter to peruse, cocked her head and pursed her lips as if to ask the daughter if she approved, a kind of "huh" look, a "would these do at $215 a stem" look. Before the daughter could respond, the mother announced they'd take a set each of sixteen—white wine, red wine, champagne and water.

"You know I've always wanted to conform, blend in," I said. I was caught, the second time in one day. She started giggling like a little girl who knows her friend's secret.

"Oh, India," she said. I knew what she was talking about. The revelation spread over her face, an understanding of who and what I'd become, a mixture of curiosity and triumph. I could have said a lot of things, but I didn't want to seem defensive, beaten. I knew I had to hang on a few more minutes.

"You went to the hedge fund guy?"

"Bonds," I reminded her.

"Oh yes, James Bond. I still don't know what a bond is. You tried explaining but it went in one ear, out the other."

The saleslady arrived with my package and the receipt for me to sign. Lily studied me. Lily the Shameless, we'd called her in grad school, the only short story writer we knew who had never actually read a short story. The girl with the perfect writer's name had spotted a target, a curiosity, an interesting subject, and now trained on her (that would be me) her professional gaze like a neon sign that said "The Writer Is In." I could almost feel her misreading me, drawing the wrong conclusions, emoting on my behalf, as she always had. There was nothing to Lily Starr. Nothing except that the Mighty Big Finger of God had descended upon her. I could feel it in the intensity of her gaze. She was eager to understand psychology while being a psychological blank slate, a turnip, a potato. My new life caused an auspicious perturbation in her that must have felt, for her, like a poem coming on, or maybe a short story, about failure, about being forced from Parnassus.

"Wall Street, that's a full-time job, right? And your writing? And after all those good reviews?" The mother paused nearby and told the daughter she looked tired. And she did, her fine blond hair catching behind her ears, her youthful cheeks paling. "Tell me you really haven't done this. I'm just not quite believing you. Did you get my message about the reviews?" Lily spoke fast, shooting questions out as rapidly as they came to mind.

"Sorry I didn't call you back."

She did look pained. My defection had become a bad omen for the trade, a betrayal of the guild—one didn't just up and leave for a world where literature was irrelevant.

"For how long?" she persisted.

"For now," I said.

"It's not right," she said genuinely. That was the thing about Lily: she was mercurial. She had no sense of embarrassment. She just laid it all out there for the world to see and think what it would. Now she almost created in me the desire for her to pull me back. But then I caught myself, stood a little taller.

"Oh please, Lily."

But she continued, taking both of my arms, looking at me closely, and it was as if we were in a tree house together making our vows to be best friends forever. We had once been good friends. We'd shared the same bed when she and her old boyfriend had had a bitter fight. We'd read each other's work in the earliest days, helped each other to believe in ourselves, to keep going. Time had driven us apart, and I'd been carried to a completely different shore. But it was the sincere eyes of my old friend who wanted desperately to yank me back, not for me so much as for herself—one can always count on self-interest—as if the slow water torture of my own career—writing and failing—somehow preserved her notion of how the world should work, that there was a system, a design. My defection wrecked her vision.

I thought of Theodor. I would need to tell him now. Immediately. Lily would be on her cell phone telling our writer friends what I'd gone and done. The news circulating with the speed of good gossip. I could hear her voice, filled at once with concern and glee and astonishment.

"Don't fret, Lily. I'm enjoying myself. It's fascinating, you know. How often does one have the chance to become something else?" And I did feel that now, Daphne in the midst of becoming the tree, the familiar parts of me vanishing—not the limbs, of course, but my own petty, writerly preoccupations.

"Oh please," she said.

"It's not what we imagine. They're actually smart and nice,

and they do read." I winked, then kissed her and told her I had to run, that Theodor was unveiling his chalice for the patron.

"Theodor. What does Theodor say?" she asked. I smiled, was all, and dashed away.

I had a dress in my bag, folded neatly and wrapped in tissue paper, an old dress, familiar to Theodor. I had planned to change out of the suit, but didn't bother now. When I arrived at the studio I took off my coat, put my bag down, gave him the package with the beautiful napkins, put lilies I had brought into a vase on the foyer table, and then I told him. He was wearing his welder's apron over a white shirt, jeans, flip-flops. His hair was wet and brushed back, the curls flattened. I knew well how those curls came to life as the hair dried, as though a part of him were waking up. I had been dishonest with every part of this man, the first time in our relationship. The flattened hair made him appear like someone else. His features were more pronounced without all the distracting curls, the lines about his eyes and lips a touch more severe. Somehow this made it easier.

"I've been lying to you," I said. He was unwrapping the napkins. They were in his hand along with the receipt.

"About what?" he asked, admiring the linen. I could see his eye catch on the receipt. He studied it for a moment and looked at me, eyes rising to pose a question.

"I've defected," I said.

"Mrs. Mysterious," he said, giving me a once-over. "In a suit, no less. You've been wearing suits, I've noticed. Part of the research?" he asked sarcastically. I sensed a reticence in him, a bracing, could tell he struggled to mask it, didn't want me to know.

"I'm a bond trader," I said, just like that and as if we were meeting for the first time. Years ago, at the New Year's party, I am certain he would not have bothered chatting with me had

I announced that I was a bond trader. Now I liked the way the words sounded, powerful. What is it? Master of the Universe, Mistress of the Universe? "I'm not writing a short story. I'm not a writer anymore. I've gone to Wall Street, took Win Johns up on that bet of his."

Theodor burst out laughing, a good hilarious chuckle, the napkins in his hand. He waved the receipt. "My sweetheart," he said and wrapped his arms around me.

"Don't be condescending," I snapped.

"What would you like me to say?"

"What do you want to say?"

"I want to laugh. This is funny news."

"You're not going to take this seriously?" The laughter made me angry. I wanted *him* to be angry. I wanted him to be furious, to feel cheated and betrayed.

"So I married a rich girl," he said, trying mightily to keep a straight face. Of course he would say that; our first evening had become the mythic base of our story, hadn't it, told to our girls over the years: the humor implicit in the notion of Theodor and a rich girl. His curls were beginning to lighten, to lift as though echoing his humor.

"You don't care?" I asked. "I've been consumed with fear, betraying you, and you don't care? I've sold out. I'm not who you married. I don't like that woman anymore. And all you can do is laugh?"

He let go of me and put the napkins down. He picked up my coat and hung it in the closet. He went to the kitchen and checked the oven, opened the fridge for a bottle of wine, which he then uncorked, took two glasses from the cabinet and poured us each one. This was the maddening side of Theodor: he avoided big discussions. He was thinking, of course. And later, when I reflected upon this moment, it would also occur to me that he was relieved, that the laughter was the expulsion of a tremendous buildup of concern. Hadn't he asked me a few nights before if I was having an affair—a concern I'd not heeded as real? My betrayal was petty compared to what he may have feared. But I didn't have so much sympathy now. I wanted to be chastised. I wanted him to feel he didn't know me, that I'd become something other, Isabella Power, her husband, of that caste. I suppose you could say that I wanted his wrath to save me, that somewhere that was the only chance I had.

Then, very seriously and very quietly, he said, "You're an artist. No matter what you do, you'll always be an artist. You can't turn your back on who you are by nature."

"I'm not following," I said. The downstairs rooms of his studio seemed smaller, closer. "I care about mortgages, what happens to them, how they're packaged into bonds, how those bonds are valued. Where's the art in that?"

"I don't know. Maybe you don't know yet. But I'd put a lot of money on your figuring it out at some point." He always had the ability to remove us from the immediate and its sticky details and bring up the larger picture. Duchamp and Warhol, the arc of one's career, how Duchamp moved away from "the retinal" to the theoretical, from the production of art, the need to create a document, to embrace the process itself. "He stopped painting and started playing chess, exhibition chess games with nude models. He sold widgets at art expos. The act of living became art for him. Warhol made a career out of pushing together art and commerce. He loved to put weird things together and sit back and watch the fireworks. You can construe this as a sellout, India, or you can see it as a phase in the arc of your career and sit back and watch the fireworks. Do what you do so well: observe."

We were standing in the tiny galley kitchen. He turned to the cabinets and started unloading plates and water glasses for the table and then he turned back to me. "Have I taken you seriously enough?" he asked with a smile. "We need to get ready," he said and placed the plates and silverware in my hands. I ran upstairs to set the table. His worktable had been cleared off to become one long dining table. The chalice stood in the center, completed, the world hanging on or about to topple, the beautiful eyes of all the beasts glimmering, the intricate painstaking work made by Theodor's hand, two years of time and labor. Fruit filled the orb, champagne grapes reclining on top of it all. Of course I knew what he meant. I was a performance piece. In some ways that was what I was for Win and Radalpieno: a stunt in a world consumed by money. I kept running up and down the stairs, setting everything up. I changed into a more appropriate outfit, the old black dress that Theodor loved, the way it scooped in the back to reveal the wings of my shoulders.

"Now I recognize you," he said.

"I felt like a spy in that suit," I said.

The kitchen smelled of roasted chicken. Cheese stood on a platter surrounded by crackers.

"Of course, a spy! That's it. You didn't think you were doing this for the money?"

"Oh, yes I did. Just because you've turned my low pursuit into high art doesn't mean I'm not doing this for the money."

"Good luck for me, then," he said. "I've always wanted sixty-dollar napkins."

"Is there anything I can do that will make you stop loving me?"

"Plenty. But taking someone up on a bet like this is not one of them. How many people get to try on something completely different in life? How many people would be as brave?"

As we continued preparing dinner, I spilled out everything that had happened in the past two weeks, telling him all about the glass palace and the photography collection and Radalpieno and the silver bell the two men kept dinging and Win and his boys and their bet and his bet and my salary and the phones and the picture of Dick Cheney, and all of this coming forth made me light and relieved and eager to describe the details of this foreign country and to see what would become of this adventure of mine.

The Texan came with his third wife on his arm and his bolo tie and his handmade cowboy boots and his loud enthusiasm for the beauty of the chalice. The wife, a lovely woman who had gotten the hell out of El Paso as fast as she could, was a good ten years older than Sullivan but seemed younger in the way she deferred to him, admired what he admired, agreeing easily with his comments. "Robot Girl," I whispered to Theodor in the kitchen as we finished making dinner. He put his mouth to my ear: "I'll bet she fucks like a robot too."

The studio filled with their presence, his booming voice and the magnum of champagne he popped open, her fruity perfume with a touch of cinnamon. He was the sort of man who assumed that the world was designed for his pleasure. In that way, all Texans are unexpected throwbacks to the Renaissance, the world revolving around their own genius. In Sullivan's case it was his penchant for amassing huge wealth, originally in the oil and gas business. He'd been a "land man," a guy who buys oil and natural gas leases, before he turned to venture capital. Now it was art, and tonight it was us—actual artists of Williamsburg. We were his entertainment, and, I'll give him credit, he enjoyed us fully, as if he'd rolled us up and smoked us, without irony—me "the author," he said, delighting in the phrase, spellbound, and Theodor, having sculpted gold for him, no less—all of us together at last, a night that the wife, Dina, would tell her friends about for a solid week.

And then Emma and Will arrived, looking beautiful as always and just the same, not changed by his new profession: she, lovely and petite in a little black dress with a ruffle at the knee, and he in a suit and shirt with French cuffs and loafers. More admiration for the chalice, a trip to the roof to see the skyline and the Texan taking Theodor aside to ask him privately if he didn't need a little tide-me-over before the big check arrived: "I don't know how you-all do it, but I'm sure this won't hurt." He pulled out his checkbook and wrote a check for $10,000, a small portion of what he owed Theodor, but that would help us enormously, would have solved many woes just a few months before. "This is how it works," Theodor had always said: "in waves. Waves of fortune. Waves of need. We just have to be steady in how we ride them."

At dinner I made everyone laugh when Theodor announced that I'd gone to Wall Street to become a bond trader, had put writing aside for now. They laughed as other people would across the years when they heard my news, always the first response—a good jolly chuckle that would remind me of Theodor's first reaction.

"The cad," Emma said, and the table quieted, attention turning to her. The room was lit only by the many candles. The light of the flames flickered on our faces, against the walls. "He got you after all my protestations."

"Who?" asked the Texan.

"Win Johns at B and B," Will explained, and then I told them the story of the bet, a prospect that sang to Sullivan's sense of the outlandish. But I could tell as I watched the faces around the table that Will, who liked to know everything but had been kept in the dark about my adventure, was straining mightily to maintain his signature poise, that air of least astonishment. "You didn't!" he said, his jaw dropping and straightening out and then dropping again as I told my story. Will, Perfect Boy, the Eagle Scout astronaut, so used to being unsurprised by any eventuality, was genuinely, comprehensively flummoxed.

"I forbade him," Emma said.

"He seduced me," I said.

"The devil," she said and entreated Will to chastise Win, to save me.

"*Ex faucibus daemonis,*" Will said. The Texan's wife screwed up her eyes to indicate what the rest of us wondered too. "From the devil's jaws," Perfect Boy explained.

"Don't fret," Theodor said. "She's a spy."

"A spy? Of course, India the observer," Emma said. "My allegiances are shifting. I feel sorry for Win."

"Don't be," Will said. "They're well matched."

To the Texan (I liked referring to him as the Texan) I said, "Ask Will what's become of him."

"And you?" the Texan said to Will, obeying me. I was ready to hear Will's news. By now all of us had had a pleasing amount of wine. Nothing mattered. Life was a funny, topsy-turvy game.

"And me what?" Will said.

"Tell him what you've become," I said.

"Oh, this is crazy," said Emma, delighted.

"He's become a writer," I blurted. "We've traded places."

"I was never a trader, India. I was much lower on the totem pole, a lowly investment banker bringing phone service to impoverished countries."

"You're all mixed up," said the wife, Robot Girl, with her deep accent and fluttering smile. For the first time of the evening declaring her own opinion. "And none of you look a day close to forty."

"He sold his novel to Piccadilly," Emma said to the table. "His agent is billing him as a new Thomas Wolfe, though he doesn't write on the top of his refrigerator. Not yet, anyway."

"I'm not tall enough," Will added.

Even though I'd been waiting for the news, it pricked a bit, and I wondered: What am I doing? Why had I done it? We had $10,000, with more on the way. I didn't need to do this. Why did Will get to become a writer? I had the urge to jot something down in that small notebook I carried around in my purse, which I'd been filling with notes over the past two weeks. Sort something out, as Theodor had said. I deflated a little, the way you can after too many glasses of drink, when it dawns on you that the sensation won't last much longer, that the party's almost over. I was glad tomorrow was Saturday, that there was still time and a chance to turn my mind around.

"Why, yes," Emma said. "Piccadilly was your publisher once, right?"

"That's right."

"Will sold not just one book," Emma persisted, "but two. Cavelli," she added. The name would mean nothing to the Texan and his wife, but to me it meant a lot. The Dashing Cavelli. Not only did Will land the best agent in town, but also the most prestigious publisher.

"You were fond of him, weren't you, India?" Will asked.

"Yes," I said simply. He was charming, dapper in his white suits, elegant and extremely smart. A Long Islander who spoke with transatlantic inflections. His offices were stacked to the ceiling with papers and books, with only the narrowest paths cleared in the corridors, which made moving from room to room nearly impossible. That old world rose before me, appealing all over again.

"My fellow bohemians," said the Texan. "How do you do it? How do you make your way in a banker's world on a writer's budget?" He made a flourish with his hands that was intended to take in the New York City skyline, which languished on the other side of the studio's exposed-brick walls.

"We hope," Will said, now squarely one of us. Everyone burst out laughing but me. I knew that response, had lived it, a quality of nonchalance about one's fate, as if one were Lermontov in a cliff-top duel, a mere character in a novel. Magical thinking, they call it. It surprised me to hear this from Will, but I suppose he was only trying on his own *vita nuova* as well. One practiced one's lines to feel how they fit. Hope? The old world disintegrated as fast as it had been resurrected. I was done with all that. I was after a different sort of animal.

The dinner ended with Armagnac, brought from the Texan's limousine, which would usher him and Dina back to their Manhattan hotel and the Chapmans to their Tribeca apartment. Goodbyes and kisses all around, and Emma, wrapped in a fur, insisted we visit them again in Maine this summer.

"A bond trader," the Texan said, shaking his head and smiling, slipping into his coat. "I think, Theodor, that your chalice has caught things at just the right moment, the tipping point. Or not. It's not made me—I'm not that smart; there are plenty smarter than me—but I always have a knack for finding the right moment. I know what it is. So I smell it here. No doubt. I think you're brilliant, old boy."

Fourteen

EMMA MOVED TO MAINE in April of that year, as soon as the temperature became bearable and snow unlikely. She flew home on the occasional weekend, or Will and the girls came to her. Now that he spent his days writing, he could pick the children up from school if he wished, had more time for them. To be prudent, they had let their babysitter of eight years go, had hired a student part-time—a painful decision, as Lolly had been part of the family, but one that made sense given the new shape of their lives. The money saved could be used to help with the new expenses of Maine. In June, Will and the girls would pack up the apartment and join Emma for the summer, their first spent entirely at Pond Point. Of course it was difficult leaving her family behind, but she was determined to make the house perfect for them.

So Emma, in Maine, passed the spring doing what she loved best, making their world beautiful. Emma's arrival, and the coincident arrival of spring, with all its associations of awakening, of renewal and, more specifically, of cleaning, fueled her for the task, which was, upon closer inspection of the house, a formidable one, but one she approached with determination and ambition, sleeves rolled, her eyes alive to the possibilities of the interior space. This was not about decoration but design, and she approached her task as if to a calling—though one perhaps not as serious as the drive of an artist. But first there was wholesale throwing out and stripping down to be done, a rendering to the bare bones, as the cottage had been bought as is. So Emma spent a long first few weeks tossing things into dumpsters—the beds, the couch, the chairs, all the pots and pans and old tins, spices and food, the kitchen appliances, the kitchen floor, the mattresses, the lamps, the switch plates, the books and the puzzles and the games and the linens, the blankets and the television and the tools in the basement and the contents of the three bathrooms, the rugs, the piano, the wreaths.

A few minutes' pause on a given midmorning gave her a chance to contemplate the new space that was emerging from under all the clutter. She could feel her mood rising with her progress, and of course this was no accident but only the most obvious of ancient principles engaged and aligned. Arranging space was nothing to be sniffed at, though most people did. But Emma wasn't most people. The Hovs, bless them, were more like most people in that they hadn't thought to change the interior of the house so there was more of a dynamic interplay between interior and exterior landscapes. To them a house was something that shut out the world, offered protection and isolation from it, so somehow filling it up added to the armor. There would be no more of that. Emma took to redefining space where she could, to let the outside in, to create new interior vistas that would, every day they were there, offer up to her family the landscape's positive, soul-expanding physiological effects.

The closing had been in late March, and by Easter five dumpsters were filled and the house emptied. The framed drawings by the children and the Bachrach photographs had been carefully wrapped in newspaper and shipped to the Hovs—a task Emma offered to do in order to speed the process along. It was gratifying to clear out the house, the accumulation not of one lifetime but of several—from the days when Pond Point had been populated by wealthy Bostonians who came by steamboat to summer here.

For a few days Emma basked in the big emptiness and in being utterly alone. She slept on a blow-up mattress in the turret, covered in down quilts (shipped up from New York), listening in the dark to the moaning of foghorns, the tolling of bell buoys, the constant, reliable tumble of waves against the shore, the cry of gulls. She ate her meals, drank her coffee, at the lobster shack in town, which was more of a hamlet: the lobster shack, a lifesaving station that had been converted into a bed-and-breakfast, a church and a general store that also happened to serve the best lobster rolls around.

The sea air and pungent pine had seasoned her blood. The horizon, the vastness of the ocean, seemed to cause her to grow, become a part of it. The surf retained its winter violence; the sea, the color of a deep sapphire, foamed beneath a lowering sky. None of the other homes were occupied, boards across the windows. She liked it this way, Pond Point unpopulated. For a few days she didn't bother calling Will or the girls. She'd walk to the lobster shack along the beach, bending with it as it reached the river. The view of the river wending its way north seemed to arrest centuries.

At the restaurant the owner and his wife were skeptical of Emma at first, this newcomer from New York City—they silently checked her out, suspicious, chins raised. New summer-home buyers were likely to import other fancy people. She drank their coffee, read the local paper, asked how the winter had been, praised the pancakes, flipped through the *Auto Trader* with curiosity, bought the Maine syrup, asked for nothing special. She understood their heavy accents, didn't need for them to repeat themselves, asked questions about the lobsters, about their clear blood, how they can regrow a leg or claw, when they molt, the variety of their colors—yellow, blue, red, and the joker, striped orange and black.

She made small talk about the weather, listened to the gossip, gleaning stories of the lives of others. A lobsterman pulling up his pot found a human thumb tangled in the rope, a mishap from an apparent attempt to steal his pot. The night before, a local scoundrel had come into the clinic one town over, missing his thumb. One thing led to another and a trial ensued. The jury failed to convict the thief. The reason: lack of evidence. Emma heard the story over pancakes. The man who told it, a skinny fireman who also delivered the mail, had emphasized those last three words, giving them enough space to make the point hit home, like some off-duty member of a Greek chorus, pouring syrup on a stack of flapjacks. "Lack of evidence," he said, underscoring for the new resident the justness of the decision—the thumbless man had lost enough.

Emma's neighbors gave her plenty to contemplate regarding the human condition. Not yet here for summer, their presence dominated nonetheless. The Coffins were forbidding the Smalls from using their driveway to gain access to their house though they'd been allowed to for years, had a variance of some sort that had been proved in court to be illegal, and the Coffins didn't like the way the Smalls rutted up the road with their enormous SUV (that gas guzzler should be illegal too). The real estate developer who lost his wife in a boating accident wanted to build a retirement community in the marshland; it was said he'd fallen in love again but that his boy didn't like the new woman. The grandson of a Prohibition rumrunner had bought the Tuttle widow's cottage, and some believed he'd taken advantage of her, and though no one could remember the rumrunner, the fact of him served well enough as an indictment of the grandson's character. The gossip described a contentious lot who were highly attuned to the tiers of their society: the oceanfront owners, the riverfront owners, the townspeople and those who lived in cottages in the pines, a small expanse of woods infested with mosquitoes and ticks which you had to drive through to get to Emma's; quite a few people living in there but you never saw them on the beach. They seemed to like to stand next to their houses in the deep shade and listen to portable radios and barbecue steaks. They liked it right where they were. Before, Emma would not have cared about all this, but now things were different. On Sundays in the summer, when the church opened again, she would like being around these people, singing their hymns, chatting with them over coffee at the parson's house after the service, knitting herself, her family, into them.

The owner of the restaurant, who was also a lobsterman, had a slender physique and boyish face, and despite being a genuine Mainer (that is, someone born here of parents who had been born here), he had the blond hair and blue eyes of a Connecticut prep school boy. His supple wife wore braces and was always busy with a chore, cleaning, cooking. She didn't smile much, but when she did, you knew you'd said something worth saying. The wife's sister, a young widow with a smoker's cough, often sat with Emma at her table even when all the other tables were empty, saying little but happy for the proximity to someone new. Here talk wasn't always necessary. Emma could shed New York—the pace, the social engine, the fears of whether Will would succeed or not—and return to her most pure self, unencumbered by concerns about her future, which vanished in the wave wash and the crisp sea air.

Everything would be fine. Will had given her fifteen years. For fifteen years he had worked a job that had compromised him so that she could have Tribeca, fancy trips, two children, private schools, lessons, comfort, security. She had not had to work. She had not wanted to work, had wanted to stay at home with the girls—compensating, as so many of us do, for the failings of our parents. As an academic her mother had never been around when needed, even if physically present. Emma had admired her mother for her devotion to scholarship, but had always been envious of the children whose mothers had the time to make them lunches, slicing the crusts off the bread, concerned with the whims and particularities of their small ones, mothers who stood on the sidelines watching the games, who did their level best to ensure their childhoods would last as long as possible.

Emma had easily shed her career in the prints and drawings department of the Metropolitan Museum, cataloguing the endless inventory—the first step on the track to becoming a curator. She stopped writing her dissertation, gave up on her Ph.D. and never looked back once the babies were born. Well, perhaps a little when surrounded by the career-driven mothers who were so beautifully defined by what they did, dressed effortlessly as district attorney, white-collar-criminal lawyer, oil analyst, editor in chief of a women's magazine, global marketing director—their days filled to the brim, trips to far-flung spots around the globe. Women who couldn't seem to comprehend what it meant to stay home, who seemed to find in that choice a defeat and a refutation of what so many women spent the past thirty years fighting for. Emma knew the worst judgments of herself were cast not by others but by herself alone. Maine was Will's last promise to her, and she knew that it was her turn to promise him.

From the café owner's wife, whose name was Nora, Emma learned to make blueberry pie with the wild blueberries Nora had picked and frozen in bulk last summer, a nice "Maine touch," but also from bags of frozen blueberries they'd carried out together, along with a dozen bags of groceries, one blistering, prematurely hot May afternoon across the Walmart parking lot in Bath. A "Maine touch" of another sort altogether, one that Emma had at first found interesting, in an abstract way. Nora's thick fingers worked the pastry, first turning the flour and butter into crumbs, thousands of doughy beads, then into one big ball. Nora had flour on her cheeks, on her apron. Her smile sparkled with the braces.

Emma loved her because she didn't know anything about Emma's New York life, the sudden changes, Lolly's departure—a bad omen, observed the mothers at school, a sign of "economizing," of the arrival of choices unthinkable in the past that were made "of necessity" in the wake of a husband's career change. Emma's role as a banker's wife was a given; her role as a novelist's wife, to many, was a disquieting, open parenthesis. The successes he'd had with his writing were invisible. A banker's success is anything but invisible. "I'm leaving for the spring to renovate the Maine house," she caught herself saying, not because it was a lie, but because it was a justification, because it suggested nothing had changed. Once she would have spoken the words honestly, without a calculated thought.

Nora, like her sister, said little but welcomed the company of someone new and interesting, but not, of course, *too* interesting. That was the balancing act Emma performed there among the Mainers. Silence between them begged to be filled, but one didn't rush headlong into it, Emma learned. No offbeat jokes about murdering the Hovs here! So Emma waited and let the idle, harmless patter flow, and occasionally her patience was rewarded. From Nora, Emma learned where the best blueberry fields were, on the cliffs that rose from the clam flats, high above the beach, with full views up the river and out to sea. From there, in the afternoon light, the tide low, you might see a man wearing waders clamming in the estuary, the pools of water turning turquoise and amber.

One afternoon when the girls were up from New York, she brought them to the cliffs, where the roots of twisted pines wrapped around the rocks like talons, and the limbs of spruce were trained inland, in the direction opposite the prevailing wind. Maine would become a part of her girls, shaping them, too. Already it had defined their summers. She and the girls wandered down a trail and stumbled upon an old graveyard hidden in the woods. There, in the pine duff, shafts of forest light fell on the tombstones. The girls were ecstatic, running from stone to stone, trying to find the oldest dates and reading aloud the family names that could still be found on store and street signs in the village—the Percys and the Perkinses and the Spinneys. Here were Ephraim, Mary and Lorenzo Spinney. "Mommy, who were they?" Ephraim had lived to be ninety-one, his wife seventy-six. Lorenzo, their son, in a marmoreal flourish, had been "claimed by the sea" at thirty-nine.

"That's sad, Mommy."

"Yes, it's sad. But they're all together now in this quiet spot, right?"

"Yeah," said the earnest, trusting Catherine, her eyes encompassing big thoughts she couldn't quite comprehend but wanted to very badly. She was pure in her privilege, and death something that happened to others, and only in old age. Elisabeth darted about the headstones, deciding that she wanted to be buried here, making Catherine, as was Elisabeth's way, face hard truths.

The dramas of entire lifetimes played out in this small reach of shoreline, the tombstones a record of love and loss and final reckoning. What a fine place to pass eternity. She'd tell Will everything she'd discovered, how much more she loved Pond Point now that it would be theirs, in a way, forever.

By the end of April Emma had a crew of six working on the house—hard-working men who loved their morning coffee, sometimes spiking it with peppermint schnapps (she believed, because they could seem a bit too gleeful), whose jovial voices recorded the sounds of progress. The roof was reshingled, the clapboards damaged in the winter storms repaired, the exterior scraped and repainted, the broken windows fixed with glass panes authentic to the period (hunted for and purchased at great expense). She had the porch rebuilt because of rot, hung a swing and cushioned it with a sturdy chenille check in tan and burgundy. Behind the house a changing room was erected with a comfortable bath and shower, a closet for a washer and dryer. The floors in the house would need to be stripped and sanded, the window sashes painted. A crew of electricians spent a week and a half rewiring, adding cable and wireless. A new kitchen was installed with white acrylic cabinets and white enamel icebox and stove and sink, a tiled floor. The toilets were replaced, the bathrooms made more commodious. The work went fast; there was little competition for the labor. Each detail she chose herself, the fixtures, the switch plates, the knobs. Every night she fell asleep early, exhausted.

In the morning she'd light a fire, make herself coffee (glad to have the kitchen) and, wrapped in a comforter, sit on the swing and jot long lists of supplies to buy, watching as the sun popped into the sky, the spring winds blowing through the porch. She took up landscaping, raking, clearing underbrush, pulling out weeds, working with the zest and enthusiasm of an owner. For anyone else the tasks would have been drudgery. She installed creamy linen curtains on simple wooden rods with decorative balls, simple tiebacks dressing the windows. She found plates and pots and glassware and silverware, chairs and a table and a stunning red couch and bureaus, at flea markets and antique stores.

She became the most delightful kind of scavenger—frugal, wise and prudent, but with a trained eye. She renovated with her own hands the pieces that needed it—sanding and staining and reupholstering some of the easier jobs. The house was an all-consuming art project, as she worked to create the kind of art she knew how to make. For the bed covers she invested in antique, hand-sewn quilts, a splash of pattern and color for the otherwise white rooms. At a sample sale in New York, while home for a visit, she bought all the linens and towels and shipped them to Pond Point. Later, opening the packages was like her own private Christmas—presents for herself. She cherished the solitude, delighted in making up the beds, ironing the pillowcases, filling the bureaus with fleece jackets and cozy pants for the girls, slippers and pajamas and swimsuits. And there was a part of her that also felt the weight of this good fortune, its fragility.

Then one day, just like that, the crew cleared out, leaving the place wonderfully desolate all over again, leaving behind new copper pipes in the basement and faucets and refurbished floors and the spectacular kitchen with the gleaming Magic Chef stove. The house was finished. The same house, but different: her house, made beautiful and comfortable and clean for her family. It was early June. There was nothing left to do but admire the lilacs and absorb the neighbors (who had started opening their own homes for the summer), who came nosing about with compliments and tangential questions, who whistled through their teeth when they saw the remodeled kitchen with the fancy cabinets that closed with a gentle click, the fixtures and the new furnace.

How much she'd accomplished in so little time! "And look at those hydrangeas!" they cried. "We have no luck with ours." If hydrangeas could thrive in Brittany, Emma thought, why not here? The way the neighbors spoke, the compliments, made her eager to unveil the house to Will. The sea grass in the dunes turned emerald and the air trembled in its purity, each day clearer than the one before, so it seemed the islands, kept at a distance by the banks of spring fog, now appeared to be advancing. The water reflected light like so many diamonds. Forever she could sit and watch the water, the tricks it played, the changing colors, a dance of blues and greens and silvers that seemed to cast a haze over the whole world. Day in, day out, boats passed, yachters engaging the season, lobstermen trolling, everything here coming out of hibernation. The air filled with apple blossoms, light and sweet and fragrant. For $195,000 she'd transformed the old Victorian on the tip of Pond Point and had staked her claim to this magnificent spot. Her house. In Maine.

Above the front door she hung a simple plaque carved with the year the house was built: 1880.

"What were you thinking?" Will asked. His voice was patient, but creases cut across his brow, the familiar furrow of worry. "It's beautiful, my darling, but just think, that's almost half my advance."

"But you said we could."

"I thought you understood the new constraints."

"I economized with every bone in my body," she said, genuinely confused because the adjustment in their spending habits was not small. Rather, it was enormous, something that would take time to accommodate to. Once she wouldn't have thought about what it cost. She had this time, she assured him, as if thought had its own column on the spreadsheet.

"I know, sweetheart, but we need to be in a different mindset now. I thought you understood." Will was concerned, more than concerned. Such spending could throw them over the edge. He'd be able to absorb this one, maybe: a snake swallowing an elephant. It would not be easy. His budget would become that much tighter. It was a relief that the girls no longer wanted skating lessons; canceling Hindi gave them more time for school. They'd been considering the public school in the neighborhood because it was excellent. That switch alone could help pay for this. Will realized just how different their financial picture had become and that for Emma it was still quaint and abstract.

"We're not relying on your advance. You told me that," she said, looking with eyes pinched together, as if trying to squeeze out the truth, if reluctantly—a sense he wasn't giving her the full story. The backdrop for this scene was their bedroom in the turret, a dark night, the girls asleep, voices hushed. No one can have everything.

By the time we arrived for a four-day weekend over the Fourth of July, the house was unequivocally theirs—the girls' art projects taped to the walls, their puzzles and games taking over the coffee table, their books arranged on the shelves, their cover-ups and hats and rain gear hanging on hooks attached to plaques with their names in a bold, colorful script, their tennis rackets, their beach towels, the new shower house with the fine soaps and lotions and bath oils, the shining cabinetry in the kitchen filled with organic products and champagne flutes and demitasse cups, the gleaming chrome La Pavoni espresso machine. Last summer the house had been a testament to all that was makeshift, make-do and temporary. In came the new regime, and a clear and directed campaign of sorts had established and unified the brand.

"It was luxuriously lonely," Emma said as she recounted her spring, regaling me with the stories of what she'd been through to get the house in order. We were sitting in beach chairs at the edge of the water, a big red canvas umbrella shading us, seagulls swooping down for their lunch of crabs, smashing them against the rocks. It was low tide. "Can you remember just a year ago? Less than a year ago, really," Emma mused.

Theodor and Will and the girls collected sand dollars, Will taking a break from his work for our visit. Of course, we'd been given a tour of his new writing studio in the basement, with its long wooden desk and leather swivel chair. He was finishing the edits to *Never Say Die.* The book was to publish in spring 2005, followed by the sequel one year later. His editor, Leonardo Cavelli, had brilliantly dissected the book, Emma told us, "like a surgeon with his scalpel. So all that work will have a double payoff. It's remarkable how easily two books came of one." A brass measuring cup from Thailand held his pencils. The room was lined with bookcases, filled with Will's summer library, as Emma put it—none of the valuable volumes. On his desk was the tall stack of his manuscript (marked up with red ink) and a paperback copy of *Look Homeward, Angel,* which, I imagined, Will had read long before but was rereading so that he could appreciate the comparisons of his work with Wolfe's. As I looked at the desk, peering into the writer's room, it did feel at once familiar and foreign, mystical and lonely, and there was not a small part of me that longed for that heady cocktail, that envied Will for always getting it right, for understanding how to manage a budget and yet live elegantly. But I also knew from experience that the outsider looking in has no true idea of what hides beneath the veneer.

And he wore his pride sheepishly, but wore it nonetheless, with a boyish grin, relishing Maine, his wife's renovation, his book, his close relationship with Cavelli, the editorial process, the long, wine-filled lunches, the risk balanced by the bounty and good fortune of his life: his well-dressed, intelligent girls, his beautiful, talented wife, who, he announced, was thinking of taking a class in interior design.

To me they seemed unchanged, on the surface anyway, by their new circumstances. Somehow I expected a transformation, a touch of the rakish artist at the very least, but not so. It had not been that long; they had not been tested yet, I supposed. How different was I, after all? I was still jotting notes in the little notebook I kept in my purse, recording the details as I had always done for the inevitable project that would someday occur to me. At dinner the night before, on the porch, amid citronella candles to keep away the mosquitoes, Will had been the gracious host, happy to use all the new toys, the accoutrements (the grill with its own gas line, the bentwood rockers) of his latest success: the house, of course. A blitz of illegally procured fireworks erupted in the dark, shooting over the water, illuminating a huddle of people standing around various bonfires that polka-dotted the beach like inflamed haystacks. Will steered the conversation toward me and my joining B&B, a notion he apparently still resisted, the idea that I'd thrown writing overboard to go for the money. With the flickering candlelight randomly illuminating small sections of his face, he pressed me on what I thought about bond traders, Win, the career change.

"The energy is thrilling, you know," I said. "My whole adult life I'd worked alone at a desk, in my imagination. I didn't know what it meant to work with others."

"And the writing?"

"I don't think like a writer anymore."

"How does a writer think?"

"Oh, come now. You know. I don't read behind the face to think what the story might be. I've stopped doing that." Which wasn't really true, but I had to make it so.

"That's too good a metaphor for me to believe you," Will said.

"I think about the market instead, what it's doing."

"Is this true?" Will asked, turning to Theodor.

"I believe she believes that," he answered. "Our conversations are certainly different. I hear a lot about the market."

"And the market?"

"Crazy, exhilarating. I have nothing to compare it to," I said. I realized too that I didn't have time to think about the nuances of people, character, as I had before.

"The truth is," Will declared, "this is one story to watch, and if you stick with it, you'll have a front-row seat. The slicing and dicing and mincing of the American dream, like taking meat and grinding it into hamburger and then shipping it off to European insurance companies, Texas hedge funds, the central bank of China. These are our houses, our neighbors' houses. These exotic mortgages are going to come due and then someone will have to pay the bill. And there're not just a few of them, so imagine the ripple effect."

"I suppose you don't think much about your old life either," I teased. He was curious, wanted to have the conversation, wanted to feel out how deeply entrenched I was by this point—could I talk the talk? And I sensed in him someone yearning for that forgotten token, lost and left behind on a past shore. The banker in him was coming untethered from the artist, eager to lift off.

"I would never have imagined that mortgages would interest me," Theodor said. "But it's the scale of this world that I find amazing. Talk about a big canvas."

"But, honey, don't we have one of those resetting mortgages? What did you call it? A 2-and-28 or something like that?" Emma asked Will.

"Yes, my sweet, but we're not stupid. It's the people who don't know what they're getting themselves into who bring the house down."

I felt a little jolt, a small crack in the wall of their finances that allowed me, just barely, to peer inside. That meant that in two years he was betting he'd have a chunk of money that would allow him to rewrite the mortgage favorably. I bit my lip and held back from commenting.

"Are you really just doing this for the money?" Will asked suddenly.

"Will!" Emma's chastening tone clearly held a previous conversation, perhaps one in which she'd made him vow not to talk about my choice. But I didn't mind. We were close enough friends, and it *was* a curiosity. I knew that.

"A few years ago you didn't think money was so base," I said to Will with a wink, then swept my hand around the porch to encompass the house. Perhaps I could have gone on to explain: the crushing burden of debt in a sea of wealth, giving up on myself, my talent. Perhaps I could have spoken as Theodor had to me, about the artist's foray into commerce. But I hadn't felt the need to justify myself. If I were a man, I wanted to say, would you question my choice?

Just then we saw an eruption of spectacular red, white and blue fireworks, one after the next, and I remembered being a little girl, sitting on my father's lap during our town's annual July Fourth display, the point at which he'd always say, "The grand finale." I loved hearing him say those words, how he savored them, how they seemed like knowledge and wisdom, elevating the last moments, the fantastic repetition of shooting and bursting, to some higher truth. The beautiful, illegal and amateur display had the same effect now.

When it was finished, it was Theodor's turn to change the subject, asking Emma about her spring, and did she think she could live up here year-round: "Never." Emma told stories about the locals, about lopped-off thumbs and lobster thieves and rumrunners and the harrowing tale of a woman torn to shreds by a motorboat—the stories she loved best, of the people she adored collecting.

"No wonder you love it here," Theodor said.

On the beach the next day, the sun warming me, the spray of the sea, I thought of the yellow plane swooping down from the sky. A light wind rippled across the water and an enormous fish jumped, then another, taut and silver. The girls ran over to us, clamoring about the seals they'd seen, twenty lazing in the sun on the rocks of Fox Island. Ruby's fists were filled with sand dollars and Gwyneth told Ruby they weren't really dollars, causing her to whine and complain. Elisabeth and Catherine kissed their mother and ran to the water, diving easily into the cold Gulf of Maine. My girls followed, diving too.

They loved it here. They were free to roam and explore. Not

far from the girls a giant tree trunk rolled in the waves. The tide would bring it to shore, and Emma would rally all of us and some neighbors to haul it to the dunes, where it would become part of the gate she was building, an elaborate stand in driftwood that marked the entrance to her house. She'd told me it was a futile effort, one they'd need to repeat the following year because the winter storms would wash it away. But she loved the exercise—it would become an annual ritual, the repetition that would define the beginning of summer, that seemingly never-ending span of time across weeks and months and years.

"After you win your bet," Emma asked, "do you think you'll stay on at B and B?"

"Who says I'll win?"

"Oh, you'll win."

"I haven't been tested yet," I said. I thought back to last night's dinner and the talk of exotic mortgages, and I looked at Emma now, wondering if I could see a fissure there, knowing that as with marriages, we never know the truth of people's financial lives no matter what they try to project. Watching her, trying to read beneath the surface of her, I felt a kinship to all the people who had studied me before when I was an artist, trying to make sense of Theodor and me, of how we afforded our lives.

"Do you miss writing?" Emma asked. She knew she was repeating the conversation of last night, pushing deeper. This wasn't about the writing, though, or about me. There was something sweet and naïve in her that I hadn't noticed before.

"Honestly, I don't have time to miss it. I love that—that there isn't enough time anymore for all the worries I could drum up."

Emma looked at me quizzically, a look that indicated that Will didn't fill his writing time with worry—or, if he did, he didn't share much of it with her. The look also seemed to indicate a new understanding of me, a sympathy, another layer revealed, that she hadn't realized how comprehensively unglamorous the "writing life" was. Perhaps I had seemed composed to her, perhaps it had seemed that my system had worked—the mechanics that had made an artistic life possible. But in this light, like shantung silk, the hue exposed another hidden shade.

"Did you go to Win because you were concerned . . . about money?" she asked.

I tried to laugh the question off, but she persisted, with her eyes on me. For the first time in our relationship I saw worry's fragile lines appear softly on her face. Or did I? Emma always seemed to have exactly what she wanted, even with her husband's huge career change. Behind her stood her regal Victorian cottage, a backdrop against which her petite figure, curled in her terry beach robe, reigned. House of cards or not, exotic mortgage or not, it was hers. She'd spent a springtime making this home into what she wanted it to be. I could see it then, as I would see it clearly later, that she was the sort of person, even in loss and challenge, who would come out ahead, with dignity—the knowledge that she was always doing right by herself and her family.

"I liked the challenge," I answered. Radalpieno came to mind, his interview, his demand that I state how much I wanted—how much I loved—money.

"I think you were incredibly brave. I can imagine the pressure you were under," she said. Then suddenly and matter-of-factly, "I spent too much redoing the cottage. Will was furious, in his way, for a few days. But it will work out. It always seems to." Then she pointed to the island floating just offshore, leaving me no space to comment on what she just offered. She said that back in the 1960s, the island had been for sale for $3,000. The land had a beach at low tide and a tall stand of spruce that protected it from the ocean. It was going for $2 million now.

"When you make your gobs I want you to buy that island," Emma said. "I want our houses to face each other. I want our girls to paddle canoes back and forth." The jump in value—of the island that would be mine so that we could be here together—was her way of explaining how it would all work: the undeniable fact that, renovated now, her house would be worth more.

I could picture the dream, our houses facing each other. A seal bobbed his head not far from shore, a fish leaped. The deep sapphire of the sea shimmered and foamed, the waves rolling in, crashing over the girls, who laughed and raced with buckets of sand to shore up their castles, startling in that clear afternoon light.

Fifteen

THE MORTGAGE UNIVERSE is divided into three areas: Agencies, Securitized and Unsecuritized. Mortgages are part of Fixed Income, which, with Equities and Prime Services, make up the division of Capital Markets. My area was Agency MBS, the most basic kinds of mortgage bonds, all agency-securitized mortgages, backed by pools of home loans acquired by regular, hard-working people. Nothing exceptional, nothing too risky.

These were not the mortgages that bought the fancy New York apartments and the million-dollar summer cottages in Maine. These mortgages had limits. In 2004, they couldn't go higher than $417,000. My desk of six traders dealt in fifteen-year and thirty-year fixed-rate Fannie, Freddie and Ginnie Mae bonds. On my desk we were both market makers and proprietary traders, but our first function was as market makers, to provide liquidity to the firm's institutional client base. But there was also a certain amount of balance sheet and risk capital committed to my business, with which I tried to make money in my sector and with the products I used to hedge (Treasuries, futures, swaps, options, Fed fund futures, Eurodollars). Among the six of us in three books, we made anywhere from three hundred to eight hundred trades a day.

Starting out, I traded things with less "lossability" so I could get the feel of things. Even so, you could lose a lot by making a simple mistake or, worse, by hurting a customer relationship. To have a basic sense of all this took about six months. I learned the language, and mostly I observed. Eventually I'd come to understand that none of the most important parts of the business could be learned. Just as great writing can't be taught. It was more elusive than, say, learning to be a bookkeeper. So much had to do with subtlety, with understanding what people were willing to pay for bonds at a range of interest rates, synthesizing recent transactions in order to establish value, feeling the dynamics of the market and, of course, getting to know the players, developing relationships. Relationships took longer.

In Win's scheme, through his connections and the fast brain he was betting I had, what he wanted to see was a remarkable ramp. He wanted me to go from $150,000 to $1 million a year. He knew I'd have some obstacles: first the learning curve, then the people who would be against me because I was an anomaly. I didn't belong there. I hadn't worked my way up the ladder for it. I was the novelist, the game, the ultimate bet, and perhaps not everyone wanted to see Win win. The challenge was to turn me into a solid trader in eighteen months. What I hadn't understood was that the bet would keep on going; he'd continue to up the ante if I performed as he predicted in the first year.

By eight months, I was just where he wanted me to be, on the desk, above the analyst but the lowest of the associates, and he was well on his way to winning the bet. I was stepping in when things got crazy, pricing and trading, working my way ever higher on the trading scale. To begin with, my trading limit was modest, but by October I'd reached the $250,000 mark, meaning I could handle trades with that much lossability. Even for an institution that could write down billions and have just as much in profits, $250,000 would be a significant loss.

In order for me to fit in, in the beginning Win instructed me to "play young." He didn't want me carrying on about the daughters or the husband, no pictures of the family on my desk, no chat of the weekend soccer games and lacrosse tailgates, ballet lessons, report cards, nanny woes. So at home April was instructed to take over. She already ran our life, but now it was official, along with a raise. She was in charge of all lessons, playdates, homework, food shopping, doctors' appointments, etc., etc. I was generous with her, one of the new perks of the job that I thoroughly enjoyed. "I prayed for you," April told me, happy with the changes. "Every night I prayed, and I taught your daughters to pray too." It is astonishing how fast we can adapt. I had thought I'd miss the girls and that it would be unbearable to spend so much time away from them. But my absence allowed for Theodor's presence, and we all settled into our new circumstances.

Play young; that is, stay focused, hungry. Only objects that would make me race belonged on my desk: hot chili sauce from Belize, for example—brought back by Kathy Park from her vacation there—to remind me that the rush was what it was all about; a jaguar figurine; a picture of the Rolling Stones from the *Sticky Fingers* days; a racecar; a pair of stilettos. Snake had his mother's curry powder in a little glass jar; Maxi had a framed pencil sketch of his favorite racehorse (before Maxi was sent back to the paddock and I assumed his seat); Tiger had a picture of his girlfriend in a bikini, staring right at him with a pleading little twinkle. Josh had his movie stars, the lassoed Clint and Winona the thief, because he liked the exhilaration of escape and the beauty of second chances. Sam had a miniature silver lacrosse stick, given to him by his dad before he'd dropped dead of a heart attack; he'd been second in command to the New York police commissioner in the 1970s. Sam also had his father's badge, which he flashed when a cop pulled him over for speeding. Gus, the Korean, had figures and equations, written in his neat hand, taped to the edges of his monitors: prepayment models, simulation-based pricing of MBS, OAS adjustment, convexity of MSR portfolios—sexy. Gus was the analyst, earnestly doing his job. Of the lot, he spent the longest hours at the desk on weekends. On my desk I also had a few Monopoly houses and hotels.

Win asked what I really wanted and how badly I wanted it. "There's no other way to put this, so I'll give it to you straight. What's going to make you hard?" he asked. "Or its equivalent."

"Wet?" I smiled, giving it right back to him. ("That's what he likes about you," Snake had said, "that you'll tell him to fuck off right to his face.")

"No. *Hard.* And fast. Welcome to the man's world."

It was like some weird tantric position involving money and risk and exhilaration and the ever-present moment of the bet. For what was a trading floor if not an organized (and legitimate) institutionalized casino, a context for transforming amorphous desire into the fungible, into substance, into certificates, into coupons, into commodities, into cold *hard* profit? TODAY COULD BE THE DAY. That's what all the trains in Penn Station say. And I was not immune. I wanted a mansion like Isabella Power's. I wanted to complain about my mirror not fitting through the door—or at least be able to if I chose to. I wanted to be a part of the conversation that had embraced New York, America: "If you own something," our President once said, "you have a vital stake in the future of our country." Weren't we all, or at least 70 percent of us, caught up in this myth? So I felt the change from the optative to the indicative. I also wanted to show—prove—that I was capable of working hard, long hours at an office like all those other people and pull in the means to afford whatever it was I wanted.

It was no longer a matter of if, just when. And this was the force of Win's question. One needed a mantra or talisman of some sort. The when, the mystery of When. The arrival of the drive and the force and the motivation and the perpetuation. The momentum. *The Mo.* It's what made the trading floor go—getting it right. Profits and losses recorded in black and white, and successes measured objectively.

By mid-fall 2004, as Win's protégée, I shined—even if I was still untested. I flushed with the desire. I wanted to be here. I had learned how to get hard. And this, this surprising inflection, in all seriousness, was why I began to dream that I'd be making the big trades, that Paramount (a client) would be calling on me, asking me to *do the deal.* This was why I got out of bed every day at 5 A.M. This was why I had no regrets telling the university that I wasn't coming back. "I'm sorry, but I'm hard," I wanted to tell the dean, the bespectacled 4 P.M. cochair of the breakout session of the Interim Committee on Curriculum Development. I was J. P. Morgan. I was Davy Crockett. *I'm sorry, I'm going to make the sun rise.* I would find the secret lever that made the world turn. I would, as they say, amass wealth. And that accumulation would generate its own gravitational pull, the way winning breeds more winning, bringing with it more money. I could smell it. It smelled of rain-washed streets and gun metal and sounded like the tumblers of a safe clicking into place for me.

What I didn't know yet was that the drive has to be tempered. Yes, it was good to be hard, but you shouldn't get crazy hard. You had to *see,* to perceive. It's a system of checks and balances, like the writer who has to constantly balance ego with self-doubt to write well. Self-doubt, however, is not a term used on the floor. On the floor we called it "mastery of emotion," and we understood, by what was not said, what we meant by that phrase. The hardest challenge is the split-second judgment you have to make, the decision that comes from some subliminal input you don't recognize. That's what makes the difference. The more centered you are, the more capable you will be of making those decisions.

You can't be trained to do that. You just have to be exposed. You develop an abstract sense of how the market reacts, an art that cannot be specified in detail, cannot be transmitted by prescription, since none exists. It can be passed on only by example, from master to apprentice. Since Win wasn't actively trading, my master was Snake. He was poised, elegant, with his sleeves always buttoned, never breaking a sweat, quiet. Sometimes in the middle of a big trade he looked so at peace you'd think he'd just finished a yoga class, had an extra-long shavasina, index finger and thumb pressed together—"dialed in," we called it, to the gods of Pythagoras and the gods of Las Vegas. It didn't matter that chaos swirled around him, that Tiger (second in command of our seat), who was riddled with impatience, kept his nervous leg pounding into the dull carpet like an outboard motor, propelling his vessel. (No wonder he didn't drink. Drink would have ignited his already boundless energy and sent him off the reservation.)

Not all traders were like Snake, in fact very few. But the really good ones were. The higher the stakes, the calmer they seemed to become, as if listening to music playing from the bottom of a well. The stories of the trader who throws chairs, screams at people to fuck off, who slams phones and kicks in walls—sure, they existed too, in larger numbers. Indeed, they weren't relegated to the past, those stereotypical 1980s traders. But Snake was one of the really good ones. The calm was his edge, his advantage, his secret, his trademark. Generally star traders don't reveal their secrets, but even if they did, it would mean little because it's a gift. Watching and listening as the trader connects disparate facts is the only possible way to learn, like the writer who studies the books she reads to understand how they are made so she can steal various tricks for her own work, applied with her own innate talent. At a certain point, therefore, the novice has to be thrown into the fray and start trading for herself to learn what her style and secrets are.

Which brings us back to used cars: Toyotas and Hondas and

Fords. No Mercedes-Benzes, no BMWs, no Bentleys—those belonged to securitized traders, the higher-value realm of the mortgage universe, the terrain of mansions and penthouses and their requisite jumbo mortgages. Toyotas—I was consumed by them. I cared about pricing Toyotas, and I was good at it. I trusted my gut, and for a streak I was correct. So I'd have a lot of Toyotas to unload. I'd know the client who wanted to sell them and the fund that wanted to buy them. I'd be asked to price the trade (say, offer 100mm FN 5s June [Toyotas]). I'd put my level on it (97-04). There'd be the dance with the client, the sweet tones and chirping, trying to get me to lower my level, wheeling me with flirtatious banter and male bravado, trying to convince me the better price was 97-02.

For example, Robert Shane, with a potbelly so big he could balance pens on it (which he did). Three kids. A wife. I'd seen him throw back one too many, many times. He was a simple guy, liked Jack Daniel's. And through his loose tongue I came to know that the petite wife with tight curls and a skinny, chiseled face found meaning in her life by running the Parents' Association at the kids' school. He had two daughters with severe crushes on Ashton Kutcher (Shane wanted me to speak to his girls, come over for a family dinner, tell them what it was like to be a woman on the Street); his boy was a toddler, already wielding toy guns and sabers, a talent that the dad perceived as a sign of his son's intelligence, how far he'd go. I sat there over cocktails and stoked the stories, asking for more details, laughing when he did, envisioning his boy, trying to make Shane feel singular, unique. My interest was genuine. I liked these people. They were good people, all out for the same end—good, hard-working souls who'd been taught the most direct route to American happiness, and here we were in a bar, stoking it with commentary on and admiration for little Bobby Shane Junior's deftness with a lightsaber. I was soft and kind, so in the beginning people thought I'd be easy to push around, but it was simply my armor.

“Sold to you,” I say now on the phone, which actually means “I don’t buy that price.” “Firm?” Shane asks in a husky tone. He’s on the wire, on speaker. Everyone around me who wants (and needs) to can hear that husky tone. They all know it’s Shane. Of course Snake’s listening, because the ante on this trade isn’t small. “I’m axed to sell,” I say. “You hit the bid,” he responds.

Immediately the bid on the follow is 97-03. My gut feel is spot-on. “Jesus Christ,” Snake says, smiling. “Okay, let’s try another. That was luck,” he says. Maybe. But not if it becomes a streak. Not if you’re consistent.

And soon I was. And soon, like statistics in baseball, it was all there for everyone to see, plain as day. I was good. The word got out. I could do this. In the beginning there were high-fives, thumbs-up, and I was grateful to these fierce, uncomplicated boys on the trading floor, to be counted among their number. “Keep hitting those singles,” Snake would say, leaning back in his chair to catch a full view of me three seats down. All the others could hear. I liked that they could hear. And those not on our desk took roundabout routes to the bathroom to pass behind us, just to hear how it was going, how I was doing, catch a telltale phrase. People knew I was Win’s, but they didn’t know I was also Radalpieno’s. At best they could guess how high up the bet went.

Getting it right, making money from your own good judgment, is a sensational emotion. Yes, there’s a mix of fear in there, like oil in sandstone—the fear needs to be there, is essential. I became part of the team, but I was simply there, too busy, swept up in *the Mo.* And in this way I rose, my trades going from singles to the occasional extra base. I was high. Everyone knows the rush of winning, the giddiness, the urge, the need for more. I wanted more, and there was more to be got, plenty, like picking apples from trees in the fall—easier even. Money was cheap. I worked ten-, twelve-, fourteen-hour days, but only as an afterthought did I ever notice it—say, in the limo home that Win had ordered for me. He was proud, which made me want to work harder. The big game no longer fazed me. Tens of millions took their proper shape—or maybe I was finding mine—and it was with these faces, laughing after hours, their ties askew in midtown bars, the people behind the trades, that I belonged, and out of this I stepped completely from myself to become something I barely recognized, and yet thrilled to behold.

Then it happened. The first time. I can remember what I was wearing that day, a blue silk blouse, a lighter shade than the pantsuit I had on. In the mirror that morning I'd thought the shirt had looked pretty; it had brought out the blue of my eyes. I can remember the date, October 15, one year almost to the day since the publication of *Generation of Fire*. The paperback was in the stores, notices were in the papers, but on the way to work none of that crossed my mind. I was thinking about the shirt, how much I liked it. Later, I'd save it as a reminder, but I'd never wear it again. The pit taught you about luck, about talismans: you never wrote with a red pen; you found a penny, you picked it up; no hats on the bed; no riding in the elevator you rode in on the day you were slammed; no ordering from the restaurant you used that fateful day. Snake wouldn't have let me wear the shirt again had I tried. "That shirt's not coming in here," he said when the deal was finished. It was the shirt's fault in the end, but in the beginning it was my fault we got rinsed, and no one was laughing.

My mistake was simple: I'd bought Toyotas today at yesterday's valuation. I'd bought quite a few, compounding my loss. Let's put it this way: yesterday, 1,000 houses were selling for 95. Overnight, some pretty big things happened in Japan, and the ripple of the wave worked its way around the world, affecting LIBOR and the rates at which a homeowner, and even I, could borrow money. In my speed to cover risk from late the day before, I didn't watch the other markets, ignored data.

I wanted the bonds. We were short the basis, and FN 5s were nearly impossible to find. I stood to gain a bundle, my biggest win to date. But because of the overnight changes, the equivalent of yesterday's 95 valuation of 1,000 houses was now 94-18. The fast calculations I did were based on yesterday's curve, spread and carry calculations, causing me to lose more than a million dollars. It's the overconfident beginning skier who smashes into a tree. Let's put it another way: ice cream is selling all over the city for $1 a cone, $10 a gallon for the fancy stuff. Overnight, the cost of cream shoots up because there's a milk shortage, a problem with cows in the heartland. You forget to check the one crucial piece of information that's going to let you know if the pricing is steady, and you think you're getting quite a deal when you sell all those gallons for $11, but the person buying is the winner, because everywhere else those gallons are selling for $14. If you failed to check on the cows—news that would be right before your eyes if you were in the business of peddling ice cream—you'd be out a crucial piece of information. If it was sunny yesterday, there is, of course, no guarantee that it will be sunny today, even if you wake up to a clear blue sky. You must check the weather report and also the feel of the air, the way it hits your intuition.

A million dollars. The realization that I'd lost came on all at once, an immediate and very visible mistake, the kind of situation in which the blood drains from your face in seconds, you feel queasy, yet at the same time you are rooted to the floor, watching yourself be killed, a sharp pain in the pit of your stomach. The whole room vanished and for a moment it was just me, alone. No one else. A relief in some measure, I closed down, shut the others out. Money that had become abstract was suddenly, miraculously, painfully real to me again. Before my eyes a million dollars slid down the drain and into somebody else's coffers. I applied yesterday's valuation to today, a rookie mistake. In my cocoon, that's what raced through my head. Then the room started to light up again, all the surrounding traders wanting to know what happened, their interest aroused more than usual because the commotion surrounded me, the phones bleating, and in the self-centered state of the loss it seemed they were signaling my failure. I'm just a novelist, I said to myself. I'd never gone this high.

"Patience," Tiger said.

I wasn't sure if he was speaking to me or if that was even what he'd said. Impatience was his character flaw, and it had become mine too. I knew better. I'd been paying attention to the mistakes of others. I wanted to get up and leave, and a part of me felt I could do that. The game's over. I lost. My writing desk, my family, they're all waiting for me. I felt ridiculous in my suit, an impostor. The laws of life finally caught up with me. You are not allowed to switch around like this. You can't become someone new at thirty-eight. I thought of all the comments of disbelief I had received, all the parents of my children's friends, astonished. When it was all over, Snake patiently but firmly asked me what had happened, how I got my price—95. He wanted me to learn. His style was cool, poised, kind.

SNAKE: What happened? How did you get that price?

ME: The 95?

SNAKE: Yes, walk me through your thought process.

ME: Well, I sold those 5.5s in June yesterday afternoon at 95-04, and the drop to July is 3 ticks, so I was just trying to cover the risk and make a tick on the trade.

SNAKE: Two problems. One, is 95 the right bid in the front month? Two, is 3 the right drop to July? Where was the ten-year note when you sold FN 5s last night?

ME: 97-12.

SNAKE: And where are they now?

ME: 96-24.

SNAKE: So with a 70 percent hedge ratio, where should FN 5s in June be this morning?

ME: 94-21.
SNAKE: And where did you get 3 on the drop to July?
ME: Well, yesterday you bought it there.
SNAKE: Yesterday's yesterday. Gone. And what's the market today?
ME: 3.25/3.75.
SNAKE: So what's the right drop?
ME: 3.75.
SNAKE: So what is the right bid side of 5.5s in July?
ME: 94-172.
SNAKE: So how much did it cost?
ME: 14.75 ticks.
SNAKE: No, on 250mm bonds, how much actual money did you just give away? Do the math.

The thing about Snake was that he was gentle. He wanted me to learn. He wanted the others on the desk to learn too. He had enough confidence to be generous. The conversation was for everyone. His tidy manner, the long sleeves of his white shirt crisply ironed, no wrinkles at the elbows, his short-cropped hair revealing a smooth, clean neck—his dark skin a contrast against the white collar. When he finished walking me through my mistake, the business was over, relegated to the past. He moved back to the trades at hand.

But on this particular day, because of the size of my loss, it didn't take Win long to come marching out of his office in a way I had not seen before, his feet thumping more heavily on the gray carpet. I realized, in the speed of his gait and the stern furrow of his brow, that I was about to meet a Win I'd not met before. He loomed above me. If Snake spent a good ten minutes on the loss, Win spent less than one, yelling at me for the first time. The first time I'd seen him mad, yell at all, his calm demeanor splitting, and I realized then that the calm was a front. He was not organically calm, in the way of Snake. Like a sudden rainstorm his wrath descended.

"No! Not the right level! Wrong level on the drop, and why would you use the bid side of the roll anyway? You *know* the 95 bid is wrong. They're offered lower than that! You should know it's stale. How could you not look at the move overnight? Not to mention the move of the curve, of the widening in swap spreads? Do you have any idea how the markets work? Are you paying attention? This job is hard enough without *giving* the money away. Tighten it up!"

All eyes were on me. The floor seemed quiet. My eyes burned. For the first and only time I wanted to cry. It was all I could do to hold back tears. He stood above me for a few seconds more. A quick check with Snake would have helped me avoid the error, but I'd been heady, had thought too much of my own talent, my own gut feel.

Finally Win left, indicating that I was to come to his office. It was the end of the day, already dark out. A canopy of only the most potent stars glittered in the clear night. If I looked into his window in a shallow way, not through it, I could see my reflection. My suit, my pumps, my silk shirt, a gold scarab bracelet that had belonged to my mother, that she'd given to me, that while writing I hadn't seen the need to wear. I hadn't seen the need to be adorned to sit alone all day. I had come to appreciate being adorned, by clothes, by jewels, by knowing I could pay for my whims: a highlight, eyebrow-shaping, a dinner out with a friend. I felt more present. Perhaps that was a common description of any giddy beginning. What had become of the woman who could sit alone all day, who could think deeply, who cared to understand the depths beneath the surface? The reflection caught me: my tidy hair, my precise bangs. Whom had I become?

Win closed the door and sat down. We couldn't hear the floor, but everyone could see us. The pain in the pit of my stomach continued to gnaw. Win swirled his chair around to face the window and then to face me. I looked him in the eye. I knew how far away I was from the shore, how difficult it would be to get back home. Something big had come to an end. I was no longer potential. Like the moment you wake up in bed with a lover, having thrown away your family, and realize he is not what you'd imagined him to be—like the husband you've left, he burps and farts and drinks too much, has flaws and a history of his own. He is not a blank slate upon which happiness can be written.

"I thought you didn't yell. You told me you didn't yell," I said. Win considered me, but did not respond. I remembered how unafraid I'd been of Mr. Radalpieno.

"I've helped you win your bet," I said. For I had. I knew enough to know that. The loss was a loss, but he'd made me into a trader, and wasn't that what he said he'd do? And he'd done it in record time, less than a year. On the floor people were leaving their desks for the day. Win continued to look at me, holding me with his eyes.

He wanted me to speak, to fill the room. But I said nothing. The East River striped the night, an enormous trench on which sailed the lonely lights of a small boat. A woman who'd vanished while walking her dog had just turned up there, the remains successfully identified after nine months in the waters. I imagined they were called the waters because of the mix of rivers and the ocean. When I was in elementary school, an upstanding mother in the community had met her end wrapped like a sausage in an Oriental carpet, tied taut and carted from Maryland to New York, to be deposited in the East River. I could remember my parents discussing it. They didn't think I was paying attention. But I was, of course. What child wouldn't have been? A woman wrapped in a carpet, murdered by her husband—at least the husband had been accused of the deed—and my father, flabbergasted, saying, "A cliché. A cliché," offended not by the murder, it seemed, but by the murderer's lack of imagination. Blue lights blinked from the tips of a pair of cranes that loomed in the dark like outsized dinosaur skeletons on the Brooklyn shore.

"You've proved to be what I'd thought you'd be," Win said. "Though it's taken you longer to fail than we'd predicted. You also lost more than we'd predicted, but to a large degree that's our fault."

"How much did Radalpieno bet I'd sink?"

"I'll lose a little here, but in the end I'm coming out ahead. You don't need to worry." I could still see my reflection in the glass, the lights of the city adding patterns to my uniform. We were all the same here. No future, no past.

Snake, though more experienced and talented and male and Indian, was no different from me. We were erased. His Hindu name was Seshnaga, which he used when he began at B&B. Seshnaga, the serpent, had been born of what was left after the universe and its inhabitants had been created. The king of snakes, he had one thousand heads, swift, gliding movements, hypnotic eyes. His heads formed a massive hood, and beneath it, protected from the monsoons, sat Vishnu as if upon a couch. Earth is said to rest on Seshnaga, and he is believed to spew venomous fire that destroys creation at the end of each kalpa, or eon. Of all the snake gods, he was the most revered. Here at B&B, Snake was not the boy who was brought to America at nine months of age by a mother joining her husband at MIT, not the boy who flew back to Calcutta twice a year to stay in the family mansion, to be waited on by fawning grandmothers who didn't like how he was being Americanized, who impatiently and with speed tried to train him in their Bengali customs so they would shape the man he was to become. Rather, here, Seshnaga became Snake, a lovely man, yes, with his crisp shirts that fit snugly round his neck. Good at numbers, kind. But he could have come from anywhere. In a different time, when a doctor's salary competed with a Wall Street paycheck, he would have gone into medicine.

"And what will you do with me when you're finished?" I asked, looking Win in the eye. Suddenly I hated this person.

"Shall we have a drink?"

"If you like."

"I'd like you to pour me a Scotch." His face was in shadow, his dark eyes like pits. I thought back to him on the beach in Maine, with his ridiculous goggles and leather jacket. I thought of him in Radalpieno's office, perhaps a little nervous. I thought of his pursuit of me in the fall a year ago. He'd got me, and had neatly turned my indifference into fear, and in so doing came to own me.

I stood up and went to the bookcase and opened a drawer, pulled from it the bottle of Macallan he kept there, poured him a glass and set it down, more noisily than I'd intended, in front of him.

"And for you?" he asked.

"Thanks for being concerned," I said. I thought of my girls, how many nights I'd been missing them, not putting them to bed. Tonight would be another. I felt the ache. Again my reflection made herself known to me. How did I allow this? I had another life. That was a truth. And had it been such a bad one? We'd struggled, certainly, but we'd always made it work. I looked at the door. How easy it would be to open it and leave. I did not pour myself a Scotch.

"I still have work to do with you yet. You'll make your mark this year, but I want to see the ramp."

"The year's almost up," I said.

"There are eighteen months. Then there's another year."

"So you'll keep stoking the bet?"

"That's how it works."

"And when you're finished?"

"I'm not following."

"Me. When you're finished with me?"

"What are you implying, India?"

I came in with my eyes open. I knew that. But I wanted to blame him for my own folly, for allowing myself to be used, then humiliated, for allowing myself to annihilate what I had spent years of struggle to create, for tempting me, really.

"You know what I'm asking. When your bet is won, where will I go?"

"My bet is won. You just said so yourself."

"Where will I go?" I persisted.

"Oh, that. You're worried, are you? It doesn't become you, India. I prefer the anger." He sat back aggressively in his chair, tipping it so that his head reclined toward the window, the sprawl of a man completely confident in himself.

"You're mad at me because I fucked up today."

"Today was nothing. It's called tuition." He sat up abruptly, placing his elbows on the desk, a new intensity in his eyes. "Yes, a lot of money, a high price, but it happens to everyone. The problem is if that's all you can do. You need to know what it feels like to lose, because then you know where the bottom is, where you don't want to go again. This is a business that's as much about losing as it is about winning. We need losers, India. There are always losers. We just need them to be somewhere else. A lot of people are winning these days, but we all know that's not going to last, and then it'll get ugly, really ugly, and there will be a lot of losers. If you stick around I'll put a lot of money on the fact that you'll see ugly. Banks will be eating each other alive. Hedge fund wonks will bet against people like us. Why? Because they can. And if their voices are loud enough, they can bring the whole operation down simply by instilling a little fear. If everyone could learn the feeling of failure, use it to his advantage, the Street would be a much more complicated and interesting place. As it is, we career from the pain of crisis to the euphoria of new opportunities. I'm paid to find the balance, and learning how to find it starts with the tuition you paid today."

He took a long sip of his drink, sloshed it in his tumbler. The pit of my stomach was now fairly empty. How fast, it seemed, these walls had become the perimeter of my existence.

"Tulip mania," he said. He tilted back in his chair and raised his glass a bit and stared into it. "You know what I want from you? I want you to go home and wear this loss like a fantastic dress. I want you to feel it in every part of you. I want it to become you."

I said nothing for a minute. Then, "And if I don't want to?"

"You don't have a choice, do you?"

"I don't?"

"I bought you. You're mine."

I flinched, but then, like a revelation, just as sudden and acute, I understood how true this was. I didn't have my job at the university anymore. I'd given that up in the summer without a second's hesitation. They'd never have me back now. I'd lost my credibility there. Without the old job, or the new one, I'd have no salary, no insurance for the family. How would I pay the tuition, April, doctors, the rent? I felt the walls and windows move in closer to me.

"And when you're finished with me?"

"You'll go back to writing, I suppose. I don't know. You're a grown woman. You'll get a job, here or somewhere else."

It had all started out as a game. I'd known that—a game I'd been eager to play, just as I'd been eager to be absorbed by the culture, the bets, the hamburgers, the late nights, the numbers. But today all that stopped, the game had stopped, for him, for me.

Sixteen

I HAD PLAYED the game because I had wanted to see if it was possible to change the course of my life. In a way, I had wanted to conform, be erased, be reborn to live the American dream, to live a life untainted by constant worry and debt. But what was it really that I was valuing, as they say on the Street, in this *vita nuova*? What Elysian Fields bloomed there? "The land of joy . . . where the blessed make their homes." Sixty-dollar napkins? Hundred-thousand-dollar mirrors? "Personal grooming experiences"? Yoga retreats and dietitians and personal trainers and life coaches and personal shoppers? Better cars? Better homes and, it almost goes without saying, gardens? Private lessons—the sacred ice time of the soul for kids, all just for them? Their favorite teachers magically transported into the living room for a little one-on-one face time with the *kinder*? Private tours of the museum's marquee shows after hours—a docent trying mightily to explain the art of Degas, Rembrandt, El Greco, Arbus and Murakami for four-year-olds? Nannies for life? Private schools, private colleges, private planes, VIP passes through gilded corridors, the world wonderfully cleansed? Plucking your pleasures and enticements as you pass them by?

It starts like this: you get a job, you want a better job; you get a car, you want a better car; you get a house, you want a better house; you have a child, you want another, then another. Crested Butte becomes Aspen becomes Gstaad. The wife? I've found another, one who makes me laugh. In a fairy tale, a hard-pressed writer—who cares only for the good, the true and the beautiful—has grown destitute because of the world's general indifference to art. In a moment of desperation, the man agrees, temporarily, to trade places with his shadow. But his shadow, who understands how the world truly works, is confident and charming and opportunistic, and becomes successful and well liked by all, even though he's only a shadow. In time, the shadow slowly eclipses the man, eventually bedding the man's wife. By the time the man comes to his senses, threatening to expose the state of things, the wife and the shadow conspire to have him killed. It's a dark parable whose significance seemed at once immediate and yet always, somehow, skittering off at the periphery of one's vision.

In Central Park, for instance, at the Conservatory Water, filled with model boats, I was with Theodor and the girls the Saturday after my first big bona fide failure as a capitalist fly-girl, thinking about Win. "Don't forget this," he'd said. "Like those bad reviews you say you always remember, the ones that pinch you awake in the middle of the night. What was it you called it? The boulder someone planted in your stomach? That's nice. If you want to survive here, don't forget the boulder."

I could feel the flush of humiliation still. After my first bond debacle, I was both the failed writer who stupidly trades places with his shadow and the shadow himself, only in this version of the story the shadow receives his comeuppance, gets knocked down by a bond market, which runs over him like a bus, to remind him, in the way that only New York City can, that he's just a freaking shadow after all.

That Saturday was a crisp fall day, and the tiny white sails of the model sloops tacked gently, hopefully into the breeze. The Lebanon cedars with their craggy limbs dappled sun like trees on Japanese screens. Uniformed attendants pushed old ladies in wheelchairs. Nannies cooed to babies in prams. Girls and boys stood mesmerized by the boats as clouds lumbered slowly across the sky like dirigibles. This sad and beautiful world—an artist with her easel stood painting it with watercolors. Some foreigners strolled by speaking gaily their own language.

"You don't have to stay, you know," Theodor said. I had asked him why we couldn't run away, live on a boat for a year, homeschool the girls. I had allowed myself to become a plaything of big-time gamblers. I could see Lily's face with its pursed and puzzled expression. She had made the same point, and I hadn't listened. I'd lost myself, even if I'd won for Win. When all was said and done, it was I who lost—and was lost. Checkmate.

Our girls had rented their own radio-powered boat and were negotiating it across the water with a fine precision, ignited by the one desire of commanding their craft. They ran up to us where we sat on a park bench (endowed by the Silversteins, in memory of Marni Rae 1909–1999) for snacks, and we popped little Goldfish crackers into their bird-like mouths and off they ran again. Ruby, with her guileless brown eyes, had announced on our way here (on bikes) that her friend Ada didn't think much of the boating here, that it was more challenging in the Luxembourg Gardens. "I want to go there instead," Ruby had declared. "That's spoiled," Gwyneth snapped, never missing a chance to chastise her sister. "The Luxembourg Gardens are in Paris." "So?" Ruby replied. "You're impossible," Gwyneth said, rolling her eyes. Then, "Mommm. Gwyneth's being mean."

Is this what I wanted them to inherit? To walk serenely untroubled through life with friends who could rate model boating on different continents? At B&B, men from everywhere—Indians and African Americans, Chinese and Koreans, WASPs and

Jews and you name it—arrived each year, but there was no diversity. The desire for money had leveled them all, honed the edges, flattened the contours into one high plateau.

In front of us a mother appeased her upset two-year-old, crying for sunglasses forgotten at home, by taking off her own Chanel glasses and putting them on her daughter. "Is that better? Now don't drop them because they are very expensive." They wore matching tan dresses and cashmere shawls. The glasses, on the two-year-old, with their bold logo on the arm, looked as though they belonged, resting on the dull bridge of her tiny nose.

"You do this if you like it. If you don't, you say *arrivederci,*" Theodor said.

"And a job? I wouldn't have a job."

"We'd work it out. This is a lark. You must remember that." The sun caught the silver in his hair, making him look older than his thirty-nine years. His sideburns were completely gray. When had *that* happened?

"If I were to leave now, it would look as if I couldn't hack it," I said. That was how the talons went in: fear of perception.

"You're kidding," he said.

Theodor's show was opening in Fort Worth in a few weeks. He'd spent the past several months on the business of his career, promoting the show with interviews, arranging for the loan of works owned by various patrons and museums. How I'd have loved to be simply an artist's wife. I could have taken care of all the business while he produced more work. Perhaps I could have been a muse. I thought of Emma. The Chapmans were back in New York now, Maine closed for the winter, Will rattled with prepublication concerns, calling to ask me if a six-city tour was good enough, to read me the advance praise, the blurbs, to tell me of Emma's plans for a surprise party given with Win and Cavelli, warning me not to let on. It was both endearing and annoying that Will valued my ear for all the news about his book. And his desire for my ear made me feel I still had a foot in a world that he was making his own, still had advice worthy of articulation, still had stock there.

"I wanted you to save me," I said. Theodor was not a sentimental man. He did not waste time on banalities. He was not the sort who would woo his woman with public candlelit dinners and roses, statements writ large for others to see and admire: look at how he loves his wife; he's having an airplane write I LOVE YOU across the sky; he's dropping five hundred grand on a fireworks display over the Hudson River. No, Theodor's sentiments were private like his kisses, and he was not the saving kind. So he laughed at me now. I thought back to our first evening together, following the Salvage Stream, as he had called it, how I'd imagined myself a castoff he'd found in those waters and picked up and resurrected, made whole again.

"You wouldn't let me save you if I tried."

I shrugged my shoulders. "I suppose not." But that was not really true. I wanted the impossible, to become something I wasn't, to be saved by a man whom I'd concocted to be something I had always known him not to be. And so I continued to sink, watching my girls in the fall light. They were free. I could see that because I'd changed my career, they'd made an adjustment in the way they faced the world, a subtle tipping, but a tipping of chance for them all the same, which they intuited more than understood. I was around less but also worried less, and in that open space they came to feel they belonged, staked their unequivocal claim and felt justified in their desires, that perhaps now their impetuous wants could be met. I recalled another mother saying once, after her husband lost his job, "But the children, they're used to a certain lifestyle. I need to be able to maintain that."

Indeed! My girls spoke of renovating the apartment so that each could have her own room—or better yet, moving into something bigger, a plan we spoke of often but which now had the weight of the inevitable. "And we'd own it," Gwen declared.

Even at their age, they understood the value placed on homeownership. The government's tax policy that rewarded homeowners had trickled down to them—through me, certainly. What was I bequeathing to my daughters? What had I become? I felt possessed by an alien force—the capital markets of the world? Again I wondered how I had allowed this to happen.

As I wallowed in my newfound despair with the *vita nuova*, Tiger and his girlfriend sauntered by—because that's what they were doing. They engaged in what could only be described as a bona fide saunter, she a bottle of uncorked bubbles in a summer shirt, all aflutter and smiling, and he gripping her hand as if to both hold her back and be carried away by her. Tiger, Snake's protégé, the second-best trader on the desk, late twenties, the girl at his side, the one in the bikini framed on his desk, there to make him race. They came to life in the dappled sunlight, as if stepping from a painting. On this Indian summer day he wore flip-flops and longish shorts that revealed well-defined calves. He had the composure of one in charge. Out in the real world, away from the legion who were just like him, he seemed more of a replica, one groomed from a young age, like so many others, to be the man that he had already become. She too had been groomed from a young age to ride on the arm of such a man, by parents who taught their girls to expect a lot, to settle for nothing less than precisely what they wanted. This was revealed in her shirt (the neckline flirting with her bust), her gait, the easy smile cast by her full lips, her confident stride. (Hadn't I been taught the same thing? But a mutant gene had early on made me desire the artistic life, and I had pursued it at all costs, and found a mate who would help realize that want.)

The pair was a particular creation of this moment in history. They'd soon appear in the Sunday paper's wedding section, their faces smiling, saying that, indeed, life was good. I wanted to poke ahead, imagine what life would do to them. I wanted to see the full arc of the story. (And they paused just then to watch the boats, he taking her hand more firmly in his.) I wanted escalation and the denouement—bitter divorce, lots of money splayed, unseemly events involving other women and a quest for the elusive Something More. I suppose I still thought like a writer, an observation that didn't make me unhappy.

It occurred to me then that I had been drawn to Win so long ago (it felt long ago, anyway) because he declared himself a seer, all-seeing, capable of reading the future. And, in kind, he had been drawn to me because I saw myself as a seer. Now, the seduction over, we were left with the reality of who we were, our failings, and the fact that the game we were playing was over. He'd asked me to wear the dress of failure and humiliation, embody it completely and come back ready to fight again. Could I do that? Did I want to do that? Did I want to continue buying into a world that created the oblivious pair in front of me, whom, I realized, I did not want to spot me, on the bench or anywhere else? If they'd stepped out of a picture and into the real world, so had I, and I wanted to stay hidden.

Theodor had gotten up and was with the girls and their boat. I kept my eyes on them, hoping Tiger and his girlfriend would saunter on by. "Play young," Win had said, and here I was surrounded by snacks and a family, playing middle age. Theodor walked back toward me and then I heard his name, called in the familiar, marbleized accent of Will Chapman's and Lily Starr's publisher—the Dashing Cavelli, Leonardo of Piccadilly.

"Theodor Larson." It was more elegant than simply eating the *r*'s. Rather, it was as if the *r*'s were somehow exempt. Then his body caught up with his voice and he stood in front of me, in a Harris tweed jacket and knitted tie and all that goes with being a well-groomed gent: a car and driver, a box at the opera, a table at Dino's. His aura spelled his flair for spotting success. He, like Win, was a cunning gambler, though of another sort, could tell which writers it would pay to boost—that singular combination of talent and superficial daring. In some ways he alone had changed the tenor of the market, back in his day, by giving placement to the cult of the personality.

Even if you had no idea who he was, he struck the image of a bold speculator of some kind or another, one who knew how the world worked and used that knowledge to extraordinary advantage. Trailing behind him was his Indian wife (a novelist and much younger and, yes, published by him) and their two young sons. Then he said my name, asking Theodor where he hid the charming India Palmer. He said my name loudly and with a flourish that legitimized his moniker. He was Dashing, extremely so. Strong broad face, suitable height, defined pose. I popped up to greet him, feeling the familiar unease I had always felt around him that spelled his power over me—that he could change my life if he wished, that he could save me with the fine publication of a book. It was as though I stood trembling before an old lover. The emotion startled me.

And then, at the sound of my name, Tiger turned from the boats toward me, and the four of us—Tiger, Theodor, Cavelli and I—formed a quartet of surprised greetings: Tiger and I a little stunned to see each other out of context, as though the sun made us palpable and real. And then Cavelli between us, trying to sort out Tiger, giving him a sweeping once-over with his eyes, sizing him up, deciding that he was from a different orbit. Tiger introduced his girlfriend, pulling her into the mix. Her name was Veronica. The name suited her simply in the way she tossed back her hair. She extended her hand to Cavelli and Theodor. Tiger introduced himself, using his given name, Robert Lippincott, which he never used. It seemed funny to hear it, as if I were speaking about a stranger—which, after all, he was to me in the clear light of day. He explained that he was my colleague. I'm sure that at first Cavelli assumed Tiger to be a university colleague. Then Cavelli and Theodor explained their connections to me: former publisher; husband. It was all very awkward—there are those moments in life in which chance encounters collide to form an avalanche. "But he's called Tiger," Veronica offered helpfully, as though that piece of information would sort it all out. "Indeed," Cavelli answered with a smile, extending his hand.

Tiger grasped it and a satisfied look spread over his impatient lips. His impatience could help him at times, but often it got in his way. Then he looked at me, and it seemed I grew—the girls raced over and hugged me and, as if on cue, I popped Goldfish into their mouths—and in this gesture grew even more, from thirty to, say, forty-five. Tiger was seeing Win's creation naked before him in all humility, and it gave him a sudden edge. All traders relish an edge, though he wasn't certain what to do with this one.

Cavelli absorbed Tiger absorbing me. In Cavelli's curious fashion he wanted to get to the bottom of Tiger, who announced to the quintet that I was a "rising star." "She'll be trading her own book by year end," he said.

Cavelli, his chin raised, asked Tiger what in the world he was speaking about. His eyes twinkled. He'd never before been so curious about me. Tiger looked at me, and Cavelli looked at Theodor with raised eyebrows, the king of my old universe, waiting for an answer. My new universe had a different king. And though Cavelli hadn't thought about me in years, he smiled and exhibited a well-timed, mildly proprietary concern that was ever so charming. I had left him, not he me. He had made a reasonable offer for the third novel and I had rejected it as paltry. But he knew how the world worked. He did not take offense. So I told him.

"I've become a bond trader," I said. It was not dissimilar to when, in the beginning of my writing career, I would tell people (when asked what I did) that I was a novelist. "I am a novelist," I would say, and I could feel myself stand a bit taller. I am a novelist. I am a bond trader. Except that most people didn't burst out laughing, as Cavelli did then. So much for elevation.

Even so, something wonderful happened, wonderful and unexpected: I had a strong desire to return to B&B, for Monday morning to be here so that I could walk back to my desk and start trading and learn from the mistake and then learn some more and take on this world again, not as a game but with a passion. I did not want to be laughed at, simple as that. I did not want to be afraid of Cavelli (and all he represented) ever again, simple as that. I held him with my eyes, watching how beautiful laughter can also be.

"You'll have to tell me all about this sometime, India," Cavelli said.

"I will," I said and offered him my most lovely smile.

Veronica, now part of the group, confided that she believed mine to be an amazing story: "It's all Tiger has spoken about for months." She gave me a genuine look of admiration, which warmed me to her, made me want to know more about her.

"I should say," Cavelli said. "That's not the end I'd have imagined for India."

I had once known Cavelli quite well, or well enough for a publisher. He liked to have long lunches with wine (on occasion, bottles) at his table at Dino's. I was not special; he did this with all the local authors, or the authors who came through town, on his list. He did not discriminate. If you were worth publishing, you were definitely worth having lunch with. Cavelli announced that I'd been an author of his who had left him for the ugly lure of money. Veronica offered me a sympathetic look, but apparently she'd had it with this encounter (*ugly money?*), and tugging gently on Tiger's hand, she told him they'd be late if they didn't get going. With farewells, they left.

Theodor was called away by the girls, and Cavelli and I stood there for a moment before his wife called for him to leave. "That was your mistake, India," he said, assuming he understood the larger picture, the route that had led me to this—what to call it?—this decision, and once again I pictured vividly the eagerness with which I would return Monday morning. I had worn the dress of failure. I would never forget how it fit. My former world would never have power over me again. I was released. I was releasing myself. For what became clear right then, falling into sharp focus, for an instant crystalline, was that I had been so willing to throw it all away because the writing had stopped belonging to me. Rather, for me it had come to belong to the opinion of others and mysterious market forces and the power and influence of money, money as the great indicator of everyone's worth. I could not work so hard at writing when I could no longer allow it to belong to me.

"We would always have published you, India," he continued. "I had great regard for your talent. I hope you don't mind my avuncular nature." Off he strolled, catching up with his wife, the boys running on ahead. As soon as I was out of his vision, I vanished from his thoughts, but he did not leave mine so quickly. What good would that have done me, his publishing me? I watched him make his way around the pond, his slow gait parting the Saturday idlers, not as a swan parting water, as once I would have seen him, but as the elderly man that he was. I had done this thing, you see, I had challenged myself here, and I was going to succeed. This did not have to do with Win now. Monday morning. My desire to return carried me aloft, for the moment, on the great wave of hope. This was a bet with myself now.

Seventeen

I WANTED ONE THING. I wanted to win.

To feel the risk, the exhilaration, the intensity of the present moment, the never-ending now. Risk created the dancing-on-the-cliff's-edge opportunity I was seeking. Without risk, you were just a schlub selling Treasury notes. A plodder. Risk became the wind at my sail, the elixir that fueled me. I came to live under the influence of its sensation, under the influence of the whirl of events flashing across the Bloomberg screen. The challenge was to be the master of it, to use it to my advantage.

The intensity could make me scared.. The speed of the market could make me scared. The large sums in play could make me scared. But as Win reminded me, you're better at your job when you're a bit scared. You just had to harness that emotion. Stay over your skis. The bumps will come—no way around that. But if you're not risking something, you're not making as much. I wanted to win, so I went big.

Sure, I'd had some small successes and had earned respect. But people seem to remember only when you tank, when you eat it or get eaten. It wasn't only for the small taste of Schadenfreude, but because, aside from tribal rituals—hamburger-eating contests and the like—the financial belly flop was the true test, which showed them who you were, whom they were dealing with. Equanimity in failure knitted you to the tribe. The trick was, then, to cultivate within yourself a fantastic and selective memory for such things, which became, with time, a lot of time—two years is a geological age in this world—like layers of sediment, the stuff that made and defined you in your own mind and in the mind of the tribe, that became the ground upon which you finally stood on your own, a made man, as the mobsters say, an equal among your fellows.

Everyone knew what the calamities looked and felt like. The knot in the stomach like a bayonet. The sweaty palms. The sense of total isolation, of being thoroughly unfit to command the post entrusted to you, while the trading floor, all abuzz with actual traders earning their way to stardom, silently mocked you as you sat on the egg you'd just laid and braced yourself for the summons to Win's office. Then the yelling, the throwing of things across the room. The boys all wanted to see that—sure, it was spectacular entertainment of the sort comedians speak of when their fellow craftsmen bomb onstage. *Now, that's funny!* Nothing in the world funnier, really. But the boys mostly wanted to watch how I would *walk through that,* how I would carry myself. This they would note with the attention of connoisseurs, because in the end we relied on each other. We were under fire together. They wanted to know whom they had with them in the foxhole.

And so, the day after the big failure I wore—into the foxhole, as it were—a skirt to work, chocolate-brown wool, a loose weave of lace at the hemline, an ivory satin shirt, chocolate slingbacks, a gold wire wrapping pink jasper (designed by Theodor, who was making his way into jewelry, mostly for me) around my neck—a style that could be called corporate chic. I wasn't going to subordinate my feminine side any longer. Most of all, I wore a big, broad smile. I knew one thing clearly: I was not going to make a career out of being a low-level associate. I swiped my security card like a pro, rode the elevator to my floor, swiped my card again, walked to my desk, said my hellos and did not look back, did not dwell anymore on the world I'd left behind.

And two years passed. My drive and determination were an engine cutting across time and its debris. Two years, from October 2004 to September 2006. George W. Bush was officially elected President of the United States. Yasir Arafat died. Hamid Karzai was inaugurated as Afghanistan's president. An earthquake in the Indian Ocean triggered a tsunami that killed 225,000 people in eleven countries. Ruby played Offenbach's Barcarolle perfectly, and like a sixteen-year-old, in her winter concert, which, as it happens, I missed, as I missed most of the girls' events. But for now this was as it had to be, and I believed it was a good lesson for them to see their mother work. And Theodor could always attend. *Brokeback Mountain* won an Academy Award. Gwyneth was invited to play goalie on her lacrosse team, and she accepted. Pope John Paul II died. Will Chapman's *Never Say Die* was published.

Let me pause here, amid the flotsam on the shoreline, to let you know that the reviews were universally spectacular. On May 3, 2005, there was an enormous sendoff for the book, hosted by Win on a rooftop terrace belonging to another banker friend of the Chapmans—champagne and canapés and men in tuxedos with gloved hands serving with silver trays, a mixture of artists and bankers who blended well, having ascended to the same plateau. Cavelli worked the crowd effortlessly. To me he said, "Ah, my bond trader. Mortgage-backed securities?" And I, "Good memory." And he, "We still need to get to the bottom of this." And I, tapped on the shoulder by Win, was swept into a different conversation. "You don't miss this world," Win said. Not a question but a command. He was dating a girl named Ginger now, a name more fitting than Beatrix somehow, sleek and young, with her eyes on him possessively as we spoke—the only girl of his

I ever met, seen at this party and not again. High fashion, long silky hair.

The reviews of *Never Say Die:* "Chapman is incapable of writing an uninteresting sentence." And "The author does not have a banal thought in his brain." And "He can write about the contours of a woman's desire like no other contemporary novelist." And "*Never Say Die* is a tour de force." And "His publisher has likened him to Thomas Wolfe, but against this comparison it is Wolfe, not Chapman, who comes up short." More than just the book pages trumpeted his "riches to rags" transformation. Will held court, his strong jaw projecting the confidence of a man who knew his way in this world. Emma was radiant, all previous signs of fracture erased by the anti-aging elixir of success and its reward.

That was all fine, if somewhat predictable. I, on the other hand, had gone the other way, done the unexpected—the skirt in Agency Fixed had become a made man, earned a reputation as a savvy trader with quick and unwavering views on market positions. My cut-to-the-chase nature was alluring to clients looking for clarity amid market ambiguity. The pace suited me. The constant need to be attentive to twenty things at the same time suited me.

"A little ADD is a good thing," Win had once said. And I now understood what he meant. Up at 2 A.M. with Japan, calculating figures, the hedge rations of MBS as the market moved. On the line with clients—Blackride, Johnson, with Texas and Georgia. I could do it. It wasn't so different from managing the family—the finances (or, I should say, the debt), the appointments, the insurance, the playdates, the sleepovers, the scheduling of school and camp and lessons and how we'd juggle this and that to pay for it all—grateful every day that those concerns no longer occupied me. I had so many balls in the air at once, and I loved it, loved catching them for an instant simply to throw them right back up there into the swirling circle. I flew to Georgia, to Iowa, to Texas, to South Dakota, to coddle clients, play a little golf. The duffer's game I'd learned under my father's tutelage I had to relearn with the help of a pro, became good enough, just, to pass. I wanted these clients to believe I cared. I listened to them talk about their children, their marriage woes, their third-home ambitions: a chalet in Aspen—was invited there with a ski tour of Ajax, led by an impossibly handsome Patagonian ski instructor. The wife of my client whisked me away from the slopes for a manicure-pedicure at the chateau, administered by an overly Botoxed mobile manicurist—her age hidden in her face like the faintest silhouette of a boat sunk in the shallows of a lake—who announced several times, "I only use French polish," and filled us in on the local gossip (a movie star, a former President, a renowned CEO and their revolving lovers), the wife believing that I'd prefer nail pampering to skiing with the boys. I pretended to keep up with their epic drinking, all of us believing (if not admitting) we were all fine—just fine!—up here, breathing a thinner air.

July 7, 2005: London's subways and one double-decker bus are hit by Islamic terrorist bombs, killing fifty-two, wounding more than seven hundred. Britain's worst attack since World War II. The Dow continues to rise, breaking records; stock options multiply. Again we vacation in Maine, spending our week in a rented house down the beach from the Chapmans', all of us falling in love with the spot, the intoxicating view working its way into our bloodstream, my daughters coming to think of Pond Point as their summer spot where they will return year after year, summers following summers to the remotest outposts of time. Hurricane Katrina slams the Gulf Coast, killing more than a thousand, displacing millions, nearly wiping New Orleans off the map. Our infrastructure begins showing signs of inevitable collapse—bridges fall, roads crumble. Saddam Hussein goes on trial, and on the same day an earthquake in Kashmir steals some seventy-nine thousand souls.

"It never stops," my mother used to say when I was a girl. "If it's not one thing, it's another. It never stops." I would look at her and wonder about the consequences of *it* stopping, of *it* all suddenly stopping.

My annual bonus doubles, then triples, then the sky's the limit: B&B stock options that start amassing a beautiful, billowy wealth. And wealth, like certain kinds of sleek sailboats, made one swifter, allowed you to sail faster than the true wind of the market.

My father tells me he is proud of me for taking responsibility for myself. "But," he asks, "what is it you make? What are you making? What service do you provide?"

My mother asks, with solemn, doubtful eyes, if this is what I truly want.

My brother says nothing. I want my brother to say something. I remember the first summer he went away to camp, remember his return. I shadowed him for days, kissed him whenever I could. It was the first time I understood that people left.

The Dow hits a milestone, topping eleven thousand for the first time since 2001. Vice President Cheney accidentally shoots his friend in the face and chest while quail hunting. Representative Tom "The Hammer" DeLay steps down, forced out of politics altogether. Saddam is found guilty and sentenced to death for crimes against humanity. President Bush and Prime Minister Tony Blair admit mistakes were made and express regret for the abuse of the Abu Ghraib prisoners.

It never stops: journalists killed in Iraq, soldiers killed in Iraq, civilians killed in Iraq, riots in Afghanistan, nuclear missile tests in North Korea, Enron executives Kenneth Lay and Jeffrey Skilling convicted, thousands dead in Indonesian earthquake, sectarian violence in the Sunni Triangle, Darfur genocide, Fidel Castro pretends not to be seriously ill, gay marriage rejected, secret court to rule on wiretaps, U.S. revises torture policy, Democrats revise primary schedule, Kenneth Lay dead, grim report on Iraq, Pluto demoted and no longer a planet.

The mortgage market frothed. Homeownership rose to a record of almost 70 percent. Three headlines I particularly remember:

June 2005:
The Trillion-Dollar Bet—Homeowners Take Risks in a Bid for Lower Mortgage Payments

May 2006:
The New Road to Serfdom—An Illustrated Guide to the Coming Real Estate Collapse

September 2006:
Mortgages Grow Riskier and Investors Are Attracted

In April 2006, Lily Starr published her second novel. It became a much-publicized bomb, panned in the daily and Sunday papers. "It took her twenty years to write the first, radiant book. Apparently that's the span of time she needs to write something worth reading." And "This inelegant attempt proves she's a one-book wonder." By June the novel was buried beneath the sediment of other books. I felt sorry for Lily; I remembered the penetrating humiliation; the reviews were likely unfair. But I did not have much time to reflect. I had taken the plunge into what made the world go round, into multimillion-dollar trades and dazzling nights. Was I throwing money away? Yes, I was. And the more I threw, the more the apparent wind behind my sleek vessel brought money my way.

Theodor had found an entirely new and powerful focus, which allowed me to see for the first time that he hadn't been so carefree in our previous life as I'd always supposed. Our grinding financial concerns had bothered him, but now he seemed released from those concerns, and this I relished and celebrated quietly every day. I loved that he was fabulously lost in his work. He'd completed two new commissions and had a show opening in Amsterdam. He'd hired an assistant—a grad student named

Harrison, who wore the same T-shirt every day and followed Theodor around like a shy but earnest puppy—and the studio was full of the lively sounds of tinkering and banging. Theodor's sketches were all over the walls, his plans for new projects expanding. In his spare time he made necklaces, really smashing in their filigree design. He would come home from the studio and we'd have long, amusing conversations over late dinners, and I'd catch myself thinking, in a blinding flash of the obvious: Hey. He's funny, this guy I married! I kind of like him.

Every day, crossing the bridges into Manhattan, the morning sunlight in all the glass, the traders wonder if today will be the day—because it might, and often is, at least for someone. Every single trader out there is waiting for that day. Again, it is not dissimilar to the writer waiting for the big moment of recognition to occur, to be hailed as great and showered with the reward. *Today could be the day.* But of course, *it* comes when you are not expecting it: the big day in the big game.

The first sign was the lights on the turret, the phone. They were blinking wildly. I knew who was calling. I could tell from the impatience of the lights. I will never forget the day. I will never forget what I was wearing. It was the skirt I'd worn on the Monday after my first failure: chocolate-colored, a different cream shirt. The skirt had a good vibe, made me feel lucky, strong in my perseverance.

Snake was in Calcutta for a funeral. So I was first on the desk, Tiger having been stolen away by another bank the year before, along with Josh. Sam had moved to the Wild West of subprime, along with the fabulously successful June Scarpetti. Gus, the analyst, was now an associate and next to me in the hierarchy. The new kids were kids, smart, sharp, going places, but still just on the threshold, freshly minted from the London School of Economics and MIT: Jon, English, a cricket star, and Pat, American, a swim team star, both white boys. They called me, with Jon's

British affect, "Mum." The tag stuck after I'd taken them into Win's office for a sit-down, spent a half hour explaining how the floor worked. Did I feel as if I were speaking a foreign language? Yes, but it was a second language, one in which I'd become fluent. Did I borrow something from the Win Johns playbook? Yes, and I may have laid it on a little thick. I was unseasoned enough to want to impress these two by baffling them. Win would not have done that, and when I was finished the young boys sat there, completely flummoxed. "Jon, Pat, you're staring." Two schoolboys in their coolly pressed white shirts, jaws agape. "Yes, Mum. Sorry," Jon said. And it stuck.

I caught hold of the blinking lights: Cerbeus from Houston on its direct line. Just then our salesperson—a thirty-year-old girl with perfectly blown-out hair, just the same every day, and smart, demanding eyes—marched over, pointed to me and said, "You. With me, now," lifting me with her finger, using that tone of the salesperson, a tone that won't quite accept that she's not a trader, that at the end of a long day she goes home in a cab rather than a town car. Okay, I thought, I'll give her this. This is big and she wants me next to her.

Perfectionism, I came to understand, is a good thing in preparation, but a bad thing once a trade is being executed. You have to be able to let go. In rehearsing for a concert, a musician practices over and over to get it right. But on the night of the performance she has to let all of that work vanish, allow the feeling to take over, for spontaneity to carry her to the far reaches of her talent.

I stood up to follow the salesperson, turned to Gus and said, "Whatever you do, don't buy another mortgage." I knew what was coming. Gut feel. The split decision that you can't be taught. It starts to seep into you, along with the squirt of adrenaline. Suddenly everything's switched on high alert. I knew Cerbeus was thinking of lightening up its mortgage holdings, so much so that the salesperson's tête-à-tête at the end of the row to warn me was completely unnecessary. I was barely listening to her, nodding in agreement, but all I could think about was how to reduce my risk. I had to, in order to take on a lot of Cerbeus's risk, which was what I was driven to do, of course. It is what all traders are driven to do, because in the end, the glory goes to the biggest stars.

The guy's name was Chuck. He was on the direct, waiting for me to pick up, to price his trade. Chuck's thick Texas drawl cut across the line, skipping all of our usual pleasantries. Indeed, he wanted to sell me mortgages, FN 5.5s with a notional value of $5 billion. I'd played golf with Chuck, a slender, dapper man who wrote poetry in his spare time (fancied himself a Wallace Stevens) and loved that I'd been a novelist. Of all my clients, he was the one who asked me most about that career, had read *Generation of Fire*. He had put money in a pool with some of his colleagues, betting that within five years—start to finish—I'd be writing books again. I didn't hear this from him. He was an honest guy. No insider deals. But I did let him know I knew, told him he was dead wrong. "This is too exhilarating," I said. "Been there, done that." He gave me a big warm flirtatious smile that seemed to indicate he knew more about me than I did about myself. We were in the dry heat of a Scottsdale golf course on business, gigantic saguaros rising with all their limbs from the dirt, and the green grass as startling in this climate as a field of emeralds. A lot of Wall Street guys had that tic, thought they knew you better than you knew yourself. I shot him the same smile back. It became our own little game of truth, a way to connect.

Now on the phone: he knew where 5.5s were trading; he had been watching the market, waiting for this last little rally before making the call. It was the start of a new quarter, and he needed to unload them and was willing to sell them at a small discount if I'd take the risk of the full size, all in one clip. Five billion dollars in one trade. It was five times the amount of FN 5.5s I'd seen traded all week. In one trade. I priced the risk 6 ticks below the bid side, 98-24 bid. "I need 98-26," he said, his tone devoid of the banter that typically accompanies price negotiations. He meant business. This was the turning point, *my* turning point.

"Done," I said, dropping the line to return to my desk to focus on the risk—my risk now—and leaving the salesperson to confirm the trade. "Well," I said to Gus, "today just got a little more interesting."

I didn't know it, but we were just getting started. The deal took three days. On the second day Chuck offered me another bundle, as big as his offer the day before, again worth $5 billion. Later that day he offered a third bundle—$6 billion in notional value. I bought all three lots.

I didn't really have a choice. With all three lots I'd have more control of pricing, no competition with other dealers for positions. The more you control the information flow, the more you know, as with stud poker: if you have three kings, and an opponent is betting as if he has two kings, you know he's bluffing. But having all three lots, I also assumed tremendous risk. Sixteen billion dollars' worth of bonds, all in one coupon. This was easily ten times as many mortgages as I'd ever had, as Snake had ever had, in risk. What if I couldn't unload them? In fact, this was the biggest single trade our desk had ever done, putting the whole Securitized Products department well over its risk limit. (The approval for me to go over the risk limit came, of course, from above, with, oddly to me at the time, Win dissenting. He was uneasy about the leverage, thought I'd succeed but didn't like the precedent for B&B, thought it invited a strategy that could prove dangerous if allowed to grow. But these were heady times.)

So what was on the line that required approval from the lofty white chamber above? If we go back to cars, you could say that I had, in effect, just bought all the new Toyotas in North America. They all belonged to me, in my chocolate skirt. It wouldn't be enough for me to say I had all the Priuses or all the Corollas. Rather, I had all of Toyota's cars. The job of selling them and making a profit was now entirely mine. The risk, of course, was that the market could decide it didn't want Toyotas anymore, not for a price that would make sense to me, that would allow for recouping what I'd laid out and, more important, what I'd borrowed. B&B didn't have all the capital that such a trade required. Actually, no bank could have had that kind of capital on hand. So here I'd have all these Toyotas that I hadn't paid for, but that I was responsible for, and that I would have to pay for if their value was adjusted down. The market could change its mind; it could decide it wanted GM's cars (with its Humvees and SUVs), could pass on my Toyotas. Of course the market didn't know I had all those Toyotas, giving me the advantage, and that's why Chuck didn't sell them around. Having all of them gave me the ability to manipulate and maneuver, to play to see what the market would bear. Now that I had priced the trade, I had to move the risk.

At the end of the second day, I set out my strategy at an after-hours risk meeting in the conference room. The head of Rates, the head of Fixed Income, Win, Snake (on a conference call from India) and Gus were there, among others. I was the only woman. I noted this fact as I always did, but had grown accustomed to the arrangement. (Honestly, the thought of my gender would be fleeting at best; with this kind of risk almost everything else seemed irrelevant. In a way, even when you are in there explaining your strategy, all you want to do is go out on the desk and trade. For me, risk like that is the only time I want to be at work. You wake up early, you get in early, you are *dying* to start trading again.)

Martin, the head of Rates, did most of the questioning. Win took a back seat, watching me navigate the waters, for this was the biggest test of all. But we were beyond the old bet. I was fully formed now, had the eyes, the hands, the legs, the heart of the trader. Win kept his dissent to himself. He wanted me to shine. Martin, in his thirties, a dad of three, who had a penchant for colorful suspenders, questioned pricing strategies. I had one, and I explained.

I was going to see what the market would bear. I was going to take the price low, push the 5.5s against myself, widen them out by a half a point if I had to. The key, I believed, was to generate interest, generate trading volume. If I waited for normal market flows to take me out, I would die a slow, painful death as rumors compounded a slow and steady underperformance. But if I found buyers 10, 12 ticks wider, and used that to push them tighter, I had a shot at clearing the whole trade in the money—and in just a few days. Sixteen billion in bonds in three days, a multiple of our weekly average.

There wasn't much chatter in the room, just quiet contemplation and the ubiquitous hum of electricity, the overbearing lights. I could see doubt in Martin's boisterous eyes, and not a little fear. His teeth were bright, whitened. But I had shown the boys that I could make money, had proved to them that I was scrappy and game. And here I'd wagered everything. I was allowed to use my strategy—one I chose because I believed buyers would come out of the woodwork. But if they didn't, if I'd been wrong about that baseline assumption and ended up having to sell as much as 16 ticks wider than where I had bought, I stood to lose $80 billion. In short, I'd be toast. But they knew they had to let me have this one, and they also knew that my fate depended on my ability to get it right. And they knew too, of course, that they'd be able to pick up the pieces—or most of them—if I went down. It was late September 2006. Times were good. There was plenty of money to be made. I wasn't going down, and I knew that, and somehow they knew that, because at the end of the day I was Win's, and he never failed.

Later, Martin would tell me that he had believed my strategy was either the stupidest or the ballsiest thing he'd ever known. He would tell me that he discussed it with his driver while riding home to Tenafly, to his ten-thousand-square-foot home perched on half an acre, with lights all over the place, climbing up the trees and fireplaces in every bedroom, gas lit and glowing for effect. Leaning forward, he asked the driver, "If you had twenty thousand shirts worth fifty dollars each, would you offer them for less, for forty dollars, just so you could get people to chase them as you pushed them up to fifty-five?"

"It all depends," the driver answered.

The next day, I did just that. I started offering the 5.5s wider, 2 ticks, 4 ticks, a quarter point. All of a sudden, the lights started blinking as customers called in, asking for offers. People started wanting them. It reminded me of the time I went fishing with my brother in Scotland. He found a bend in a stream where you could drop your hook and pluck out fish after fish in seconds. We were pulling them out of the water. The littlest kids, even the two-year-old, were pulling fish out.

This whole period in the financial world seemed like that; drop the hook in and pull out money. I, a former novelist, no business school experience, could drop the hook in just as easily, just like everyone else, better perhaps. Then I started moving the price back up, pushing mortgages tighter, creating my own reversal.

I took my style from Snake's playbook. I was calm. I took off my shoes. Only those closest to me and those who needed to know, because of how my trade may have affected their own positions, were aware of the ongoing deal. The guys from the risk meeting were standing behind me. At 10:45, Win whispered, like a father, "Atta girl." And no one breathed, because they were all thinking the same thing, without a trace of condescension, because they were watching me, at my little desk, slowly move an entire market. They were, as they say, very deep into this play. *Atta girl.*

At one point Radalpieno descended to the pit and quietly stood behind me with the rest of them, like spectators in an operating theater. When he came down, others on the floor began to sense that something very big was up and that I was at the center of it, like Jack LaLanne swimming up the Hudson, pulling a barge with his teeth. Radalpieno did not stay long; there wasn't much he could do. There wasn't much any of those guys could do. They didn't know the clients, the flows, the routes to unload, the way I did.

I remained quiet. I was in midperformance now. I was feeling the fear, and it was mixing beautifully with the moment, keeping my senses alert and alive. Everyone was still buying—remember, I had $16 billion to unload. The whole market was moving. You could see it happening on the screens. I recalled the day in Radalpieno's office when Snake had made the screens move, and I confess that I swelled—in a controlled way, but I swelled all the same—from all that I knew and from all that I had learned. I was proud of the results and surprised at the same time. I was good. I could feel it. I recalled Miss Fine reading my essay on my bedroom to the class, all the students attentive, listening to my words being read in Miss Fine's dulcet tones. They were rapt; they were mine. Now I remained calm. Chuck, at Cerbeus, had loved that I'd been a novelist. Having been a novelist had given me the advantage here. Having been a novelist had finally paid off.

But I didn't have much time to think. I was in high demand from salespeople and from customers who wanted to know my "thoughts" on the market. The rumors had started. The market knew that something had happened, something big, but more than that, they knew I was at the center of it. Me. Someone who, just a year earlier, wasn't even on the radar screen. Now, if you owned a mortgage, I probably knew more than you did about your risk. Knowledge was power, and my knowledge of who had kings (to return to our poker analogy), and who didn't, made my views critical to anyone trading the market.

We were almost out of the risk—within striking distance of just a few billion left, an amount that even I could sleep through the night with. Win and Martin were beginning to relax behind me. Gus and I tolerated the small jokes that replaced their tense silences, though in reality we stayed focused on the risk, communicating with hand signals and in our own shorthand as we managed the book.

"Pick up Mitchell," said our head of Pass-Through Sales. Mitchell was an important client, with Samson. He had a sense of what I had, and he wanted to buy. I picked up.

"Indy, Indy, Indy," he said, his voice lightly cajoling. "You *have* been a busy girl this week, haven't you?"

"I do what I can," I responded sweetly. "That is, after all, why I'm here—to trade. How can I help you?"

"Listen," he continued, our small talk already over. "I know you need to sell these pigs, and I can see why—they're clearly not the cheapest things out there. But I have a little cash I can put to work. I thought I could help you out. Why don't you sell me one billion Fannie 5.5s. I can sell you ten-year notes on the other side. Say, 99-26, I'll buy the mortgages, versus 101-04 on tens. I'm just calling you, trying to do you a favor here."

This was it, the last billion, to take me back under my risk limit. If I printed this trade, we were home free. But the price—I knew his bid was too low. FN 5.5s were 99-27+ bid. No one else would sell a billion within a tick of that. I knew he expected his persuasive banter to weaken me, but I wasn't the same person I had been the first time I walked into this building nearly three years ago. "99-276 offer versus that strike," I said.

"India!" He tried to sound shocked. "I'm trying to help you out here." Then, with a sigh, as if he couldn't believe what a bad decision he was making, "How about 99-26+?"

"Mitchell," I responded firmly, feeling Win's doubt and Martin's skepticism, "276. You know you're not going to get them there from anyone else. It's my best level, and my final offer. Take it or leave it." That 276 was a three-quarters increase, an odd figure, but I could get Mitchell there. I could hear management behind me—Win and the others—suck in a collective breath, tense as I was, as I fought for an extra $390,000, when just two days before this risk could have cost millions.

"Why the three-quarters?" Martin whispered.

I didn't bother turning to face him. I remained focused, as if I were in a yoga balancing pose, tree pose, half moon, keeping my third eye trained. A beat passed.

"Done," Mitchell said, and the group exhaled.

Martin slapped me on the back. "Bingo!" he shouted. The deal was executed, and with my three-quarters I sailed to the finish line, selling all the 5.5s, moving risk for an important customer and earning more than $14 million for the company. Not bad, when I could have lost $80 million. Not bad at all.

"Three-quarters, that was great. Just dynamite," Martin would say for days.

"Three-quarters," Win would say, catching me at the elevator, a twinkle in those beautiful brown eyes. I could think of many things, among them that this would be my year, that this year I'd get a bonus that could accommodate not one house, but a few. I'd rolled the dice and done more, it seemed, than merely win. It was not a giddy feeling. It was the sensation of invincibility.

"Are you happy?" Theodor asked soon after, as we walked the streets of Chelsea on a Saturday without kids. He held my hand in his. Was I happy? He never asked me questions like that. Too direct and simple for him. The fact that he really had no idea what I did all day, I supposed, had reduced the caliber of his questions to the most elementary level. Are you happy?

"Yes." In a word. Yes. Yes, I was happy. I was exhilarated. I was cool. I was smart. I was savvy. I had brains, fast brains. It's a lie that money is more interesting for those who don't have it than for those who do. It's too fun to spend. Radalpieno secured and tripled my bonus. Tuition was no longer a struggle. We could keep the out-of-network allergist my older daughter loved. I did not fret about a parking ticket, the groceries, how we'd pay April each week. We asked Janine, the cleaning woman, to come four times a week. We started looking at townhouses. Having lived the other life, I knew the difference, knew that I now preferred to worry about my trades, other people's money rather than my own, rather than all I had struggled to afford. And spend? I booked a Christmas ski vacation in Telluride for the family: our own house, chef, valet, skis brought to the door, ski on ski off, sitter for the girls, private instruction, chauffeur—just to see, in part, how it felt. It felt as if I were getting away with something, enjoying a pleasure that wasn't quite mine. But it *was!* I donated to the girls' school, to museums, literacy programs, the public library, to all the prizes I'd won and been nominated for. I sent April home to her island, brought her family here. I loved being generous. I remembered that long-ago day, publication day of the last novel, remembered hoping that it would do well so that I could be generous. I could be so now.

In a store window in Chelsea I spotted a lovely dark blue wool dress, fitted, falling to just above the knee, three-quarter-inch sleeves, mother-of-pearl buttons running down the back—Cuban-born designer. Theodor asked me to try it on for him. I did, spinning before him as he stood, hand resting on chin, appraising me. He liked me in the dress, wanted to unfasten the buttons one by one. I bought it. I did not look at the price tag. I did not feel the guilt, the concern over how I'd scramble to pay for it. We ate a long lunch with wine on a rooftop terrace where people also splashed in a heated pool, and the Hudson River lay before us with all its happy sailors and in the distance the Statue of Liberty with her torch and her song of freedom.

We walked along the river to Tribeca, dropped in on the Chapmans, surprising them—Will at his desk, Emma straightening up. They were tanned and relaxed; the summer in Maine still glowed on their skin. The girls had an art project spread out, some papier-mâché concoction, and they were up to their elbows in flour and goo, working assiduously at the long kitchen table. They didn't bother to look up and greet us until chided by Emma. What a good mother she was, I noted, with this project, clearly of her design. I admired her, her organic effort. With dishes in the sink and the place a little untidy, Will in bare feet and a T-shirt, I could see them as if suddenly new, different, no longer on the pedestal upon which I'd placed them. Rather, the Chapmans were just people. Nice, good, hard-working, loving people. They didn't know more than I. How had I ever thought that? Will offered us drinks and the four of us sat before the big windows of their living room as the sun went down into New Jersey and the planes lined up from the north to land at Newark.

Was I happy? The question lingered above like a bubble in a cartoon. Yes. Yes. I was happy, calm, tired in a luxurious, sensual, freed way. I was free. And it felt as if it would never end. I was happy that it would never end.

Dinner with the bosses at Bon Soir to celebrate: Radalpieno was there, telling the story of my first meeting with him, describing me as feisty and flirty, wearing an outfit that was a writer's idea of corporate, the black velvet suit that he'd have liked to take off of me, Win ringing the bell all the time. Lots of laughter. Oh, yes, that bell. Martin and Snake and Win and several others were there. "The diversity bell," Martin offered. Radalpieno continued with my appearance. I'd made quite the impression, nails a little messy, shoes and an old handbag. "A real Eliza Doolittle in need of a good washing." "The what?" I asked Martin, still caught on the diversity bell. I'd forgotten about it. "To keep the boys in line, watch our tongues. When you're guilty of a slur, you get rung. A hundred dollars goes to a charity of your choice every time it rings. There's a direct-deposit form you fill out. Miss Lane keeps a tab, which we pay every month." Plenty of wine and endless courses. And Martin with his colorful suspenders repeating for the tenth time his conversation with his driver over shirts, his wonderment at my stupidity or my balls. "Where's the bell?" I asked. "If I had the bell on my desk it would be ringing like a fire alarm."

"The bell's yours," Radalpieno said. "I'm bringing it down first thing in the morning. Hand-delivering it myself." And on they spoke until enough was drunk and enough was eaten, until one by one they left, Radalpieno asking me several times if I was happy, satisfied, telling me I was his now. And they were all gone and I was alone with Win. Just the two of us at the big table, his brown eyes illuminated by the candle flames.

"Everyone loves you," he said.

"For today," I said.

"You're not wrong about that," he said after a pause. Waiters busied about. The restaurant emptied. Win refilled our glasses.

"Today," I said. "Isn't it always all about today, anyway?" I was giddy with my success. On top of the world. Mistress of the Universe.

"You've got to keep an eye on tomorrow too. The trick," he said.

"There're always tricks. You can't ever let anything go."

"Not if you want to stay in the present."

"Hmm. A riddle. Keep your eye on tomorrow to savor today."

"To make today last," he corrected.

"Always a sage." I took a sip of wine. "Wise one," I said, "read the future now."

"You want to play that game?"

"It's fun."

"Yours or the market's?"

"Both."

"The market is easy. We have a year to gradually reduce our exposure to some of the absolute crap out there, subprime and all of that. Scarpetti's finished."

"Really?" I said incredulously. A few months before, a year before, I would not have been surprised, but something had changed in me. I'd gone deep, and so I couldn't see wide and long. I didn't want to anymore. There was no fun in that in the realm of what I did. I'd gone inside Plato's proverbial cave, and in there you can't see reality directly. Instead you see reality's shadow dancing around in the figures on the computer screen—that's as close as the trader wants to get to what's real. All the trader needs to know about are the trades at hand, how to price them, manage exposure. "Subprime's so hot," I added.

Win spoke evenly in that way of his. "Everyone's got his head in the sand. Not a smart place to be. Even a deal like yours wouldn't happen six months from now."

"We'll short swaps," I said, half question, half statement. There was always a way out of everything. Instruments and products and systems and techniques and models had been created to get everyone out of everything. Riskless risk.

"Short. Exactly."

This was the payoff, the conversation, at this level Win completely trusting me. I had entered The Inside.

"We're being too serious." I raised my glass to him and he poured more into it. I was feeling the buoyant effects of the drink. He'd grown on me over the years, his looks. There was something tender in the shine of his cheeks. Life at this level of play was fantastically sweet, and I had just been celebrated by some of its main players. The meal was enormously expensive. The head of B&B came to dinner for me, was hand-delivering a silver bell to me in the morning. I'd ring it the moment he gave it to me, because he'd certainly give me reason to, and he'd laugh and say something more inappropriate, and the floor would take note of this exchange. I could see myself rising in the hierarchy and I liked how it felt. I was ambitious for more. I understood how people came to love power, needed it to thrive. Once you get a taste of how delicious it is, it would be impossible, I imagined, to suddenly start a diet.

"And now, my future?" I said boldly.

"Give me your palm."

I gave it to him. A waiter came over but we ignored him. We were the only diners left in the restaurant. We owned it for the rest of the night, having just dropped so much money. We could stay as long as we wanted. It was after midnight. Win held my hand, turned it over, palm up, brought a candle closer to it. His hand was warm and soft and moved me to come in closer to him. Our shoulders touched. His eyes zeroed in on the trident of lines, their tributaries. "Well?" I said.

"Are you scared?" he asked.

"Of course not, Mr. All-Knowing Seer." We turned to look at each other and our faces were quite close. He studied me for a while and I could see the cloud of seriousness wash over him again, blocking out the bright and splendid sun. At the time, I was impatient with him. We were celebrating, after all. You know those moments: there is only one direction, and its end is the rainbow with its promised pot of gold—nothing less, nothing more. But now, looking back on all of this, I can see Win there at our table, see his beautiful eyes reflecting the candle flame. He had made me, and like a parent who suddenly realizes how vulnerable his child is, his mood switched. For he himself had been where I was, swimming in the heady pool of success, believing in his invincibility. Oh, surely I knew that such moments don't last. I would have said so myself, had I been asked. But I hadn't been.

"I'm proud of you," he said. If I was on the inside—that is, if I'd gone deep inside the cave—he was not. He was on the outside. He had the ability to always stay outside, so that he could see long. He had warned me of this. It was his singular talent always to know the long view. And this was why he continually won.

"The palm," I persisted.

"Do you know what you pulled off?" It was a game of dare now, a match with our eyes, who'd do what or turn away first.

"I do," I said. I didn't blink. "The palm, is it scaring you?"

"Isn't it more fun to not know?"

"You're afraid," I said. He seemed to be, as if he wanted something he didn't know how to ask for. "Of that crystal ball of yours? I've never seen you afraid." I can remember him now, the warmth of his hand holding mine, the very serious nature of his composure—the game over, the desire to speak clearly and be heard. But what teenager listens to her parents? It was on that night that he began to see through me. He had created me, but I was no longer his and there was little he could do to protect me.

By then Win already had his plans to leave B&B, I would understand later. He was reading in my palm whether or not he wanted me to come along. He was weighing things: my raise, my rapport with Radalpieno and the others, if I would say yes, if I'd take the risk, if he'd want me. He was joining a hedge fund, had a nifty plan to go short on all the nonsense, do the research, figure it out and be positioned when the whole operation went down. He'd be quoted later as saying that he hadn't understood the fine points, the entire structure, the complexity, but he'd had the gut feel that Wall Street, the financial world, had created a doomsday machine—a machine that people around the globe were oblivious of because they believed we knew what we were doing over here.

"Things change fast" was all he said, pulling back, deciding: he would not ask me to come along.

"Do you think I don't know that?"

"You haven't seen it." A waiter hovered, poured us some water. "Do you ever think about tulips?" he asked. "I think about tulips all the time. My mind is filled with tulips, the colors and variations." Another waiter blew out the candles on surrounding tables.

I yawned. I was tired but wasn't ready to go home. I wanted to stay there all night. "I don't think about tulips," I said. We sat there a bit longer, looking into each other's eyes, an unnerving sensation that requires no small amount of trust. The game of dare was over. Now it was simply a reckoning. In the end, I had enjoyed the notion of being caught up in a Pygmalion story. I had not minded being the rough stone for another's design and love. But under the microscope of his penetrating gaze, as hard as I tried not to become uneasy, I became so. I was no longer India Palmer, novelist, nor India Palmer, trader. I had mutated into a less flattering creation as I became for Win a metaphor. I tried to regain my composure. "The party's ended," I said and gently slid my hand from his, but he would not immediately let it go, as though he too were trying to stay tethered to the present.

Eighteen

The February 2007 issue of *Woman:*

Walking the Wire:
Novelist turned trader India Palmer travels the distance from high art to high finance

by Simone de Savoy

You know the story line—successful banker turns photographer; hedge-fund manager cashes out and heads to Vermont to milk goats and make cheese; CEO turns tail to help the starving in Darfur—these "change of life" stories all work in one direction: tassel-toed capitalist chucks it all to do good. It's almost a cliché.

Leave it to India Palmer, occasional boldface name and author of the critically acclaimed *The Way We Do Things Here* and most recently *Generation of Fire,* to turn that cliché on its head and surprise the publishing world by giving up on books altogether to become (wait for it) a bond trader. Trend alert: Zadie Smith is now heading the arbitrage desk at Credit Suisse. Richard Serra is appearing tonight on *Fast Money.*

I'm kidding! Sort of. At least in the case of Palmer, the move from the world of Maupassant to mergers, acquisitions And All of That Rot is true. Your Girl has word from a reliable source inside the Towers of Mammon that Palmer has been spotted looking earnest and wearing a smashing set of new It Girl business suits while being shepherded around by none other than cutie-pie tycoon Wayne Johns, aka "Win," in the trading pit of Bond & Bond Brothers on the 33rd floor of the Winchester Building. But she's no intern, it seems, and this is no research "stint" for a next novel. No, India Palmer has, indeed, put her shoulder to the capitalist wheel and made her way up the ranks, from lowly first-year associate to MD (that would be Managing Director to you, bub). And this after only three years on the Street. Her spectacularly swift rise has ruffled a few feathers in the Government-Sponsored Entities division of mortgage-backed securities at B&B, my sources say, but they also confirm that she's no paper tiger. She's actually pulled in some big deals and is making money despite the grumbling. I'll be honest, though—the idea of bonds, or a pool of bonds, is something that makes me go glassy-eyed, so I set out to track down the New India Palmer to see what was what.

On a balmy late-October day I meet with her at Boulon to discuss her monumental career change. Surrounded by mothers who lunch in Louboutin heels and Balenciaga's techno-prints, Palmer, a statuesque blonde with sky-blue eyes, dressed hippie-conservative with style flair—Jimmy Choo slingbacks and a soft, easy skirt made from a tablecloth (fabulous) by Behnaz Sarafpour and curvy small jacket designed deliciously by Celine—entered late, apologizing profusely. So much for the suit, I thought. Her outfit was accented with a Larson necklace of large blue sea glass wrapped in gold leaf and linked with gold chain, the work of Theodor Larson, India Palmer's fabulously handsome sculptor husband. *Would you two please just stop!* I shouted. She laughed and demurely covered her mouth with the back of her hand.

"I don't subordinate my feminine side," Palmer said of the

testosterone-infused universe she now inhabits. "I'm very open about being a girl. I have great conversations with the boys about my outfits. They'd never admit it, but I think they like the change of pace."

One observer, who wished to remain anonymous, said, "It's given them a new focus to distract them from all the bodies she's stepped over—guys who didn't get promoted because she did." *Meeow!* You go, girl!

Palmer, who had taken the afternoon off from B&B, sipped a Château Lefrois white Burgundy (her selection) and said, "You're here to find out What In The World Was She Thinking?" I was, indeed. "The switch was easy," she said. "Everyone around me was making gobs of money and finally I wanted to make gobs of money too. I wanted to prove to myself that I could. Theodor helped," she said with a laugh. "He called it my Duchampian Experiment."

Duchamp she did. Just four weeks before our meeting, Palmer made an astounding play that is gossiped about (one of B&Bs largest rate trades ever, is the rumor). But Palmer is mum when I ask for details. She dismisses me with a chuckle. "You don't discuss these things. I'd be put in the box forever."

Would Duchamp have approved? She paused and took a sip from her glass. "This is about money, dear," she said with a smile, and then, sitting back in her chair, a bit whimsically, "Wouldn't that make a title? *Dear Money.*" She savored it, then added, "It's actually a British financial term for money that's tight, hard to get—frozen credit markets."

Dear Money: Perhaps this is a kind of obituary—though, as one who sobbed her way through freshman orientation at Swarthmore reading *The Way We Do Things Here,* I can't quite let India Palmer go so easily. I want to fight for the winner of the Washington Award for fiction. (She won when she was only 26.) I want to celebrate a writer whose books never sold in breakout numbers, though she had earned for herself a solid literary reputation and high regard among critics.

You'll forgive me for recalling that, 14 years ago, I found myself assigned to write, a little staggered and daunted, a short profile of Palmer for these pages. I stammered and read from a list of 35 prepared questions, but Palmer couldn't have been more gracious. With her next novel, India Palmer was stolen away from Deutsch, her first publisher, by Leonardo Cavelli for Piccadilly. This move began a trend that persisted until her last novel was published, in 2003. She leapt from one publisher to the next, receiving ever-bigger advances (at least initially) and promises of being introduced to the wider audience that all writers long to find.

"In some ways I was too ambitious to be a novelist," she told me at our recent lunch. "Lots of ambition, no hope."

Now she has wandered into unfamiliar territory indeed, but that fierce ambition is still with her. "I don't believe in flittering around the edges of things. I guess I was never a voyeur by nature, which seems like a kind of job requirement for a writer. I simply decided I wanted to be surprised, to surprise myself, not by watching on the sidelines, but by doing."

It all started on a beach in Maine, "out of the clear blue sky," as she likes to say, when a new career literally fell in her lap. Through a friend, the acclaimed novelist Will Chapman (he was an M&A guy at the time), she met the hunky Win Johns—famous for shorting Silver Star in 1999 and making several hundred million for the company overnight. Johns brought Palmer on board more or less on a whim, says Palmer. "He admired my work, I admired his. One thing led to another." (Johns could not be reached for comment.)

What has changed most for her? "The grueling 16-hour days. The intensity, the pressure of being absorbed into competition. Oh, yes, and all the silly office pranks and the side bets that go on here."

Side bets?

"Everyone bets on everything. It's like being stuck with a bunch of numerically gifted gambling addicts who will bet on absolutely anything. What tastes better, Perrier or Pellegrino? That was a recent office bet. Who can eat the most hamburgers—I won that one—not the betting part but the eating part. People were betting on—or against—me, and I won. That victory sort of put me on the map, in terms of accelerated hamburger consumption," Palmer said with a grin, "as someone to be feared." All of the silliness, Palmer confided, is about building morale. "High jinks are a needed contrast to the intense pressure. It's all very locker room," she explained, "but I don't know what would happen if we didn't have that kind of pressure-release valve."

Still, it was hard to imagine the author of *Scion* gulping down burgers. I wanted to know if she missed writing, missed the process of working through one of her gorgeous chapters. "I had a professor whom I adored in grad school," she said. "He used to say to the class all the time—a bit too much—that if we could imagine ourselves doing anything else, anything at all other than writing, we should do it." She looked me squarely in the eye. "So, the short answer is no. I don't miss it at all. I found something else I liked doing as well, perhaps better."

I also couldn't resist asking, "What does this say about our culture?"

Rolling her eyes, she dismissed me: "I don't know. Ask an anthropologist. Or a novelist, maybe."

Nineteen

CAVELLI'S CALL, which came a day after the latest article about me hit the newsstands, arrived like a kind of fickle but predictable weather. Caller ID announced *Piccadilly Publishers.* At any other time in my life, my heart would have skipped. Such calls could tilt the balance of things ever so slightly in one's favor.

"India," Cavelli said in his Locust Valley lockjaw, drawing the name out as if it had been minutes and not years that had passed since we'd last spoken. "India," he said. "I'm beyond fascination, my girl. I'm dying to hear more about this Wall Street experience of yours. Fascinating! Brava!" What was there to say about creatures like Cavelli, who, as someone once said of a certain charming President from Arkansas, always had one arm draped around you in an embrace while the free hand was busy pissing down your trousers? "Leonardo," I said, "what a surprise."

"Now don't be cross with me, dear girl," Cavelli said. I could hear him smile as he fired a mild warning shot across my bow, just in case I was angry at him—which I wasn't, of course—for being out of touch with me. I knew as well as he did the way things worked. I'd left him, after all. But he was always hedging, always in control, even when he held a bad hand. There was something to be said about watching the man, as a kind of human spectacle, operate. "The whole fucking business is going to hell," he said, "and you had the sense to get out when you could. Well done."

"It's always going to hell."

"Well, you've got a point there," he said. I could hear the creaking leather of his swivel chair as he leaned back, this habitué of the always oncoming season of new things under the sun. Not so for the author, for whom, after publication, although she'd poured every fiber of her soul into the enterprise, the future of her book stretched no further than the expiration date on a gallon of milk. Cavelli's office was a testament to the processional sway of the future—the desk stacked high with fresh manuscripts; the ceiling fan, its blades furred with dust, slowly circling above his head; the morning light aslant through a pair of windows that looked out on a wooden water tower. "You've got a point," Cavelli repeated, as if this were the first time he'd considered the notion. "When, my dear girl, do I get to hear about this excursion of yours?"

In a world filled with capricious sentiments, Cavelli had managed, by comparison, to approach a kind of dignity. He had stood by me when he was my publisher, no matter what. After I left him, he'd call, keep his hand in, as it were, with me. Wanted to know what I was up to, until seasons came and went and time swept us farther and farther apart. I'd always thought that I would try again with him, that he'd give me a fair reading, that if I was willing to take a small advance he might be willing to buy my book. For me, though, it was pride. I'd been stupid, perhaps, easy to believe in retrospect. If I'd stayed with him, my career as a writer could have had a much more certain and favorable face. Now, with his exaggerated diction, his elided *r*'s, Cavelli wanted a one-on-one with me, wanted me to explain what was happening in the mortgage universe, wanted me to explicate high finance. I didn't have the time for such a visit just then, but of course I made the time. I wasn't as immune to his summons as I had hoped to be if ever the time came.

"What do you propose?" I asked. The floor was buzzing around me. Cavelli, with his slow, cool attitude, had no idea what he was asking of me. It was eleven in the morning. The markets were insane. Some banks were showing signs of trouble, hedge funds going under, others beginning to fracture, billions of dollars in write-downs. Two hedge funds at Paul, Smart & Smith, Will's old firm, had shuttered their windows. Cavelli wasn't wrong to call. It was a curious time.

How did this mess get started? Where was it headed? I was the one with the crystal ball on this fine day in the middle of 2007—or so Cavelli thought. Perhaps I could predict what might go down, but in truth I was just trying to ski ahead of an avalanche. Not much time to speculate on the long view. Short term was all a trader had time for. And now came the roller coaster ride of volatility. One week of free fall. The next week you were back where you started, as if the previous week hadn't happened. As a joke, somebody left a parachute in the office kitchen. The guys in subprime were writing lyrics like this one, sung to the "American Pie" tune:

A long, long time ago,
I can still remember
How that yield spread used to make me smile.
And I knew I had my chance,
Those CDOs I could finance,
And maybe pay my bills for a little while.

But February made me shiver
With every press release Bear delivered.
Bad news in my e-mail—
Would I collapse that last deal?

I can't remember if I cried
When I saw the CFC slide,

but something touched me deep inside
The day the subprime died.

So bye, bye, repo money supply.
Sent my collateral to four dealers
But they all asked me why.
And good old boys were on a crack-induced high
singin' "This'll be the day the loans die,
This'll be the day the loans die."

Did you write swaps on B/C loans?
Did you blow bucks on new iPhones?

Did that nut Cramer tell you so?
Now do you believe in rate control?
For a Fed cut, would you sell your soul?
And is response to your bid list mighty slow?

Well, you try to widen that spread, my friend.
Your sales force has gone off round the bend.
And Bernanke's on the news,
But Greenspan lit the fuse.

I was a paper-rich middle-aged broncoin' buck
With a master plan and a lot of pluck,
But I knew I was out of luck
The day the subprime died.

So bye, bye, repo money supply.
Sent my collateral to four dealers
But they all asked me why.
And good old boys were on a crack-induced high
singin' "This'll be the day the loans die,
This will be the day the loans die."

I was waking up almost on the hour to check where the markets were overnight. Every day was like going to war, and I had the sense that things were going to get worse. But it was only a sense. We traders didn't have the larger, universal picture of all that was under and on top of us. It didn't work that way. All the songs and high jinks were just fun, as if by acknowledging the ominous with a wink we could keep it at bay. Simply, you had to be quick, nimble, decisive. I'd listen to playlists the girls and Theodor would make for me to psyche me up—*Come As You Are, Don't Forget to Dance.* (I never actually saw the family, had no time to miss them.) Some days would end and everyone would stand there like zombies, shaking their heads. The terror of the abyss followed by the exhilarating comeback.

On the other end of the telephone line, in his publisher's cocoon, with a fluorescent light ballast buzzing somewhere off in eternity, the pressure, the flop-sweat swamp of the trading pit meant nothing to the Dashing Cavelli. He would want to know, like everyone else, if I'd seen this coming. And of course I'd think of Win, of his departure for the hedge fund, all of us in Rates feeling betrayed—he'd seen it coming. But what was *it,* really? Was Win poised in his short position? Cavelli, like everyone else, would want to know what we'd do about it, how we'd manage it. It was all over the news since February: "U.S. Investors Worried about Subprime"; "As Mortgage Crisis Begins to Spiral, Casualties Mount"; "Crisis Looms in Mortgages, Upbeat Analyses"; "The American Dream's Rising Cost"; "Prospering in an Implosion"; "Debtor Nation; Big Investors Jumping Back into Shaky Home Loans"; "When Does a Housing Slump Become a Bust?"; "Another Crash of '29?"

Plenty of indictors: smart friends, friends who should have known better, didn't know the details and fine print of their mortgages. Shorters circled B&B like so many hyenas around a wounded animal. (Win left us alone.) The bets were on that many of us would go down—that our leverage was too high, that our exposure was too vast, that Radalpieno's risk threshold would send us down. (I recalled Win's leverage warning when I'd made my big trade, no one paying it heed.) Here's an analogy: You're a family, mom and dad. You own a house. You believe the value of it will keep going up, so you renovate the kitchen, send your kids to private school, take those biannual vacations—spring break and Christmas. It's assumed you'll get a raise, get a bonus. (Bankers are like waiters; the big pay is the tip.) There's only one direction at this age (midlife), and that's up. So you don't mind the debt you've racked up; you'll pay it off with the bonus, start paying it down with more frequency, take out a home-equity line of credit.

In short, we'd been fools, the whole lot of us. But it's hard to predict when things will fall apart. And then, when it does, you're just trying to stay alive in the avalanche. You have to know when to face off against the market. According to Win, women can make great traders because they are more sensitive to their own weaknesses and failings. They are likely to objectively reevaluate a position and get out of a bad trade rather than stand against an avalanche. But there were only a handful of women trading on the Street. Now the avalanche was coming down the chute and Cavelli wanted to chat.

"What do you propose?" I asked.

I knew what he wanted. There was only one thing a publisher could want.

"Can I lure you to my offices?"

"When?" I thought flirting with the notion could be a curious way to spend some time. I had enough of the writer left in me to want to peer down an old alley. Call it a hedge. Maybe I was looking for an alternative way in which this story of mine might finish.

"This evening? After work, that is. I imagine you might be quite busy."

"How's Thursday afternoon? I'm taking the day off."

"Divine, my pet. A date."

The company's offices had been in the same building since the 1940s. The elevator let you off on the fourth floor, the entirety of which was Piccadilly's—a labyrinth of manuscripts stacked in small towers and books and unopened boxes and piles of papers—a firetrap, and to think that once upon a time the place was blue with cigarette smoke. Black-clad assistants darted about. Nothing fancy, nothing glamorous. Fancy happened at Dino's, Cavelli's Italian watering hole around the block, where he had his table and his usual order of oysters or mussels and his bistecca alla Fiorentina with a spritz of lemon and his two carefully measured glasses of Barolo, where he held court with his authors and other editors and agents in his dapper suits. Here in the offices, his editors sat hunched at their desks, in their cubicles, bent over books, the phone. A strong smell of coffee permeated the air. A wall was devoted to plaques for various awards—the Washington, the International, the Eiseman, the Nobel. And, of course, books from the recent past faced outward along the halls, some behind glass, others stacked hip-high in the reception area.

Miss Barthelme appeared, a white-haired elderly woman, poised and elegant in a lavender summer skirt-suit, who, though older than Radalpieno's Miss Lane, seemed to be cut of the same cloth, from a forgotten time when women prized the job of devoting their lives to holding up a great man.

"India," she said, kissing me lightly on the cheek. "It's been far too long." She led me through the maze. I followed, obedient as a schoolgirl. Then, stopping, Miss Barthelme turned to admire me, as if in afterthought, as if, as we made our way through the stacks of papers and books, an image of who I'd been came to memory and jarred with who I was now, in my expensive jeans and crisp linen blouse, expensive sandals, pretty jewels, finely cut and colored hair.

"You don't look like a bond trader," she said, "whatever that is." And she continued on to the outer reaches of the floor and Cavelli's office. Again, books and all the rest smothered the waiting area outside his door. The door was closed, but I could hear his voice, rising, lulling, rising as it penetrated the thin wall. "May

I get you a drink—some wine, water, coffee, tea? I suppose it is teatime." She held me with her hazel eyes, Miss Barthelme—a good, sound literary name. She extended her hand, gesturing to a frayed leather couch on which I could wait. I obeyed, gently moving aside some books. She vanished with a warm smile.

As soon as I sat down, Cavelli's door opened and there he stood, a little hunched, a little older, but graceful still, in a linen suit, his dark, peppered hair slicked back, his brow furrowed into a confident smile. "India," he intoned, long and full and sweeping me across time and continents. "India. So good of you to come."

He kissed me on both cheeks and we entered his crowded office. On his desk sat a 1940s-style black telephone, reminding me of the one Radalpieno had on his desk. Yet I was certain that Radalpieno's was a retro model and Cavelli's the genuine artifact, which had been ringing on this desk since Piccadilly opened its doors.

He sat down in his leather chair across the desk from me, moved some books aside and shuffled some papers. The enormous water tower outside his window seemed comically proximate, like some sort of artist's statement about the importance of drinking water in our modern world. It partially blocked the windows of another office building, in which I could make out a few people meandering about their business—dressmakers or makers of curtains. Large swaths of fabric held up and measured and studied. Bolts leaned against the walls. But the water tower obscured a better understanding of their endeavors. For all I knew, they could have been making confetti for the party everyone was going to have when the world came to an end. On the floor above, a man approached a window and stared out of it. Light squeezed between the two buildings, splaying itself frugally.

I remembered coming to Piccadilly for the first time, feeling a sense of arrival in the hunkered, dimly lit but official hive and manufacturing hub of American literary stardom, feeling buoyed up by it, chosen, rescued.

Cavelli regarded me for a moment, smiling. "How's Theodor?"

"Terrific," I said, showing off a pair of earrings he'd made me.

"Very nice," he said. "Patel says Larson Designs has arrived." Patel was Aruna Patel, his Indian success story and wife. He always referred to her by her last name. I took note of the fact that he and his wife had discussed us. I warmed to that fact.

"He's pretty busy," I said. "But tell her I can get her a good deal."

"Hmmm," he answered.

"He's testing the commercial waters too," I said.

"Isn't success lovely? In the beginning, artists always underrate money. How many times I've seen that scenario play out."

I could have spent an afternoon listening to Cavelli enumerate every last writer of that description, if only to feel the pleasure of their company, but I asked instead, "And your boys?"

"Splendid. Rambunctious. Testosterone, you know."

I can't say I felt nothing, sitting there. The words of the best writers in the world rested on his desk, in the bookshelves lining his office walls. But it was Cavelli's business acumen that I appreciated most—how he turned his imprint into the brand authors sought, so much so that when a recent Nobel laureate asked for too big an advance, Cavelli responded with a simple "Fuck you," knowing full well that his author would dine out on that story for the rest of his life. "And your girls?" I was touched that he'd remembered their gender.

"They're well, but I don't see much of them these days."

"Is it worth it?" he asked, suddenly and sharply. I was taken aback.

"Is it worth it for you?"

"Touché," he answered.

"I haven't had time to ask if it is," I conceded. "I'm just trying to keep up, stay over my skis, you know."

"The story is that you knew nothing about Wall Street, that this escapade was a lark between two bankers with too much time and money on their hands."

"That about sums it up."

"Was writing that bad?"

"Don't get me started."

"Your mentor in all of this, Johns—he won the bet?"

"That's right too. But from my point of view the bet is history, water under the bridge. I mean, yes, I suppose they can call it to mind if they want to, or if it serves a purpose. Then I'm a story that burnishes their image, which is important in that world. At that level, money as a marker of distinction has almost no value. There's just so much. But, I guess, as a story to trade on, it's going to be hard to top what they did with me."

"I don't suppose you had anything to do with that."

I noticed that Cavelli's head had developed a bit of a palsied wobble. He raised his chin to me and smiled serenely. I shifted in my seat and, out of nowhere, felt a strong desire to light up a cigarette. "Leonardo, why am I here?"

"Let me ask you something. Is Johns a good man?"

"He's a smart man. He's left B and B. He believed we were going to hell. And yes, he's good."

"Are you—good?"

"Am I good? Are you kidding? I'm as good as I can be, considering." My BlackBerry was vibrating away like a dark little gremlin in my purse. "Win would recommend cash positions for investments."

"It's that bad?"

Cavelli's phone rang. He picked it up and said his name, then said no and put the receiver back in the cradle and looked at me. "You know why you're here."

"Do I?"

"Of course you do."

"The bubble is bursting," I said.

"They've burst before. How will this time be different? What's the story?"

"Do you want optimistic or catastrophic?"

"I suppose catastrophe makes for the better tale. Doesn't it? When you're writing a story, where's the fun in optimism? Everyone getting along and having a jolly grand time? Of course, you need a touch of that at the end."

He seemed to have all the time in the world for me. I could feel my BlackBerry vibrating again. With anyone else I would have responded to the messages. But maybe this was the last time I'd ever be here, talking with this man.

"You know our mutual friend Will Chapman?"

"How's Will?" I asked.

"Writing as well as ever, but he's having a little mortgage trouble. Seems he got in too thick with the place in Maine and needs to sell."

"You don't say?" This was news. I thought of Emma. I thought of how much she loved Maine, remembered her telling me that Will had been furious with her for spending so much on the renovation. I remembered the exotic loan. It had come due. I felt a jolt of fear for them and then relief for myself that this was not my concern. But I'll confess, I also felt an instantaneous justification in my own belief that you couldn't want such things and also want to be a writer.

"They're in a tough place," Cavelli said, darkly, but with that sense of having information that could be of interest to the person with whom he spoke. He was reading my face. He could see intense curiosity there. He was as bad a gossip as the rest of us. "Apparently he'd been relying on stock options from his old firm, but they plummeted before they were vested. I hadn't understood that a third of those annual bonuses are stocks you can't touch. Why in the world would bankers loan money to people who have only a promise of money, who can't pay it back? None of what I read makes any sense."

"Tulips," I said, just as Win had that night in his office, then again at dinner, celebrating my big trade, as if the word alone could explain where we stood today. I'd felt unexpectedly relieved when Win left the firm, though I admitted it to no one. I'd never imagined there'd be a "post-Win" period, but here it was, and with his departure came that relief. My own sense of being a cardboard cutout had departed. We talked occasionally, Win and I, but not much since I knew he was shorting the market. The guy who'd flown into my life on a biplane and bet a bundle on me was now actively trying to bury us all. I wanted to know about Will and Maine. In how much trouble were they? I'd heard the rumors—Paul, Smart & Smith. But after closing the hedge funds they'd assured stockholders they'd recover. Things could turn around yet for Will. This was just part of the roller coaster ride.

"Tulips," Cavelli said, smiling, leaning forward to let me know he understood the reference and to hear more.

I carried on for a bit about tranches and Alt-A's and no-docs and CPOs and rating agencies, about the market creating the value. Then I threw in credit-default swaps just to make things really crazy. And to make things impossible to understand I mentioned deregulation and derivatives. I tried to give Cavelli the catastrophe, because it seemed that's what he wanted to hear. In the end, of course, tulips hadn't fared so well. If the Chapmans were losing Maine, that wasn't a good sign for the market. If Will, as a former banker, had underestimated his ability to make payments, or overvalued his future earnings, what was the rest of America, those with less knowledge of finance, thinking?

"And the characters," Cavelli said, fingers stroking his chin. "Tell me about them."

I thought for a moment and then smiled. "Who'd inhabit this book?" I asked. He was playing a game now. He wanted me to populate the story. "Well, there's Win, swooping down in a yellow biplane to turn an art-house novelist into a billionaire banker, and a wife and her banker husband who wants to be an art-house novelist, and the CEO of B and B, who has too much time on his hands and wants his men to bleed green, and who rings a little sterling-silver bell every time he makes a sexist, racist or otherwise politically incorrect comment, and who rules from a glass tower."

"I like it," Cavelli interjected.

And I continued: all the contests and my win with the hamburgers and Toyotas and bacon and so many billions of dollars. As the details poured from me, of this ridiculous, absurd, glittering world, they almost made me excited. The storytelling reminded me of when I told Theodor for the first time about my defection—in the end it had been comforting and refreshing. I thought of Theodor's chalice, the world resting on a fragile limb about to topple—or not—the Texan's boisterous "You're brilliant, old boy." Theodor had let go of the sculpture, sent it into the world, his no more. This was how it was supposed to be. And I will confess here, I paused, wondered in a fleeting moment, the way so many ideas and notions can occupy your mind in a flash: I wanted to go back; I could go back; I could make it mine as it had been in the very beginning, oceanic stretches of time, an entire summer's worth, deeply immersed in a world of my own making, belonging to me alone, the way Theodor's sculpture had once belonged to him. I felt both a pang of regret and the fullness of possibility in a life lived creatively, in which all that is sacrificed is compensated for in the desire to make and think and understand. I had the urge to write a sentence, craft a paragraph. I could feel the engine trying to turn over, catching, engaging like a car left idle for a long winter.

Cavelli's eyes concentrated on me. He was smart and literary and attentive, chin resting on palm, peering through the portal opened by me and my words. I hadn't felt this passionately in years. I could feel my skin warm, my cheeks flush. I wanted to get inside this, understand. I missed this. I could have talked with him for a long time.

Miss Barthelme knocked and cautiously opened the door. "Your next appointment is waiting."

I uncrossed my legs, ready to be dismissed.

"It will be a minute," he said. She left, closing the door quietly behind her.

"And they thought they could take you, just anyone, and graft you into this world?"

"You know," I said, crossing my legs again and sitting back, "they did. And in the beginning it felt dirty, like a raunchy affair, illicit, exciting. But that was just me, it turned out, indulging my own prejudices. I discovered it was a much more complex world, of smart, educated people, children some of them, readers too." He smiled, sharing the inside joke of those outside finance—that we all believe them to be illiterate. "And so I surrendered to it all." I *could* imagine the story. I was writing it in my mind. I looked at his office door. Outside someone was waiting. I was making someone wait. I wanted that person to wait forever so I could remain in here, in this sweet memory.

"Don't you feel that defines a fatal flaw?"

"Surrendering?" I asked.

"To money," he said.

That snapped me back from my reverie, sharpened my sense of clarity. "Isn't that what's happened to so many of us? We all wanted the money, believed so invincibly in ourselves that we mortgaged our futures for the Mercedes today, the new kitchen, the addition, the trip to Europe. Isn't that what America has done?" But it was more than that. I understood what it was just then, for me. I felt as if I belonged now, that I wasn't scheming anymore, trying to get away with something in order to afford my life. I belonged now, to the school, in a house, at the movies with my kids even, in stores, at my daughters' doctors, to this world that made me.

"A fatal flaw," he repeated.

"I suppose it could be," I said. "I got caught up in the frenzy in my own special way." I thought of Will and Emma and their house in Maine.

Our conversation continued for a good twenty minutes, veering back to the mess that he apparently found my role an emblem of. He was convinced this would be a nuclear financial explosion and suggested that I was particularly well positioned to tell the tale, one with my own intriguing backstory.

"And how will it end?" he asked.

"The bankers, they'll all be obliterated. No one will be able to look at them. Tarred and feathered," I said. He gave me a pleased smirk. "Of course, it will end with the bankers just where they were in the beginning, creating new products that do the same thing that bundle and pool potential, slice it and dice it and ship it off around the world, and the frenzy will start all over again. It won't be houses but something else. College tuition plans, life insurance—they'll be gambling with your life. They'll never lose." I smiled at him. "The rich live differently," I said.

"Who do you think would be interested in writing this?" he asked with a half-cocked smile.

"Don't you think there will be many?" I asked. "Financial wizards will have proposals by the thousands, no?"

"Not that kind of book," he said. "I'm talking about a book of witness."

"Written by a bystander," I said.

"India," he said, standing up at last and stepping around his desk to give me a hug. "Think about it, won't you?"

That little engine of possibility turned over again, but quickly stopped.

"Not a chance, Leonardo, as tempting as you are. I'm very happy. For the first time in my life I am extremely happy with what I do."

I'd said no to Cavelli, and as I did my writer's studio flashed before me. I'd held on to it all this time, still paid rent on it, though it remained unvisited, gathering dust—there just as I had left it. I said goodbye to Cavelli and shut his office door behind me and stepped into the anteroom, where I stood blinking for a moment. Hunched over a manuscript, red pen poised in her hand, sat Lily Starr. Then I saw the grade book and noticed that the "manuscript" was a stack of student papers. It was late June. Summer session, no less.

"Lily."

"India," she said, smiling and tossing her purse over the stories. "What in the world?"

"Just a visit."

"How crazy is this? I'm just here to talk to Cavelli."

"Crazy," I said. "Are you teaching?" I gestured toward the stories.

She rolled her eyes and stuffed the papers into her bag, the blue alligator handbag with the little silver feet.

"You look so good," she said.

We both stood there, her compliment of the kind one sometimes hears at reunions or funerals—an indirect, public avowal that time, gravity, entropy, the IRS, alcohol, a thick stack of student papers waiting to be read and deficiencies of character one couldn't surmount alone had all conspired to make you look as if you needed, at the very least, a long hot soak and a good airing out in high-desert sun, possibly with a feathered shaman or two to help guide you back from where the wheels had come off your caboose.

"I read in a magazine that you bought a house in Southhampton," I said, not really sure of what else to say.

"Springs," she corrected, apologetically. Her lips curled into a frown. "But we have to rent it out all the time. You know, mortgage payments." She paused. "Crazy," she said. Then, unable to resist: "New book?"

"Honestly," I said, "I'm not really sure why I'm here."

A flash of relief in her eyes. "I miss you, India. It's been so long," she said, as if trying to sort something out for herself. Why had we thrown each other away?

"We're all so busy," I said. "I'd love to catch up. Have you finished another novel?"

"A memoir. The fiction's on hold."

Cavelli opened his door with a booming welcome for Lily. "My Starr," he declared.

"Good luck to you," she said. "Call. Please."

Twenty

HOW DO YOU KNOW the end is near? When shoeshine boys are giving you stock tips. The trouble is, the only way you really understand this is after the fact. Yesterday it was the shoeshine boy. Today it's your mother-in-law. The joke and its punch line live in the land of perspective and hindsight. But if you live moment by moment in the present, if you're a fire-breathing, hamburger-eating numbers guy, as I'd become—"India Palmer, just one of the boys"—then all one sees is numbers.

We were all about reality, and numbers were real and studly and all the rest of it. Numbers allowed you to see beyond the distracting fabric, the shifting veil of illusion that most people mistook for reality. But even if one of us were to disclose our quantitative methods to the public at large—say, blaring them with a bullhorn from the back of a truck driving down Broadway—it would be the listeners who'd die of boredom or bafflement. I wasn't a "quant," a Princeton Ph.D. in economics, not even close, but I learned to speak their language. I'd come to take it as an article of faith that 99 percent of the time I could lose no more than the bet I'd made. If the bet was $50 million, 99 percent of the time that was the most I could lose. And the numbers, like the ground beneath my feet, bore me up.

I walked as if on a mighty earthen levee and noted with satisfaction how the waters were held at bay. I noted the people, how small they were, living their lives oblivious of the levee. This was the 99 percent. It worked. It was fundamentally sound. You could believe in it the way you believed in the Army Corps of Engineers. It was convincing in its daily utility. It was durable. Its mighty engine thudded convincingly. Over time, one simply took it, like the fact that the sun would rise tomorrow, as part of the given.

But riding out across the ever-narrowing asymptote of chance, at the far periphery of thought, at the remotest end of possibility, a cold, dark number was ever so occasionally rumored to exist. This was the One Percent Chance that the levee would break, that the supercollider experiment would somehow form antimatter that would fuse everything—the air, the trees, the oceans, all of us—into a solid, ever-expanding ball of destruction. The One Percent was Kali, the destroyer goddess, riding on a theoretical comet of the apocalypse. You could not, if you wanted to maintain your credibility as a numbers guy, simply dismiss her, because, after all, she was a number. You could not truthfully say, "This is not possible." Because it *was* possible. All you could say, in truth, was that it was not probable.

The One Percent was where the dragons lived. The people who forswore the pallet-loads of money that everyone else was making and stuffing into their own accounts, not because it was right or prudent but because they could—the antinomians who kept their eyes on the realm of the dragons, who thought about what terrible, wholesale destruction the dragons could do—these people collectively would not have filled a small elevator. Nobody invited them to the party. They were cranks of catastrophe. They were out of step with the times. And who among us wants to say goodbye to a good time?

The only way you understand is after the fact. Unless you're Win Johns. When Win lit out for the territory, wild rumors circulated: he'd racked up some heavy losses; he'd been caught money-laundering for the Man in the Moon; he was a kingpin of the white slave market in Romania—such outrageous stories swirled in the wake of his departure from Bond & Bond. To where? To short the market, of course. But to all of us it may as well have been to Fiji, to Oz, to the bottom of the Aleutian Trench.

Amazing how the pace of the market made Win's former place in it a distant memory. Nobody cared. There were nondisclosure agreements and contractual clauses and noncompete provisos guaranteeing that Win would remain, in terms of his relevance, on Pluto. And as if from that recently decommissioned planet, he could look back on the tiny speck floating in the darkness that was us, our busy brew, but he could do nothing or say nothing that would be heard against the feverish pitch of the galaxy, which moved and would always move, as we all knew, despite the occasional disquieting glitches, in one direction only. One didn't bet against the galaxy. And what mattered in the galaxy we'd created—the substance of our dreams, our deals, and the fabulously spinning noncorrelated assets we'd invented, those curious cycles and epicycles derived from dreams—was something that had always mattered. It was something beyond logic or reckoning. Something firm beneath our feet. Something that kept us warm at night and the rain from falling on our heads. Something to look out upon, some landscape to survey and assess and regard. Something real. Real estate.

There was no bidding war between Emma and me, as Win had predicted. I bought the house because they needed to sell and because I could buy. They'd made mistakes with mortgages, as so many others had. I bought the house because I could. And, because I could, I planned to tear it down and build it back again as it had been, the same design but better, sounder, more polished, more comfortable, each room a bit more commodious, the bathrooms large enough for tubs and showers, insulation for winter visits, a fireplace that didn't hog the views. I wanted not to mess too much with history, to keep the integrity of the house's original design but modernize it, so you couldn't tell, if you'd known the house across the years, whether anything much had changed.

But there was something else at work inside me. Maybe I would make two turrets instead of one, for balance, each with a door onto second-floor balconies. I would make the attic and basement livable. "To the unknowing eye, it will appear that the house has had no more than an excellent paint job," said Sims, a New York architect who had done some work in the Hamptons and was known for his stone-and-glass façades and for being mindful of the carbon footprint. "It will look as though now someone cares for it just a bit more." I did not mention that to Emma.

To one so new to having money, to its power to transform, to its—how shall I say—enchanting melody, the plans to merely restore and remodel the house at Pond Point slowly began to seem slightly, peevishly foreshortened. For weeks I looked over Sims's shoulder as he drafted. Everything was at my disposal. I could reposition the house. I could open it up to admit the eastern sun. I could extend a deck into the sea grass, add a Jacuzzi. Because he was young and hungry, and because he had read me well—seen that I too, in my own way, was hungry—Sims introduced more radical plans for an entirely new sort of house, a *rara avis* sort of house, an eco-friendly, sustainable assemblage of cubes and parallelograms and solar panels, a polyhedral cathedral, like some ship heading out into the Gulf of Maine and built to outlast the ravages of time and tide. It would ruffle feathers from Sebasco Cove to Gilbert Head. Yachtsmen would use it to mark their position off the coast. Passing lobstermen would pause in wonderment—or call it blasphemy.

I did the numbers, and the numbers sang their enchanting song. My accounts were a mountain. This was a foothill. It was more than just doable. It was done. I could spend a winter on Wall Street amassing—I loved the word—*another mountain*, and by spring I could move into Shangri-la. It was heady stuff. So we worked on it, Sims and I, a step forward, away from my original intention (the same but improved) and toward his (an Ozymandian assertion): advance, retreat, until temptation won and I had a pile of blueprints to tell the story.

The sale of the house was matter-of-fact. It had been Emma's idea, mentioned first on my family's annual visit. "Why don't you buy it?" she'd offered, as if to a co-conspirator, our feet pushing into the sand, books in our laps that we weren't bothering to read. "Better you than a stranger." The girls ran around on the beach. Theodor and Will were on a jog. I'd imagined this moment for Emma, had envisioned a rupture of some sort, but I hadn't imagined she'd have been this placid. "We can't afford to keep it, alas. Ah, the compromises one makes for art! Who would have thought?"

"I'm so sorry," I said.

"Don't be sorry," she said. "It's just a house." All the sounds washed over us, the waves and the gulls and the P-3 Orions, turboprop planes lumbering overhead on their practice sorties from the new naval base—big, hulking, ominous, like circling sharks. Round and round they cruised. "If you buy it, it'll still be in the family. I mean, you'll invite us up."

"You'd have your own room," I said, imagining the picture along with her. I meant it, in a way.

"I had thought Pond Point would never change," Emma said contemplatively. I noticed a few strands of gray in her dark hair, caught by the sun, a revelation of another sort. "Each summer we'd return, and the place was just as it had been the year before, nothing changed." Emma was staring out at the horizon, her voice like a guitar tuned up an octave. "The arms of sand would stretch to the islands at low tide; the dunes would always rise as dunes are meant to do; the beach would be wide and the rivers would run their course; the tides would always be low in the afternoon. The moon red in the evenings above the little island there." She pointed to the island where ornithologists had erected tents from which to study the piping plover. White-capped waves rolled toward us from the island, rhythmically, calmly.

"But of course it wasn't that way," Emma continued. "Every summer there would be a new surprise, something different—less sand here, more sand there; the spit to Wood Island completely submerged at low tide so you had to wade out to it, pulling the girls, when they were young, on rafts; the small river cutting across the other spit to Fox. The place was alive, growing, changing, dying, regenerating. My girls changed. The only thing that seemed to remain the same was the house. It had been there forever in the same spot, through storms and coastal blizzards, nothing shaking it. Other houses had come and gone, but not our house. There were dramatic stories of houses being swept out to sea. But not our house. Several generations had summered here. Where are they? They're all gone. Even we'll be gone. But not the house."

I thought then she might break. But she didn't. She never broke. We agreed to buy the house and she did not break. What did I want? Did I want to watch, from the comfortable perspective of the person I'd become, Emma making the kind of sacrifices that I'd once had to make? Perhaps a part of me did, but I pretended that wasn't so. I held her by the shoulders in an attempt to comfort her as we sat in silence, looking out onto the waters, but she didn't need the comfort. She'd accepted the loss, moved on.

Quietly, in the house, Emma packed up the belongings she wanted and shipped them to New York, eventually transferring the title of her dream to me. Her dream was for the simplicity of the eternal summer, preserving her children, keeping them forever small. It was sentimental and quaint, and when they had money the ramshackle house seemed to provide (I understood now) a counterpoint to the luxury of their lives. I understood, too, what I couldn't have then—that I didn't need or want a counterpoint to luxury. I wanted money to do exactly what money could do. For that reason I'd been carried aloft by Sims and all his blueprints. Through local gossip, Will had learned my plans, and when his e-mails and phone calls with his inevitable pleas began, I couldn't return them. But events propelled me to the final act, a day I was mildly dreading, when Will would see firsthand all that I was about to do, or undo. It was hard to miss; it had made the *Sagadahoc Bugle.*

The girls were back in school, caught up in their busy lives, and Theodor was in Italy for an exhibition of his work. I came to Maine alone to handle the closing with Will and then to prepare the house for demolition. It was Friday, September 21, 2007, the first day of fall, though it still felt like summer, with a strong offshore breeze. A few people played on the beach, hanging on to summer, here for the weekend. Kites dipped and dived. Our small driveway was cluttered with machinery: a bulldozer, a hydraulic excavator, a crew milling about, hammering enormous bolts to the legs of the old Victorian house. (I hadn't realized that a house could have legs; pilings, I guess.) The bolts had hooks that would hold cables that, once bound around the house, would, with some heavy pulling, take the house down.

Will Chapman stood there, dressed in khaki shorts and a pink polo shirt, sunglasses resting on his head. "It's not for me to say, India. But I wish you wouldn't," he said simply, respectfully. The ocean slapped against the shore. A sudden freshet of rain sprinkled us. In minutes the sun would shine, sending up columns of steam on the beach. Then, perhaps, a downpour.

"I promise you'll love it," I said, smiling, believing he would when he saw the finished house. "Sims is first rate. His houses are becoming important. Everyone's tearing down houses, replacing them."

"Oh, come . . ." He was going to say something more, but didn't. He looked at the house and then to the long dumpster hauled in to receive the wreckage.

I didn't want him to be mad at me. I didn't want people to be mad at me. I wanted them to love me and think I was good, though under Win I'd become much more accustomed to disregarding the opinions of others.

"It's not about the house," he said, turning back to me. He brushed the hair from his eyes, rustled by the breeze. "I guess"—he paused for a moment—"I guess you've never understood that." All around was the view, the spectacular view. The workmen were waiting for me to give them the go-ahead. I had stopped them out of respect for Will. I wanted Will to say his piece. I missed Theodor suddenly. I wished he were here. Some of the workers banged away at the piles supporting the house. "You know, we envied you, India. You had drive. You had commitment, determination. The life you made for yourself, Theodor, the girls."

"And I don't have drive now?" I asked. I was teasing. I knew what he meant, but it was easier to make a joke of it.

A group of college-age kids came piling out of a house down the beach, a little ranch that had replaced a Victorian that had long ago washed out to sea. "The fun people," Emma had called them, because they were always engaged in some active sport. They carried sailboards and kayaks, a half-dozen young men, raring to go, in wetsuits. I was becoming a bit impatient with Will.

"It won't always be like this, India. This isn't the end, either, you know. Markets change."

He stood before me in that rarest of moments in life, a true reckoning, the moment before the firing squad, the chained-to-the-bulldozer moment when no matter whether you're right or wrong, it was time to say what you had to say and to hell with the consequences. But he couldn't say it all, because who among us really can? I could see myself as if from above, standing in the drizzle. My hair was pulled back with a clip, and I wore gray yoga pants and a white T-shirt and flip-flops, my toenails red. Behind me the bulldozer and hydraulic excavator stood poised for demolition.

"We wanted to be you, India. Maybe we hadn't spoken about it or said it directly. But we understood each other. You made it look possible. You gave us courage." Then he was silent, letting the last words sink in. We were at the breach point. After this, all would be "after." I would exist in the past, in the third person. *There had been an instant when he first met her*—I could almost see it as the opening of a longer work—*in the Tribeca park with her little girl and Theodor, and he knew he wanted to save her. He sensed in her something fragile,* the story might continue, *something he wanted to set free.*

"You don't understand," I said. I thought of my meeting with Cavelli and realized it had been Will who had put Cavelli up to it, to calling me. A flash of revelation, evaporating just as fast, for what really did it matter? I let the strength of my will absorb the prickling sensation in my nose and eyes. I had proven I could do it. I had what I wanted. I wasn't lying anymore. I would not let him steal that from me.

"You want to know something ridiculous, India? Emma and I used to laugh about this. For us, you and Theodor were always . . ." Will broke off, looking at the house again, and laughing suddenly. "The Joneses," he said. "You were the goddamned Joneses."

And then Will was gone and I was alone.

It started raining harder. The workers called it a day. The contractor told me to let him know in the morning, told me it was worth it for me to think hard. His thick Maine accent swallowed multiple letters and sounds. Told me, warned me, that once the house came down, it couldn't be put back. He was a big man with streaked rosaceous cheeks. He turned his baseball cap around, beak to the back, as if for emphasis.

I brought out a beach umbrella and opened it in the rain and propped up a chair beneath it and covered myself with a blanket. The fun people in their kayaks had poked around intrepidly but were now gone, had taken shelter. The rain became heavier, the day grayer, the wave crests snow white. A renegade gull flew happily in the downpour. Water leaked through the umbrella, splashing on the blanket, reminding me of the leaky roof of what soon would become my old apartment. We were buying a loft in Tribeca. I listened to the soothing patter as the rain slowed. The afternoon was still in front of me, and when it came the sun would cut through the clouds and the tide would pull back into the ocean, revealing the full wide swath of the beach, and the fun people would again spill from their house with footballs and Frisbees.

My house rose regally from the dunes. It was a striking house. Perhaps, if I squinted, I could see why Emma had adored it so. A loft in Tribeca, a summer house in Maine, made my new career, my new life, seem less dreamy. I'd taken a risk and would again. It so often felt like jumping off the high board at night, a sensation you become accustomed to, a thrill you develop a taste for, especially when you end here in the sand with the horizon before you and a house you can tear down or build up as you choose because you've made the leap. Real estate, sweet real estate. The September afternoon, the clouds now white, billowy cushions against the cornflower-blue sky. Everything was aligned.

Perhaps the story begins with a house. *And the rain passed as it always did, and out came the fun people again, to collect wood for a bonfire,* which I knew meant a display of fireworks as soon as it was dark, little bonfires dotting the arc of the beach for as far as you could see, everyone gathered around a bright, crackling light in the sand, while satellites streaked across the darkness and the markets turned. I would sit back and watch the show, note with pleasure what fun the fun people made for themselves, and I would have some fun of my own. I would direct the new regime to begin. Would it be cables tightening around the legs of the house, or something else? Either way, it would be mine. And tomorrow I would do exactly as I pleased.